MEN OF BONE

MEN OF BONE

A THOMAS BERRINGTON TUDOR MYSTERY

DAVID PENNY

20220601.1447

ALSO BY DAVID PENNY

The Thomas Berrington Historical Mysteries

The Red Hill

Breaker of Bones

The Sin Eater

The Incubus

The Inquisitor

The Fortunate Dead

The Promise of Pain

The Message of Blood

A Tear for the Dead

The Thomas Berrington Tudor Mysteries

Men of Bone

A Death of Promise

The Thomas Berrington Prequels

A Death of Innocence

The Thomas Berrington Bundles

Purchase 3 full-length novels for less than the price of two.

Thomas Berrington Books 1-3

The Red Hill

Breaker of Bones

The Incubus

Thomas Berrington Books 4-6

The Incubus

The Inquisitor

The Fortunate Dead

Thomas Berrington Books 7-9

The Promise of Pain

The Message of Blood

A Tear for the Dead

Unit-13: WWII Paranormal Spy Thriller

An Imperfect Future

For Meggie, again and always.

ENGLAND, SEPTEMBER-NOVEMBER 1501

ONE

Thomas Berrington had avoided much in the way of trouble for several years, so it came as a surprise how easily it found him again on his return to England. Not that it was his fight when it came. Such had never concerned him in the past, but the last few years his mind had changed on the matter. He had seen too much of death and bloodshed to welcome more.

When the trouble came, the circumstances were mundane. Thomas needed a haircut and a shave; nothing more.

He had arrived in England three days before, grateful that the late September weather had been kinder than feared. The waters between northern France and southern England seemed rough enough, but the crew only laughed when he commented on it. They told him to come try it in November or December.

A good south-westerly had brought the small crayer from Fécamp to Southampton in only two days. Once the crayer was safely tied up, Thomas stood on a narrow gangplank and stared at the cobbled dock, a strange reluctance filling him. One step and he would stand on England for the first time in forty-seven years. He feared that once that step was taken he might never return to where he had come from. This was meant to be an assignment of limited duration, but so had been his leaving of England at the age of thirteen.

"Move on, sir," said a voice from behind. "Unless you have changed your mind, but it will be the same price to take you back as it was to bring you."

Thomas took the step. The world continued to turn. The sky did not fall. Though after the crossing, the cobbles beneath his feet seemed to move.

He found a stable that would sell him a horse and paid the price asked without haggling, which confused its seller no end. The ostler told Thomas the horse's name was Ferrant, but he could change it if he wished. He saw no reason to do so. It was a placid beast, which pleased him, and answered well to his touch.

Thomas's mind stilled as he rode away from the bustle of the port town of Southampton. Three days later it grew anxious again when he saw the smoke-stain and church spires of London ahead. He reached into his jacket for a scrap of paper and read the two words he had written in far off Spain: *Bell Savage*. It was the name of an inn he would find if he followed the road into London from the west. He had instilled the same name into his family two months earlier, before leaving them to journey north on his own. He could think of no other means of them finding him other than to seek the same lodgings and ask his whereabouts. An English nobleman had provided the name of the inn when he came to witness the grandeur that was Granada and the palace of Alhambra.

As he approached the walls of London, Thomas still had no idea if the man had intended to make a fool of him or not. So it came as a surprise to discover the Bell Savage was a large establishment consisting of thirty well-appointed rooms, together with stabling for sixty horses. It sat near the Fleet, on a wide thoroughfare named after the river, but far enough away to avoid the stink of its putrid water. The inn was a hundred paces from Ludgate, which offered entrance through the city walls. Thomas handed Ferrant over to a young stable-hand and took his saddlebags inside, together with a leather satchel almost black with age, which contained some of the tools of his trade. Thomas was a physician. A surgeon trained in the best infirmaries of Moorish Spain. When it still existed, which it had not done for over nine years.

Inside, the goodwife showed him to a room and handed him a heavy iron key for the lock, with a promise it was the only one so his belongings would be safe. Thomas dropped his saddlebags on the bed and set the leather satchel beside them.

"Are you hungry, sir?" asked the goodwife. "I can send food to your room, or a fine table is set downstairs. Four pence either way."

Once more, Thomas did not know if the cost was reasonable or not, but he had no hunger. The small meals he had taken since arriving in England had not enamoured him to its cuisine.

"Can I ask you something?"

"Ask away, but ask quick. My customers complain if I am away too long."

"Then two things. First, do you know if the King is in London? Second, do you know where I can get a haircut and shave?"

The woman laughed. "Both simple questions to answer, sir. Yes, the King is in town. And there is a barber's shop less than two hundred paces along this road."

Which is where Thomas found the trouble.

When he reached the shop it was busy and he had to wait. As he did so he had more questions, which he directed at the man standing beside him, who was waiting his own turn. There were two barbers working, one an older man with very little in the way of hair on his own head, the second a young woman with luxuriant black tresses and a pretty face.

"Tell me, sir, for I am newly returned to England after some time away, what is the fashion these days? Do men wear beards? Do you know how long the King wears his hair?"

"The King?"

Thomas nodded. "King Henry, I believe."

"You are right in that, sir." The man looked Thomas up and down. What he saw was a man taller than most, rising to a good six feet. Strangely dressed, with a long blue scarf wrapped around his neck and shoulders. A face that carried a scar or two, but none recent. Hair that was too long and beard the same. "You need only look around to judge the fashion for beards, sir. Few gentlemen sport them these days. As for the King's hair, I do not believe I have ever seen him."

When his turn came, Thomas asked the young woman who had called him to a chair about the King.

"He wears it to his chin," she said. "Though it is thinning these days."

"And clean shaven?"

"Of course." She examined Thomas. "Will you need a shave too?" She ran her fingers through his hair but made no comment on its quantity or quality. Thomas had stripped and washed his body, including hair and beard, the night before in a river he believed was the Thames. Watching the other clients, it appeared cleanliness was not something required by either of the barbers.

The woman picked up her scissors, the two blades hinged with a curved steel hoop which required some strength to use.

"How much shorter do you want it?"

"I want it as short as the King wears his."

"A good four inches, then."

She began to work, starting with the shave before moving on to his hair. She cut the bulk of its length off quickly, then returned to apply some measure of style to what was left. There was no mirror, so Thomas had no idea how good a job she was doing. She had used the same scissors to remove most of his beard before scraping away the rest with a sharp blade. She was almost done when she gave a gasp and her hand jerked to inflict a small cut on Thomas's cheek.

"I am sorry, sir."

Thomas glanced at the door to see what had bothered

her. Three men entered the shop with a swagger, all dressed in similar clothes, with red felt caps on their heads. Several of those standing to wait their turn found themselves unwilling to wait longer and eased past the three to leave.

One man went to the male barber and pushed him backwards against the wall. A second came to the woman and put a hand on her breast. She made no effort to push him away.

Thomas did not know how much trouble there was in this and had lost the spirit to respond to such situations several years before. Even so, the assault on the young woman brought him to his feet. He wiped his face with a linen cloth.

"I was not finished with my haircut," he said to the man. "And the lady would like you to release her."

The man turned to look at Thomas. "You are finished now. Leave if you know what is good for you."

Later, Thomas would wonder why he acted as he did, but supposed it was instinct. There had been many years when he thought nothing of protecting others. A strange reluctance held him back for a moment until the man snatched at the girl's dress and ripped it to reveal her breasts.

Thomas hit the man square on the nose, feeling a satisfying crunch as bone shattered. At one time, he would have taken his life without a second thought. Now, life held more value for him; the lives of both the innocent, the vulnerable, and the guilty.

The man raised both hands to his face and gave a great cry.

Another who had waited at the door came at Thomas, a short blade appearing in his hand. Thomas waited then, as the blade struck out, he caught the man's wrist and twisted hard, forcing him to drop the weapon. Thomas kicked it away, then hit him even harder than the first man, this time on the side of the head. The man's knees went and he fell to the stone floor, unconscious. The last of their small group released his hold on the barber and came at Thomas. As he approached, the man with the broken nose stopped wailing and put his arms around Thomas to hold him in place. Thomas pushed backwards as hard as he could, smashing the back of the man's head into the wall. When his arms went slack, Thomas twisted to avoid the blade coming at him and lashed out. His heel caught the attacker's knee and he heard it pop out. It was an easy enough injury to fix, one Thomas had done on many a battlefield, but never without significant agony. The man screamed and hopped away. He dragged himself to the door and disappeared through it.

Which is when the young woman punched Thomas hard on the cheek. When she reached for the shears she had cut his hair with Thomas caught her wrist before she could pick them up.

"What do you think you are doing, fool?" she said. "Your meddling has killed us all."

The male barber came across. "You," he said, pointing a shaking finger at Thomas, "get out of here and never come back." He looked at the young woman, then the men on the floor. "Do you think they are dead, daughter?"

"Both alive," Thomas said, "but they will be sore when they wake up."

The barber ignored him. "We have to get them out of here before they come round. Take his feet."

"I will take the other one," Thomas said.

The man looked at him. "Why are you still here? Do you want to die?"

"Not particularly." Thomas knelt and lifted the larger of the two men beneath his arms and dragged him out through the door. By the time he had leaned him against the wall outside, the barber and his daughter had brought the other out. The street had been busy when Thomas entered the shop. Now it was almost deserted.

"Where do you want them?" he asked.

"We should toss them in the river," said the woman, but her father shook his head.

"Drag them down the alley, then we must come back and lock the doors." He shook his head. "They will be back soon enough, and more of them next time." He stared hard at Thomas. "This idiot does not know what he has done."

"We have to leave," said his daughter. "We cannot stay here now."

"This is our living," said the man.

"There is work for cutters of hair and pullers of teeth everywhere. All we need are the tools of our trade. I have heard Oxford is better than here, and there are no bonemen."

The man went inside, leaving his daughter standing beside Thomas. He could see little resemblance between father and daughter, but that meant little. Neither Thomas's son nor daughter looked anything like him.

"Show me this alley," he said, lifting the larger man, who was showing signs of waking.

The woman led Thomas along the road a short distance. A narrow alley ran away between two houses, the roofs so close a man might step from one to the other. They left the unconscious man half-way along the alley, then went back for the other. They dropped him beside his companion, his head cracking against the flagstones. The alley stank of discarded food and worse.

"Who are they, and what did they come for?" Thomas asked. "Was it nothing more than trouble?"

"They are bonemen, and they came for their monthly payment. Same as they have done this last four years. Oxford will be better, I am sure."

"What payment?"

"You must be a stranger to this town if you know not what I speak of. Once a month the bonemen visit our shop and all the others in this street. They demand a shilling from some, a penny from others, each to their ability to pay. We are told it is to protect us from villains; but they are the villains."

"Does everybody pay?"

"If they value their lives they do. You should get out of town before they make an example of you. The one who escaped will run back to his master to report your resistance."

"I don't think he is capable of running," Thomas said. "A fast limp at best."

As they approached the barbershop, the man emerged. He carried two small hemp bags and handed one to his daughter. "Come then, let us run from here while we can.

It will not be long before they are back, and there will be more than three of them when they do." He glanced at Thomas, then turned away, uninterested in his fate.

Thomas watched them walk away towards the west. All around him, the busy life of the street began to start up again. Soon, the unconscious attackers would wake. Thomas wondered if they could describe him. For a moment, he considered entering the alley and killing them both. It would take no time at all and put an end to any chance the bonemen could come after him. But Thomas had grown tired of killing. He had turned his back on it years ago. He only hoped it would now turn its back on him in return.

TWO

When Thomas passed the barber's shop the following morning he stayed on the opposite side of Ludgate Hill. He knew word had spread regarding events of the day before when he saw a workman removing the barber's pole, while others carried crates inside. New tenants were moving in, the location too good to be left vacant for long. Despite his careful examination of those he passed, Thomas saw none wearing the scarlet hats he assumed identified a boneman. He knew a little more about them from Peggy Spicer, the goodwife of the Bell Savage, a buxom woman in her thirties with a ready laugh. She had leaned across the table after bringing Thomas an excellent stew, her impressive cleavage deliberately displayed for his enjoyment should he care to look. She seemed in no hurry to return to her work. Other women passed by as they served the patrons.

"Yes, I know about the bonemen," she said. "Every innkeeper, trader and establishment in London knows of them. Why do you ask?"

When Thomas told her, she stared at him with eyes wide.

"Why did you do such a foolish thing, sir? I wish I had never sent you to that barber now."

"I would like as not have got into trouble wherever I went. I cannot stand aside and watch when a woman is being assaulted."

Peggy Spicer laughed. "You are in the wrong town for that kind of chivalry."

"Do they call on you, these bonemen?"

"They call on everyone. As you can see, we are a busy establishment. We consider the payment we make to them the cost of doing business, no different to paying the King's tax."

"And the name? Do they call themselves bonemen, or a name given to them?"

"You don't want to know," said Peggy Spicer.

Thomas leaned across the table. "But I do."

She looked around the room and then, as if satisfied they could not be overheard, and she was not required for some urgent task, pulled out a chair and sat.

"I think it is a name given them but one they have taken as their own because of the fear it brings." Another look around. A lean across the table which displayed even more of her cleavage. Thomas tried not to stare. "They are amenable enough most of the time, but—"

"Those I met earlier today were not."

"Most of the time," she said again. "But if you refuse to pay, or you cross them, there are punishments. Beatings. Rapes. Cuttings. For serious transgressions, death. And when they have inflicted their punishment, they leave a single piece of bone."

"Human?"

"You would need to ask that of someone else. I have never seen one of these bones, only heard tales."

"Do the authorities know about them?"

"Everyone knows about them."

"So why is nothing done to stop them?"

Peggy saw Thomas's pewter goblet was empty and refilled it from the jug of wine on the table. "No doubt they have better matters to concern themselves with. I don't know why they take no action, but they will have their reasons. Did you enjoy the stew?" Peggy stood, making it clear no more information would be forthcoming from her.

"It was excellent."

"My recipe. Now, do you want me to send a girl up to your room later? They are all clean, all willing. Only four shillings a go."

Thomas shook his head, suppressing a smile. "My thanks, but I have no need of a girl."

"Someone more mature perhaps?" She gave what she no doubt intended as a sultry smile, which was lost on its intended subject. "You are a good-looking man, so perhaps you think you do not need to pay. But men always pay."

"I have a friend you would get on well with."

"Is he handsome, too?"

"He is the most handsome man you will ever set your eyes on."

Peggy looked around the room. "Where is he? I would like to meet him."

"He is probably somewhere in France by now. He is bringing our two families to England, so I expect you will meet him soon enough. I gave him the name of this establishment and told him to come here asking for me."

"That is fine good of you, sir. Why the name of the Bell Savage?"

"It was given to me by someone before I left Spain."

"You don't look Spanish."

"That is because I am not. I was born in England sixty years ago but have not set foot on its soil in over forty-six of those years."

"You don't look to have sixty years."

"Now you try to flatter me, but I know how I look."

"Why are you back in England, sir?" Someone called Peggy's name and she raised a hand in acknowledgement but waited to hear his answer.

"I am hoping for an audience with the King tomorrow."

Peggy laughed and turned away, shaking her head. Clearly, she did not believe him.

Now, on a fine morning where overnight rain had washed the streets clean and a westerly breeze carried some of the stink away, Thomas dismissed all thoughts of the bonemen from his mind. After what Peggy had told him, he knew they preyed on the entire city, and he was but one man. Besides which, this was no longer his country, and this was not his fight. He would hand the message he carried in his jacket to King Henry, finish the task Queen Isabel of Castile had set him, and return to the warmer climate he had grown accustomed to. Only six months, though he would have preferred those months not to be mostly winter. He had bad memories of English winters.

Thomas ignored the majesty of St. Paul's Cathedral, the spire reaching into the sky as though to pierce it. Instead, he turned right and headed for Cheapside. The alley he took was narrow with the roofs of houses to either side almost meeting overhead to cut out the daylight and enclose the fetid odour. Thomas picked his way carefully, avoiding what he could, but could not do the same for the stink. Those he passed appeared not to notice it at all.

One of Peggy's girls had drawn him a map, a simple sketch but more than adequate to take him to the Tower. Thomas had been informed the King would reside there until they completed his new palace on the river at Richmond. Both Peggy and the map-drawer warned him from venturing too close to the river. Thomas found the number and closeness of the churches a surprise, though their presence should not have been. Like Spain, England was a devout Catholic country with a devout ruler. Thomas knew he would have to bear that in mind and make a pretence at devoutness himself. He knew the words and actions, but the peace and glory they had once brought him as a boy had long since been scoured from his soul.

As Thomas approached the Postern Gate, two guards blocked him from entering. Others were being allowed through with a nod, but Thomas understood he was a stranger here. He only hoped his accent would not complicate matters. Peggy had already commented on his manner of speech. He knew the English words but had forgotten the right way to sound them.

"What is your business, sir?" asked a guard.

It pleased Thomas to hear the 'sir'. He had dressed as well as he could. He had almost not worn the tagelmust that had become second-nature to wrap around his shoulders and head, but examining other men he had twisted it into a passing resemblance of a chaperon.

He took a step back as he reached into his jacket, in case either guard thought him reaching for a knife. He drew out the letter he had carried ever since Isabel handed it to him several months before. It was creased, but the royal seal remained intact.

"I wish to present a letter from her Royal Highness Queen Isabel of Castile to His Majesty King Henry. It concerns her daughter, the Princess Catherine of Aragon, who arrives shortly to marry Prince Arthur."

The guard stared at the letter. Thomas saw he wanted to reach for it but could not now the words had been spoken. Stilted and formal, but deliberately so. As he wended his way through Spain and France, Thomas had honed the words over and over until satisfied they were the best he could conjure. Now the time and place had arrived to see if they would be good enough or not.

"And you are?" The guard looked Thomas up and down, but did not appear concerned at what he saw.

"I am Thomas Berrington, Duke of Granada." These words were easier because they were the truth, even if he could scarce believe it himself. Isabel had elevated his rank and set him as the ultimate authority of the city he had once called home. Perhaps, he hoped, he might one day call it home again.

"Berrington is no Spanish name," said the guard.

"Indeed, it is not. I was born in England."

"And now you are a Spanish Duke?"

"It is a long tale, sir, and best kept for the King." Thomas held the letter out, a little reluctant to do so because he had carried it for so long, and the last fingers to touch it other than his own had been Isabel's. But this place, and the King within, was its intended destination.

The guard took it before handing it to his companion. "Take this inside and pass it to someone who can make sure it gets to the right person." When the other guard had gone the man turned back to Thomas. "If I may say so, sir, you do not have the look of a Duke about you, Spanish or otherwise."

"It is a title, nothing more, and does not define me as it might others."

"You wear no jewels, no ermine. Are the customs so different in this place you call Granada?"

"Indeed they are, but to explain them would be another lengthy tale."

The guard gave a nod, as if grateful he would not have to hear it. "You can wait over there with the others." The man stared at Thomas, a challenge in his eyes because he had deliberately not used the correct form of address for a man of stature.

Thomas smiled and moved away, unconcerned. There were times he forgot what Isabel had turned him into. He would have it stripped from him if he could, but knew in this place the title would carry weight. With good fortune, it would allow him to do what he had been sent to achieve. To protect Catherine with his own life if necessary.

Thomas purchased a warm bread roll from a street-seller and bit into it, relieved to discover it palatable. He had left the inn without breaking his fast, so ate the roll in three bites and bought a second. He tore off small chunks as he sat on a low stone wall and watched the bustle of foot-traffic in and out of the Tower. Men and women, a few children. Some carried goods. Some were well-dressed and clearly people of stature. The others were dressed as most were in London, the manner of dress different to that of Spain. Less flamboyant here for those of importance. Somehow duller for those who were not.

The Tower was a solid, square structure set hard on the banks of the Thames, where small boats were pulled up on a shingle beach to unload supplies. The outer wall was high, with only a few heavily guarded entrances offering access to a second level of defence. From within rose a substantial square tower with bright pennants flying from each corner. Thomas did not know what they signified, but was sure someone would tell him if he asked. Not that he would ask because he did not care. Only one thing concerned him, and had done so for many years. That was the young woman who was even now making her way to this country to marry the King's son.

Thomas heard the many church bells stutter to ring off the hour of prayer before a tall woman with sleek dark hair emerged and spoke with the guard, who had passed his time watching Thomas when not dealing with more urgent matters. Thomas rose and walked across to them.

"Is this him?" She looked Thomas up and down, her expression showing little welcome.

"It is. He claims to be the Duke of Granada."

"Then perhaps that is who he is." The woman turned to Thomas. She almost matched his height, which would place her close to six feet. She was slim, dressed in a long, dark dress that hid her feet. Her hair was as black as the dress and hung long down her back, caught in a clasp at the base of her neck. "I am Philippa Gale. Come with me." She spoke sharply, and Thomas wondered if she had been called away from some more important matter to deal with him. He noticed her hands were empty. Isabel's letter must lie somewhere inside the Tower walls. He followed her through the outer guard-post, then through a second into an inner ward.

"Are you taking me to see King Henry?"

"King and Queen both. You have created quite a stir, Your Grace." Unlike the guard, she used the correct form of address. The one Thomas hated.

They passed through another gate into an open court-yard, a further wall to the right. Ahead, the square tower loomed up, but that was not their destination. Philippa Gale led Thomas to yet another entrance set close to the base of the tower and they entered a grassed area. Seated to one side were two boys, one close to being a man and, if Thomas judged correctly, even closer to being a married man. A second boy sat beside him as they played a game of checkers. Thomas assumed this was the young Henry, Duke of York. His age was right, as was the description. Two jugglers tossed flaming batons into the air, throwing them from one to the other. A small group of musicians played lutes, while another banged a ragged beat on a small drum. None of them were particularly skilled.

Philippa Gale wrapped her fingers around Thomas's wrist and drew him towards where a man and woman sat side by side, watching the entertainment. She released her hold when they were twenty paces away and allowed him to proceed the rest of the way alone.

Thomas bowed low. When he straightened, the woman motioned him closer. The Queen was in her mid-thirties, with lustrous blonde hair, her clothing elegant. A small red hat sat on top of her hair, held there with a long silver pin. The King was perhaps ten years older. His dark hair was cut to just above the shoulder, as promised by the barber, and starting to show traces of grey. His face was stern, but whether this was his usual expression or a response to his unexpected visitor, Thomas did not know. The King's eyes tracked him up and down with little sign of welcome. Thomas directed his own gaze to a point between the two, knowing better than to meet their gaze. Not yet, in any case. He needed to remember this king and queen were not like Isabel. His relationship with her, honed over many years, was far closer than it had any right to be. Thomas saw Isabel's letter grasped in Queen Elizabeth's hand, which she lifted to make a show of reading.

"Do you speak English?" asked the Queen. "We can manage French and Latin, of course, but Spanish is beyond us. Though my son is trying to learn a little for when his bride arrives."

"Princess Catherine speaks passable English, Your Grace. I taught her myself."

"And this letter, did you also write it yourself? Do you know it is also in English and describes a man of unusual, if not suspicious, talents?"

"I believe Queen Isabel wrote it with her own hand, Your Grace, and its contents are unknown to me. The Queen also speaks passable English. She has a fascination for this country. I believe it derives from an interest in her ancestors."

"John of Gaunt." The King spoke for the first time, his voice softer than Thomas expected. "Who is also an ancestor of mine, as he is of my Queen. Do you play chess?"

Thomas suppressed a frown. "I do, Your Grace."

"Good. Play a game with me. How about a wager of a crown?"

Thomas stared at the King until remembering himself. "A crown? I do not know that coin, Your Grace."

"When did you leave England for Spain, sir?"

"At the age of thirteen. Forty-seven years ago."

"Then that is why you do not know it. I had it minted barely six years ago. I suspect you do not possess such a coin, so how say you to a shilling? There must be a wager, otherwise what is the point of the game?"

"I can afford a shilling, Your Grace, but have no money on me." Thomas made a show of patting his jacket. He saw the Queen smile.

"I expect I can trust a man who claims to be the Duke of Granada for a shilling, just as he can the King of England. So what do you say, sir?"

"I say yes, Your Grace."

King Henry rose and offered a hand to his wife. As they moved towards one of the buildings lining the square, Thomas heard the music fade into a chaotic ending and the jugglers let their flaming torches fall to the ground where they stamped them out.

Thomas felt another touch on his wrist as Philippa Gale came to stand beside him.

"Can you really play chess?" she asked as she led him after the King and Queen.

"I can. I prefer mandala, but I play chess well enough."

"I don't know this mandala you speak of, but the King plays chess well enough too, and he loves a wager. Whatever you do, Thomas, do not lose to him deliberately, thinking it will please him. He will know if you do and you will lose any slight chance of friendship you may have."

Thomas had not considered friendship with the King, though why not was an interesting question.

"Does he win often?"

Philippa laughed as they entered the building. "No, not so often. I may have exaggerated his skill. He even lost a game to his son."

"Arthur?"

Philippa gave another laugh. "Young Harry, who has only ten years but is sharp for his age. As is Arthur, of course. You have come to talk of the marriage, have you not?"

"Marriage and other matters, yes."

"Other matters? What can be more important than the joining of two great powers?"

"Can I ask you something?"

"It depends what manner of question it is. Try me and see, Your Grace."

"Only if you stop calling me that."

"But you are the Duke of Granada. Is it not expected?"

"Not by me."

"Very well then. I shall try to remember your request. Should I call you Thomas?"

"That sounds like a good idea." Thomas was unsure if she was flirting with him or not. He was too out of practice in such arts to be sure. If only his companion Jorge was here, he would know in an instant. Except if Jorge Olmos was present, then the beautiful Philippa Gale would not be flirting with plain Thomas Berrington.

"I ran across a little trouble yesterday and I am curious whether the King knows of the perpetrators of it."

"I am sorry you had a poor experience of London, Thomas, but like all cities there is both good and bad here. What happened?" Once more, she touched his wrist, her fingers warm.

"I ran into some people who call themselves the bonemen. It seems they are extorting money from every trader, inn, tavern, and business in London. It is the kind of affair the King should know of. But I expect he already does and is putting measures in place. It is not my business, is it?"

"No, sir, it is none of your business." Philippa Gale's face had lost all trace of flirtation. Had Thomas any expectations he might have felt disappointment, but he had none. "I suggest you make no reference to it. Play your game of chess. Win or lose, it matters not which as long as you have a shilling if you lose. Then tell the King and Queen about this Catherine of Aragon. What she is like. How pretty she is. What manner of wife she will make for their son. That is what you are here for, and nothing else."

THREE

The King sat at a narrow table while a page laid out the chessboard. The man placed the white pieces on King Henry's side. Thomas crossed to the table and waited until the board was complete and Henry nodded for him to sit. The first move was a pawn, of course, and Thomas countered to free up his second rank. When Henry brought a second pawn to sit beside the first Thomas hesitated a moment, then took it.

Queen Elizabeth settled into a chair at the end of the table, Philippa Gale at the other. The Queen raised a hand to call a servant across.

"Bring us some of the good wine," she said. "Unless you prefer ale, sir?"

"Wine is most acceptable, Your Grace."

The Queen placed Isabel's letter in front of her. Thomas saw it comprised two sheets. He recognised the tiny, elegant hand of its author.

"Queen Isabel of Castile appears to have a high regard

for you, Thomas Berrington. An uncommonly high regard. Is it deserved, sir?"

"I am not the one to judge that, Your Grace, but it pleases me she does." When Henry brought his bishop out, Thomas moved his queen as far as he could on the diagonal, putting Henry's king in check. His skill at the game had improved since he had been in Isabel's employ. She enjoyed the game as a relaxation of an evening and they often played together while Catherine sat and watched, by far the most studious, as well as pious, of her children.

"You are close to both her and her husband?"

"I have served alongside them for fifteen years, Your Grace, and given what best service I can."

"As one mother to another, the Queen has been most candid. She tells me that without your skill, Princess Catherine would have died at birth, and most likely her mother too. She also tells me you are the best physician in the whole of Spain." Elizabeth shook her head at the notion of such a ridiculous claim. "And that for some time you lived among the heathen Moors."

"I did, Your Grace." Thomas knew better than to attempt a lie. "I learned whatever skill I may possess at the great Infirmary in Málaga, training under Moorish physicians and scientists."

Elizabeth glanced at the letter once more. She was silent for a long time. So long that a footman set down a tray of glasses and two bottles of dark wine. Henry sucked air through stained teeth and moved his king one square to the right. Thomas brought another pawn forward.

"Queen Isabel asks something in this letter—a letter intended not for me but my husband—that is highly unusual. She asks that you can accompany her daughter, Princess Catherine, when she comes to England. Will she not have her own people to take care of her? Not to mention my own son's guards and soldiers. Why you, a lone man? Or are you not alone?"

"I have family and friends following behind me, Your Grace, but at the moment there is only myself." Thomas was aware of two games taking place here and hoped he could respond to both.

"I see." There was an uncomfortable pause during which Thomas wondered what thoughts might run through the Queen's head.

"Your Grace…" He waited until her eyes met his. "Whether I am granted this great honour Isabel has asked of me or not, I intend to watch over Catherine and keep her safe for as long as I might live."

"Isabel and Catherine, is it? Not Queen and Princess? Exactly how close to the royal family of Spain are you, sir?"

"They are my family now, Your Grace." Thomas felt the conversation slipping away from him and feared he had handled matters badly. He wished he could start over, but it was too late for wishes. "And yes, Your Grace, when in their company I use their given names, I freely admit it. As do my son and daughter."

"What ages are your children? And their names, if you will?"

Thomas smiled, on safer ground now the Queen was curious about his family. Not such safe ground if he told her all the truth, but he hoped he would not be that stupid a second time.

"Will is the name of my son, Your Grace. William Berrington. And my daughter's name is Amal. It is a Moorish name, as her mother Lubna's name was."

"You are married to a Moor?"

"I was, Your Grace. She died."

"I am sorry to hear that. Have you taken another wife? A Spaniard, perhaps?"

Thomas moved chess pieces without thought. He had discovered Henry a limited player of the game and saw how his ten-year-old son had beaten him. Instead of concentrating on the chess game, Thomas gave most of his attention to the other game taking place with the Queen. He did not know why she was so interested in his personal life, but was grateful her questioning was at least friendly.

"I have no wife now, but was married to the daughter of a Northman until recently."

A smile appeared on the Queen's lips and made it as far as her eyes. "I see you are a cosmopolitan individual, sir. Both Moorish and Northern brides. Did this second wife also die?"

"She grew bored with me and found a more exciting husband, Your Grace."

The Queen looked as if she was about to laugh before she controlled herself.

"I understand you left England at a young age, in the company of your father."

Thomas glanced again at the letter the Queen held. It was not nearly long enough to have outlined his entire life story.

"I did, Your Grace. You are most well informed."

"You are wondering how I know so much about you, are you not, sir?"

"You are the Queen of England, Your Grace. No doubt you need to know a great many things, even about a poor orphan such as myself."

The Queen smiled, making her even more beautiful than she already was.

"I like you, Thomas Berrington. You aren't afraid of me, are you."

"Should I be, Your Grace?"

The smile remained. "We are in the Tower of London. Men and women have disappeared inside these walls, never to be seen again. As I know only too well. If I click my fingers, the same might happen to you."

Thomas waited, but the Queen did not click her fingers.

"Did you not wonder why we kept an important man loitering outside for so long? The Duke of Granada, no less." The Queen waited while a servant poured wine into their glasses. She lifted hers and sipped, gave a nod of approval. "Queen Isabel gave us your name and your title. We maintain excellent records in England, so it was easy enough to track you down. Made easier because of those you accompanied when you left this country. Your father was Sir John Berrington and fought alongside John Talbot, the Earl of Shrewsbury, at Castillon. It was before I was born, sir, but England lost many good men that day." Her face offered a sour expression that was nothing to do with the wine, which was excellent.

Thomas gave his attention to the chess game and saw he would be the victor. As he had been a victor so many times in his life. He counted the pieces on the board. Twenty-four remained. Fifteen belonged to him.

Henry had three moves that might threaten Thomas's king, but he could counter all. Henry reached for his knight, then withdrew his hand without touching it. Instead, he brought his queen forward to check Thomas's king. It was an arrogant move which might have won the game, but Henry had missed Thomas's own knight. He set his finger on it and as he did so, he saw the realisation in Henry's eyes.

"Damn it, sir. Do it, then."

Thomas moved his knight, lifting Henry's king from the board and laying it on the table.

"Good game, Your Grace," he said. "You almost had me a few times there."

"You flatter me with your words, Sir Thomas." The King smiled. "Yes, we know that about you as well, and what you did on the field of battle at Castillon. What age were you?"

"Thirteen, Your Grace."

"Were you, by damn? I would say too young for such an honour to be given, but the records do not lie. What was the fighting like?"

"Bloody, Your Grace."

"Battles always are." The King leaned forward. "It was before my time, but everyone knows it is where the French beat us after England had been victorious for a century of skirmishing. I would like to hear your story some time, sir, and how you came to be knighted on the field of battle, but not today. We have other matters to discuss, and you must give me a chance to win my shilling back." The King clicked his fingers and a servant hurried across to be instructed.

"How long have you known Queen Isabel?" asked the Queen.

"I first met her in the year of our Lord fourteen-hundred and eighty-three, Your Grace, when I treated her son for a badly mended leg."

"So it is true you are both physician and soldier?"

"It is true, Your Grace, though everything that happened to me was little more than one accident after another. I had no plan to do any of it. Being a soldier was thrust upon me rather than through any conscious choice."

"But do it you did, sir," said King Henry. "That shows character."

"I had an uncle travel to Spain during the expulsion of the heathens," said the Queen. "He told me he fought alongside King Fernando at Málaga."

"There were many Englishmen there, Your Grace, and all fought bravely."

"And for a just cause."

"As you say. What was the name of your uncle?" Though Thomas believed he already knew.

"Richard Woodville, the third Earl Rivers. Did you ever come across him, sir? Two Englishmen in a foreign land?"

"I did, Your Grace." Thomas knew he was walking on eggshells now. He wondered how much the Queen's uncle might have told her about their encounter during the savage siege of one of the great Moorish cities of al-Andalus.

Queen Elizabeth's eyes tracked his face. "He mentioned meeting several Englishmen while he was there, but your name is not familiar to me if he did, but it was a long time ago so he may have done."

The chessboard was set up afresh, Henry still playing white. The servant he had spoken to returned and softly lay a shilling coin on the table beside Thomas.

"That will be mine soon enough," said Henry, and laughed.

His wife smiled softly at him, a clear affection between them. "I believe all the coins in the land are yours, my love."

A softness had settled across them, which told Thomas he might have some chance of success in what Isabel was asking of him. He wondered if he could allow the King to win the next game without letting it show. Before either could make a move, two figures entered the room. Arthur, Prince of Wales, and his brother Henry, Duke of York. They approached the table, Henry with more swagger than his elder brother, despite being five years his junior.

"Can I ask you something, Sir Thomas?" said the Queen.

"I am at your command, Your Grace."

"Indeed, you are. My son is sore curious about his bride to be, which is natural in a man. Word is she is beautiful, but when we sent our own artist to Spain, the portrait he made shows her as uncommonly serious."

"Catherine is devout, Your Grace, but she is also one of the most beautiful creatures ever to walk this earth. I recall when the man came to court and am afraid to say she took against him at once."

"You know her so well?"

"As you are already aware, I have known her since she was born. She is clever, brave, and loyal."

"That pleases me to hear."

Thomas glanced at Arthur and made a decision. "If I may, I would like to show you how beautiful Catherine truly is. Queen Isabel is fully aware you want to know what manner of woman your son is to marry, so she had Antonio del Rincon, who has been artist to her court these last twenty years or more, to paint Catherine exactly as she is."

The Queen looked at Thomas without expression. Her son leaned forward, a tension in him.

"Do you have this miraculous painting in your possession, Sir Thomas?"

"I have it on my person, Your Grace." Thomas slipped a hand inside his jacket. "If I am allowed?" He waited for permission.

Arthur took a step closer. The young Henry was moving chess pieces around randomly.

"Show it to me first," said the Queen.

Thomas withdrew a small block of wood only six inches by five. He had carried it over all the miles between Granada and London because Isabel had known this token would be required. He hid the image it held from Arthur as he handed the block to Queen Elizabeth.

She held it up. Her eyes came to Thomas, back to the painting. It was small, but Thomas knew it was a perfect representation of Catherine. As it was of him. That too had been Isabel's idea.

"Why are you in this picture, sir?" asked the Queen.

"Are you truly as close to the Spanish royal family as this implies?"

"I think I have already explained that, Your Grace. Queen Isabel knows as well as you how marriages, especially royal marriages, may be arranged without either party meeting. She also knows from personal experience the images sent to prove suitability are often, shall we say, lacking in a necessary authenticity. By adding me to the painting, she hopes you see Catherine is truly as beautiful as claimed, set as she is beside my plainness."

The Queen continued to look between the painting and Thomas. Finally, she handed it to her husband, who made a grunt of approval. He passed it to Prince Arthur, whose already pale face paled even further as he took in the image of his bride-to-be. Thomas tensed himself to rise, sure the youth was about to faint. The moment passed when the young Henry snatched the wooden block from him and laughed.

"She is indeed fine handsome, Arthur," he said. "If you decide not to marry her, I think I might."

His father reached out and slapped the back of Henry's head.

"Thomas is too good a player for me, Harry. Perhaps you can beat him and earn yourself a shilling."

FOUR

Thomas had returned to his room at the Bell Savage only moments before when there came a rap on the door.

"It is open," he called out, balancing on one foot as he tried to pull his too-tight boot off the other.

It surprised him when goodwife Peggy Spicer entered. She came in, closed the door behind her and pushed him so he sat hard on the bed.

"Let me do that for you, sir."

Thomas grew uneasy. Peggy was a handsome woman, with a voluptuous body, but he was not looking for diversions. He might have in the past, and he might again in the future, but at the moment other matters pressed on his mind.

Peggy knelt and tugged at the stubborn boot until it came free. Then she worked on the other before standing.

"Four bonemen came while you were out." She appeared to notice his manner of dress for the first time. "My, but you look like a gentleman now, don't you?"

"Which is why I need to change before coming down to eat. Did these men call for their stipend?"

"It was not payment they were after, not yet at least. That is due next Monday. They were looking for a man who fought back while he was having his hair trimmed. Does that sound like someone you know?"

"Did they come because they know I am staying here? If so, I apologise for bringing trouble to your door, Peggy."

"They described you good and fine. A tall man with hair greying at the sides. Hair that had been recently cut and face cleanly shaved. A good fighter, they said. That I did not know about you, but I can see how it might be true. They are asking at all the inns within a quarter-mile of the barbershop. I told them I knew no one who matched that description, but I am sure they will be back when they fail to find you. What happened, Thomas?" She used his name deliberately, but then why should she not? He had called her Peggy.

"One of them assaulted the barber's daughter. It was she who cut my hair and shaved me. I thought I had left all such things behind, but it appears not to be so. What should I have done, allowed the man to rape her and then the others take their turn?"

"They will do that now anyway, in punishment for what they regard as resistance. They will need to be seen to do so, and when finished they will set a single bone between her naked breasts."

"That will not happen. The girl and her father left for Oxford immediately after the altercation. I saw someone

36

else moving in as I passed the premises this morning. How many of these bonemen are there?"

"Why do you want to know? Too many to fight, if that is what you are thinking."

"How many?" Thomas rose to his feet, uncomfortable at having her stand over him. He walked to the window to put some distance between them and tried to recall how long since he last lain with a woman. Months most like, certainly not weeks.

"More than a hundred, possibly double or treble that number. London is a big city. I see the same faces come here often enough, but each group has their own territory."

"Do they have a base?"

"Do not even ask that," said Peggy. "You cannot fight them."

"I don't intend to, but does the King know about what they are doing? I meant to mention them to him but was warned off in no small manner."

Peggy laughed. "King Henry would not bother himself with the troubles of small men and women such as myself."

"The authorities, then. There must be some form of law here."

"Yes. The King's law, which is mostly concerned with much tax he can squeeze from commoners so he can spend it building his new palace out Richmond way. That or gamble it away. Henry likes a wager, but he rarely wins is what I hear."

Thomas smiled. "That I am already aware of." He

reached into his pocket and drew out the two shillings he had won. One from the father, the other from the son. He tossed one to Peggy, who caught it with the ease of long practice.

"What is this for?" She made an attempt to put on a sultry expression but failed.

"I won that from King Henry today. You are right that he likes a wager, as does his son."

"Now that I did not know, and it surprises me. I hear Arthur is too serious for his own good."

"His other son. And that is for the trouble I brought you. I will leave tonight if you can recommend somewhere as good as the Bell Savage."

"There is nowhere as good as this house, and there is no need to scurry away. Stay in your room for a night or two. I will send your food up, and a bottle of wine." She tried for sultry again, with the same result. "And if you need anything else just ask for me."

When she was gone Thomas turned the key in the lock and undressed. He used a linen cloth to wash his body, then dressed in less ostentatious clothes. He wrapped his tagelmust around his neck and coiled it over his head so he could easily arrange it to hide his face if necessary. He had no plan, no idea of what he intended to do, but he felt a need to be in the company of ordinary men and women. His shoulders remained tense after being in the presence of the King and Queen, of making sure every word carried the right meaning and was spoken using the correct protocol. He hesitated at the bottom of the stairs, but Peggy was deep in conversation with a group of gentlemen who had taken a corner table. Thomas slipped through the back door and walked past the stables into Ludgate Hill. He watched the passers-by for a while until he was sure no bonemen were among them. The throng was thick with people, horses and carts entering and leaving through Ludgate. Thomas checked once more before making his way to the far side of the road to disappear down an alley leading south. Peggy had warned him from venturing too close to the river, so it was there he headed. Thomas was unafraid of being accosted. His own reaction in the barbershop had come as a surprise, but also sparked something he thought might have been lost to him—his talent for fighting. It had always been with him, even as a boy, and his life since had honed it into something he gave little thought to. He could fight, it was as simple as that. He could *still* fight.

The alleys grew narrower, twisting and turning in a confusion of directions. Thomas tried to pick his way through the detritus discarded by those who lived cheek by jowl then gave up, otherwise he would have made no progress at all. When he came to the river he turned east, the road a little wider here and open to the water on his right. Despite the approach of night men continued to work, loading and unloading ships, and wherries carried people to and fro across the water. Eventually, Thomas found what he was looking for. A sad looking alehouse stood on the corner of two roads. Workmen stood outside drinking because there was no inside, only a rough hole in the wall of a house from which ale was passed out in leather or wooden pots. Thomas searched his pocket for the smallest coin he could find, but even that resulted in the tippler having to make change. The ale was sour, with a strange, rancid aftertaste, but Thomas knew he had to drink it if he wanted to fit in. He was looking for answers but knew better than to ask questions. Instead he fell into conversation with two men who approached him to ask if he was in the right place. Despite wearing his oldest, most repaired clothes, they recognised a stranger. Thomas wondered if he should not have bothered washing before he came out.

Thomas told them he was a stranger in town, recently returned from fighting abroad. He was thinking of setting himself up in a small business such as an alehouse. It was all that was needed. Every man in London likes to think himself an expert in all manner of subjects, even those he has no expertise in. It helped when Thomas bought more ale when their pots were empty.

"Of course, you will need to account for the tax," said one as he sipped the top from his pot.

"The King's tax?" Thomas asked. "Do they even bother to collect it from a place such as this?"

The man laughed. "Not the King, sir, the bonemen. They tax every premise, even one such as this, though not so much as they might ask of a smart establishment such as a tavern."

"Do you mean they demand payment?" Thomas asked.

"I do, sir."

"In exchange for what?"

"They say they will attend if you ever have trouble you cannot deal with yourself. Of course, they never do, not so far as I have ever heard."

"Why don't people simply refuse to pay?"

"Well, then there will be trouble. They are hard men and have been known to kill an entire household to set an example. Women raped, even children put to the sword. Nobody wants that bone set on their hearth." The man spat on the ground. "I am glad to be an honest worker unloading cargo, though I expect my master must pay his stipend every month, the same as everyone else."

"Why do the authorities do nothing about it?" Thomas had asked the same of Peggy, but he believed he might get a more honest answer from these men.

"Why do you think, sir? And yes, another ale would be most welcome. I have a fair thirst on me this evening."

Thomas went to the hatch and returned with full pots. He nodded to let the man know to continue.

"I hear rumours the bonemen pay those in authority to look the other way. It is good business for both sides. So you may want to consider setting yourself up in some town other than London. Or perhaps just accept, like everyone else, that some of your profit will end up in the bonemen's pockets. What you need to remember is—" It seemed the man was warming to his subject when all at once he turned away. He and his companion found something fascinating on the far side of the street.

When Thomas glanced around he saw two men approaching. He did as the men had and crossed the street. He stood hard against the closed door of a house and watched the two men approach.

They stopped at a shop selling felt hats and some coin changed hands. They stopped again at a butcher's shop, and once more money was exchanged. When they reached the hatch in the wall they demanded two pots of ale and a ha'peny. It was far less than the shilling asked of the Bell Savage, but more than enough considering the difference in their circumstances. The two men had a short conversation with the tippler before moving off.

Thomas allowed them to get fifty paces away before he crossed the road. He slipped a penny across the counter, which quickly disappeared.

"What did they want?"

"They wanted their two farthings." The tippler studied Thomas. "They also asked if I had seen a tall man with shoulder length hair. A man who might look a little like yourself, sir."

"And what did you tell them?"

"That I had seen no such man. Whoever that man might be I would recommend he keeps his head down for a while."

Thomas slid six pennies across. "Ale for everyone as long as that lasts. My thanks."

The two bonemen had turned the corner at the far end of the street by the time Thomas started after them, which suited him fine. He caught sight of them ahead as he turned the same corner, then stayed well back, finding something of interest each time they stopped at a premises. Three more streets away they approached a man who stood at the side of the road with a small wooden barrow. Instead of demanding money from him the waiting man opened the neck of a hessian sack resting in the barrow and both men emptied coins from their pockets into it before moving on.

Thomas watched them go, then decided to stay where

he was. Whoever the man with the barrow was, he had the money. The bells of the multitude of nearby churches rang out another prayer hour in mis-timed strikes before the man started away, pushing the barrow ahead of him. He made no effort to avoid those coming the other way, expecting them to avoid him instead; which all did.

He reached the gate leading onto London Bridge and passed the guards without paying. When Thomas reached them they demanded a farthing to cross. He had no intention of crossing but paid the farthing anyway.

A third of the way across, the barrowman stopped in front of one of the tall houses that lined the sides of the road. To its left towered the chapel of Thomas á Becket, while on the right a shorter, wider house sat. The man banged on a wide door, and when it opened pushed his barrow inside.

Thomas ran hard so he could see inside the house before the door shut. He had just enough time to glimpse a wide interior lit by oil-lamps, enough time to see a sturdy table piled with all manner of coin being counted by half a dozen men. One man sat on the far side with a ledger, recording the night's haul. And then the door started to close.

It stopped and a man came out onto the road. He stared hard at Thomas.

"Move along, sir, if you know what is good for you. There is nothing to see here."

A hidden voice from inside called out, "Who is it?"

"A nobody, Galib, poking his nose where it don't belong."

Thomas offered a nod and continued south along the

bridge. He would take his time before returning, and make sure the door was shut before he passed. He considered himself fortunate the man had not been offered a description of who the bonemen were searching London for.

FIVE

When Thomas arrived back at the Bel Savage, Peggy Spicer caught up with him as he tried to pass unnoticed through the main room. Her husband looked up from serving ale and watched her come across to him without expression.

"Someone called for you, Thomas," said Peggy as she accompanied him into the rear hall leading to the stairs.

"More bonemen?"

"No, a woman. A beautiful woman. Well-dressed. She gave me this for you."

She reached beneath her blouse and drew out a note. When she handed it to him it was still warm from lying against her fulsome breast and he suppressed a smile at the blatant attempt at seduction. No wonder her husband had offered little welcome on his return.

The wax seal was broken, and she saw him note the fact.

"It was that way when she handed it to me, I swear.

You saw the King, did you? He wants you to return on the morrow at the stroke of ten. Are you really a Duke?"

"I am afraid so."

"Do you want me to wake you early, Thomas? Or perhaps I should come up with you now to make sure you are comfortable."

"I would be poor company tonight; perhaps another time."

Thomas looked past Peggy to where her husband continued to stare at them, then turned away and climbed the stairs. In his room, he turned the key in the lock and placed it on the bedside table. Then he searched his belongings until he found a knife. It was six inches long; more than long enough to kill a man should such be needed. He slipped it under his pillow, then undressed and slid beneath the blanket. Peggy was going to be a problem, he knew. Once he had seen the King he should think about finding another inn, perhaps closer to the Tower. Only as he turned to blow the candle out did he recall the note. He got up again and found it in his pocket.

It was short and to the point, no doubt written by someone other than King Henry. The man wanted to see him, as Peggy had correctly stated, no later than the stroke of ten. He had a proposal to make.

Thomas wondered if Philippa Gale had been the woman who delivered it, and if so was it she who broke the seal to read the contents—no doubt assuming he would put the blame on Peggy Spicer. He set the note on the shelf beside the candle before blowing it out. His mind buzzed with a myriad of thoughts, but eventually sleep came on its stealthy feet. It was dark when something woke him and he reached out to light the candle but knocked it to the floor. With a curse, he sat up. Someone was trying the door, with no luck. Then he heard something that should not be possible. A key being inserted on the far side. Peggy had assured him each room possessed only the one key. He had been a fool to believe her.

Thomas reached for the knife as the door opened and three men entered. One was the landlord, holding a lantern aloft. The other two wore scarlet hats, visible even in the meagre light entering from the corridor. None of them spoke, but the landlord stood with his back to the door while the other two approached the bed.

"Stop where you are," Thomas said. "I have no wish to hurt you."

A coarse laugh sounded. "Good. Trouble is, we want to hurt you. Hurt you bad. Maybe too bad to survive is our order. Leave you outside on the street as an example. We were told to strip you, but I see you have saved us the trouble."

The man came at Thomas as soon as he stopped talking. His companion circled to the side, both of them with swords in their hands, which pleased Thomas. In the confined space, they would prove difficult to use.

"Your last warning," he said, but got no reply. He had not expected one, and knew he would have to kill at least one if not both of them. In that case, best to get it done he told himself.

Thomas ran at the man who had spoken, on the assumption he was likely the one in charge. The man took a step back, surprise on his face. No doubt he was used to his victims not fighting back. He raised his sword but caught the tip on the low roof. His strike when it came was weak, but the sword would still have cut into Thomas's arm. Except when it descended, Thomas was no longer there. He darted to one side and thrust his knife into the man's side. Not deep enough to kill, but deep enough he might think himself dying.

The man grunted and went to one knee. His hand clutched at the wound, but to little effect. Blood, dark in the gloom, ran down his side onto the floor. Thomas knew he should have gone for the heart but had pulled his blow instead, and he did not know why.

He turned to the second man, who was backing away.

"Are you going to see sense?" Thomas asked.

The man nodded as he continued to move towards the door.

"Tell your master not to send anyone else unless he wants them dead next time," Thomas said. "This stops now. Understand?"

The man nodded again.

"Take your man and go, he needs a doctor. Find a Moorish one if you can."

Once the man had dragged his companion through the door, Thomas walked to the innkeeper and grabbed his hair. He pulled him away from the wall.

"Did you send for them?"

"Don't kill me, sir. They came and asked about you. I knew what they would do to me, to Peggy and our girls, if they found out I lied to them."

"How much did they pay you?"

"Nothing, sir."

"Such a small sum to die over, don't you think?"

"Please, sir, no."

Thomas let his breath go, the anger leaving him with it. The man was a weak fool. He deserved punishment, but Thomas no longer felt capable of inflicting it. Instead, he picked up the candle, lit it, and started to dress.

"You are to make no mention of this to anyone, understand?"

"Yes, sir. Of course, sir. Nothing happened here." The landlord started for the door.

"Wait."

The man stopped, half-turned away as though he did not want to see the blow that killed him.

"Cross me and I will make sure you pay. And pay a lot more than you do the bonemen. Remember that. Now go."

As Thomas turned away, he trod on something sharp and drew back. When he looked down, a small pale object lay on the floor. He knelt and picked it up, turned it over. It was a small bone, one he recognised as being the upper part of a finger above the knuckle. Had the bonemen succeeded, then this is what they would have placed on his body as a warning to others. Nobody interferes with our business, and if they do, this is their punishment.

Thomas packed his few belongings into the saddle-bags. He was about to leave the room when he turned back and picked up the finger-bone from the table beside his bed and slipped it into the bag. As he descended the stairs, he met the landlord coming up with Peggy behind him. As they passed, she avoided Thomas's eyes and he knew she had been in on the plan. So much for seduction. He saddled his horse and rode out into a dark London, its streets almost deserted. His mount turned east and Thomas let it carry him towards the Tower and whatever the morning might bring. He no longer cared about the bonemen. They were not his problem. Let London deal with them or not. Thomas had a princess arriving shortly, and he had vowed to protect her.

SIX

Despite dawn having not yet broken, the guards at the Postern Gate took pity on Thomas and allowed him to pass. They told him where the stables were so he could leave his horse. A second set of guards took longer to examine Thomas's letter under the light of a lamp, but eventually passed him through the next set of barriers. They warned him he could proceed no further until his meeting, so Thomas curled up on a stone bench. He wrapped his cloak around himself and tried to sleep, recalling many other nights when he had lain on hard ground. Recalling men he had killed. The thought made him wonder why he had stayed his hand tonight. He had no expectation of finding sleep, so it surprised him to be shaken awake to discover daylight bathing the courtyard, grateful to escape his dreams. Thomas washed a hand across his face and sat up to see who had disturbed him, expecting a guard. Instead, Philippa Gale leaned over him, a spark of amusement in her dark eyes.

"I like a man who comes early for an appointment, but this might be taking matters a little too far."

Thomas's dreams had been of killing, of being chased, which is why he said, "What do you know of the bonemen?"

The amusement drained from Philippa's face. "Why do you ask such a question?"

"Because I injured one of their number last night when he came to my room. The innkeeper betrayed me."

"You attacked a boneman?" Philippa pushed Thomas along the bench and sat beside him. She gripped his wrist as she had done the first time he came to the Tower. "You said they came for you. Why?"

"I crossed them when I went for a haircut."

The mundanity of it made Philippa laugh. "They are evil men, but I have not heard they have taken against the cutting of hair. Why did you injure him?"

"Because he intended to kill me. I let his companion take him away, but my old self would have slain them both."

Philippa stared at him. "Perhaps that is what you should have done. Those men will report to their master, and the next time they come for you there will be more than two of them."

"They dropped this when they left." Thomas leaned down and searched in the small panel on the side of his saddle-bag before drawing out the finger bone. He held it in his palm to show Philippa.

She looked at it, no revulsion on her face.

"Is that what it appears to be?"

"That depends what you think it is."

"The bone from a finger."

"Then you have a good eye. They meant to lay it on my body after they finished with me. But there will be no next time. I intend to find out what the King wants and then travel south to meet my family. I will not have them come to London if it can be avoided."

"I know some of what King Henry wants, but not all. I will let him tell you himself." Philippa released his wrist and rose to her feet, once again making Thomas aware of her height, her slimness, and the curves that lay beneath the elegant dress. "You cannot wait out here until he sends for you. Come with me and I will take you to the kitchens. I am sure they can find us something to break our fasts, and it will be warmer than sitting here."

The kitchens were indeed warmer. Thomas started to sweat as he and Philippa sat at a table in one corner and ate whatever the kitchen staff were preparing for the court, which was rather a lot. A range of meats, fruit, and still-warm bread made with the finest flour, as befitted the kitchen of the King.

A flush had risen in Philippa's cheeks, so she must also have been feeling the warmth.

"Tell me about your family, Thomas. You said you married twice. Do you have children?"

"Two." He considered it wise to omit mention of any others. The explanation for them would take too long, and Thomas was finding this clever woman attracted him. And, he believed, she him. Why, he failed to understand, for there had to be thirty years between them, and he knew he was no great catch.

"Boys or girls?"

"One of each. Will is almost a man now, and taller than any man you will ever have seen."

"I have seen some very tall men, though I admit few who tower over me. And your daughter?"

"Amal has fourteen years, and with each she grows more like her mother. She is sweet and clever and loving. A man could wish for no better a daughter."

Philippa's hand came out to touch the back of his. "I can see the hurt in your eyes when you speak of them, but also the love. And your son, what age has he?"

"Eighteen years."

"You are a lucky man indeed." Still her hand remained. Thomas turned his over so their palms lay one against the other, and Philippa smiled. He did not know what his intentions were. He expected nothing of her. Nothing at all.

"Tell me about yourself," he said. "Are you married?"

"I am not, nor ever have been."

"I would ask why not, for you are a handsome woman, but no doubt you have your reasons. How long have you worked for the King?"

"Not the King but the Queen, though I expect it is one and the same these days. My mother worked for Lady Elizabeth Woodville, the Queen's mother. I was born eighteen months after the Queen and we grew up together, more like sisters than servant and mistress. Then mother died and father brought me to London and set himself up in business."

"That does not explain why you are part of the royal retinue now."

"Shortly after the Queen married I went to her at

Elsyng Palace, when she was carrying Arthur. She was pleased to see me and we talked long into the night, and in the morning she offered me the post of tutor to her children. She was so sure there would be more, and in that she was not wrong. These days I spend my time with Prince Arthur, tutoring him in the language of Spain, though he is not good at it despite being intelligent."

"*¿Hables español?*"

"*Claro que sí.*" Philippa smiled, her expression that of a young girl showing off her knowledge. "But we should speak English while we are in the Tower."

"Where did you learn to speak the language?" Thomas asked, intrigued even more by this woman.

"My father came to England from Holland, but he went there from Spain. He was—" Philippa cut herself off abruptly and withdrew her hand. "No matter what he was. He taught me his language almost from birth."

"I would like to meet him," Thomas said.

"He is dead." Philippa showed no expression, no sorrow, nothing.

Thomas examined her face, making no pretence at hiding the fact. He saw small signs. The darkness of her eyes. The sleek blackness of her hair.

"Was he Morisco?" he asked, seeing the tell in her eyes and the twitch of her lips. He spoke to her in Arabic, expressing his sympathy.

"I thank you, but my grasp of that tongue is not good. Yours, however, appears to be perfect. Do you have a past, Thomas?"

"We all have pasts, do we not? Even if they are dull and uneventful."

"But yours is not, is it?"

"Some would think so, but to me it has been my life, nothing more or less. You cannot judge your own life, can you?"

"But you are the Duke of Granada, an elevated title for an Englishman, even one who speaks Spanish and Arabic. French as well, no doubt." She smiled when Thomas nodded. "Oh, but I would like to know you better."

"You said you tutor the Prince in Spanish. Do you also teach Henry?"

"Harry," said Philippa. "We all call the little scamp Harry. And yes, a little, though he is less interested than Arthur, obviously."

"Does the King know about these bonemen who attacked me?" Thomas asked, watching as the good humour drained from Philippa's face.

"He is protected from such matters. If he needed to know of them someone would inform him, but others deal with these things."

"Except they do not appear to be doing so. What others?"

"Why are you here, Thomas? I need to know the reason before I offer information that may have nothing to do with you."

"Do you have much knowledge?"

"I live with the royal family of England, so of course I do. I am a servant, but one close to their power, who hears many things. It also helps that I am a woman, and eminent men do not consider a woman likely to understand their reasoning when they debate each other."

"But you are a clever woman, are you not?"

It relieved Thomas when she smiled. He wanted to please her. He had not wanted to please anyone outside his own family for a long time. Except, as the thought came to him, he knew it to be wrong. There were two others he wanted to please. Queen Isabel of Castile, and King Henry of England. Perhaps more than two if he included Henry's wife and children. Thomas wondered how his own children might get along with those of the King, both sons and daughters, then shook his head. He was getting above himself. England was not Spain, and his relationship to the King here was not the same as his relationship with the Queen in distant Spain. Far from it.

Philippa rose to her feet and smoothed her dress. "When the King makes his request of you, then we may see more of each other. If we do, then we can talk about our pasts. I will tell you of mine and you can tell me of yours."

"And if King Henry does not ask me what you think he is going to?"

"Then we will see; but you should know that I like you."

"Why?"

"You are more interesting than most men I meet. The palace is full of many who lack charm or humour, or those who lack any trace of intelligence. Often enough, they lack all three. You are not like them. You also strike me as dangerous, which I also find myself attracted to."

Thomas rose, his eyes only an inch above hers. "Not as dangerous as I once was."

"Except you attacked and injured a man last night, so perhaps a little dangerous still. Come, Thomas, it is close

57

to striking ten and it will not do to keep the King waiting."

There was no need to go outside because Philippa knew all the twists and turns that led them before long to the rooms Thomas had stood in the day before. Philippa held him back, her hand once more around his wrist as they waited to gain entrance. King Henry stood at a table that had not been there yesterday, his knuckles on the surface as he surveyed a scatter of papers. Two other men were with him. One was of similar height to the King and stood at his side. He was dressed in good robes and wore a chain of office around his shoulders. His face carried a sour expression that seemed baked on. The second man Thomas recognised, relieved to see Rodrigo Gonzalvo de Puebla, one of the Spanish ambassadors to King Henry's court. Thomas knew him from Granada and liked the man. There were rumours he was a converso, a Jew who now prayed in the Catholic cathedral converted from the grand mosque, but in Thomas's eyes that only made him more interesting. The other ambassador, who was not present, Don Pedro de Ayala, was less to Thomas's liking —a vain and proud man who saw almost all others as beneath him. There had been times Thomas believed this attitude extended even to Queen Isabel and King Fernando.

"I know Rodrigo Gonzalvo, but who is the other man?" Thomas asked, his voice low.

"Sir Richard Empson," said Philippa. "He is the King's master of taxation; also councillor to Harry. Don't cross him, for he has both a temper and a long memory. We must wait here until they conclude their business, however long it might take."

Which may have been all day had not Queen Elizabeth approached with her two sons trailing behind, her two daughters following on.

"What are you doing standing out here, Pip?" she asked.

"Sir Richard is with the King, Your Grace."

The Queen peered around them then laughed. She entered the room and spoke with her husband, who gazed at her with a softened expression. Their conversation did not carry, but when it was concluded Sir Richard Empson and the Spanish Ambassador left. Sir Richard swept past without acknowledging their presence, though he offered a curt nod to Arthur and Harry. Rodrigo Gonzalvo offered a few brief words of welcome to Thomas and shook his hand.

Philippa drew Thomas into the room. The papers remained on the table, but Thomas deliberately averted his eyes.

"I understand you were born in Lemster," said the King, surprising Thomas.

"I was, Your Grace."

"It lies close to Ludlow, does it not?"

"Less than an hour on horseback."

"My son is due to leave for Ludlow Castle on the morrow. As Prince of Wales, he manages the borderlands and beyond in my name. I would ask that you accompany him on his journey."

Thomas almost blurted out 'Why?' until he realised it

was not an appropriate question to ask a king. Instead, he said, "What are my duties to be, Your Grace?"

"Talk to him. Tell him of his bride to be. Tell him what manner of woman she is and what manner of wife she will make."

"I can scarce judge Catherine as a bride, Your Grace, but I will do what I can. You are aware Queen Isabel has asked that I remain close to Princess Catherine when she arrives, if such is possible. She trusts me to keep her safe."

"I think my soldiers can do that without your help. But Queen Isabel vouches for your good name, and soon our countries are to be joined by marriage, so it may be possible to grant your request. You are a stranger in this land, a blank sheet of paper, which may serve my purpose. When you reach Ludlow, there is a minor task I ask of you. There is a Justice of the Peace by the name of Hugh Clement. He owns extensive holdings in the area and was appointed to his post two months since, so has the balance of the year remaining in his position. I hear rumours he is not up to the job of Justice and is using it to line his own pockets rather than mine. I need someone on the ground who knows the area and knows men. Preferably someone not associated with me. I want you to tell me what you think of this Hugh Clement. I need to know is he reliable or not."

"You put a great deal of trust in me, Your Grace."

"You are exactly what I need to judge this matter on my behalf. Most men I could send would flatter me with what they believe I want to hear. You are not like most men, are you, Thomas?"

"Not so different, Your Grace."

"A good sword must be beaten and thrust steaming into cold water before it becomes strong. Over and over again. You will be my strong sword in this matter. Agree and I will grant your request. You may accompany Princess Catherine, but from a distance. I will give you some position that makes it seemly."

"Perhaps you can appoint me as assistant to Prince Arthur's physician, Your Grace."

"Perhaps I can, even if my own physicians would berate me for doing so, but it will be a position, granted. Do we have an understanding?"

"We do, Your Grace."

King Henry held out his hand. Thomas knelt so he could kiss the hand, but Henry shook his head.

"Shake my hand, Thomas. Seal our understanding man to man."

Thomas took the King's hand with a sense of stepping across some invisible line. Had he just made a pact with a good man or bad?

"Can I ask something in return, Your Grace?"

"By damn, but you are a brave one. Ask if you must."

"I ran into some minor trouble when I arrived in London. It seems there is a gang of ruffians who name themselves the bonemen. They demand payment from traders in return for their protection. I wondered if you had heard of them."

King Henry continued to hold Thomas's hand in an iron grip. "I know nothing of what you speak, but will have someone look into the matter. If anyone is taking trader's money in this city it should be me, and properly recorded. Commerce is to be encouraged, but only the King can tax people."

King Henry turned away and left the room beside his Queen. Young Harry came and tugged at Thomas's hand.

"I demand a rematch, Thomas," he said. "I want my shilling back."

"And if you lose again, Your Grace, do you have another shilling to pay the debt?"

Harry only laughed and ran off to set up the pieces, too impatient to wait for a servant to do so.

"It is lucky he is the second in line," said Philippa, still close beside Thomas. "He is too headstrong, and too easily distracted, to make a good king. Arthur is like his father. Careful and shrewd. He will fashion his England into a fine land once he is king." She touched his hand briefly and cast a glance at him. "A land where a man and woman might raise a family."

Thomas moved away to play chess with Harry, still bemused by Philippa's attentions.

SEVEN

Thomas knew he could have reached Ludlow in three days had he ridden alone, but he was not alone. In the company of Prince Arthur and three score men and women, carts and horses, hangers on and the curious, the journey had taken almost two weeks. A further eight miles remained before they reached their destination when Thomas urged his mount to the front of their caravan to fall in beside Prince Arthur. At his side rode his senior advisors, Gruffydd ap Rhys and Sir Richard Pole. Thomas liked the one but not the other. Sir Richard Pole had been aloof during their journey and Thomas gained the impression the man disliked him. Gruffydd ap Rhys was the opposite. Despite being the son of the ruler of half of Wales, he acted as a mortal man, with the ability to do whatever was ordered of him without question. Thomas hoped he never fell out with him because beneath the friendly exterior he sensed someone who would run an enemy through without a second thought, and the skill and strength to do so. He had spent evenings with Gruffydd in fine manor houses, all honoured to host the Prince of Wales even if the cost would take a year to pay off. Thomas had spoken of Catherine, of Spain, but little of his own past. Philippa had often been present. Now, as he fell in beside the Prince, she rode several paces behind in the company of Sir Richard Pole's wife, Lady Margaret who, unlike her husband, was sweet-natured and generous.

"I have a request if I may ask it, Your Grace?"

"Ask then." Arthur looked tired. The journey had been long and the weather often wet. Rain had greeted them that morning, but the sun had come out a little after noon to steam the ground.

"I would like to make a detour before returning to Ludlow this evening."

"A detour where, Thomas? This is fine farmland, but sparse in places worthy of a visit."

"I was born not three leagues from here, Your Grace, as I believe we spoke of when we rested in Oxford. I would like to see the town again, more out of curiosity than anything else."

"Lemster, is that what you told me? I recall the place. I have visited twice, the last time when we rode to Hereford a year since. Is that right, Sir Richard?" Arthur looked at his advisor.

"You are correct, Your Grace, as always. A small burgh with little to commend it." Sir Richard Pole's eyes were on Thomas as he spoke. "When did you leave this place, Thomas?"

"Forty-seven years ago."

Sir Richard barked a laugh. "I don't suppose it will have changed much, or that anyone you know is still alive, but I don't think we need you for anything, even when we reach Ludlow."

Thomas knew Sir Richard would not have allowed him to join their company if it had been left to him. The fact bothered Thomas little because he had yet to see much to respect in the man. He had long since given up respecting anyone simply because of a title.

"Then you may go, Thomas," said Arthur. "You will return tonight?"

"I will, Your Grace." Thomas was turning his horse away from the stone bridge spanning the Teme, the only crossing for several leagues, when Philippa rode across to him and the Prince.

"Can I accompany Thomas, Your Grace?" she asked. "I have heard him speak of this town and am curious to see if it matches his description, though I doubt any place could be as depressing as he makes it out to be."

"Do we need Pip?" Arthur asked Sir Richard.

"Not until tomorrow, Your Grace."

Philippa urged her horse towards one of the uniformed men surrounding Prince Arthur. She leaned over and said something to him. A moment later she turned away, and the man rode off at a gallop.

"What was that about?" Thomas asked when she joined him.

"Arthur is hopeless, as are the others. I thought Lady Margaret might have made arrangements but it seems not, so I sent someone to tell the castle the Prince is likely to arrive tonight. There are preparations that have to be made."

Which is how it came to be the two of them rode away to the south-west, following a good road that rose and fell over low hills that sparked faint memories for Thomas as they crossed them. As did the villages they passed through. Cresting Leysters Hill, the view west opened up to show half of Wales, hill after hill fading into a distant haze. Closer to, Lemster sat beyond the river Lugge.

"Is that it?" asked Philippa. "It looks rather pretty from here." She had chatted constantly, firing off a series of questions, all inconsequential. She had dressed more casually for the journey, even wearing clothes that matched Thomas's so she rode as a man, astride her mount rather than side-saddle. Her long hair was wound up and captured beneath a brown cap.

"Perhaps it has changed since I have been away."

Philippa laughed. "Perhaps it is improved by your absence."

"That is more than likely. We turn aside soon; I want to see my old home."

"But we will visit the town, will we not? Perhaps we might conjure a delay and have to take rooms at a local inn. What if it is full and they have but one room, Thomas? Would that cause a scandal?"

"Not in Lemster."

A short time after passing through Kimbolton Thomas led them across Cogwell Brook, all the names, all the landscape growing in familiarity as if he had been away mere months rather than years. The ridge of Eaton Hill rose ahead, but his destination lay on the western slope. The track to his old house remained the same, but much else had changed. Not in major ways, but more subtly. Someone had planted a new wood of oak, ash and hazel. The trees stood tall now, some of their trunks thick around. The slope they rose from had been used to graze his father's sheep the spring before they left. Thomas recalled selling a flock of fat lambs for a shilling a head and the subsequent trouble that had come, not because of the sale, but he would always associate it with that trade. As they turned along the side of the hill, he stopped and let his breath go.

Philippa came up beside him. "What is it, Thomas? Are you unwell?"

"I am fine."

"What, then?"

He nodded to where the ruins of a house stood a hundred paces ahead. The cause of its dilapidation was not clear, but Thomas thought it might have been fire. The roof was gone and the side and rear walls had crumbled to almost nothing. Thomas turned in his saddle and surveyed the town lying below. Yes, this was his old house, the view the same as he recalled. He had come expecting the land to be sold, for there to be another family living in the old Berrington home. He had not expected this. It felt like some judgement on his life. He had turned his back on this place and, without his attention, it had crumbled into the landscape.

Thomas dismounted and held his hand up to assist

Philippa. She came down into his arms, his hands grasping her slim waist, and for a moment they stood inches apart before he turned away.

"I need to see it."

"This was your home," said Philippa. "You should visit on your own."

Thomas nodded. Approaching the house from the side its dereliction grew ever clearer. He did not try to enter, barely needing to, because he could see the interior through gaps in the fallen walls. There was no furniture. No doubt when Thomas and his father failed to return, people would have taken whatever they wanted. There would have been coin inside too, hidden but not well enough to stop someone with determination. Losing any coin did not concern Thomas, because he would have more than enough of his own when his companions arrived from Spain.

He walked to the rear of the ruin and climbed the slope until he came to the family graveyard. He only identified it by two oaks that grew there, now both taller than those held in his memory. One had lost a branch that lay on the ground, half mouldered away. The grass was long, more than knee high, and Thomas had to push through it but failed to find what he was looking for. Somewhere here lay graves. He had dug the last two himself, made crosses of wood and hammered them into the ground One for his brother, John; the second for his mother, Catherine. There were other family members as well whose deaths had come at more natural ages. His grandfather and grandmother, an uncle, two aunts. This was where the Berringtons had always been buried since coming to live on the side of Eaton Hill.

Thomas turned and looked over the top of his old house to the town below. The silvered waters of the Lugge and Kenwater marked two boundaries of his father's holdings to east and north. The Priory loomed large, beyond it a jumble of black and white houses, fields, and farms. A trail of smoke in the distance marked a place Thomas had once known well, as well as the girl who lived there. The brickworks remained, and he wondered whether the Brickendens still worked it, or did it have new owners. He turned to see Philippa waiting patiently beside her horse and made a decision.

As he walked towards her, he saw a mounted man coming from the same direction they had, not in a hurry, but clearly headed for the ruined house. Or them.

Thomas reached Philippa as the man approached. He was broad and short, his feet barely reaching the stirrups hanging from his saddle. His face was florid, no doubt from working outside his whole life, and drinking in The Star most nights.

"You are trespassing," he said, his voice hoarse. "What are you doing up here? Nobody lives here no more but all this land is mine now. Get off it before I throw you off."

Thomas smiled at the bluster but understood it. His own father would have been exactly the same if a stranger came onto his land.

"We are going, sir, but first I have a question if you would be so good as to answer it."

"Why should I?"

"Because I have a right to know. Who are you, and how did you purchase this land?"

"Twas abandoned more years ago than anyone can remember. No purchase needed. I went to the local Justice and pleaded my case. They parcelled the land out between three of us. Forty acres each. And what my name be is none of your business, unless you tell me yours and what interest you have."

"Did you burn the house down?"

"Not me. It has been that way a long time. And you have still not told me what you are doing on my land."

"My land," Thomas said. "This was my land. This was my house. The Justice, whoever he was, had no right to parcel this land out to anybody."

The man shook his head and grunted, the sound perhaps meant to be a laugh. "T'aint your land anymore, boy. I got deeds signed away all fair and square. Take me to law if you want, but you will lose."

Thomas smiled and offered his hand to Philippa, who used it to swing into her saddle. Thomas pulled himself into his and urged his horse forward. As he passed the man, he said, "We will see about that the next time I speak with King Henry. Come, Lady Gale, the Prince of Wales awaits us in Ludlow Castle."

They had reached the main road north to Ludlow before either of them spoke, and it was Philippa who broke the silence with a laugh.

"I think I enjoy being Lady Gale. Did you see his face when you mentioned the King?"

"I did."

"Are we not going into the town?"

"If they are all like that man, there is nothing here for me now."

"That land was all yours? What was it, one-hundred and twenty acres? A man could live well on that. It looks good land, too. Sheep, even wheat and barley down by the river. Did your holding extend that far?"

"To the banks of the Lugge and a little beyond." Thomas glanced at Philippa. "You have a good eye."

"My father raised sheep in Northamptonshire when he first came to England, before he went to work for the Woodvilles. The land was not as good as the land here, and not one-hundred and twenty acres, but enough to provide a living. He raised sheep, for the wool mostly."

"That man was right. This is not my land anymore."

"They conspired to steal it, Thomas. Speak to Henry and he will restore it to you."

"They believed me dead." A thought came to him. "My sister lived when I left, but I do not know if she still does."

"Then you must find out. What age was she when you left England?"

"She had less than three years, but was sweet, clever and beautiful." Thomas frowned. "I left her with my aunt in Ludlow. My aunt must be dead by now, but Agnes would have fifty years if she lives. I expect she will have married and moved away, but there may be records." He smiled. "I will endeavour to find her, though I doubt she remembers me. Children that young don't, do they? Were you born in Northamptonshire?"

"I told you I was. It is where the Queen was also born."

"How does a girl from the shires become so elevated?

Particularly one whose father is not native to this land. That is what you said, was it not?"

"Do you doubt me, Sir Thomas?"

"Not at all. I am merely curious, Lady Gale. I also appear to have been elevated without even being aware of it."

"You are elevated far higher than me. I am a servant, nothing more. Northamptonshire is where my mother and father started working for Queen Elizabeth's family."

"You mentioned your father, but this is the first time you have spoken of your mother. What happened?"

"She died at the moment I was born."

"You never knew her."

Philippa shook her head. "And never missed her either, I suppose. Lady Elizabeth Woodville was like a mother to me and her daughter like a sister. We ran wild in the fields around the manor house."

"Did you miss it when your father took you to London?" Thomas saw three men approaching along the road and kept an eye on them. There was nobody else in sight. He was not expecting trouble, but knew it better to be prepared than not.

"I missed Lizzie." Philippa raised a hand to her mouth. "Oh, did I just say that? Sometimes I forget myself and her elevation. Did you miss Lemster all those years you lived in Spain?"

Thomas laughed. "Not at all. At first, after my father died, I suppose I did. But then my life took many strange turns and I almost forgot where I came from. I certainly forgot my native language."

"Is that why your accent is so strange?"

"Most likely. I used to talk like all the other boys around here, but that was a long time ago. Come to my other side, Philippa."

"Why? And you should call me Pip, like everyone else does."

"I am not sure I like the look of these three approaching us."

Philippa looked ahead, but she fell back and came around on Thomas's left. He eased them over to the side of the road so her horse walked on the rough grass at the edge of it.

"They look like ordinary enough men to me," said Philippa.

"Indeed they do, but they are observing us. They are three and we are two, and you are a beautiful woman."

"Do you really think me beautiful? Thank you, but I have not seen this suspicious side of you before."

When the men were a hundred paces away, they urged their horses into a canter. Thomas laid his hand on the pommel of his sword.

"Neither have I for some time, but if there is to be trouble I am grateful suspicion remains a part of me. There is a narrow track into the woods coming up on your left. Take it until they have gone past. Do not look back."

"What about you, one man against three?"

"Yes, I know. It is unfair. But there are only three, so I will have to make do with that. Besides, they are no doubt entirely innocent. Now go, and ride fast. Only return when you hear me call out." Thomas slapped the rump of Philippa's horse and it took off at a gallop. He saw one man turn away from the road to intercept her, but she was too fast, too good a rider. She reached the narrow track first and glanced back once before disappearing into the trees. Thomas cursed when he saw the man follow, but there was nothing he could do about it until he had dealt with the other two, who were almost on him. He wondered, if it came to it, whether this time he would pull his strike in mercy or not.

EIGHT

Thomas drew his sword but kept it at his side as the two riders eased their mounts to a walk, then stopped, one either side of the road with not enough space between them to pass.

"Where is your woman off to in such a hurry? Not scared of us, is she?" The man stared at Thomas, no trace of humanity in his eyes. "Or perhaps she should be scared."

"What do you want?"

"Want? We want you to give us whatever you are carrying. That sword would be a start. It looks like a fine blade. And then you will have some coin about you, I am sure. Perhaps your clothes as well, they look workman-like. And I like your scarf."

To the death then, Thomas thought. So be it. He had no sympathy for men such as these, but would have preferred to let them live another day if he could. The man doing all the talking was short, but that meant noth-ing. Thomas had a companion, a mercenary, who was also short but more dangerous than any man alive. The second man appeared softer, but there was something sly about his features. Thomas had another companion who would recognise the intention in both of them with no need of talking, but he was not here. He missed the presence of both now trouble had found him. Both men wore green felt caps tilted to one side and similar jackets, but not so alike as to make it a uniform. It was clear they were arrogant men, used to getting what they wanted.

"Who do you ride for, or are your hats nothing more than an unfortunate choice?"

"Who we ride for is none of your business. If you want to see the sun set, then you do as we say."

Thomas tried to identify the accent, to place the man, but knew he had been away from England too long to do so.

A high-pitched scream came from the woods, and the two men laughed.

"Looks like your filly's been caught. Now, if you will be so kind as to dismount, we will take your horse and leave you with your clothes. I expect your woman has already lost hers. When you have gone on your way, we will find her and send her along to Ludlow—that is where you are going, is it not? We will send her after we have all taken a turn. She looks like a fine filly. Thoroughbred, no doubt… or she will be." There came another laugh.

Thomas slid from the saddle as if doing as asked, preparing for what would come next. He recognised the lie when they told him he could keep his clothes and ride away. He stayed close to Ferrant to make it more difficult for the men to come at him from both sides.

They were too sure of their own power, which is what Thomas counted on. The man who had done the talking came at him, trying to trap him between Thomas's horse and his own. All Thomas needed to do was lift the tip of his sword and the man did the rest. The blade slid into his chest, Thomas guiding it expertly so it pierced the heart to emerge from his back. The man was already dead but stayed in the saddle, held there by Thomas's blade until he pulled it free.

He turned to the second man, who was already backing away.

"It was nothing to do with me, sir. Rafe is headstrong. I saw nothing here. Nothing at all."

"Who do you ride for?"

"Nobody. The hats were Rafe's idea. He says—" The man glanced at his companion, who slid from the saddle to thump onto the dusty roadway. There was little blood because his heart no longer beat. "He said they made us look important. I told him I wanted nothing to do with this."

"If I let you ride away, who are you going to tell about what happened here?"

"About what, sir? I saw nothing. If I were you, I might be minded to go and see what is happening to your woman and let me ride on."

Thomas wanted to kill the man. He knew it would be a mistake to let him live to tell others what had happened, but his advice was sound. He needed to find out what was happening to Philippa. It might be too late to save her honour, but he could punish her attacker.

"Go then," he said, swinging into the saddle. "Mention a word of this and I will come after you."

He kicked the flanks of his horse and thundered along the track Philippa had taken. He had gone only a hundred paces into the trees when he found her.

Philippa sat on a thick carpet of pine needles, her knees raised, arms clasped around them. The neck of her shirt was torn to display her shoulder and upper chest. Thomas thought she might be crying.

There was no sign of the man who had followed her into the trees, but Philippa's horse tugged at a patch of shaded grass as if nothing had happened here.

Thomas dismounted and knelt. Philippa flinched when he put his arms around her, then gave a loud sob and clung against him. Thomas held her until the sobs faded, then took her face in his hands and stared into her eyes.

"Tell me what happened."

She tried to shake her head, but Thomas held it firm. More tears trailed along her cheeks.

"You need to tell me," Thomas said. "The healing can only start once you do."

She jerked away and turned her back to him. Thomas wrapped his arms around her, pulling her against him, her back to his front. He leaned close and kissed the side of her cheek.

"Did he touch you?"

Philippa shook her head. It took her a while before she could find her voice. "He did not get a chance, but he would have. I could see it in his eyes. When he heard your horse he mounted his own and fled."

"I heard a scream."

"I hoped you would." She half turned and looked at Thomas. "What about the others?"

"One is dead. I let the other go."

Philippa showed a moment of shock. "Why?"

"Did I kill one or let one go?"

"Let one go. I recognise their type, but Ludlow has been safe for years now. They were evil men, and both deserved to die."

"I grow tired of killing men, but in this case I had no choice. It was me or him." He released his hold on her, hoping she was coming through her shock. "Take a minute to gather yourself. I need to move the body of the dead man."

Thomas mounted his horse and rode back to where the man had fallen, only to find the body gone, together with his horse. For a moment he wondered if he had been mistaken and the man had not been dead, then shook his head. He had never made that mistake before and knew he had not this time. He dismounted and examined the ground until he found a faint trail of blood leading away. He looked along the road, but the man he had allowed to escape was gone. Presumably together with his dead companion. Thomas returned to the woods and Philippa.

"You should get drunk tonight and sleep without dreams."

Philippa shook her head. "Tonight I will get drunk, agreed, but I want to sleep beside a brave and courageous man."

Thomas laughed. "Where do you intend to find such a paragon in Ludlow?"

"I am sure I will find one somewhere on this road if only he stops being so chivalrous and admits to his own desires."

"My own desires have never brought me much happiness, all except one time."

"Then let us attempt to make it twice, Thomas." She met his eyes, her gaze demanding a response, and eventually he nodded. Philippa Gale was beautiful. She was willing. And he would be a fool to refuse her.

Afternoon was edging towards evening when Thomas and Philippa rode through Ludford Gate and climbed the steep slope into Ludlow. They made their way to the castle which loomed over the town, only to discover Prince Arthur had not yet arrived. The guard who informed them of the fact knew nothing more, nor the reason for the delay.

"What do we do?" Thomas asked Philippa. "Enter the castle anyway, or see if we can find out where they are? How can they not have arrived yet?"

Philippa dismounted and stretched her arms above her head as she twisted. She appeared to have recovered from her shock, which Thomas considered showed either strength of character or lack of empathy. He knew which he preferred to believe.

"You know why he is late," she said. "The same reason we never reached our planned destination on at least half the days of the journey. Princes travel exceedingly slow. They are not fast like you and me. And no, we cannot enter the castle before Arthur does. We will have to find alternative accommodation in the town." She smiled innocently. "I have made this journey three times in his company and twice he stopped at Caynham Manor. It is under the jurisdiction of the Abbot of Wigmore, and Arthur likes to pray there before arriving in Ludlow. I wager that is where we would find him if we decided he needed finding."

"How far to this manor?"

"No more than a league."

"So we could reach it before dark."

"We could, but it is owned and managed by monks. You would sleep in a dormitory with them, probably sharing a bed, and they would banish me to a house kept for the wives and daughters of visitors."

"So you suggest we stay in Ludlow?"

"I do."

"Should I banish you to a house somewhere?"

"If that is your wish, Thomas." Philippa lowered her gaze in a show of false modesty. "But The Rose and Crown offers the second best rooms in Ludlow after the Castle, and goodwife Constance Sparrow hosts the second best bill of fare. Both suitable for a man in your position, I am sure." Her eyes rose. "We can play games until midnight or admit to what we both want."

Thomas opened his mouth to ask what that might be, then closed it again. There was no point. He knew that a closeness to death often demanded a reminder of life.

"People will talk," he said eventually.

"Let them. I do not listen to gossip, nor respect those who do."

Thomas slid from his horse and led it through the market square, surrounded by mismatched houses and alleys leading off, until they reached the stables behind the Rose and Crown. A square church tower loomed over them, which seemed close enough to touch. They left their horses and Thomas carried his saddlebags over his shoulder as they entered the inn. Philippa had nothing to carry. All her goods were still on a wagon in the company of Prince Arthur.

Thomas asked for the best room for himself and his wife, while Philippa stood meekly behind him.

"It will cost you a shilling a night," said the goodwife in warning.

"Then I hope it is fine indeed," Thomas said. He set a shilling on the table and watched it disappear.

"You paid too much," said Philippa when they were in the room and the goodwife had gone.

Thomas thought she was probably right. The room was not large, but the bed was wide and hung above with tapestried drapes that could be drawn together to keep out the light or prying eyes. A small window offered a view out to the square church tower. There was no key for the door, but there was a bolt which Philippa threw across before undressing.

"Are you sure this is what you want?" Thomas asked, watching her.

"Do not tell me you have changed your mind after spending an entire shilling. Here, untie the laces at my back." Philippa turned away from him.

"The shilling was for the room, not you."

"I know, but it would be a shame to waste it."

Thomas pulled at the long ties, revealing Philippa's slim back and smooth skin. When she was naked, she turned to face him without shame.

"I hope you do not intend to keep all your clothes on, Thomas, or I will be sorely disappointed."

"I should warn you I am not looking for a relationship," he said. "As soon as Catherine is settled, I intend to return to Spain."

"You need more practice at wooing a woman, don't you?"

"I have been told that several times before in my life."

"Neither am I looking for anything other than tonight, but you fascinate me. I want to lie with you to see how it might be between us. So take off your clothes." She turned and pulled back the heavy covers on the bed, then lay on it without drawing them back over herself.

Thomas looked at her, an unfamiliar stirring in him he had suspected he might never feel again. He undressed and joined Philippa. The day had been long and strange, and he needed to lose himself with her as much as she appeared to want to lose herself with him.

NINE

When Thomas woke, he found himself alone in the wide bed. Outside, full dark had fallen, but the sound of voices drifting from below told him it was not yet late. Within the room, three candles burned. Philippa had lit them earlier because she said she wanted to see him and be seen in turn. Now she sat on the floor, still naked, her back to him. For a moment, Thomas admired the slim strength of her before realising what she was doing. His dark leather satchel, the one he had owned for most of his life, sat in front of her. The top was open and Philippa was selecting items from within.

Thomas watched her, delighted at the illicit nature of his study without her knowledge. He saw her retrieve a book from within the deep confines of the satchel. She flipped through pages that comprised drawings of the human body, the descriptions written in Arabic. Thomas carried the book with him everywhere, but it seemed of less interest to Philippa. She closed it and set it aside. Next she drew out small stoppered bottles. Thomas watched as she opened some and sniffed. He was ready to call out if she opened something that might cause harm, knowing full well what each contained. They were the liquors of his trade. Essence of poppy. Distilled alcohol. Liquid hashish. Salves created by Belia, who was travelling to England to meet him.

Philippa sniffed, stoppered the bottles again and set them beside the book. She shifted position, crossing her legs with ease as if she sat this way all the time—though perhaps not naked as she now was. Thomas wondered what it would be like to live with Philippa Gale, but even as the thought came he knew it was not what he wanted. Women had scarred his soul in the past. All but one, and now she was gone and still he bore the scars of her loss.

Philippa drew out a wrap of red velvet tied around with a linen cord. The material of both was faded and worn. She untied the cord and rolled the package open. She drew one candle closer and leaned over to examine the contents. The indentations along her spine showed as she did so. Thomas pictured the bones within her, intimate with each of them. The extra rib she possessed. The wider pelvis. He had studied bodies, male and female, since the age of eighteen when he had entered the Infirmary in Málaga as a student.

When she picked up a slim metal rod tipped with a cork, Thomas said, "Take care, that is sharp."

Philippa showed not the least sign of surprise and Thomas realised she had been aware of his study of her all along, and smiled. She pulled the cork from the small blade and held it close to the candle.

"What is it for?"

"Cutting," he said.

"Cutting what?"

"What do you think?"

"People." she said.

"Yes. People."

She turned around without rising, sliding across the rough wooden floor so he feared she might catch a splinter in her perfect flesh.

"Why do you have all these things in here?"

"It is what I do. I am a physician. A surgeon."

She stared at him for a long time, her breath coming softly, chest rising and falling. Her hair, unclipped and loose, hid her breasts. It was no attempt at modesty, for they had explored every inch of each other before exhaustion took them. Or rather, took Thomas. He believed Philippa might have been more than willing to continue until dawn.

"A surgeon?"

Thomas nodded.

"I thought you were the Duke of Granada."

"That too, but if pressed to say what defines me, what makes me, I will always say I am a healer."

"Is that why Queen Isabel sent you to England, to keep her daughter healthy?"

"Part of the reason, yes."

Philippa moved the small clay bottles. "And these?"

"Some of them dull pain when I have to cut. Others help with healing. Some ease the breath in a man's lungs. Some help a woman who aches during her bleeding. A friend of mine made most of them."

"In England they would call you a witch if you were a woman."

Thomas thought of the woman who was travelling to join him, who knew more about herbs and tinctures than anyone he had ever met. They would almost certainly call Belia a witch, and the thought caused him a moment of concern.

"What would they call a man?"

Philippa laughed and shook her head. "I don't know." She rose and stretched, unashamed at displaying herself. They were lovers, and lovers should carry no shame between them. "They would call him a fool, most like. Are you hungry? I am starving."

The sound of people talking, the clatter of plates and mugs, drifted up from three floors below.

"I expect I was earlier, but you seem to have distracted me."

Philippa smiled. "I think it was you who did the distracting." She turned away and gathered her clothes. "With luck, the food will be as good as the bed and the company I shared it with. With even more luck, Arthur will not have arrived and we will have to spend the rest of the night here."

Thomas slid from the comfort of the bed and found his own clothes. He tried to recall how long since he had made love with a woman, and could not, only who. But he had no clear recollection of when. He and Helena had drifted apart over the years until they barely saw each other. The last Thomas had heard, she had married a rich Count and lived in Valencia. There had been no talk of the son she had borne Thomas going with her, and his daughter was nothing to do with her.

"You are no longer in this room with me," said Philippa. "What are you thinking of?"

Thomas shook his head. "Old memories, that is all." He crossed the room, took Philippa in his arms and kissed her. She was slim inside his embrace and returned the kiss willingly.

It must have been later than he thought because when they entered the main room downstairs only a few people remained. Constance Sparrow told them the kitchen was closed, but she would see if she could find them something. Thomas led the way to a small table close to the fire. It consisted only of pale embers but offered a welcome warmth. Thomas glanced around at the remaining customers, all of them men. The majority were asleep. A group of three sat at a table with their heads together as they discussed some matter. One was dressed as a gentleman, complete with sword on show. Another was short, wiry, with long hair tied back and wearing a leather vest as if ready to fight. The third was slim, well-dressed without being flamboyant, his dark hair neatly cut and face clean-shaven.

Constance Sparrow returned with two bowls of something brown, two earthenware mugs, and a jug of wine.

"I will add it to your bill," she said, before returning to her place at the long table where she had been standing when they came downstairs.

Thomas tasted the stew. It was lukewarm, but better than he feared. Philippa ate her own food fast before pouring wine for them both; it was not as good as the food.

"Those men who attacked us," said Philippa. "Why did they do it?"

"They demanded money from me, and you know what the one who came after you wanted. You did well."

"I had a knife and would have used it had you not come. I have done so before."

"You killed someone? Who?"

"I have my secrets too, Thomas. Maybe I will tell you when we know each other better."

"Don't we now?"

"Upstairs?" Philippa smiled. "That was discovering each other's bodies, not minds. Minds are far more interesting."

"I agree about the minds, but must admit I found your body rather interesting too."

Philippa laughed, making one man at the table glance at her. His eyes remained on her for some time before he leaned across and spoke to the man in the leather vest.

"And I yours. One day you will tell me how you got those scars. So was it only theft and rape on the minds of those men, do you think? If so, it was a dangerous course they took. We were alone, but anyone could have come along."

"We were better dressed than most in that district, so no doubt they took us for people likely to have silver and gold about our person."

Thomas saw the man in the vest rise and start across to them. He dropped his hand to his waist only to find he had brought no weapon. He looked around, planning what he would do if it came to a fight. Use the table. Perhaps throw the jug of wine at him.

"How are you, Pip?" said the man, and Thomas let the thoughts of violence spill away into dust. "Is Prince Arthur returned to the castle?"

"Still at Caynham Manor, Daniel. Is that Hugh and Peter with you?"

"Hugh told me to ask if you wanted to join us." The man smiled. "I suspect our wine is better than what Constance brought for you." He glanced at Thomas. "Your companion as well, of course."

Philippa turned. "Thomas?"

He looked to where the two men were still talking, their attention on their own conversation. If he was right, the one purporting to be a gentleman was Hugh Clement —or at least he hoped he was. This chance encounter offered an opportunity to sound the man out.

"It would be a pleasure."

The man, Daniel, nodded and went back to his table.

"Are you sure, Thomas? We could just climb the stairs and then climb atop each other again if you prefer."

"I would, but if that is Hugh Clement—"

Philippa smiled. "Of course it is. And I recall what the King asked of you. I stood beside you when he did the asking. Now is your chance to introduce yourself. But use your title to impress him. He is arrogant enough to need reminding of his position."

"Which title would that be?" Thomas rose and offered a hand to Philippa.

"Sir Thomas, of course. I doubt Hugh even knows where Granada is, let alone if it has a Duke."

Hugh Clement rose as they approached and Daniel brought two more chairs, sturdy and comfortable with curved backs. Clement offered his hand and Thomas shook it, unimpressed at the strength of grip and clamminess of the touch.

"I am Hugh Clement, Justice of the Peace for the district." He glanced at Philippa. "Who is your friend, Pip?"

"This is Sir Thomas Berrington, Hugh. He has been appointed to assist John Argentine as physician to the Prince."

Thomas saw the third man glance at him at mention of his name.

"Have you by damn," said Clement. "Argentine could use some assistance. I hope you know a little more than he does."

"I believe I do, sir."

"Sit, sit. You have already met Daniel Lupton, who is my second-in-command. My other companion is Peter Gifforde. He works for Wigmore Abbey."

Thomas took a seat and accepted fresh wine from the jug on the table. It was indeed of better quality than their own. He watched Hugh Clement as he greeted Philippa. A peck on both cheeks, one hand at her back, an easy familiarity between them.

Clement confused him. King Henry had said the man was weak and possibly corrupt, but the man sitting in front of him gave every appearance of being urbane and sharp. As did his companions. Daniel Lupton was handsome, with the effortless grace of a fighting man. The other, Peter Gifforde, was also handsome, better dressed, but had said nothing yet.

"Thomas was born in Lemster," said Philippa.

"Berrington." Peter Gifforde spoke at last. "My grand-father mentioned a Berrington to me many years ago, when he still lived."

Hugh Clement laughed. "It would be difficult for him to mention it after he died."

Peter Gifforde offered a tight smile.

"Are you from the same family, Sir Thomas?" asked Clement. "Is that why you are here in Ludlow?"

"Who was your grandfather?" Thomas stared into Peter Gifforde's eyes. Nothing in the man reminded him of any Gifforde he had ever known.

"My grandfather's given name was Walter. Walter Gifforde. And if you are who I believe you to be, he knew you." There was no expression on Peter Gifforde's face.

"And if he is who I think, then I knew him, too. He was close to my age, so must have died young."

"He had a hard life. He caught the pestilence as a lad and told me he never fully recovered."

"I caught it too. Over half of Lemster did, and half of those died of it. Your grandfather was lucky. I left the town before I knew whether he lived or died."

"We should sit down together sometime and talk of the past," said Peter Gifforde. He lowered his voice and leaned close so that only Thomas heard the next words. "But not tonight. We should not spoil your return to the district with tales of what you did."

Thomas spoke as softly. "I agree. And I can tell you a different truth if you have the ears to listen."

Peter Gifforde sat up and smiled. "Yes, we should do

that." He glanced at Hugh Clement. "Perhaps we should ask Thomas and Pip to dinner at your house, Hugh."

"A capital idea, I will arrange it. Are you staying here or at the Castle, Pip?"

"We are staying here tonight," said Philippa, making it clear they were together. "But we will be in the Castle tomorrow once Arthur arrives. He will want to see you when he does, I expect."

"More likely Sir Richard Pole and that mad Welshman," said Hugh Clement. "They like to question me half to death while the Prince looks on with that benign smile of his."

"Not much passes Arthur by," said Philippa.

"If you say so. I hear he is too studious and does not much like to fight."

"Perhaps that is what England needs these days," Thomas said. "A little time to recover from the madness of the years before Henry came to the throne."

"I heard you went away," said Peter Gifforde. "What do you know of those years, Thomas?"

"You are right, I did not live through them myself, but news reaches even as far as distant Spain."

"And Arthur is to marry a Spanish princess, I hear," said Hugh Clement. He made a coarse gesture. "Is she beddable, do you know?"

Thomas made no reply. He had changed his opinion of the man and decided he did not like him. Did not like him at all. Urbanity hid a coarse nature which he despised. He glanced at the others. Daniel Lupton was staring away at one of the serving girls and she was smiling at him in return. Peter Gifforde was looking at Philippa with a strange intensity on his face.

Whether or not she caught the look, Philippa rose and offered her hand. "Come, Tom, it has been a long day and our bed awaits."

As they ascended the stairs, Thomas said, "Could you not have been a little more circumspect?"

Philippa laughed. "Hugh Clement has a mind he can woo me and I wanted to see his expression when I spoke as I did. I am ready to renew our exploration of each other, so hurry, Tom."

"Is there anything left to explore?"

"I am sure I can find something. As I am sure you can."

TEN

When Thomas woke the following morning he rose from bed before Philippa could distract him again. Which she did anyway, sprawled uncovered across the bedclothes.

"I am hungry," he said as he searched out his clothes, which appeared to be scattered across every corner of the room. "And by the look of the light coming through the window, we might be too late to break our fasts."

"Constance Sparrow will find us something."

"If you intend to stay and disport yourself, I will go down and see if she might find something for me."

Philippa grinned and did something that almost changed Thomas's mind.

Downstairs, the girls—and from what Constance Sparrow had said they might be her daughters—were sweeping the floor.

"I am sorry, sir, it is too late to break your fast here," said one when Thomas enquired. "The kitchens open again at noon if you can wait."

"Where is Goodwife Sparrow?"

The girl shrugged and returned to her sweeping. Thomas looked around and pulled out a chair in the part of the room that appeared to have been already cleaned. He waited, and eventually Philippa appeared. She was dressed as the day before, as was Thomas, because they had nothing else with them.

"I was told food is finished until noon," he said.

"Stay here." Philippa turned away and went through past the wide serving table and disappeared. She came back a few minutes later and hooked a finger for Thomas to follow her.

Constance Sparrow was in the kitchen talking with a girl of only sixteen who carried a basket far too large for her slight figure. In the basket lay bread, rolls, and pastries. The freshly baked smell of them filled the room.

"You can have some bread once I have paid for it," said Constance. "And there is cheese and possibly a little pork left over from last night." She nodded at the big table which took up most of the centre of the room and Thomas sat. Philippa drew her own chair close to his so their arms touched.

"How do you do it?" Thomas asked.

"People like me. You like me, don't you?"

"I do."

"See?" As if that explained everything; and perhaps it did.

The girl left with her empty basket and Constance cut slices of still-warm bread and set them on a plate. She found cheese and, true to her word, there were even a few thick slices of pork which had been marinated in mustard seeds. It was a meal fit for a Prince, and Thomas briefly wondered what Arthur had eaten to break his fast, and where the lad was now.

One girl came to the door and told Constance there were men who wanted to speak with her. She brushed her floured hands on her skirt and went out. Thomas leaned back and watched, curious, then rose when he saw the face of one of the men. When Philippa looked up at him, he motioned her to stay where she was.

Thomas went to the doorway and stood beside it so he could see out and hear what was being said, because the face he recognised belonged to the man he had allowed to ride away.

"You are too soon for food or ale," said Constance Sparrow, though her voice was welcoming enough.

"It is not either we are after." It was the man Thomas knew who spoke, his voice familiar, still with a hint of threat to it. "We are calling at all the inns in search of someone."

"Good for you." Constance's welcome had worn thin.

The man leaned forward. "And it will not go well for you if you lie to me, goodwife. A man and woman, both tall, the woman handsome, the man not so much."

"I have men and women staying, of course," said Constance, "but none as I recall who match your description. Do you not have names?"

"Not yet, but we will soon enough once we find them." The man leaned closer, his voice even colder. "If I find out you are lying to me, I will be back." He smiled, but there was nothing of warmth in it. "I will be back later today or tomorrow in any case, with a business proposition."

Constance Sparrow said nothing. The men turned and

left, deliberately turning over two tables and several chairs. One of the girls who remained cowered away from them.

Constance Sparrow stood where she was, her shoulders tense, then turned and came back into the kitchen. Thomas caught her arm as she passed.

"There was no need to lie on our behalf. I could have taken care of any trouble if they started it."

Constance looked down at where he held her and Thomas released his hold. She continued on and sat at the table. She reached out and took a corner of bread and chewed it.

"I did not lie for you, I lied for me. For my business. If word got out I gave my customers away to men such as those, how long do you think before I lost them all?"

"Do you know who they were?"

Constance Sparrow shook her head. "Never seen any of them before."

"They said they would come back. Do you know why?"

Another shake of the head, but Thomas was wondering if he might not know. If so, the idea confused him. Three men approaching a profitable inn. Just as they approached the Bell Savage on Ludgate. Did that mean the bonemen were planning to set themselves up in Ludlow as well as London? And why Ludlow? It was an insignificant town on the edge of Wales; but it did house Prince Arthur and all that came with his presence. Thomas pushed the thought to the back of his mind where he knew it would marinate by itself until ready to tell him something. He reached for more of the bread.

"This is excellent."

"Agnes Baxter's shop in Market Square. Best bread in Ludlow. Perhaps the best bread in Shropshire."

"Agnes Baxter? The last time I visited Ludlow, the bakery was owned by Joan Baxter and her husband."

Constance Sparrow laughed. "My, that must have been some time ago. Joan died thirty years ago and left the shop to her daughter."

"There were others, were there not? Boys and girls."

"It was before my time, sir, so I am only passing on what I have heard second-hand. But the way I heard it was none of them wanted the hard work involved in the baking of bread. It means rising before the sun and often enough not going to bed until long after it has set. But Agnes does not seem to mind." Constance Sparrow looked at Thomas. "Are you from around these parts? You don't sound as if you are."

"I have been away a long time." Thomas glanced at Philippa, who had stopped eating and was now listening to their conversation without contributing. That was unusual enough for him to wonder what the reason might be. Unless his and Constance Sparrow's conversation was so fascinating, she wanted only to listen. Or she was tired from their efforts of the night.

"What is your name? Will I know your family?"

"I doubt it. My name is Thomas Berrington and, as far as I am aware, am the last of that name. I left my little sister with Joan Baxter forty-seven years ago when she had not yet three years. Her name was Agnes, so perhaps aunt Joan gave the name to one of her children."

Constance Sparrow stared at Thomas for several seconds before saying, "Agnes told me once she used to have a different name, but had not used it since she was a child. But I would not have put her at having fifty years, sir."

Thomas returned the stare, some emotion between shock and excitement curling through him.

"Agnes Berrington?"

Constance Sparrow made no reply.

"Is Agnes Baxter your sister?" said Philippa. "I know Agnes, and her daughters, but have never spoken to her regarding her past." She reached out and took Thomas's hand. "We must go there now and see. Would you recognise her?"

"I doubt it. She was too young and will have changed completely by now. She was such a pretty little thing, with a sweet nature."

"So we introduce you," said Philippa.

"Not until I am sure."

Philippa went off to find out where Prince Arthur was and Thomas stayed to question Constance Sparrow without making it too difficult. He wanted to know more about Hugh Clement, and she appeared to know him well enough. As she had already told him, a goodwife knows everything going on in a town.

It was a half-hour before Thomas stood on the far side of Market Square across from the bakery, watching people come and go. The square was busy with trade; stallholders selling clothing, cloth, cheese, meat and fish, as well as spices, herbs, vegetables and fruit. Several stalls were piled high with that season's apples and pears, as well as plums and damsons. Men sat outside the taverns lining the square drinking ale and enjoying the entertainment.

A woman appeared at the entrance of the bakery and twisted to ease an ache in her back. Thomas watched her, a familiarity settling through him. He had not thought he would recognise Agnes, not from the almost three-year-old he had abandoned, but the woman across from him looked so much like his mother she could be nobody but his sister.

Still Thomas made no move. Agnes came out into the square and wandered the stalls, stopping to talk with several of the vendors. She came all the way around the square until she stood only yards from Thomas. He studied her pale hair, as blonde as Catherine Berrington's had been. When she turned, she glanced in his direction with no sign of recognition, and Thomas knew he was right not to approach her. Agnes had been too young to remember the brother who abandoned her when he sailed to France to fight.

Thomas waited, watching as she walked away. When she reached the far end of the stalls, she stopped and turned again. For a moment, her eyes met his and this time, a frown troubled her smooth brow. His sister, Thomas realised, was beautiful. He saw how Constance Sparrow could mistake her for younger than her years. Thomas wondered who she had married, because men would have wanted Agnes as a wife. He realised he was staring back at her and turned away, almost colliding with Philippa as she came the other way.

Philippa grabbed his arm to steady herself. "No, you

don't. Go across and tell her who you are. If what you say is true, you are the only family she has, and you her."

Thomas felt himself pulled by forces he did not fully understand. Was it better to leave Agnes in ignorance of his return? Knowing could bring nothing good, but it might prove difficult if he stayed in Ludlow.

"What news of the Prince?" he asked, to gain a few moments for thought.

"He has reached the outskirts of town but stopped to eat. Half a league from the Castle and he takes lunch. No wonder our journey took so long. So, are you going to introduce yourself to your sister or not?"

"She does not know who I am, or even if I am alive. She was too young when I left to remember me, so best she remains ignorant of my presence now. I was thinking a better use of my time while we wait for the Prince is to look at where this Hugh Clement lives."

"Are you thinking of buying his house? You will need somewhere to live, but I doubt you could afford a manor house, even a small one."

Thomas smiled. "I think my funds, when they arrive, might stretch far enough." Provided, he thought, Jorge was bringing their wealth with him and had protected it through the arduous overland journey.

"Shall we knock on the door and make him an offer? We could live there together."

Thomas made no comment. He liked Philippa well enough, but wondered if she had expectations he was unwilling to satisfy. Buying a house and living together implied marriage, and Thomas had no intention of ever marrying again. Better to disappoint her. Except he wanted to see the manor house, and her idea might prove a sound one. If it worked.

"Goodwife Constance Sparrow told me the house lies at the end of a road by the name of Linney," Thomas said.

"It leads to a gate in the town walls and then down to the Corfe, and I know the manor house of which you speak. Do you see some manner of conspiracy here? How exciting."

"I see nothing yet, but it is worth looking into. You can return to the Castle if you wish. I intend to take a stroll and see where the man lives and who else may be there."

Philippa reached out and took his hand. "I will come with you. Perhaps we can find a leafy glade where we can rest awhile."

Thomas crossed the square, heading for a narrow opening on the far side, but Philippa pulled him towards the bakery.

"I am still hungry," she said. "Let us see what there is we can eat while we walk."

"No." Thomas tried to pull away, but Philippa's grip was stronger than expected.

"You said she will not recognise you, so what harm is there?"

There was a small crowd outside the shop, which boded well for the quality of its produce. The bread eaten that morning also promised the same. It relieved Thomas his sister was nowhere to be seen. Instead, the young woman who had brought the basket of bread for Constance Sparrow, and another of the same age, stood behind a table with shelves of bread, pies and cakes arrayed behind them.

"What is good?" asked Philippa.

"Depends what you like," said one, her local accent broad. "Is it bread you are after or something sweet? We have some fine fruit pies baked only this morning. Is it for you and your husband, or your children as well?"

Philippa smiled. "Only my husband and myself. What is that?" She leaned over and pointed to a sugar-dusted tart with a lattice covering through which dark plums showed.

"You are in luck, my lady. It is one of our most popular items and that is the last one. Do you want it?"

"I do."

The girl turned and reached for the tart, set it on the table.

"Anything else, my lady?"

"Four of your sweet rolls."

Thomas looked at the goods and picked up the tart. "We could do with something to carry these in. And a little cheese would be good to go with the rolls."

"And a jug of ale," said Philippa.

"Indeed, a jug of ale, but only the one." Thomas paid for the tart and rolls but left them on the table. He walked across to the market, sure he would find what he sought. He saw the cheese first, but left it while he searched for a woven basket. The stall selling them, together with hanks of cloth, hats and doublets, offered a choice. Thomas picked one of middling size, paid and took it back to get the cheese and goods from the bakery. He was smiling as he approached Philippa, then stopped dead. She was talking to Agnes, who had come out to see who had bought the last of the fruit tarts.

Agnes looked up at him and the same frown touched her brow as before.

Thomas knew he could not stand where he was so started up again. As he came closer he heard Philippa say, "Berrington? How strange, for my companion also goes by the name of Berrington. Is it common in these parts?"

"Not now, my lady, and not for many years. I go by my aunt's name these days." Agnes's eyes were still on Thomas. "There is only myself and my daughters left in the area that I know of. Sickness took almost everyone else, and my brother died somewhere abroad. Is that your companion with the basket? How did you find a man willing to carry a basket? And he has ale and cheese, if I am not mistaken. Hold fast to him, my love."

Philippa turned, though Thomas was sure she knew he was there. A glint of mischief showed in her eyes.

"Thomas, come and meet another Berrington. Her name is Agnes."

He hesitated, then came the rest of the way. "I know well what her name is."

Agnes stared up at him and sudden tears came to her eyes when she heard his name. "Tom?" she said.

He nodded.

"But you are dead. Everyone told me you were dead, so it cannot be you."

"It is me, my sweet. And as you can see, I am not yet dead. But surely you cannot recall me?"

"I do, Tom, I do." She came closer and her hands came out to grasp his that did not hold the basket. "You brought me here on Bayard. Aunt Joan sent to Lemster for him after you and father left. He became my horse until he died. A good horse he was, too." Agnes shook her head. "Listen to me, wittering away. I want to know everything about you, Tom."

"And I you, but not now."

"Yes, now. You cannot disappear on me again. What if you never come back?"

Thomas knew it was a powerful argument, particularly considering recent events. Which meant Hugh Clement would have to wait.

ELEVEN

Thomas sat beside Agnes on a wooden bench set against the stone wall of the small courtyard behind the bakery. Philippa had returned to the castle, saying she wanted to be there when Prince Arthur arrived. They had eaten warm bread rolls with cheese, drunk ale, and Thomas had told his sister a little of what had happened to him in the forty-seven years since he had abandoned her in this courtyard.

"When I left you with Aunt Jean you were trying to climb the wall," Thomas said.

Agnes smiled. "I used to get told off all the time for it, even when I grew older. I do not recall that time, though."

"How can you remember me at all? You had not even three years when I brought you here. I remember nothing before I was four or five, at least."

"I think I do." Agnes reached for his hand and nestled it in her lap. Sunlight spilled over the roofs of adjacent houses to fill the courtyard with bright warmth. It caught in her hair to form a glowing golden halo around her head. "I am sure I do, but it might be nothing more than stories Aunt Jean told me about. I am proud of you, Tom."

"And I of you. You have built a good business here."

"Aunt Jean built the business. All I did was inherit it."

"You told me some of her children died and the rest moved away. Did they want no part of it?"

"Two came back and said I owed them money because the bakery should have been theirs, even though they did not want it. The work is hard and you have to rise before dawn, even in the summer. They would have sold it."

"Did you pay them?"

"Not what they asked, but a little. It must have been enough because they never returned."

"Constance Sparrow told me you married."

"Once, when I was in my thirties. Late for these parts, as you must remember. Late for most parts, I suppose. He left me when I fell pregnant for the second time. I thought he was a good man, then discovered he was not. All I have of him are my daughters. I love them dearly and forgive them his blood they carry."

"They are fine girls," Thomas said. "I did not recognise you in them or I might have guessed before."

"They favour me a little more the older they grow, but they do not have my hair. I expect I have changed a lot since you last saw me." Agnes gave a sad smile. "Oh, but I would have loved to have grown up with you in my life, Tom."

"And I you, but I am back now. And I did recognise you, just not at first. I saw you frown when you looked at me across Market Square."

"You were older when you brought me here, and I

think I saw something in you. I think it was the way you stood rather than how you looked. Upright, like you always did, as if you intended to take on the entire world."

Thomas laughed. "You would never have seen that in me at three years of age, sister, but you are not altogether wrong. I seem able to find a fight where nobody else can. Did you never marry again?"

"I lost trust in men after my husband left me and never felt the need for that other thing a man can offer a woman. Not enough to give up my independence. What brought you home, Tom?"

Thomas wondered if he had come home or not. It did not feel like home. He wondered if it ever had. While they ate he had told her a little of his story, but neglected to mention those things that would bring no pride in their telling. He knew Agnes must wonder why he had not returned after the battle at Castillon. The battle where their father had died, together with hundreds of English and Welsh men. But Thomas had no explanation. He did not know himself why he had not, other than the passage would have proven difficult, and for some time after the battle he was not himself. The fighting, the bloodshed, the horror of it had changed him. Ending the life of his father to prevent greater pain had changed him. Now he wondered how much to tell her of the reasons for his return. He had told Agnes of Isabel, Queen of Castile. Told her of her pretty daughter, Catherine of Aragon, who would come to live in Ludlow. But of himself? Enough, but not enough.

"Isabel asked me to return to England," he said.

"To come home?"

"What do you know about Prince Arthur and his bride to be?"

"Everyone knows she is a Spanish princess and they will live in the castle here in Ludlow. I would like to see a Spanish princess. Do you know if she is beautiful, Tom?"

"She is." There was an entire lifetime he wanted to tell his sister about, but suspected it would take another lifetime to tell it all.

"Why did this Queen Isabel ask you to return?" Agnes gave a laugh. "Are you as close to her as you make it sound?" She shook her head, as if the concept was too strange to believe.

A score of answers ran through Thomas's head, but which to offer? The truth he could not tell. Some semblance of it, perhaps.

"We became friends," he said, making Agnes laugh again.

"Friends? Like you and Philippa are friends? I see the way she looks at you. Like she wants to eat you all up."

It was his turn to laugh. "I may have taken on more than I can handle there, sister. But no, the relationship between Isabel and myself was a meeting of minds. And of equals, I like to believe."

Agnes squeezed his hand. "Do you love her?"

"I assume you ask about Isabel, in which case my answer is yes. I would die for her. I have almost died for her more than once, and would do so again."

"That was something else Aunt Jane told me about you. You were always too brave, too loyal, for your own good. It got you into trouble more than once is what she said."

"Guilty as charged." Thomas squeezed his sister's hand. Across the courtyard, Agnes's two daughters sat at another table, their heads together in conversation. They were sisters, not twins, but still Thomas found it hard to tell them apart. Pretty girls with darker hair than their mother.

"Do you ever visit Lemster?" Thomas asked.

"Not for many years. There is nothing for me there now. Did you know our old house burned down? They sold the land off when you and Pa failed to return."

"I went there on my way here. I intend to return soon and move the graves. Where to I don't know."

"When are you going to leave again, Tom?" Agnes's voice was soft.

"I don't know that either. Isabel has asked me to protect Catherine, and I will do so as long as I have the strength. When I no longer can, I expect Will is going to take my place. To be honest, he would be better to do it from the outset. He is six times stronger than I am. When that day comes, I hope to return to Spain. I still have a house there, and people looking after it for me. I would end my days in Granada, if I can."

"Listen to you, Tom, talking as if you are old. You don't look old."

"Oh, but you have a flattering tongue on you. I thought I had grown weak but have discovered I can still fight when called on."

"Don't fight, Tom. I want you around for a long time yet. Now you are back, I want to see a lot more of you."

"You will, sister. I thought of you often, how you were, how you had grown, who you had grown into."

"And what do you think? Will I do?"

"You will more than do."

Agnes smiled, but there were tears in her eyes. From beyond the courtyard walls, a great hubbub sounded, and one of the girls ran out to see what the noise was about. When she returned, she announced that Prince Arthur was riding through the street.

Thomas rose and embraced Agnes. "I will have to follow him to the castle. Are you coming out to see him pass?"

"I see the lad all the time. I will come when your princess arrives. That I want to see. Go, Tom, do your job, but never be a stranger."

"I won't." Thomas kissed her cheek and went out.

Cheering people thronged the marketplace. Thomas was impressed by the obvious adoration given to Arthur, then he saw one reason for it. As he rode astride a tall white charger, he reached into a velvet bag and drew out handfuls of small coins which he flung into the crowd. It meant nothing to him and everything to those who benefitted from his largesse. Thomas saw Philippa on the far side of the square, talking with Sir Richard Pole's wife, Margaret, who oversaw the household. Perhaps she was asking to have the pair of them assigned to the same room.

Thomas half-hoped Philippa would fail in her endeavour. They had grown too close too fast for his liking, and he believed she was keen on them growing closer yet. It confused Thomas why he even questioned their relationship. Philippa was a pleasant companion, both beautiful and wicked. She was also clever, which Thomas admired when he found it in either man or woman. There were too few clever people, he often thought, or not enough willing to admit to their cleverness.

As Thomas watched Philippa move away in the company of Lady Margaret Pole, he turned aside to take up his interrupted task.

Linney was a narrow lane shaded by houses that stood close on either side. As Thomas passed through the high town walls using Linney Gate, the ground ahead fell steeply and the view opened up to the north. The winding Corfe showed only here and there as a glint of silver between wooded banks. To the right, dense woodland grew. Oak, elm and ash. An occasional pine rose above the rest, and there was a small copse of birch. It was to the trees he headed. When he heard horses approaching from behind, he veered off into their cover and waited for the riders to pass. Five men, each dressed in similar hats as those of the day before. Hugh Clement's men?

When the track was clear, Thomas continued but stayed within the shade of the trees, soft loam beneath his feet. He smiled at Philippa's suggestion they should bring their food to eat among the trees, knowing she had been suggesting more than just food.

Hugh Clement's manor house sat back from the river on a patch of higher ground, no doubt to avoid the floods that would rise come winter. It was, as promised, small, but still larger than most houses in these parts. It rose two floors, with a tower on the western side rising to three and topped with a short spire. A walled stable-yard was set to one side and Thomas saw the five riders passing their mounts over to a stable-hand who led them away before the men entered the house. Thomas settled against the bole of an oak that might have stood on that spot for two centuries. Every now and again, acorns fell to the ground as a stray wind scurried through the branches. Thomas would have preferred to be closer; close enough to overhear whatever conversation went on within the house. But he knew such was impossible. Instead, he sat and waited, watching for movement, and tried to stop his eyes from closing. He wondered what he was doing here, but knew the reason. It was what he had done many times before. King Henry had asked him to investigate Hugh Clement, so here he was. But this was now more than simply acting for the King. Men had attacked him and Philippa. They would have killed them both, Thomas was sure. Without being aware of exactly when the moment came, this task had become personal. He was not altogether sure what was going on in Ludlow, but was determined to find out. The men who attacked them wore the same hats as those who had entered the house below. There was something here he could not turn away from. He would dig until he found that something, or nothing. In either case, he would report back to King Henry. What the King did with the information would be up to him.

Thomas woke with a jerk to find a man squatting in front of him. At first he thought it was one of Hugh Clement's men, but as he came fully to his senses he saw it could not be. A long blade was stuck in the ground between the man's feet. His clothes were coarse and many-layered. On his head sat a wide-brimmed felt hat from beneath which long strands of thick grey hair hung down. At least the hat was neither green nor red. The beard on his face matched his hair in both length and thickness. His brown eyes were sharp, hinting at an intelligence at odds with his appearance. In his hands, he held a stick with a heavy knobbed end. Cherry, it looked like; a good solid wood for a stick that might also serve as a club. Beside him lay four fat rabbits strung on hemp twine. So a poacher, then.

"I was about to leave you sleep, but am glad you woke. I thought you might be one of Clement's men, but now I see you are not."

"I assume neither are you."

The man nodded and grinned, showing a surprising number of teeth. "You be right in that. You are Tom Berrington, ain't you?"

Thomas sat up straighter and wiped a hand across his face. For a moment he wondered if he was still dreaming. How could this man know who he was?

"Who is asking?"

"No secret about my name. Everyone calls me Jack Pook these days, but I used to be Jack Brickenden. You were sweet on my sister once. Long time ago that was, but you ain't changed so much, I reckon. Where you been, Tom?"

"Bel never told me she had a brother."

"Black sheep of the family, me. I expect that's why."

"Is she... is Bel..." Thomas could scarcely get the words out. "Is Bel still alive?"

"Of course she is. She got that sickness, same as you did, but she's been hale since."

"Married?"

"She was, but her husband died a few years back."

"Children?"

"Seven. Five of 'em still alive, too. She did good, our Bel. She talks about you now and again. Less so now than she once did, but that's only natural, ain't it? What with everyone assuming Tom Berrington be long dead. Not many came back from that war you went off to."

"What are you doing out here in the woods? Did you come looking for me? Are you one of Hugh Clement's men after all, come to whack me with that stick?"

"I told you, I am no Clement man." Jack spat on the ground. "A free man, I am. Likely too free, some might say, but it's how I like it. You look a bit the same as you used to, Tom, but not so much I'd have recognised you if I hadn't heard you were back. Arthur Wodall said he saw you up at your old house. He made sure he got the third of your land that had your house on it."

Thomas stared at Jack. "That can't have been Arthur Wodall. The man would be in his ninetieth year by now."

"This is Arthur the son. They had two more children after you left

Do you think I could forget such a thing, Tom? What with you and Bel both involved? The Wodalls had two other children after you went away. Alice, and a boy they called Arthur after his father. They never forgave you, Tom. Still don't. The whole family believes you guilty."

"If that was Arthur Wodall why did he say nothing? I even asked him his name and he did not tell me."

"Way I heard it from Bel, you and the Wodalls weren't friends. Far from it. I don't even think Arthur wanted your land, but he took it because it was yours. He does nothing with it. P'raps you can buy it back off him." Jack cackled a laugh at the thought. "It was Arthur who burned the house down."

Thomas examined his own feelings on the matter and discovered he had none. Too much time had passed, too much life experienced. Jack spoke the truth. The male Berringtons had died out in France. If not for Isabel's request, Thomas would never have returned to England.

"Where do you live, Jack?" Thomas rose to his feet. The afternoon was fading into a fine evening, sharp with the promise of frost before dawn. The air held the soft scent of loam and bark. Fires had been lit in the manor house and smoke rose in spirals from three chimneys.

"It's a fine house, ain't it?" Jack ignored Thomas's question as he rose to stand beside him.

"It is."

"You stayin' around these parts, Tom?"

How much to tell this man he had not even known existed? And then, because Thomas had carried a flame for Jack's sister all those years ago, he said, "I am staying in Ludlow Castle at the moment."

"I heard Arthur was back. What're you doing in the Castle?"

"Do you know he is getting married?"

"Entire district knows that."

"I am to watch over his bride-to-be when she arrives in England."

"You?"

Thomas nodded and started to walk. Jack fell in at his side, the rabbits swinging from the string wrapped around his left hand. He used the cherry stick to help him walk, though Thomas saw no limp.

"I know her mother," he said.

"This girl Arthur's marrying is a princess, I hear. So do you know a queen, Tom?"

"I do."

Jack shook his head at the wonders of the world beyond Ludlow and Lemster.

"I expect you must know King Henry as well, then."

"I do."

"Should I tell Bel I seen you or not? She's like me and don't hold with important folk who have airs and graces. Not that you look like you have those, mind."

Thomas walked on for a score of paces, wondering how to answer. Then tossed the dice to see where they fell.

"Tell her, Jack. And if you do, send her my love. Tell her I think about her too, but like you said, not as often as I once did. Now I want you to tell me what you know about Hugh Clement, and whether he is up to no good."

Jack laughed. "He's a nobleman, so of course he's up to no good. All the same, they are. No offence intended, if that's what you are now, though you don't dress like one. Are you a nobleman, Tom?"

"I honestly don't know. Tell me what Clement is up to."

"It will cost you a few flagons of ale and a fine meal, but not in Ludlow. The town will be thick with folk now Arthur has arrived. There is a fine tavern down Overton way, and the landlady has great big paps on her a man can stare at for hours if he has a mind to. I'll tell you what I know about Hugh Clement, and you can tell me what you have been up to all these years."

TWELVE

It was late by the time Thomas returned to Ludlow and the castle, grateful for the remnant of a half-full moon dropping towards the west which allowed him to find his way. He had left Jack Pook at the tavern in Overton, still trying to persuade the landlady to offer him a bed for the night. Thomas's head swam from too much ale and too much information. What Jack did not know about the district seemed barely worth the knowing. Thomas had no idea where he was meant to sleep so went in search of someone who could tell him. The kitchen was always a sensible place to start so he tried there first, following his nose. When he found it, a single lamp burned and only one woman remained. She was scrubbing at a pot with sand to clear the debris of dinner from it.

"You are too late if it is food you are after," she said over her shoulder.

"I am not after food but a bed for the night."

The woman snorted a laugh. "Well, if it is mine you are

after you will be out of luck, though you are handsome enough, and I like the way you talk. Are you foreign?"

"If you consider Lemster foreign, then perhaps so. I am with the Prince's party but was detained. I don't know where I am meant to sleep."

"You need Lady Margaret Pole, but she will be in her own bed these last three hours. You might try her husband. He was in Mortimer's Tower not so long since, talking with that Welshman."

"Gruffydd?"

"That is the one. Half the Prince's party seems to be Welshmen these days. Not like it used to be, I can tell you."

"I expect not. Where is this tower?"

The woman sighed and put down the pot. "Go back across the drawbridge and turn right. You cannot miss it. It is a great big tower. You will find them right at the top. The pair of them like to drink and stare out across the countryside in the belief they control it. But don't tell them I said that."

Thomas found the tower easily enough; it would have been difficult to miss it. It was the only structure of any height to rise from the defensive wall of the outer bailey. Stone steps led up in a spiral, and when he had climbed half of them he heard voices from above. He came out into a small chamber set with a table and chairs, but no roof. One wall sat lower than the others. It was here that Sir Richard Pole and Sir Gruffydd ap Rhys stood. They did indeed appear to be looking west across the moon-washed countryside they believed lay under their control. The moon reflected from rapids close by

Dinham Bridge. Gruffydd turned and nodded at Thomas.

"You have good feet, Tom. We only heard you the last ten steps."

"Then I must remember to take more care next time. Lack of practice, I expect."

"There is wine over there if you want some. Have you come for a reason or just to talk? We can do that right fine up here where nobody can hear us. I take it we can trust you?"

"You can." Thomas needed no more wine but poured himself a cup all the same. He wanted to keep in favour with these men. He had spoken with Gruffydd on the journey west and liked him. The man was blunt and straight-talking, sometimes too straight-talking. Sir Richard Pole was different, but also dedicated to Prince Arthur's welfare.

"So what is it you want with us?" asked Gruffydd. "Apart from the pleasure of our company, that is."

"Two things." Thomas walked across to join them at the balustrade. "First, and of little import, I don't know where I am meant to be sleeping tonight."

Gruffydd laughed and slapped Thomas on the back, making him spill some of the fine red wine. "With Pip, I expect. Is that not right, Richard?"

Sir Richard gave a curt nod. "She came right out and asked my wife to assign the pair of you to the same room." The merest hint of a smile touched his lips. "I thought Maggie might faint away there and then, but Pip had her way, as she usually does. As you appear to be having your way with her." Sir Richard winked, causing Thomas to change his opinion of the man. He had known others who put on a stern face to reflect their status, but often enough if a man dug beneath the surface he would find the thread of humanity which ran through them, just as it did in most. Not all men, but most.

Thomas was glad he had climbed all those steps to reach this platform and these men.

"I don't suppose you have any idea which room that would be?" he asked.

"I don't, but there is a plan posted in the office next to the gatehouse," said Sir Richard. "You could have saved yourself a climb if you had thought to check there first."

"Then I would have missed the pleasure of your company and this fine wine."

"It is good, isn't?" said Gruffydd. "You said two things, Tom. What is the other? Unless you meant the pleasure of our company, of course."

"How much do you know of what King Henry tasked me with?"

"We wondered why you were part of the company, but Henry knows what he is doing so we did not question your presence. Besides, you have the look of a man who might be handy in a fight."

"Do you expect any fighting?"

"I always expect fighting. Better to expect it and be ready than have it come at you without warning."

Thomas nodded his agreement, coming to a decision. King Henry had told him the matter of Hugh Clement was to be kept from Prince Arthur, but Thomas believed he could trust both these men.

"I have been learning about Hugh Clement."

"Ah," said Sir Richard. "I told you that might be it, did I not, Gruff?"

"Indeed you did. What have you been finding out, Tom? That the man is a rogue using his position to line his own pocket? Not such an unusual state of affairs among Justices, which is why I suspect the position is only for a year. The title is unpaid, so a man must find some way to fund the work. Not that Clement does much in the way of work."

"I think it may go a little deeper than that, Sir Gruffydd."

"Now you intrigue me. And call me Gruff, though Richard here might stand on protocol and insist on the Sir, even from a man who is a Spanish Duke."

"Do you recall when I left the royal party at Tenbury?" Thomas waited for a nod of acknowledgement. "Pip and I rode to Lemster. I wanted to see my old house, but it lay in ruins. That is not the story, though. As we rode north to join the Prince's party men accosted us on the road."

"By damn, Tom, what happened?" said Sir Richard. "This is a peaceful town. We will not stand for vagabonds. Do you know who they were?"

"One of them. Another ran, and the third is dead."

Gruffydd smiled. "Did you kill him?"

"I did. It was kill or be killed. I expected to have to kill the other who had gone after Pip but he ran scared when he heard me coming."

Gruffydd looked at Sir Richard. "I expect she could have managed well enough without your help. I always believe her capable of killing a man. What makes you think these men belonged to Hugh Clement?"

"I don't, not for sure. Perhaps I am just plucking evidence from thin air. But the King sent me to look into Clement's affairs, told me he might be doing something underhand, and then we were assaulted. The two I saw wore similar jackets—not quite a uniform, but close, and green felt hats, but that does not make them Clement's men. When you failed to arrive in Ludlow yesterday, Pip and I took a room at an inn. Hugh Clement was there talking with two other men and invited us to their table."

"Daniel Lupton will be one," said Sir Richard, "and I suspect the other was Peter Gifforde."

"You are well informed."

"It is my job to be well informed. Pip knows them all, so it does not surprise me they invited you to their table. I expect the wine was good, was it not?"

"It was. Daniel Lupton works for Hugh Clement, does he not?"

"He does."

"But Peter Gifforde indicated he is something to do with Wigmore Abbey."

"Administrator." Sir Richard went to the table and poured himself more wine. "It puzzled us all when the appointment was made because usually one of the order takes the role, but I have to admit he is making a good fist of it. The Abbot is growing old and his mind lies elsewhere. The Abbey holdings are being better managed than they have ever been. There is money to be made there and Gifforde seems to pull it in these days." Sir Richard smiled. "The Abbot joined us at Caynham Manor, but slept through most of our meal there. Come to think of it, Peter Gifforde was there too but left early."

"Would he have business with Hugh Clement?" Thomas asked.

"More than likely. The Abbey is the largest landowner in these parts, even more so than Prince Arthur. It is reasonable Hugh Clement and Gifford's interests would coincide."

"And Daniel Lupton? Does he have interests?"

"Daniel's interests are Hugh Clement's interests. He fixes things for him. Collects debts owed, administers some kind of justice when needed. After all, what is a Justice of the Peace meant to do if not that? Without Daniel, nothing would happen. Hugh is amenable enough but lacks the wits to be effective. The appointment will have been political, but who made it I don't know. Though I expect I should." Sir Richard glanced at Gruffydd, who had been steadily drinking. "Do you have any idea, Gruff?"

"Most likely the Abbey, which explains why Gifforde was there. Hugh is beholden to him, no doubt. His appointment came not half a year after Gifforde got the job. Not that Hugh would ever accept the fact, or even recognise it. Perhaps it is Gifforde who pulls Hugh's strings and makes him dance. If he wants a Justice he can control and direct, then Hugh is the right man to appoint. No doubt next year he will seek another similar. There are enough nobles around here with money and land, but little in the way of brains, to provide an endless supply."

"There are also some who like to make trouble," said Sir Richard.

Gruffydd smiled. "Aye, agreed, but we know who they are, and they know we know. Things have settled down under Henry. About time, too. England could not face many more years of civil war and the coming and goings of kings. The country has been quiet for a while now. Burgundy has stopped her attempts to stir up trouble, and the Scots have withdrawn north of the border."

"And this new connection to Spain will steady things even more," said Sir Richard. "As soon as Arthur has a son the line of Tudor succession will be safe."

Gruffydd laughed. "Don't kill Henry off just yet. The man has twenty years left in him."

"Agreed, but all the same a son or two for Arthur will send a powerful signal."

"If what you say is true," Thomas said, "and I agree with you, why has the King asked me to look into Hugh Clement's affairs?"

"That is specifically what he asked you?" said Sir Richard.

"It is."

"Did he offer any clue what you are looking for?"

Thomas shook his head.

"The two of us wondered why you were with us. Now it makes sense, but what does not is why he asked you and not one or both of us. Or any of us. There are good men under our command who could do what is being asked of you."

"Perhaps he asked because I am a stranger. Though that only makes the task harder."

"Except you are from around these parts," said Gruffydd. "Maybe Henry thinks you will have a better sense of what is out of place than someone else."

"Then he is wrong in that." Thomas held a hand up

when he saw Sir Richard scowl. "Yes, I know the King is never wrong. Which is why I will do whatever I can. This will not be the first time I have brought a wicked man to justice."

"And if Hugh Clement is not wicked?" said Sir Richard.

"Then I will have had the pleasure of your company, your fine wine, and Pip's bed. Which is where I should be now."

Gruffydd barked a laugh and slapped Thomas on the back. "Any other man would have been there hours since."

As Thomas descended the steps, he thought of the conversation between the three of them perched high atop a castle tower. He had learned a little, but was not sure it did him much good. He knew he was an interloper, and men of power did not as a rule much like interlopers.

Thomas went to the gatehouse and found a sheet of paper nailed to the wall showing the room allocations. He found where he and Philippa were sleeping and made his way there, surprised at how much excitement he felt to be with her again. He would ask more questions about Hugh Clement and his companions in the morning, but morning remained a long way off yet.

THIRTEEN

Rain had come overnight to outstay any sparse welcome it might have had. Thomas sat astride Ferrant, his tagelmust wrapped over his head. He had covered half the distance to Lemster but so far not seen a single soul on the road. When he left Ludlow, the rain had been heavy. Now it was only miserable. Soon it would be bearable, and then it would stop. Thomas surprised himself with how much he recalled of the rain in England, but he supposed there had been a great deal of it to teach its lessons and vagaries. At least it was warm rain. Soon, October would slide into November, the last of the russet leaves would fall, and winter would offer its chill promise with early frosts. Philippa had remained in bed when Thomas rose, offering only a mumble as she turned over. Rather than wake her, Thomas left a note, brief but accurate. *Gone out on business. Back later.*

Until Catherine arrived, it pleased Thomas that King Henry had asked him to look into the dealings of Hugh Clement because it gave him something to occupy his

mind. It was possible the man was doing nothing unto-
ward, but Jack Pook hinted there were things it would be
useful to uncover.

By the time Thomas reached the bridge over the Lugge
and entered Lemster, the rain had stopped and a weak sun
was showing through. Mist rose from the fields to drift
past at shoulder height on Ferrant. There were more
people now and some turned, curious who the tall
stranger was, no doubt wondering why he dressed so
oddly.

Thomas tied Ferrant to a rail and entered the grounds
of Lemster Priory. He had several questions and considered the Priory a safer place to ask them than Ludlow. A
mere four leagues separated the towns, but Thomas knew
people rarely left the place they were born in. As a boy, he
had only done so occasionally, and then because his father
was squire to John Talbot, Earl of Shrewsbury. A service
that brought about both his own death and that of the
Earl.

Within the Priory grounds, several brothers worked.
The extensive vegetable garden needed constant attention
if it was to feed the twenty Benedictines. They set any
excess outside the western gate for the townsfolk.
Thomas had been a frequent visitor to the Priory when
young. Not for any religious reason, though at that age he
still believed in God's glory, but to learn. He devoured the
knowledge held in the Priory library. It was a trait his
father failed to understand but which his mother
encouraged.

One monk working a vegetable plot rose and
approached, his sandalled feet heavy with mud.

"Can I help you, sir?"

"I would like to see the Prior if possible."

"Do you have business with him?"

"That I don't yet know, but if I do then it is the King's business as well as mine."

The monk looked at him without expression. This was a house dedicated to the worship of God. Kings came and went, but God and Priories would go on forever. Or so they believed, and Thomas saw no reason to doubt that belief.

"I will see if he is free. Your name, sir?"

"Thomas Berrington." He watched for any recognition but none came. Much time had passed since he last stood on these grounds.

He watched the hustle and bustle of managing the property while he waited. He knew that as well as the gardens, carp ponds lay on the far side fed by the Kenwater, which diverted the waters of the Lugge for that purpose. The Priory, like Wigmore Abbey whose control it fell under, owned much of the land around Ludlow and Lemster. They rented most out, and the rents were reasonable, unlike those of other landowners.

The monk who had gone to inform the Prior of his visitor returned faster than he had left.

"He says he will see you in his office." The monk seemed disturbed that Thomas was granted an audience so easily. Perhaps it had been the mention of the King's business that did it.

Thomas followed the monk, who led the way. Once within the stone walls, their long distant familiarity brought a sense of times past and opportunities lost. Also of alien opportunities he had grasped with both hands. Other lands, other languages, two wives, children, friends, the love of a Queen and the hatred of a King. Thomas wondered what he would have become had he returned to Lemster, or never left it. He might have run away, abandoning his father without regret because he had hated the man. John Berrington was a hard man and a bully. His self-belief had resulted in his death on a battlefield outside the small French town of Castillon.

The sound of an exclamation brought Thomas back to himself and he looked up to see a tall figure at the end of the long corridor. The monk stopped in his tracks, once more uncertain at the breaking of protocol.

Then the Prior came forward and said, "It cannot be you, Tom, you are dead. Praise be to the Lord you are not."

Thomas stopped a few feet from the man who had taught him so much, challenging him and disciplining him in equal measure.

"Bernard?" Thomas said, then ducked as a hand came out to slap his head, but the blow was soft and done with love. Just as it had been the last time this man had done it.

"Prior Bernard now, Tom." The Prior tilted his head, his still sharp eyes examining Thomas.

"I expect I have changed, haven't I?" Thomas said.

"You have, but not so much I cannot make out the boy beneath the mantle of the man." The Prior's eyes left Thomas for a moment. "It is all right, brother, I know Thomas like I know myself."

Only when the monk had left them, when the door at the far end of the corridor had closed, did Prior Bernard close the space and embrace Thomas. His arms were still strong, but Thomas knew the man must be in his eighties. When the hug finally ended, Prior Bernard held Thomas by the shoulders, unshed tears glittering in his eyes.

"Is this real? It seems more like a dream, but here you are. Come, Tom, I want you to tell me everything that has happened to you." The Prior shook his head. "How long is it now? What age have you?"

"Sixty years, Bernard. I have sixty years. You must have eighty or more, yet still you look hale."

Prior Bernard laughed. "What age were you when you left for France with John Talbot? Thirteen, was it not? I suppose I may have seemed old to a boy of thirteen, but I was only ten years older than you. So no, I am not eighty, Tom, but I feel every one of my seventy years. God has been kind to me and all my aches are small ones. But you…" He examined Thomas again and laughed. "You are taller than me. You always were tall, but now…" A shake of the head. "And strong. Are you still fast?"

"Fast enough."

"I expect you must be to have lived this long. What are you doing back in Lemster? Have you come to stay? Listen to me, question after question. Come to my study and you can tell me everything."

"That might take a month."

"Then let it."

They settled on wooden chairs facing each other. Sharp sunlight fell through a tall leaded window to make patterns on the floor between them. It was Thomas's turn to examine Prior Bernard. He discovered signs of the years since last he saw him, but it surprised him how few they were. His tonsured hair was greying but not white, and other than the shaved pate it appeared to all be present. His body remained as lean as it always had been. There were lines etched in his face and around his eyes, but Thomas knew he possessed those himself.

"You have come here on some purpose, I expect. Are you surprised to find me as Prior?"

"Only surprised to find you still alive. You always were the most able."

"And the least modest, I was often told. I try not to be, but it comes hard. I expect you know all about that, don't you?"

"I freely admit to being proud of my lack of modesty, and teach my children to be the same. If a man has talent and ability, he should use it, not be ashamed of it."

Prior Bernard laughed softly. "You have not changed much, have you, Tom?"

"Do any of us?"

"I believe I have. You know well that I fought in the Holy City as well as against the Moors in Spain, but I turned my back on my past and have lived a contented life here. There is an hour yet before Sext, so tell me why you are here. The rest can come later. I will see you again, will I not?"

"Of course."

"So you are staying?"

"That I am not sure about, but staying for a while at least. Until Prince Arthur weds and settles into married life."

"You work for the Prince?"

"And his father, which is why I am here, and even

more pleased to discover you are Prior because I trust you."

"You always were too gullible. But ask what you want and I will answer if I can."

"I am trying to tease out information about a man called Hugh Clement. He has a small manor house north of—"

"I know Clement," said Prior Bernard, his reply curt.

"From your manner of speech I take it you don't much like him."

"Do you know why I always liked you so much, Tom? Why I let you get away with many things I would never allow in others? Because even at thirteen you were competent, and you were curious, and you wanted to learn. Those things will get a man a long way in life if he is also honest. I take it you are that, too? I would be sorely disappointed if you are not."

"I try to be. Am I to take it Hugh Clement is none of those things?"

"You are right. Worse, he has power but does not know how to wield it other than to benefit himself."

"I arrived in Ludlow only two days ago, but already I have come to the same conclusion. I know nothing about the man, which is why I came to you."

"I am the head of Lemster Priory, Tom. What makes you think I have knowledge of dealings by the current Justice of the Peace?"

"Are you saying you do not? The man I knew all those years ago always had an eye on the welfare of those he considered his flock. Besides, when I talked with Hugh

Clement there was another there you must know. Peter Gifforde."

"Ah, yes. Peter. Of course I know him."

Thomas stared at Prior Bernard, trying to judge his expression. It was too bland. Too neutral.

"And…?"

"Are you not curious about his name?"

"He told me who his grandfather was, if that is what you mean."

It was Prior Bernard's turn to ask, "And…?"

"I assume the man is dead by now. That is what Peter claims."

"Yes, he is dead. And I am still waiting."

"If I tell you something, can you promise not to reveal it to anyone else?"

"Are you offering to make confession? In which case you need a priest, not a Prior."

"Not my confession. Walter Gifforde's, when he thought he was dying."

"Is it to do with the murder of Raulf Wodall?"

"It is." Thomas gave a shake of his head. "Did you ever believe me guilty of killing him, the same as everyone else in town?" As he spoke the words, Thomas realised he had carried a sense of that judgement through all the intervening years. He had been innocent, but not even his own father believed him.

"Never," said Prior Bernard, and in that one word Thomas felt a weight lift from him. Perhaps this was a confessional after all.

"So it will come as no surprise that Walter Gifforde killed

Raulf. I worked it out and went to see him when he was in the throes of the sickness, same as over half the town. He told me what he did. If you believe me, you do not need the details."

"I would not wish to know them," said Prior Bernard. "But Peter Gifforde is the grandson, not the man himself. Are you making some connection here, or what?"

"I don't know. I am gathering information, nothing more. What did you think about it when they made Peter Gifforde administrator of the Abbey?"

"It surprised me, of course, but he has proven himself to be proficient in the position. The Abbey brings in almost a quarter more in revenue than it did before he came, and there are fewer arguments over land and debt. Abbot John is pleased with him, and if the Abbot is, then so am I. There is no secret plot here. Peter came home and settled into the role that might have always been meant for him. He deals with Hugh Clement because it is his job to deal with many people, and I trust him." Prior Bernard gave a deep sigh. "I know you, Tom. You need proof, don't you?"

"I would welcome something."

"Then I can show you the contracts for all the land Hugh Clement has acquired, as well as those handled by Peter. As you know, a copy has to be lodged with the Abbot, and they always send a second here in case the original is lost. Most of these acquisitions came about before Peter or Hugh took up their current posts. I can leave you to examine them while I pray, then you will eat with us and we can talk more."

"Will the brethren not wonder who I am?"

"They will, but I will tell them you are an emissary

from King Henry. Which sounds close enough to the truth to even be the truth. Can you still read Latin? Most of the documents are in English, but not all. A few are even in French."

"Yes, I still have some Latin, as well as French, Spanish and Arabic."

"I once had a little of each of those, but doubt I could recall any other than the Latin and French."

"You always were coy about your past," Thomas said.

"As befits a man of the cloth. We must put behind us all that we were, and that is what I have done."

"Do you never think of it?"

"Of course I do. But when the memories come I set them aside until they fade. They have no place in a house of God." Prior Bernard tilted his head. "Do you have your demons, Tom?"

"Too many, but my family and friends keep me sane."

"I am sure you said you have children."

"Two. A boy and a girl. Will and Amal."

"Amal is an Arabic name, is it not?"

"Her mother was a Moor."

"You remain married?"

"She died a long time ago, but Amal is so much like her it almost feels as if she has been restored to me." Thomas felt his voice catch and coughed to cover the emotion, but he saw Prior Bernard notice.

"And your son, is he also a Moor?"

"Different mother, same grandfather. Will is half a foot taller than you and has hair as white as the snows of the Sholayr." The familiar words came without thought to Thomas.

Prior Bernard frowned as he worked out the relationship and found it wanting in probity.

"Their mothers were what, cousins?"

"Sisters."

"And you married both?"

"I did." Thomas watched Prior Bernard, knowing he had revealed more than he meant to, and that the revelation might change everything.

"Did you sin, Thomas?"

"It never felt like a sin."

"Sin never does. That is its siren call. Have you confessed your acts?"

Thomas stared at Prior Bernard without replying and saw a change pass through the man.

"Did you convert to their religion? Is that why it was no sin to have them both?"

"No, I did not convert, but neither do I believe in sin anymore. I was not married to both at the same time. When you knew me, I was pious enough. I believed in God, the Church, in the Holy Spirit and prayer. Somewhere between then and now it has all leached from me. I realise what saying this means and am sorry if it hurts you, Bernard, but I cannot speak anything but the truth; not to you. I used to respect you more than any man in my life."

"And now? Who do you respect now?"

"I still respect you, but you are right, there have been others over the years. The grandfather of my children is one. I have been fortunate in my friendships."

"And your enemies?"

"Most of my enemies have been unfortunate." There was no inflection in Thomas's voice.

"You have killed."

"As I know you will have, because you were a soldier."

"It is what soldiers do, Tom. We kill, but only when ordered to do so, and only our enemies."

"I have killed no one who did not deserve to die, and many I allowed to live even if they did not deserve to. It is possible too many died, but I stayed my hand when I could. I am not an evil man, Bernard, but there are times my thoughts are darker than they should be. I strive to be good, but sometimes a man has to act and do what is right, to stand up for what is just."

Prior Bernard ran a hand across his head and let his breath go. "Your words might have matched my own at one time, but no longer. Perhaps you are right, and I have spent too many years cloistered within the walls of this Priory. There is a real world out there but I have turned my back on it. That might have been a mistake, but I believe God asked it of me. I serve Him now. You serve the King, who is closer to God than any other man in this land, so you are also doing God's work, even if you feign no belief. Sometimes God makes demands that do not sit well, but do them we must. The world needs men who can serve what is right and just. Is that you, Tom?"

"Perhaps."

"I think it may be. But always remember your goodness. You had a surfeit of it at one time. Does it still exist?"

"There was a time I lost it, I admit, but it came back to me and these days I hold tight to it."

"Good. Then I will help with what you ask. You have

been honest with me and you might not have been. I respect an honest man."

"As do I."

"Then come with me, Tom." Prior Bernard rose to his feet. "I will take you to the documents."

As they walked side by side along the corridor, Thomas asked, "Do you still keep them in the same place?"

"We do. You so loved the sacristy, as I recall. Let us hope it holds at least a little of what you seek. And I will pray that one day you may rediscover the faith you once had."

FOURTEEN

Thomas had no idea how much time passed before Prior Bernard returned and leaned over the large elm table scattered with documents, sketches, and maps. There were copyhold records and court leets, together with lists of villeins subject to Hugh Clement's jurisdiction. There were also gaps in the records that became apparent only when the rest was known.

"You have been mighty busy, Tom. I hope you intend to tidy all this back where you got it from before you finish." Bernard picked up the book Thomas had been writing his findings in.

Thomas felt thirteen years old again under the Prior's chastisement. He looked at the table and saw he could have been better organised.

Prior Bernard laughed. "What is this scribble? I cannot read a single word. Your script used to be better than this."

Thomas smiled. "It is Arabic, which I am sure you

know. It comes more naturally to me these days, and has the advantage nobody else can read it."

"And if somebody kills you? Who will know what I hold here?"

"It has not happened yet, and enough have tried. But I will produce a copy in English and lodge it with you. It would be good to have a second pair of eyes go over it to see if they agree with my findings."

"In that case make it Latin, for I read that better." Prior Bernard laughed when he saw Thomas's expression. "Come on, Tom, it will be good for you to stretch that mind of yours and stop it growing old."

"Too late for that."

Prior Bernard pulled a stool across and sat with a sigh. "Age does not come quietly. You will find that out soon enough."

"I already have."

"We have an hour before we eat our main meal. You will join us, won't you? I want the others to see you sitting next to me. It will make a statement."

"Of what?" Thomas pushed some papers together, trying to sort them into the order they had been when he took them out.

"You said you work for King Henry. Prince Arthur too, I assume, if you are here. It does the brothers good to be reminded they live as they do by the grace of both God and King."

"Do you have trouble here?" Thomas twisted to ease an ache in his back.

"No trouble, but you know how it is in a closed order. At least you should, you used to visit often enough."

Thomas laughed. "I was thirteen, Bernard, and in love."

"With Bel Brickenden, as I recall. Along with half the town. Do you think I could forget such a thing? Do you know she still lives at the brickworks?"

"I do. I met her brother only the other day, though when I knew Bel I did not know she had a brother."

"Jack Pook, yes. I assume he told you he was the black sheep of the family?"

"He did, but he also said Bel still talks to him. What did he do so wrong to exile him from the family?"

"He was always getting into trouble of one kind or another when he was young, and for a long time after. These days, not so much. Probably worst of all, he did not want to become a maker of bricks. Jack is too independent to settle for a steady trade. The family wanted nothing to do with him, but Bel always kept in touch. She has a soft spot for the rogue. Did he know who you were?"

"He did. Said word had got around about me looking at my old house."

"Jack hears everything. He still has some of the devil in him, but he is a good man to know if you can put up with that. I cannot, of course, but you are a different matter."

"I tried to look up the records of my old house but could not find anything. Jack told me Raulf Wodall has the deed now, but if so it is not here."

"Do you want the house and land back? I can probably arrange for it to happen if you do."

"My thanks, but no. It holds few good memories for me. What I do need is permission to dig up the graves and move them. My mother and brother lie behind that shell, as well as my father's parents and some of his sisters, I think."

"I can find a place for them here if you wish it," said Prior Bernard.

"I would rather bury them on land I own. Which I have also been looking for amongst these." Thomas shuffled through a smaller pile of papers set in the top corner of the table. "All this land is under the jurisdiction of either the Priory or Wigmore Abbey. I want to own the land I intend to live on."

"The church does not sell its land. I can rent you some, but sell it? I am afraid not, even for you."

"Which is what I expected. But does the Abbey have records of freehold?"

"I am not the man to ask. You would need Peter Gifforde for that. I expect he would have the information at the tip of his fingers from what I hear tell."

"Then perhaps I will call on the Abbey soon."

"If you let me know when I will come with you. An introduction from me will ease your passage to the knowledge you seek. And it will do me good to get out into the countryside for a few hours. In the meantime, I can set someone to looking through our records to see if we have anything for you."

"I will pay for their time, and—"

Prior Bernard cut him off with a raised hand. "No payment. You can contribute alms to the poor of the town if you wish, but I need nothing from you for this. Oh, except perhaps I do. I am curious. It is a failing, I know, but tell me if you found out anything about Hugh Clement amongst all of this."

"That is easy enough." Thomas touched a separate pile of papers, all related to the dealings of Hugh Clement. "He has become a tenant in chief for large swathes of land north and west of Ludlow, and continues to gather even more to himself. He gained the latest only this summer. Most of it is sub-let to villeins. Some papers show how much rent they pay. Add them all up and it comes to a handsome sum. And that is only those where monies are shown. Hugh Clement is a wealthy man. Wealthy enough to employ his own army if he wanted to."

"Except the King does not allow a man to do that."

"Jack Pook says he thinks that might be what Hugh Clement is doing."

"Jack and I have little in the way of conversation, but if that is what he told you I would take his word for it. Jack is a rogue, but an honest rogue. You say there are gaps in the record that interest you. What are they?"

"I found several parcels of land, some small, some middling, none large, that have fallen through gaps between the church and the law. They appear to have no owners, even though the church should own everything that is not the King's. I intend to ride the boundaries and find out what lies there. If people work them, I will ask who they pay rent to."

"And if nobody works them, that will also prove interesting," said Prior Bernard. "You were here when the pestilence came and know full well the toll it took. I suspect some of these parcels were owned by families who died out in their entirety. It was a time of chaos, so it is understandable if things were missed. The Priory lost a quarter of our brothers to disease. But enough of land deeds, come and eat with us. Leave the papers as they are. I will have a brother tidy them later. I am sure I can find several who need a penance." Prior Bernard picked up the pages holding Thomas's Arabic script. "And translate this for me. Latin and English, if you can manage both."

Thomas smiled. "I expect I can, though these days the English might be more of a challenge than the Latin."

"I like the way you speak it now, Tom. There is a colour to your speech that is most pleasant." Prior Bernard handed the pages to Thomas. He opened his leather satchel and slid them inside to the sound of metal sliding against metal.

"What do you have in that abomination, Tom?"

"Tools of my trade."

"You have become a bricklayer? I expected more of you."

"Bricklaying is an honourable profession, Bernard. But no, I became a physician. A surgeon. It is where I learned my Arabic, in the infirmary of Málaga."

"A Moorish physician mended a wound for me once when I fought in the east. They are skilled, I admit, if misguided in their religion. Are you skilled, Tom?"

"I have been told I am."

"You haven't changed so much then, have you? You always were the cleverest lad I knew. Now come and eat. I have honoured your presence by asking for fish cooked in the Jewish manner. I take it you are familiar with that, coming from Spain?"

"If you mean battered and fried, then yes, I am. Though I have no recollection of telling you I lived in Spain until this moment."

Prior Bernard rose to his feet and Thomas saw him try not to grunt.

"Where else would the Duke of Granada live? And I know fine well where Málaga is. I too am not stupid."

Thomas knew he should be riding north to Ludlow. Instead, he stood beside Ferrant and stared at a cluster of buildings set close to the waters of the Lugge. Smoke spiralled from three chimneys which rose from a long open-sided barn. This, Thomas knew, was the brick-works. A solid black and white house stood at a safe distance from the furnaces. There were stairs against an outside wall, and Thomas knew they led to a large room where once he had lain beside Bel Brickenden. Thomas had seen three strapping men come and go around the works, but none were in sight at the moment. He had decided not to approach the house, knowing it would be a mistake. Reacquainting himself with an old lover was pointless. He had been thirteen, Bel barely two years older. They had been little more than children, and both had lived full lives since. First love might taste sweet on the tongue of memory but could prove rancid when the bottle was opened years later. Thomas knew such from bitter experience.

As he turned away, a whinny from Ferrant halted him. One man he had observed appeared from the tree-line with a solid length of wood in his hand.

"We told you last time to leave us alone. Told you what you'd get if you came back, so now you're going to get it."

Thomas heard a sound from behind. When he turned, he found a second man approaching. He, too, carried a club.

"You can put that down. I am a friend."

"Not to us, you ain't. We won't kill you, but you're going to take one hell of a beating to teach you not to mess with the Brickendens."

Thomas tensed himself for the attack, running moves through his head, aware there was a third man somewhere. Still at the house protecting the women, he hoped. Which reminded him of why he had come.

"Are you Bel's sons?"

"How do you know Ma's name?" The first man frowned, unsure now.

"Is she down there in the house, with the third of her sons looking out for her? Dutiful sons you are, in that case. She must be proud of you."

"Who are you?"

"Go tell your mother Tom has returned to Lemster."

"Just Tom?"

"She will remember or not. I will stay here. If she does not want to see me, I will ride away."

The man shook his head. He walked away down to the house and disappeared inside. His brother remained where he was, his eyes never leaving Thomas.

Long minutes passed. Thomas patted Ferrant's neck, and the horse turned its head in appreciation and gave a snuffle. He bumped Thomas's hand with his nose, asking for food, but was good-natured when none was forthcoming. Below, the door of the house opened and a woman came out. She looked up at the man and horse on the slope, then started across. Even at a distance, Thomas recognised her.

She stopped an arm's length away and glanced at her son.

"It's all right, Edmund, I know Tom. We are old friends. Go down and tell the others I'll be just fine with him."

She waited until her son offered a grudging nod and turned away, but only after casting a threatening glance in Thomas's direction.

"You have strapping lads, Bel."

"I do. You have grown tall too, Tom. I was going to ask if it is truly you but I can see it is. Even fully grown and your hair starting to grey I can see it is you."

"You have not grown so much."

Bel smiled. "I've grown in a few places I expect. Are you home for good? Everyone thought you were dead when you did not come back. I waited, you know. Two years I waited, just in case. Had plenty of offers, like you'd expect, but I waited two years for you. Except you never came back. Was that long enough, Tom?"

"You should have forgotten about me sooner."

"How could I after what we did together?" She smiled when she saw his expression. "Not only that. Saving your life as well. Just like you saved mine."

"You were sick the last time I saw you. I did not know if you would live."

"You stayed with me when I was sick, Tom. Most people would not have done that."

"Of course I stayed with you. I loved you. Who do

your sons think I am, Bel? They threatened me with a good beating."

Bel laughed. "And if they tried, you'd have fought them off, wouldn't you? You were always fast and dangerous, but never with me. We had a couple of men around a few weeks back. They wanted to know all kinds of things. How many bricks we sold. How much we made from the business. Edmund and the others didn't like them and neither did I. There are funny goings on around here lately, but whoever it was knows better than to try coming back."

"Did they say who they worked for?"

Bel cocked her head to one side, her eyes sharp, as they had always been. "Why do you ask, Tom?"

"I am doing something for…" Thomas's voice trailed off. He did not want to tell Bel he was working for King Henry. It sounded immodest and barely believable. "… for someone. It involves an important man in the area."

"We have a good few of those, what with Prince Arthur living in Ludlow Castle. You might have to be more specific if you expect an answer. But they never said who they worked for. We thought most likely they worked for themselves, trying to see what they could squeeze out of us. I heard they had been around a few other places doing the same and getting the same answer."

"If they scared some of the others, they might not want to say anything about it."

"Is this something to do with whoever you work for?" Bel shook her head. "Do you know what I find most puzzling about all this? You working for someone. The

Tom I used to know would never bend his knee to anyone, rich or poor, important or not."

"I am not that boy anymore. Are you the same girl, Bel? I expect not."

"Having children and losing a husband is enough to change a girl. Even so, it is good to see you doing so well, even if you are working for someone important. They will be important, will they not?"

"They will."

"Good. I was making supper if you would like to eat with us."

"I would, but I have to be somewhere. I should be there now, but when Brother Bernard told me you still live here I had to come and see for myself."

"Prior now, Tom. I hope you did not call him brother."

"I might have, yes."

Bel grinned. "You've not changed much, then. Don't be a stranger, Tom. You've got nothing to fear from me. I'm done with men these days. I got plenty of offers when John died, but I did not want another husband."

Bel came close and lifted up, but Thomas had to lean down so she could peck a kiss on his cheek. He watched her walk down the slope and enter the house without once looking back.

FIFTEEN

Thomas lay curled against Philippa, a deep sense of contentment filling him, when there came a harsh knock at the door. He glanced at Philippa, who drew the covers up before Thomas called for whoever was outside to enter.

One of the gate guards came in, halted when he saw there were two in the bed, though he should have known from the posting of accommodation he must have consulted. He recovered enough to recall he had come for a purpose.

"Are you Thomas Berrington?"

"I am."

"There is a woman at the gate asking for you. She says it is important."

"Did she give a name?"

"Agnes."

"Agnes?"

"That is what I said. She is demanding you come down to see her. I said it was too early, but—"

"Let me dress. Tell her I will be there as soon as I can."

When the man was gone, Thomas threw the covers back and pulled on the clothes he had removed the night before. He was aware his new position close to Prince Arthur demanded he dress better, and as soon as he could find time he would search out someone to make him a more suitable outfit or two.

"What are you like with men's attire?" he asked Philippa, who continued to lie in bed.

"I like it when I take it off you, Tom. Why, are you coming back to bed?"

"It occurs to me I should dress better. Can you ask around and find out who is reliable in the district?"

"About time. I know several tailors who will make you some fine outfits. What do you think your sister wants?"

"How am I supposed to know that? I will see you later, but when I do not know."

"Do you want me to come with you?"

"Not yet. If you are needed, I will send a guard to fetch you."

Philippa threw back the covers and stood. "In that case, it might be a good idea to put some clothes on."

Thomas found Agnes pacing up and down outside the outer gatehouse. He realised he did not know what the time was, but the streets were growing busy.

"What is wrong?" he asked.

"I knew I was right coming to you, Tom. No how are you but straight down to business. All right, then. Two men came to the bakery first thing this morning as I was firing up the ovens." Agnes took his hand and drew him away from the castle. "Come, I will show you and tell

153

you as we walk. I need to get back for when they return."

"Slow down and tell me what happened."

"Nothing and something." And when Thomas frowned, she said, "Well, they wanted something, but they couched it in such terms that if I reported them they could pretend they meant something else. They came straight into the bakery even though the shop was open. We always put out the stale bread from the day before so the poor can help themselves from beyond the back gate. Except these were not poor men; they dressed well, like gentlemen."

"Two, you said?"

Agnes nodded. They crossed Market Square to the bakery, where a small crowd had gathered to purchase its freshly baked produce. Agnes's daughters were busy at the serving table.

"Did they make threats?"

"Not right out. They hinted more than made them."

They entered the shop, and Agnes drew him through to where the brick ovens worked their magic. The air was thick with the scent of flour, yeast, pastries, and fruit. The heat was almost overpowering, but Agnes seemed not to notice. This was her domain, and she would be well used to it.

"I was here." She released Thomas's hand and went to stand in front of an oven. Beyond her, Thomas saw loaves inside the oven rising and turning crisp. "They came in from the courtyard, so must have opened the side door. Usually it is locked last thing at night but I have not checked it yet. Sometimes the girls forget."

"Then let us check it now. You can tell me what they said and did just as well outside as in here. Or do you need to do anything first?"

"Not for a while." Agnes led the way out.

Thomas noted they passed through the door from the bakery into a short corridor. A door halfway along on the left was closed, but Agnes ignored it. Another door at the end granted access to the courtyard.

"The door to the street is there." Agnes pointed to a solid oak door set into the stone wall.

Thomas crossed to it and pulled, but it stood firm.

"Are you sure they came in this way?"

"The door we left through is where they came into the bakery and this is the only way to get to it."

"What about the other door we passed?"

"It gives access to the upper rooms. There is one other door to the outside, it is the way I brought you yesterday, but I know that was locked because I check it every night." Agnes looked around. "Could they have climbed over the wall?"

Thomas examined it. "You tell me. You said you used to get told off for climbing it."

"From the inside, yes, though I could do so no longer. But the mortar outside is better and there are scarce few places a man could gain a hold. Besides, there were two of them."

"So they came through the door. Left though it as well, most likely, and locked it behind them. You said you did not check it last night?"

"I do not recall. Usually I would, but it is like all such things that become a habit. You think you have done something but have no accurate recollection of the act. Perhaps I forgot."

"Or perhaps they picked the lock. I have a friend who can get through any door. Come and sit, tell me what they said to you."

"It was not their words as much as the way they acted. As if they could do anything they wanted to me. Anything they wanted to the shop. And then they said..." For a moment, Thomas thought Agnes could not go on, but she firmed her shoulders and took a deep breath. "... they said I had two pretty daughters and it would be a shame if anything happened to them. I almost hit them with a kneading board. They wanted to know if there had been any trouble lately and I asked what kind of trouble? Did they mean pickpockets in town, men fighting, or what?

"They said anyone watching the bakery or this house. I told them no, not that I noticed. I thought that was the end of it. At first I wondered if they were constables checking on the safety of the town, but as they went on I saw my mistake."

"Go on." Thomas reached out and took Agnes's hand, enclosing it within both of his. For a moment it felt strange to hold the hand of the sister he had not seen in forty-seven years, but then the strangeness faded. Some things are just right.

"One of them picked up an apple tart and bit into it. I told him that would cost him a farthing, and he laughed. Then the other did the same, but he dropped his on the floor and ground it beneath his boot. It was then I started to be afraid."

"What were the two girls doing while this was going on?"

"Opening up the shop at the front. They had taken the unsold bread from the day before to hand out. Cleaning the shelves. Getting ready to serve customers as soon as the first loaves were ready."

"I assume you start work before sunrise. Was it still dark outside?"

"Getting light, but only just."

"So few people on the streets?"

"No, not many, but I never have time to check. The ovens need feeding into life, then once they are hot enough the charcoal has to be scraped out and transferred to the other oven before I put the first loaves in. It is my busiest time of day."

"You do all of this on your own, the three of you?"

"We do. We mix the dough the night before and leave it to rise. I spend most of the afternoon making it up and the girls help. Trade slows once noon passes and we start preparations for the following day."

"I take it this is a good business?" Thomas said.

"We do well enough, yes."

"So you are well-off?"

"In terms of coin if not time."

"Did they ask for money?"

"Not outright, but they mentioned it. They told me strangers have been seen in town and they suspected trouble might come to Ludlow. They had been sent to talk to the townsfolk and ask if they wanted to contribute to a force they were forming to protect the town."

"A force?" Thomas said. "What kind of force? No,

never mind, tell me if there has been any increase in trouble in Ludlow."

"Not that I have heard about, and if there was, I would hear. There is always trouble. You must remember what Lemster was like. Aunt Jean told me when I was older that you were always getting yourself into one scrape or another. But there has been no more trouble than usual."

"Did they say how much would be an appropriate contribution to this force?"

"They did not. I asked, but they said they were only sounding out local businesses. They told me they would be back later today, when I was less busy. Which is when I came for you. I could not think of anyone else. I thank the Lord you were in the castle."

"Did these men say who they worked for?"

"I did not ask, and they did not volunteer. Is it important?"

"I don't know for sure, but suspect it might be."

"Will you stay here for when they come back?"

"I have some business in the castle, but will return as soon as possible. When do you think they might be back?"

"I do not know. When the shop is quieter, so after noon makes sense."

"I will return before then. In the meantime, ask your girls to keep a lookout for anyone acting suspiciously. If they see the men again, get one of them to come for me."

"Do you know who those men work for?"

"Possibly, but I intend to find out for sure before I return to you." Thomas released Agnes's hand and stood. "If I am held up, close the shutters and lock the doors."

"You are scaring me now, Tom."

"Don't be afraid. Whatever this is has not started up yet. I intend to make sure it does not have a chance to. This kind of thing might work in London, but Ludlow is small enough to kill it at birth."

Agnes accompanied him to the front of the shop and kissed his cheek.

"Have you eaten today? You look too thin." She pressed a still-warm meat pie into his hand.

Thomas ate it as he walked through the streets. He was looking for the men who had come to Agnes's shop but saw none that might be them, or companions of them. He doubted there would be only two going around the businesses, taverns and inns of the town. When he arrived outside the Rose and Crown where he and Philippa had spent their first night in each other's arms, he had not thought it his destination until he got there.

Constance Sparrow met his eyes as he entered. They were the only two people in the large downstairs room where he and Philippa had shared wine with Hugh Clement.

"Did you forget something, sir? I saw nothing when I checked your room."

"No, I am here for something else."

"Another room for you and Pip?"

"Not that either, comfortable though it was. I want to ask you if any men have been here asking for a contribution for some kind of force to protect the town."

"If you mean Hugh Clement's idiots, then yes. Late last night when we were trying to lock up."

"Did they threaten you?"

"Not in so many words, but they made their meaning

clear enough. Pay up and they would ensure there was no trouble here. Refuse and they could not guarantee our safety."

"They said those words?"

"I never lie to a gentleman, sir."

"How do you know they were Hugh Clement's men?"

"One of them was here before when they asked about you. And they wear those silly green hats." Her eyes looked beyond Thomas and he turned, but it was only two of the pot girls come to start work.

"What do you intend to do when they return? Pay up or refuse?"

"What do you think we are going to do, sir? Paying types like that never leads to any good. I intend to send them packing."

"You and the girls?"

"I have other resources I can call on."

"Then do it. Do it now."

"I will when I am ready. I can take care of myself." She reached beneath the table and drew out two objects. One was a short sword, the blade razor sharp. The other was a crossbow, a bolt already placed but not yet tensioned.

Thomas knew it was not enough, but did not say so. The sword was her best option. The crossbow would take too long to draw. A man could run from the door to the table before she could raise the weapon and fire.

Thomas heard the door behind open again, louder than when the girls had entered, but ignored it. Early customers or someone looking for accommodation. Only when the woman stepped back did he turn to discover three men crossing the room towards him.

One was a man who had sat with Hugh Clement when Thomas and Philippa ate in this room. Another was the man he had allowed to ride away after the attack on the road. Thomas suspected it was an oversight he might come to regret.

SIXTEEN

As Thomas turned to face the interlopers he reached back to place his hand on the hilt of the sword Constance Sparrow had brought from beneath the table. He took in the three men. They were all shorter than him, but then most men were. Thomas knew he could defeat them, but not sure if he could do so without the spilling of blood. Their blood, of course. Such action had not bothered him in the past, and a fleeting thought crossed his mind to wonder why it bothered him now. Old age? A different country and language? Different people? Or his elevated position, perhaps. He had given little heed to the titles Queen Isabel had bestowed on him, but supposed they must have changed him in some ways—if only in how others treated him. Thomas released his grip on the heavy blade and took two paces away from the table.

"Is it ale you have come for, boys?" He used the term deliberately, pleased to see a spark of anger in the eyes of one; the man he had let ride away. A coward backed up by others was always dangerous.

"Goodwife Sparrow knows why we are here, but we will take a pot of ale to quench our thirsts if you are offering, sir. And then you can leave so we can discuss our business." Daniel Lupton, who had been in conversation with Hugh Clement the night they arrived, spoke. He had been dressed in a mail vest that night. Today he wore a dark blue velvet doublet and the obligatory green hat. Thomas assumed he was the leader of this small group. His presence also offered final confirmation of Hugh Clement's involvement.

The man Thomas let ride away leaned close and whispered something into his ear. Whatever was said caused the false expression of friendship to fade from his face.

"My friend tells me he has been looking for you. Best then that you stay until we complete our business with the goodwife." The men waited, and after a moment, Constance Sparrow poured three pots of ale and set them on the table.

"One for our friend as well," said Daniel Lupton.

"I thank you, but it is too early in the day for me, and I have business to attend to when we finish here." Thomas remained where he was, the heavy blade within reach. It lay in clear view next to the pots of ale.

The man Thomas had allowed to live knocked against his shoulder as he came for his ale, made brave by his companions. He picked up all three pots and handed them out before draining half his in a single swallow.

"We have come with terms." Daniel Lupton looked around the wide room, the tables and stools, the fine fireplace where embers continued to glow from last night's fire. "One shilling paid on the twenty-fifth of the month seems a fair price to keep this fine establishment free from both trouble and damage." He smiled as though he was a reasonable man and not a rogue. "Today is the twentieth, so we will return in five days. And our thanks for the ale." He drained his pot and set it on the table before picking up the heavy blade. "A fine weapon," he said. "A little weighty for a fair woman, but in the hands of someone such as myself it could take a man's head clean off his shoulders." He swung the blade fast towards Thomas, who did not flinch, and Daniel Lupton laughed.

Thomas fought the instinct to hit him. He did not want to bring trouble to Constance Sparrow, but knew trouble would come for him soon enough. He was content to wait for it, sure in his own ability to fend it off. Even more confident after what had happened on the road from Lemster. His fine clothes and exalted position in Granada had made him forget what he was once capable of. He was grateful to these men for reminding him. He set a coin on the table. It would pay for the three pots of ale four times over.

"Do you intend to resist?" asked Daniel Lupton.

"That depends what you want of me. I suggest you leave before you answer, in case your answer is not acceptable."

Daniel Lupton appeared amenable on the outside, but there was a coldness in his eyes. He touched the shoulder of the man Thomas had allowed to ride away on the road from Lemster.

"Oswyn here says he has more than enough questions for you once we are somewhere more private."

"And if I do not want to go somewhere more private?"

"Then we can ask them of you here, in front of the goodwife. Is that what you want?" Daniel Lupton stared into Thomas's eyes before giving a shake of his head. "No, I thought not."

He reached into his jacket and drew something out, hidden inside his hand. He pushed past Thomas and set the object down on the table. It was a small sliver of bone. Not a finger-bone, but something from an animal. Sheep, possibly, Thomas thought. Not a finger-bone, no, but the meaning was clear enough, to him at least. These were bonemen.

As Thomas started after them, Constance Sparrow called out to him. "Should I send a message to the castle, sir?"

"I think I can handle these three myself if need be." Thomas continued walking, his mind working on this new discovery. What were the bonemen doing in Ludlow? Had they been sent? And if so, why?

Outside, the streets were filling, men, women and children bustling past. Two oxen pulling a cart of straw meant they had to press against the walls to avoid both its wheels and the beasts. Thomas knew he could take advantage of the situation to escape, but he wanted to know who was behind the attempt at extortion. Hugh Clement, he was sure, but he needed proof if he was going to accuse the man. He was Justice of the Peace for the district. As such, he was responsible for law and order. He would be a hard man to accuse without the accusation coming back against the person who made it. Thomas also wanted to know how many men Clement had working for him. Almost certainly more than the three he saw here. And then, of course, there were the bonemen. The same, or some poor copy?

When the cart had passed, the men continued north on Mill Street. One led the way while the other two followed close behind in case Thomas tried to run. When they entered Market Square, Thomas was sure they intended to take Linney all the way to the Corfe and Hugh Clement's manor house. Instead, Daniel Lupton entered the grounds of St Laurence's Church. From within came the sound of an organ and voices raised in a chant. The men made for the left side of the substantial building, then stopped between two buttresses that sheltered them from view of the street.

Thomas pressed his back to the cold stone of the wall, preparing to use it to spring at them when an attack came. A cold leached into him he had not felt for many years. He thought he might have lost it for good when he became a civilised man, but here it was again, offering its icy promise of mayhem.

"I want to know what are you doing in Ludlow," said Daniel Lupton, "poking your nose into matters that are none of your business."

"I serve Prince Arthur and King Henry, who has asked me to be here." It was worth a try mentioning both Prince and King, but Thomas saw Daniel Lupton was unimpressed. Did Hugh Clement believe himself above the law of even the King, or was he an even bigger fool than Thomas had already taken him for?

"What are you to goodwife Sparrow that would be worth taking a beating for?"

"Is that what you intend, a beating? What have I done to deserve such?"

"You killed my friend," said Oswyn, stepping closer.

"I believe that was kill or be killed." Thomas stared into Oswyn's eyes, which he saw fight hard to hold his gaze. "Now I see it was a mistake to hold my hand and not kill you as well."

"Murder, it was," said Oswyn.

"Self-defence."

"It will come down to Oswyn's word against yours if the matter comes before the Justice," said Daniel Lupton. "For all your boasts, you are a stranger in this town, while Oswyn is well known. And if need be, I can find others who witnessed this altercation and will testify it was yourself who started the fight. Oswyn barely escaped with his life, is that not right?"

Oswyn nodded. His fists were clenched, and Thomas saw he wanted to attack him but could not until set loose. The other man was of more concern. He hung back, relaxed but ready, the tallest of the three and the strongest. He had the appearance of a soldier, made more so by a scar that ran from above his right eye to the corner of his jaw.

"I let him ride away because I don't enjoy killing weak men." Thomas was pleased to see Oswyn tense. "And seek your witnesses, sir, as I will seek mine. One of whom is tutor to Prince Arthur."

"Philippa Gale?" said Daniel. "A woman's word is worth nothing against that of a man."

"I would take the word of any woman against yours,

all three of you. Or the word of your master, Hugh Clement."

"Who says we work for Hugh Clement?"

"I sat with him and you but three days ago," Thomas said. "At the time I thought you no more than local harlequins, but you changed my mind when you left a bone on Constance Sparrow's table." Thomas saw a frown on Daniel Lupton's face and realised the man might not recognise the full significance of what he had done. "Who told you to leave it as a threat? Because you are no boneman, none of you are."

"What do you know about bonemen?" Daniel Lupton's frown deepened. He reached out to lay a hand on Oswyn's shoulder. "Step back and give the man space. I want to find out how much he knows."

"He knows nothing," said Oswyn. "We should kill him now. You know we cannot let him live."

"Who is going to do it, you?" Thomas asked.

"Yes, me," said Oswyn.

"Come on then, kill me." Thomas waited, ready.

"No!" Daniel Lupton tried to stop his man, but it was too late.

Oswyn launched himself at Thomas, a blade already in his hand. His first mistake was to hold it above his head, ready to strike down. His second was coming too fast.

Thomas caught his arm and deflected the knife, then used Oswyn's momentum and added to it so his head cracked into the stone and he fell to the ground. Thomas felt something prick his back and knew he had made a mistake. He had assumed the other two would do nothing. In that, he was wrong.

He turned his head to find the third man close behind. The tip of his knife remained unmoving, the point breaking skin so Thomas felt blood run down his side. He examined himself, calculating that a thrust would pierce a lung even if it missed his heart. He had made a big mistake.

"Have you killed Oswyn?" asked Daniel Lupton.

"Stunned, nothing more. He will have a knob on his head as big as a fist and a headache for a few days, but it is fortunate he lacks any wits to lose."

"Why did you not kill him when you did the other?"

"Because I grow tired of killing, and he struck me as a weak man too easily led." Thomas glanced down at Oswyn, who had not moved. He continued to watch until he saw his chest rise and fall, then turned back to Daniel Lupton, ignoring the man who still held the knife against him.

"He is easily led, I agree," said Daniel Lupton. "But sometimes in my business easily led men have their uses."

"And what business is that?" Thomas asked.

"Not yours, for a start. I ask again how you know about the bonemen."

"Do you expect me to talk with a knife sticking in me? Call off your dog and you and I can have a discussion. But I expect information in return."

Daniel Lupton laughed. "You are a strange man, Thomas Berrington. You look strange, you talk strange, and you act strange. I expect some of this is because you do not know who you are dealing with, so I will tell you. But only the two of us. Step away, Rowland."

The knife withdrew instantly. Thomas resisted the

reflex to put his hand beneath his jerkin to check the wound, knowing it was not serious and to do so would only show weakness.

"Take Oswyn back to the house," said Daniel Lupton. "Can you manage him, or do you need to fetch others, or a cart?"

"I can manage."

They were the first words Thomas had heard him speak. His accent was not local; possibly not even English. There was an undertone to it he was sure he had heard before but could not place. He had visited so many lands of late and it could be from any of them. He watched Rowland squat, then work his hands beneath Oswyn's shoulder and heave him to his feet. He leaned the slack figure against the church wall, then tipped him across one shoulder before turning to stagger away.

"He is going to need a cart," Thomas said.

"He will find that out soon enough. Now, do you want to talk here, or should we find some tavern and conduct our business like civilised men?"

"Just you and me?"

Daniel Lupton made a show of looking around. "Do you see anyone else?"

Thomas wondered how long he had before someone decided he was missing. Days, he suspected, if not weeks. He was a new member of Prince Arthur's retinue and had not yet found his place among them. With luck, Philippa would be the first to realise he had not returned and raise the alarm, but that might not be for some time, after the note he left her. Thomas considered these problems as he walked beside Daniel into Corfe Street, not sure what he might come up against. One thing he was sure of was that he could not trust the man. He expected them to turn towards Linney, but instead Daniel Lupton strolled in the other direction. They re-crossed Market Square, then turned down a narrow alley cast in deep shade by the overhanging eaves of houses on either side.

"This will do," said Daniel Lupton.

A sign showing a badly painted black bull was set above a narrow doorway. A single window opened inwards, and when Daniel rapped on the side of it an old man appeared.

"Is the back room free?"

"Tis for you, Dan. Ale and food? The wife made a nice lamb pottage last night. Shall I see if there is any left?"

"Two bowls, and fresh bread if you have it. And ale, of course."

Daniel Lupton entered and Thomas followed him along a narrow corridor until they came to a second door at the far end. It opened for Daniel Lupton to lead the way into a room set with a small table and four chairs. There was a fireplace, but the ashes had gone cold. A single window offered a view into a yard.

"Is this where you usually drink?" Thomas took a chair on the far side so he could watch the door. He more than half-expected Rowland to join them before long, in the company of more men. If he did, Thomas had already worked out his escape route. The window was glazed, but badly. He would throw himself into the yard and hope it offered a way out. If not, it would be better to fight in the bigger arena.

"The ale is good and the food even better, but no, I

usually frequent rather more upscale establishments. Those such as the Rose and Crown. I have a position in town to maintain. But The Bull is quiet at this time of day and the landlord knows how to be discreet." Daniel Lupton smiled. "Should I need to make an example of you."

"Only you? Are you sure? I assume Rowland will know you have come here."

"He will."

"Then best we discuss matters before he finds us."

"You are under my protection for the moment, Thomas. I can call you Thomas, can I?"

"If I can call you Daniel."

"Just as if we are best of friends. Do your friends call you Tom?"

"Some do. Good friends."

"Thomas it is, then." A woman a third the age of the landlord entered with a tray. She set it down and turned to leave. Her hand came out and stroked the side of Daniel Lupton's face, then she was gone.

Daniel Lupton poured ale from a jug into two pots.

"Now then, Thomas Berrington, tell me what you are doing in Ludlow, and whether you are going to be a problem that I need to take care of, or whether two pounds might make you look the other way."

SEVENTEEN

"Are you bonemen?" Thomas asked. "Or do you call yourself something different here?"

"What do you know of bonemen?" said Daniel Lupton. He took a bowl of pottage, tore a chunk of fresh bread from a loaf, dipped it into the sauce and lifted it to his mouth.

Thomas watched him eat, wondering what approach to take. And then, as he usually did, decided on honesty. He wanted to know what was happening in Ludlow, and playing games with this man would teach him nothing. He reached for the second bowl and some bread. When he put it into his mouth it was rich from the sauce, which was more heavily spiced than expected. It reminded him a little of the food of southern Spain, which was coloured by the influence of the defeated Moors.

"I know little of them," he said. "And if I had not gone for a haircut and shave, I would likely know nothing of them at all."

"A haircut and shave?"

"In London. I thought I should be presentable when I met King Henry." He considered it worth getting that information in early to set a stake in the ground. He knew the King. Knew Prince Arthur. So not a man whose disappearance would pass unnoticed.

"Tell me about this haircut."

"In exchange for answers from you," Thomas said. "I tell you something, you tell me something. Agreed?"

"Why should I?"

"Because you need to know how much I know. You need to know whether I am a threat to what you are planning to do in Ludlow. You and Hugh Clement."

"How do you know we are planning anything? Or that it involves Hugh?"

"I am not a stupid man."

"It surprised me when you knocked Oswyn out so easily. He is not our best fighter, but he is big and strong."

"Sometimes big and strong is easier to defeat. My haircut was almost finished when three men entered the premises. The barber's shop was set on Ludgate Hill, in case you ever visit London and need a haircut. Though thinking on it, it is no longer a barber's."

"What did these men want?"

"Money, of course. Just as you and your men hope to collect money from goodwife Sparrow on the twenty-fifth of each month. A shilling, did I hear? More than they demanded of my barber."

"Goodwife Sparrow has a higher income than a barber, even one in London, though I have never been there. And there is no hope involved. We will accept a shilling from her on the twenty-fifth of each month. Less from some establishments, more from others if we can get it. Every business in Ludlow will soon pay me and my men."

"Don't you mean Hugh Clement's men?"

Daniel Lupton offered neither confirmation nor denial. "What did you do when these bonemen demanded money?"

"I was foolish. It was nothing to do with me, but one man assaulted the barber's daughter. It was she who cut my hair, and cut it well."

Daniel Lupton smiled. "This must have been some time ago, then."

"Several weeks, I admit. I knocked two of them out and chased the other off. Then the girl who cut my hair hit me. Hit me hard."

"She was happy to pay, I expect. As people in Ludlow will be happy to pay for our protection."

"It is a strange manner of protection that meant they attacked her. Just as my female companion was attacked as we rode from Lemster to Ludlow. I made a mistake when I allowed Oswyn to ride away. What is it you are offering to protect the folk of Ludlow from? As far as I can tell it is a quiet town."

"Trouble can come even to peaceful towns." Daniel Lupton finished his bowl and set it back on the tray. He poured more ale for them both. He had been right in his earlier judgement. The ale was excellent.

"I am still waiting for an exchange of information from you, my friend." Thomas knew the response he received would tell him much; most importantly, whether or not Daniel Lupton intended to kill him.

"What is it you want to know, Thomas?"

"If you are bonemen."

"You keep on coming back to that. What if I say we are not?"

"What if I say I don't believe you?"

"Then you show a disappointing lack of trust."

"Then let such be, for I don't believe you. Why should I?"

"Because I am an open and honest man."

Thomas laughed, then drained his ale. He turned the pot upside down, because not only was the ale excellent, it was strong and he could feel the effect of it. He wondered if that had been Daniel Lupton's intention, though the man had drunk more than him.

"We are not bonemen, because those in London you call bonemen do not call themselves that either. It is their customers who gave them the name."

"Customers?"

"Yes, customers. I am a civilised man. A businessman who offers a service in exchange for fair payment."

"And if these customers do not make payment?"

"Everyone has a choice. Why are you here, Thomas Berrington? Has someone sent you to spy on us?"

It was so close to the truth of what King Henry had asked of him Thomas wondered if someone had betrayed that confidence. Except, as far as he knew, only Philippa, Sir Richard and Gruffydd were aware of his mission, and he was sure no betrayal had come from any of them. Was it only a lucky guess on Daniel Lupton's part?

"I have not come to spy on you. It is your own actions that drew my attention, and then I recalled what happened when I was in London. The bonemen have that city under their control."

"Did you report to anyone?"

"To the King himself."

"Have you truly met him?"

Thomas could not work out if Daniel Lupton was impressed or not.

"I have. Have you met Prince Arthur? He will be the next king."

"Yes, I met the boy and liked him. He has a sweet soul, but will not be hard enough when he is King. I hear he is to marry a Spanish princess."

"Catherine," Thomas said. "Her mother sent me to England to offer her my protection."

Daniel Lupton shook his head. "You are a strange man. You do not look important, or even someone who has important friends, but you appear to be familiar with those who rule this land. I have a proposal for you."

"Propose it then, but if it is what I think do not expect me to agree. I will not help you. Not for two pounds, tens or even a hundred."

"I admit I was going to seek your help in exchange for a stipend paid once a month." said Daniel Lupton. "Enough for a man to live on, as well as his wife and children. I realise you are a man who knows how to protect himself. A man with firm principles. Such a man might be a problem for my master—"

"Hugh Clement." Thomas spoke over Daniel Lupton, watching as his eyes grew hard.

"Yes, my master is Hugh Clement. And you once more

show why you are going to be a problem. I assume you intend to refuse my generous offer?"

"I do."

"So what am I to do with you? What would you do if you were in my position?"

"I would never be in your position."

"Again you make things difficult for yourself. I ask again. What am I going to do with you?"

"You think you are going to have to kill me. Or at least try to. If so, I should warn you that better men have tried and they now lie in early graves. If they were fortunate, that is. I left others to bleed out on the side of the road."

Daniel Lupton smiled. "What if I told you I have two score men I can call on?"

"I would tell you they are not enough. Not unless you can call those forty men here right now." Thomas stood. "I intend to leave. I thank you for the pottage. It was indeed excellent. And for the ale, which was also good. If you want to talk to me again leave a message at the castle."

Thomas walked past the table, expecting Daniel Lupton to lunge at him, but no such attack came. Perhaps Thomas's boasting had achieved its intended effect, and if the man believed only a quarter of what he claimed it still made Thomas a dangerous man.

Thomas found the reason for the lack of concern as soon as he stepped into the alley. Four men blocked the way in one direction, another four in the other. Daniel Lupton came out and stood beside him.

"So," he said. "We are nine and you are but one man. How many have you defeated, Thomas? I take it you will have a blade about your person, but so do my men. One or two of us even have swords. It is time my master spoke with you to see if he agrees with me you are too dangerous to leave alive."

"Why should I come with you rather than attack you now?"

Daniel Lupton smiled. "Because if you do, you will bleed out in this alley. Just as you have let men bleed out on the side of the road. I too can be dangerous."

"And if I come with you, I will die. Which would you choose?"

"I would choose to live as long as possible. Who knows, perhaps Hugh will decide to be merciful, and then you will have thrown your life away for nothing."

Thomas considered his position. If it had been four men plus Daniel Lupton he might have risked his hand. But nine? He thought not.

Besides, he was curious what else he might find out if he went with them. Provided he managed to stay alive.

As they walked through the town they made a strange sight. A tall man with a long blue scarf wrapped around his neck, surrounded by eight men with a ninth leading the way. They stayed in the narrower alleys, making everyone get out of their way. Thomas saw in the reaction of those who fled how these men were regarded in Ludlow. He wondered why nothing had been done about them. The town was home to Arthur, Prince of Wales. It ought to be better policed than this.

When they reached Market Square there was no alternative but to cross it, but the reaction of the townsfolk remained the same. They turned their heads away so as not to see anything. They left a space around the group.

Thomas glanced towards Agnes's bakery. She was not in sight, but her two girls stood at the serving table. One of them raised her eyes, saw what was happening, and turned away. Thomas inwardly cursed.

They passed St. Laurence's church for a second time and passed out through Linney gate, the ground ahead falling away to the river. As soon as they were beyond the town walls, the men crowded close around Thomas and taunted him. One or another would throw a punch, which Thomas avoided as best he could without retaliating. He suspected that was what they wanted. To start a fight out here would provide them all the excuse they needed.

"Don't kill him, lads," said Daniel Lupton, from the head of the group. "Hugh will be mighty displeased if we bring him a corpse that cannot be questioned. Mess him up a little, nothing more."

As soon as the words were out, one of the bigger men crashed his fist into the side of Thomas's face, almost sending him to his knees.

Thomas spat blood and walked on. It soon became clear how close the men intended to push their order not to kill him.

EIGHTEEN

When Thomas regained consciousness he kept his eyes closed, partly to judge the situation, partly because only one of them felt capable of opening. He was sitting on a hard chair. Ropes bound him, cutting into his chest, his legs and arms. He accepted he had made a mistake in not fighting back outside the tavern. Whatever beating they might have given him could not have been worse than the one he got.

Thomas wondered when the order would change from 'don't kill him', to 'kill him'. He regretted he would never see his children again. He even regretted he would never hear Jorge's voice, nor Belia's. Not even sweet Catherine's. Philippa Gale barely crossed his mind, which brought a different manner of acknowledgement. She was beautiful, she was clever, but she was wrong for him. Their ambitions differed too much. At least she might mourn him for a short while before moving on to someone more suitable.

When Thomas heard boot-heels cross a tiled floor he

opened his one good eye to find Hugh Clement standing in front of him. He was dressed in a loose linen shirt and dark hose, but wore no doublet or jerkin. His head was bare to reveal red-brown hair thinning on top. The man might have been part-way handsome had he not carried such a scowl.

"Awake at last then, Berrington. I wondered if my men had been too enthusiastic. You are not a young man, after all."

Thomas twisted his head from side to side. It was a mistake. He ran his tongue around inside his mouth, relieved to encounter no broken teeth. The beating seemed to have been mostly to his body, which would be black and blue come nightfall. If he lived that long.

"I have been hurt worse," he said, glad the words emerged without slurring.

"Have you, by damn? I will chastise my men in that case, but I suspect you were younger then."

"A little, yes."

Hugh Clement snapped his fingers and Daniel Lupton appeared with a chair. He set it four feet from Thomas and waited until his master took it, then disappeared again. Thomas suspected he was standing behind his chair but had no sense of him, which disappointed him.

Hugh Clement leaned forward, his eyes sharp as they studied the damage to Thomas that was visible.

"I hear you have been causing problems for me."

"And I hear you intend to cause problems for Ludlow."

"Oh, quite the opposite. I merely plan to offer a service not currently available to the businesses of the town. And not just Ludlow. Once the system is running smoothly I may look to extend the service throughout the two counties. Perhaps even as far as Worcester and Gloucester, once I have built up enough capital."

"When I tell King Henry what you are up to he will put a stop to your plans."

"Do you think so?" For a moment Hugh Clement appeared to show genuine puzzlement. "I suspect the King has more pressing matters on his mind. The marriage of his son, for one. His continued arguments with France and Holland. He created his reign through force and has seen little peace since the battlefield at Bosworth. I was there, you know."

"On which side?" Thomas saw the answer when the man's eyes flickered away for a moment.

"Which side is of no importance now I have earned the trust of the King. Why else would he appoint me Justice of the Peace?"

Thomas laughed, raising a scowl from Hugh Clement.

"It was my appointment that gave me the idea. There is little peace in the area because there is nobody to enforce it. My life is a constant distraction of crime, both petty and large. Robbery, murder, embezzlement, counterfeit coinage... I could go on but fear I would only bore you."

"You don't strike me as someone clever enough to have come up with such a scheme on your own." Thomas's words were barely out when Daniel Lupton hit him on the side of the head from behind. He ignored the blow. "Was it the bonemen approached you, looking to expand their reach?"

"The who?"

Once again, Thomas saw the tell.

"Perhaps you came across them when you visited London. No doubt an important man such as yourself is called to the capital occasionally. Do you have an invitation to the forthcoming wedding?"

"Of course not. I am a mere Justice in an out of the way place. When the wedding will be is a mystery to all, I hear. This Spanish Princess seems exceedingly slow reaching England. Or perhaps she prefers foreign cock to that of a proud Englishman. Well, I am sure Arthur will show her what she has been missing. The sap rises hard in a lad of fifteen, even one as unworldly as Arthur."

Thomas wished he was free so he could hit the man, but that opportunity might yet come.

"Or do the bonemen know nothing of what you are doing here?" Thomas saw a change in Hugh Clement's face, a tension in how he sat, and knew he had discovered the truth of it. He laughed. "Oh, but that is a fine thing indeed. They know nothing of you, do they? Was this all your idea?" Again the tell. "Of course not, you are not bright enough to come up with such a scheme. But that might be why you have done so, because an intelligent man would realise what would happen when the bonemen discover his duplicity. And discover it they will, have no doubt of that."

"You may be right, Berrington, but they will not find out about me for some time yet. News passes slowly in the shires, and I am sure those in London have more than enough to keep them busy without worrying about what happens in Ludlow. By the time they do we will be too strong for them. Even now we have men coming from Wales to join us. Hard men. Fighting men. They will—"

"Hugh." Daniel Lupton spoke the single word from behind Thomas and Hugh Clement's mouth shut with a snap. That one word, and Hugh Clement's reaction to it, told Thomas more than all the conversation so far. Hugh Clement might believe he was the leader of this conspiracy, but Daniel Lupton was controlling him. The question was whether he was being controlled in turn?

The other information Thomas gleaned was of even more importance. To him, anyway. Hugh Clement had already said too much to allow Thomas to live.

"Kill me and there will be consequences."

"I agree, but only for you. And I will not kill you, Thomas Berrington. That pleasure will go to someone else." Hugh Clement looked past Thomas to Daniel Lupton, still standing behind him. "I take it Oswyn still wants to do the deed?"

"He does," said Daniel, his voice close. "He demands it."

"Take care, then. I do not want this man escaping. Nobody will believe his mad tale, but better if nothing of it comes out."

"Agreed," said Daniel Lupton.

"Men know where I am," Thomas said.

"I do not believe you."

"Believe what you like. They saw me leaving Ludlow in the company of your thugs. I expect Gruffydd ap Rhys is leading a group of soldiers here even as we speak. Now he is a hard man. Clever too. Too clever for you." Thomas did not know if there was any truth in the words he spoke. Had either of Agnes's girls seen him? And even if they had, did they get the message he tried to send? Somehow, he doubted it. Which meant he would die at the hand of a man he should have killed. He suspected Oswyn would want to draw out his death, but he had experienced pain before and it always ended. Except this time, his own death would end it.

Hugh Clement rose to his feet and Thomas thought this was the moment. Instead, he spoke to Daniel Lupton. "Check. Send a man up the road on a horse to report back. Tell him to go as far as the castle and stay there if he sees nothing, but come back at a gallop if he does. Send Oswyn and three others back here when you go. I don't trust this man for all that we hobbled him."

Thomas heard Daniel Lupton leave. For a moment, there was only himself and Hugh Clement, and he knew this was his only opportunity. He had worked on his bindings as they spoke, so one hand was almost free. Almost but not quite, and he suspected he had little time to effect an escape. So he threw himself backwards hard. The chair crashed to the floor and did as he hoped. It splintered into several pieces, encouraged by the slight movements he had been making.

Thomas rolled to one side, scattering wood. He rose to his feet and ran at Hugh Clement, who was backing away with hands raised.

"Help! Help me!" He called out, but nobody came.

Thomas wrapped the rope around Hugh Clement's fat neck and pulled it tight, cutting off his breath. Thomas knew the human body, knew how to injure it as well as how to heal it. A little more pressure and he could cut off the blood flowing to Hugh Clement's brain. The man would die in less than a minute.

Thomas turned Clement around so they both faced

the door and dragged him backwards until his legs came up against the sill of the window. Just in time as four men crashed into the room.

Thomas released the pressure and heard Hugh Clement draw in a great breath.

"Tell them if they come at us I will snap your neck."

"You have nowhere to go, fool."

"Tell them!" Thomas jerked the rope tight for a moment before releasing it.

"Stay back," said Hugh Clement.

Thomas saw one man start to edge towards the door.

"Stop there or he dies," he said, and the man came to a halt.

Thomas did not know what to do next. He could try leading Hugh Clement out the same way the others had entered, except he had no idea of the layout because he had been unconscious when they carried him in. He could throw himself backwards through the window and hope the glass broke. It was made up of small leaded panes. Sometimes the lead was poorly soldered and would break. Other times, it formed a barrier that needed more force than that of a man crashing into it. But, Thomas wondered, what about two men? He pushed aside the aches that wracked his body and moved away from the window. Hugh Clement stumbled and almost fell, which would have brought the four men down on them. Thomas kept him on his feet, but the effort sent a sharp pain through his side that weakened his hold.

Hugh Clement must have sensed the loosening of the rope because he pulled away. Thomas allowed him to go because it meant what he intended to do might work even better. He let the man get three feet away, then jerked him hard. Thomas swung him around on the rope, pulling it tight now, no longer caring if he snapped Hugh Clement's neck. The movement carried the man towards the window, then past it. Thomas pulled again until Hugh Clement was tight against him, then heaved the two of them back into the glass.

It broke.

They fell out in a shower of shards and another sharp pain lanced through Thomas as Hugh Clement landed on top of him. He pushed the man off and rose to his feet, turned and ran as fast as he could away from the manor house. Except, as he turned the corner, he found a dozen men running to meet him. Everyone stopped. Then Hugh Clement arrived, wheezing, and pointed at Thomas.

"Kill him."

"Soldiers are coming," said one man, then Thomas saw Daniel Lupton push his way through.

"It is that mad Welshman, Gruffydd," said Daniel Lupton. "He has fourteen mounted men with him. Even if it was just him we could do nothing, not now."

Hugh Clement had other ideas.

"Hold Berrington tight and draw him around front so they see him as soon as they arrive."

"Give it up," Thomas said.

"Not yet. Do as I say."

Four men came forward and gripped Thomas. He knew he could break away, but there were too many others, so he allowed himself to be led around the manor house to an open yard with stables to one side.

Gruffydd ap Rhys rode at a fast canter to pull up on the far side of the yard.

"What's all this then?" he asked, his Welsh accent strong.

Hugh Clement came to the front of the group of men, attempting to pull his clothing into some kind of shape.

"I am arresting this man for murder. He killed two of my men."

"Only one," Thomas said, his voice too quiet for Gruffydd to hear.

"What do you say, Tom? Hugh is Justice of the Peace. I am sure he would not make such an accusation without proof."

"There are witnesses," said Hugh Clement.

Oswyn came forward from the group to stand beside him.

"I saw it all," he said, a quaver in his voice. "This man killed two of our men on the Lemster road. We gave him no provocation. It was in cold blood." The words came out stiff against his tongue, as if he had memorised them by rote.

"You said witnesses," said Gruffydd. "I see only one man."

"There are others, but they are not here. They will give the same evidence."

"What say you, Tom?"

"Yes, I told you I struck a man on the Lemster road, but only because we were attacked. And it was only one man, who would have killed me. I also have a witness to vouch for the truth. I let this man," he pointed at Oswyn, "ride away with his life because I felt sorry for him. It was a mistake. One I intend not to repeat."

"You know I am going to have to take you to be questioned further, Tom?" said Gruffydd. "Now that the Justice has made an accusation."

"Understood."

"You look like you have been in a fight. Can you walk?"

"Not a fight, a beating. And I can walk if I have to."

Gruffydd turned in his saddle and pointed at one of his men. "You, share with someone else. Give your mount to Tom."

The man slid down without question and someone else offered a hand to pull him up behind them. Thomas walked to the horse and set his foot in the stirrup. He steeled himself, then lifted onto the still warm saddle, his teeth clenched to hold back a scream of pain that wanted to fly out. He settled himself and stared at Hugh Clement, and knew there would be repercussions.

NINETEEN

Thomas rode alongside Gruffydd at the head of the column of men. He felt safer now soldiers were between him and Hugh Clement's thugs.

"Looks like you took a good beating, Tom. Was it Clement's men did it or Clement himself?"

"His men."

"I thought so. Hugh never gets his own hands dirty. Is this to do with what you told us about the other night?"

"It is."

"What about his accusation? Did you kill two of his men? You said one when you spoke in the tower, and claimed self-defence. Which is it?"

Thomas had hoped the questioning would not come as soon as this. So... the truth or not? He had already admitted to killing a man, but he did not want Philippa involved as anything but a witness.

"I killed one man, but not two. He would have killed me, then he and his companions would have raped Philippa, before killing her as well."

Gruffydd shook his head. "God's teeth, Tom, what are we going to do about this accusation? Hugh is going to spread it all over town."

"They came upon us on the Lemster road and it was kill or be killed. I had to protect Philippa."

"Is she your witness?"

"She is."

"Good, Arthur likes her. So do King Henry and the Queen. Even Henry's mother likes Pip, and Margaret Beaufort likes nobody." Gruffydd gave a rueful shake of his head. "I made a pitch for Pip myself a few years back, but she turned me down. She told me she never messes with married men. You are a fortunate man, Tom. A very fortunate man. You know you are going to have to repeat all of this in front of Richard, don't you?"

"Only Richard?"

"We can hardly call in the Justice, can we? Richard and myself, I think. We will call Pip as your witness and hear what she has to say, then decide. But I suspect I already know what our decision will be."

"Do you know Clement has men coming in from Wales?"

"I do not. North or south?"

"Does it matter?"

"It does. I am from the south. Pembrokeshire, just like Henry, even if he spent years in France. The south is for the King. The north still harbours a grudge because the English killed their prince."

"Llewelyn ap Gwyrdd," Thomas said, causing Gruffydd to turn and look at him.

"That's the one, but how do you know about him?"

"You forget I was born in Lemster. The border of Wales is a few bare leagues from there. Everyone in the Marches fears the Welsh. But all that happened a century ago."

Gruffydd barked a laugh. "The Welsh hold grudges longer than any nation I have ever known. Them and the Scots. Do I need to worry about these Welshmen Clement is bringing in?"

"I don't know. What do you think?"

"What I think is that my life and that of Ludlow used to be a lot simpler before you came along." Gruffydd held a hand up. "Not your fault, Tom, I know, but others have noted the fact and may not be so understanding."

"It may be my fault," Thomas said. "It has happened often enough before to make it likely, I am afraid. Trouble seems to follow me around like flies follow a horse's arse."

Gruffydd laughed. "Damn it, but I like you, Tom. God knows why, but I do."

"I have another question," Thomas said. "Do you know a man by the name of Jack Pook?"

"Yes, I know Jack. Had occasion to warn him off poaching on the Prince's land more than once, not that I ever caught him in the act. He's a damned good poacher, so I expect he has taken the odd deer or boar. Should hang for it, but as long as he leaves enough for the rest of us we turn a blind eye. He can be useful if you want a man who can pass through the land without leaving a trace. Why do you ask, Tom?"

They had come to the stables, and men were dismounting. Thomas did the same and passed his borrowed horse over to a stable-boy who would wipe it down before taking it to graze in the fields beside the river.

"I went to look at Hugh Clement's house after we were attacked and met Jack in the woods. He might prove a useful ally if I can persuade him to help, especially after what you just told me about him."

"You wouldn't have to pay him much, either," said Gruffydd. "What do you want with him?"

"You already said it. Jack can pass almost anywhere without being seen."

"Raise the suggestion again when we talk to Richard." Gruffydd looked Thomas up and down as they entered the inner bailey. "You need to change, and it would be an idea to have someone look at your wounds. Shall I send John Argentine?"

"No, I can check for damage myself. I will know I have been correctly treated if I do."

"Argentine's not a bad medic, but as you wish. Pip told me you were physician to the Spanish Queen for a time."

Thomas tried to recall if he had ever told Philippa about what he had done for Isabel and her family, but could not. They had talked about a great deal on the long-drawn-out journey from London, so he supposed he must have. He left Gruffydd to whatever duties called him and climbed to the room he shared with Philippa. He expected it to be empty but discovered she was there. She sat in a wooden chair near the window, sewing a repair to one of her many dresses. She rose at once and crossed to him, intending a welcoming kiss, but stopped when she saw his face. Her hand rose and cupped his cheek.

"Who did this to you?"

"Clement's men. I am glad you are here. I want you to examine me and check there is nothing more than bruising. I hurt everywhere, but can only check my front myself."

Philippa offered a coquettish smile. "Does that mean you will have to remove all your clothes?"

"It does, but don't get any ideas I cannot deliver on. It might take a few days before we do that again."

"I will just have to find another man then until you are ready."

Thomas eased from his shirt but found he could barely reach around enough to do so. Instead, he stood in the middle of the room while Philippa undressed him. Then he continued to stand as she ran her fingers across his back and legs, searching for anything more serious than bruising.

"They did a good job on you, didn't they? You have a small knife wound to your back, but it has barely broken the skin. How many did this to you, Tom?"

"A dozen, I reckon. Too many for me to fight off even if I tried. I thought I might get away with less damage if I let them do what they wanted, but I am sure they intended to finish me."

"Something will have to be done about this attack on you. Wait here while I go for hot water. You need to be cleaned. Sit in the chair, I don't want you staining the bedclothes."

After she was gone Thomas remained on his feet. He stretched his arms above his head, then bent at the waist to restore some flexibility in his spine. He was not sure if it worked or not, but when Philippa returned he felt better than he had. She washed him with warm water, soap and a linen cloth as he stood passively. When he became aroused, she laughed.

"Well, it looks to me like you may have recovered already."

She dried him, then helped him dress in clean clothes.

"Throw those others away," she said, staring down at his tattered clothes.

"Not yet. Keep them until the end of the day in case Sir Richard wants proof of what happened."

"You are all the proof he needs."

"Perhaps. Gruff said they are going to want to talk to you as well. You are my witness to what happened on the road from Lemster. Hugh Clement accused me of murder, but I am sure Gruff did not believe a word of it. Sir Richard is keener on evidence and witnesses. I am sorry, I did not want you involved, but there is no one else."

Philippa took Thomas's hand and raised it to her chest. "You have nothing to apologise for, Tom. I will do as you ask."

"Gruff told me he set his sights on you at one time and was rebuffed."

"He did, but does not hold it against me. Did he tell you why?"

"He did."

"And you told me you are not married."

"I have been, but at the moment I am all yours."

Philippa grinned. "Just don't forget it. You don't want to find out how I deal with men who cross me. Now, I want to finish repairing that tear in my dress, and then the Prince needs me for his lessons. You should rest on the bed. I will bring you some broth when I am finished."

Thomas almost told her he had no intention of resting but suspected it would only lead to an argument, so he nodded and did as she told him. Philippa took her seat at the window and picked up her needle and thread again. Thomas watched her work, the easy skill of what she did, and knew she might prove a fine assistant if he needed one. He had not much used his medical knowledge over recent years and felt the lack of practicing it. He wondered if that might change now he was in England. Thomas knew the level of skill he possessed was not always welcomed, particularly by other physicians. He tried to avoid contact with Prince Arthur's physician, John Argentine. He had spoken only once with him as they journeyed from London and found him as set in his ways as most others in his profession. They went little further than bleeding, applying leeches and examining a man's water. Thomas knew there was far more that could be done. He wondered if he might return to his profession if he set up home here in Ludlow or Lemster. He was unaware of falling asleep, only of coming awake when Philippa stroked the side of his face. He sat up, but she put a hand on his chest and pushed him back down.

"I should have let you sleep. I am going out now. Try to rest a few more hours if you can. Sleep is the best medicine for you."

Thomas smiled, thinking of his musings before he had drifted off. Everyone, it seemed, was an expert. He remained on the bed for a quarter hour after Philippa left, then rose. There were people he wanted to question, and others he wanted to check on to make sure they were safe. But questions first.

The afternoon was almost over before Thomas knocked on the side door of Agnes's house. The bakery was closed, but he was sure someone would be inside, even if he was less sure they would answer the door. Thomas had gone to every alehouse, tavern and inn, as well as a third of the businesses in town, to hear the same story from each. Small groups of Hugh Clement's men had visited them over the previous week. Sometimes three, but most often two. The request had been the same in each case. We will return shortly for your payment to protect your livelihood. The sums asked differed depending on the size and trade of each, and the timings meant the callers would have to visit less than a dozen establishments a day. Butchers, haberdashers, tailors, seamstresses, stables, mills and every varied manner of business required of a town hosting the Prince of Wales reported the same. The bonemen had come calling with their proposal. Standing outside Agnes's door, Thomas calculated that Hugh Clement's men would collect near two-hundred shillings a month if everyone paid. And he was sure almost everyone would pay in the end. A few pretended otherwise. Some would fight and be made examples of, a single sliver of bone left as a warning.

The door opened a crack and one of the girls peered out. When she saw it was Thomas, she opened the door wider and he stepped through.

"Is Agnes home?"

"Eating dinner in the courtyard. There may be some left if you are hungry." The girl stared openly at Thomas's face, his bruises growing darker as the day progressed.

"I have come for conversation, not food, but my thanks. Was it you who took a message to the Castle? If so, I thank you again." Thomas had difficulty telling the two girls apart.

"It was Jilly, sir. She said she saw you being bustled along by those men who came demanding money from us. They said they would return next Monday for payment."

"You know about what they ask, then?"

"Mother keeps nothing from us."

Thomas knew he needed to find out more about Agnes's girls.

"What is your name?"

"I am Rose, sir." She gave a little curtsy. "And you are Thomas Berrington. Mother told us you are her long-lost brother, so I expect we should call you Uncle Thomas. We did not even know she had a brother."

Thomas smiled. "Everyone thought me dead. I hope my bruises don't scare you too much."

"Why would they scare me, sir? Mother told us you are the bravest, cleverest man there is. This way, Uncle."

As Thomas followed, he said, "If I really am your uncle, I think you should call me by my name."

"Uncle Thomas?" she asked.

"Just Thomas, or Tom—there is no need for the uncle. It makes me feel old."

Rose stopped and turned to look at him. "If you don't

mind me saying so, Tom, you do look a little old. Especially at the moment."

Thomas laughed. "I expect I do."

The other girl, Jilly, sat at the table in the courtyard where three places were set. Agnes rose and came to greet Thomas, but stopped short when she saw his bruises.

"Was it those men?" she asked.

"It was. I believe I have Jilly to thank for saving my life. Hugh Clement would have seen me in the ground."

"She came and told me what she had seen, and I sent her to the castle. I am glad someone came to find you, but it looks from the state of you they should have come a little sooner. Are you eating with us?"

"I cannot. I have been away from the Castle too long as it is. There are questions I must answer as well as information to give. Have you had any more trouble?"

"Today has been quiet." Agnes returned to the table and sat, her meal only half eaten.

Thomas brought another chair and sat across from her.

"I think I was their primary object of attention today, but they will be back on Monday. You should pay what they ask. I gave the same advice to the other businesses in town. Pay for now while I work out how to bring Hugh Clement down."

"It will not be easy, Tom. I hear rumours he is recruiting men from Wales. Soon he will have as many under his command as there are soldiers serving Prince Arthur, and they are more ruthless, I reckon. He also knows every man of substance and every man of evil for twenty miles around. Often enough they are one and the same." Agnes picked at her food, her eyes on Thomas.

"I have dealt with evil men before and defeated them. They were hard men, too."

"I expect you were younger then."

Thomas wondered if everyone in this household considered him too old for the task he had set himself.

"All I need do is convince Gruffydd ap Rhys and Sir Richard Pole of the case against Clement and our forces will be evenly matched. More than evenly matched if there are men in Ludlow and Lemster willing to fight alongside us to protect their livelihoods."

"You might be unlucky in that. Most are used to bending the knee to Hugh Clement, and he likes it that way. Demands it, I would say."

"And you?" Thomas asked. "Do you bend the knee to him?"

Agnes smiled and patted Thomas's hand. "Perhaps we are both a little alike, brother, even if I have seen nothing of you for all these years. I bend the knee to no man or woman, other than the King or the Prince. And God, of course."

"When they come, pay them what they ask, sister. I am going to stop them, but I need time, and I need Ludlow peaceful."

"There will be some who refuse, you know there will."

"They will hurt nobody much at the start, but if some continue to refuse, then the punishments will escalate. That will be Hugh Clement's undoing." Thomas hoped he was right because he had proven little of a threat to the man so far.

TWENTY

Thomas returned to the castle to be informed by a guard at the gate that Gruffydd and Sir Richard were waiting for him in Mortimer's Tower. The day was ending and torches had been lit, their light dancing across the roughly hewn table. To the west the sun touched the wooded hills in a blaze of colour that promised the possibility of rain before morning. There was bread and cheese on the table, as well as a jug of wine and another larger one holding ale.

"Sit, Tom," said Gruffydd. "We sent for you several hours since, but it seems you had gone out. What was the point of my rescuing you if you leave to walk the streets of town where anyone can see you?"

"I wanted to know what was happening."

"As do I," said Sir Richard. "I have sent a message for Philippa to join us as your witness. This accusation against you is serious and we cannot dismiss it without some investigation. You may be one of us now, but we will show no preference. If you are guilty of murder you will hang for it."

Thomas stared at Sir Richard, whose expression was set hard. When he glanced at Gruffydd, he saw a little more compassion, but knew he too would follow the law in this matter.

"While we are waiting for Pip," said Gruffydd, "this came for you." He handed across a note, the seal broken.

"Who opened it?" Thomas asked, unfolding the stained paper.

"I did," said Sir Richard. "Not that it did me any good. It is a child's scribble no man could read, and no doubt meant as some kind of jest."

Thomas smiled as he scanned the content.

"My son wrote this, and the only problem he has is having to duck when he enters a doorway. It is written in Arabic, which both my children consider their first language, though I have been teaching them English for the day they arrive. Which it seems they have now done."

"So not a scribble," said Gruffydd. "What does it say, Tom, or is the letter private to you?"

"It is for me, yes, but I see no harm in telling you its content. He sent this from the Bell Savage in London three days past, which is where I told them all to go. I had hoped to be there to greet them but matters brought me here."

"I have stayed at the Bell Savage," said Sir Richard. "It is a fine establishment, and Peggy Spicer an excellent goodwife."

"I thought the same too at one time. If he sent this three

days ago they must be almost here by now. I will need to find somewhere for them to stay. Outside of Ludlow would be best if there is going to be trouble." Though as Thomas spoke the words, he thought of his son, Will. Tall. Strong. Handsome. He had handled trouble before and not been found wanting. Except Thomas would prefer a life less filled with incident for his children than his own had been.

"There is the matter yet of your guilt or not of the accusation against you, Thomas," said Sir Richard.

"How many children do you have?" asked Gruffydd, the less accusatory of the two.

"Two. Will and Amal."

"Amal?"

"It is a Moorish name, given to her by her mother who died in childbirth." Thomas considered it a simpler explanation than the truth. That his wife Lubna had been murdered by the crazed son of an Abbot in Málaga during the brutal siege of that glorious city. "There will be friends coming with them as well, but how many I cannot be sure of. We discussed who should or should not come before I left Granada, so I suspect between seven and nine."

Gruffydd shook his head, a smile on his face. "Why am I only now learning about your family, Tom?"

"We haven't spoken of such things between us, have we?" Thomas was aware such matters were discussed between friends. He was sure he would never call Sir Richard Pole a friend, but Gruffydd was a different matter. Thomas liked his bluffness, his lack of airs and graces. None of that meant he would not watch as Thomas took his last drop on the gallows.

"The Prince also received a message this morning. It

seems it is a time for families re-uniting. His bride-to-be landed at Plymouth a week since."

"Catherine is in England?"

"If you mean Princess Catherine of Aragon, then yes," said Sir Richard. "Arthur is readying to leave to meet her, but the arrangements are not yet completed. The message also mentions you. Princess Catherine has asked if Thomas Berrington will accompany Arthur to their meeting. The implication being it is her wish you do so."

The expression on Sir Richard's face showed that such was not his wish.

"I suspect she seeks a familiar face. She is an able girl, but still young."

"Older than Arthur by near a year," said Gruffydd. "I hope she is not too worldly because the Prince can be overly courtly. The sooner they have a boy the better for the country."

"Let them marry first, man," said Sir Richard.

"Of course. Though as all of us know, such is not always necessary."

"It is if the boy wants to inherit the crown. Bastards don't count."

A female figure emerged onto the platform, but it was not who they were waiting for.

"Where's Pip?" asked Gruffydd, rising to his feet.

"She left in the company of a man an hour since, sir," said the woman.

"Who was he?"

"I know not, sir. The guards at the gate may."

"Very well. When she returns, tell her to come to us at once if we are still here."

The woman bobbed a curtsy and turned back to negotiate the descent of the tower.

"Do you have a rival for Pip's favours, Tom?" asked Gruffydd.

"Perhaps. Does she have friends in Ludlow?"

"Pip has friends everywhere she goes. She may have grown tired of waiting for your return, as myself and Richard were beginning to." Gruffydd glanced at Sir Richard. "Can we make any progress without her?"

"We can try, at the least. Tell us what happened. Your version of events. And then we may need to speak to Hugh Clement and hear his side. You had best be with us while we do so, but that can wait until the morning. Tell us your truth."

Thomas did, or as close to the truth as he was willing to go. He told them how three men attacked them as they rode north from Lemster. How it had been self-defence, and how he had killed one of their number.

"Why?" asked Gruffydd when the short tale was told. "Why not kill them all?"

"Because one took no part in the attack, and the other fled when he heard me coming to Pip's aid." He met Gruffydd's gaze. "It was a mistake, I agree. One that led to me being beaten today and might have brought about my death."

"What happened to the body of the man you killed?" Sir Richard picked at the bread and cheese, a jar of ale in the other hand which he used to wash down the food. His voice was soft, without accusation. "It might prove useful to see it as a confirmation of what you say."

"While I went to help Pip his companion took the

body away." As Thomas told the story, he realised how artificial it sounded. "Both horses were gone. I don't see what you might learn from the dead man other than he had a sword wound through the heart."

Sir Richard looked at the square of cheese between his fingers, then placed it back on the table.

"I suppose you are right. Why did you not come to tell us of this attack rather than omit mention of it? If the events are as you claim, then no blame would fall on you, and certainly none on Pip."

"You were still at Caynham Manor with the Prince when we returned to Ludlow. By the time you arrived, it seemed of little importance. I had dismissed it from my mind."

Sir Richard stared hard at Thomas. "You have killed so many men you forget taking the life of another?"

"Perhaps. I know I have lost count of how many I have killed, but none who did not deserve to die. Those men would have killed me without a second thought. Pip too."

"We have all done the same, Richard," said Gruffydd. "You know we have. It only makes me respect Tom the more for speaking as he has."

"The man deserved a Christian burial if nothing else."

"Perhaps he had one," Thomas said. "We should ask around the local churchmen to see if they have buried a medium-tall man with a hole in his chest."

"Pip came to your bed that night, did she not?"

"She shared my bed, yes, but it was at her instigation, not mine. I had no expectation of her."

"Pip always goes after what she wants," said Gruffydd. "Some might call her cold-hearted, but I admire her for it.

She obviously wanted you, Tom. You are a lucky devil is all I can say."

"I hope I live to be luckier still."

"She will not marry you, you know," said Gruffydd. "She has had other lovers and never wants to marry them. Make the most of it while you can. I expect she is worth the effort, is she not?"

"Do you expect me to answer that?"

Gruffydd gave a great laugh and slapped Thomas on the shoulder, apologising when he saw him wince.

The light had leached from the west and bright stars sparked the heavens by the time Thomas descended the winding stone staircase.

"Don't flee or it will go ill for you." Sir Richard's words followed him down.

When Thomas entered the room he shared with Philippa, he found she had not yet returned. He went to the gatehouse and enquired if the guards had seen her entering the castle, but neither had. Going out, yes. Coming back, no.

"I heard she left with a man," Thomas said. "Did you see him?"

"He stood where you are while I sent a message, so of course we did. They went off together when Pip came out. They seemed to know each other. Knew each other well, I would say." There was a challenge in the man's eyes as he spoke, and Thomas supposed everyone knew about Philippa and him.

"What did he look like?"

"One of those monks from the Abbey," said the man.

"Tall, though not as tall as you. He wore a long white robe with the hood pulled up."

"A monk? Are you sure?" It made no sense.

"I am hardly going to mistake a monk, am I?"

"Did you hear a name mentioned?"

"I did not, but Pip seemed to know whoever it was well enough. I overheard her asking where they were going and he told her to the cottage."

"What cottage?"

"I watched them leave, and they made their way north to Hugh Clement's land. The only cottage I know that way is set hard alongside the woods with a stream in front of it. Good fishing in the Corfe, there is."

But the man was talking to empty air as Thomas crossed the drawbridge and began to run.

TWENTY-ONE

Thomas slowed as he approached the cottage, which sat exactly where the guard at the gate had described. He had not seen it before and wondered why not, because it lay in plain sight on the edge of the woods where he first encountered Jack Pook. It was illuminated now by a newly risen moon. He only supposed he had missed it because his attention was on the manor house.

Flickering light showed in the single window as Thomas approached, taking care where he placed his feet. He was trying to come to terms with what he had heard: that Philippa had left willingly with her caller. The guard told him they appeared to be friends. Which raised the question of why she might be friends with a monk, or a man who lived in a cottage on Hugh Clement's estate. Thomas was aware she knew Hugh Clement, but enough to answer his summons, if such it was? He tried to recall any slip Philippa might have made that would show she knew the man better than she had communicated, but nothing came to him.

He approached the single window set beside the door, trusting darkness to hide him as he came close to peer inside, unsure what he might see.

There were no shutters covering the window. No doubt whoever lived here assumed little need of them here. They would not expect a man to be standing outside looking in. What Thomas saw was a half-naked Philippa on the stone floor with two men standing over her, both with knives in their hands. As Thomas watched, one blade released a drop of blood which spattered against the floor.

Thomas stepped to one side and aimed a kick at the door. He expected it to be locked, but it crashed back so hard it almost slammed shut again. By the time he entered the small room the two men were turning at the interruption, and he recognised Oswyn and Rowland.

Thomas wanted to go to Philippa but could not yet. She would have to wait a little longer. Not too long, he hoped, as he felt a coldness settle through him. The room became crystal sharp, the men predictable as Thomas's old skill returned as though it had never gone away. He had no weapon, but did not need one.

The men came at him together, which was a sound move. It meant he had to deal with both at the same time and made it more likely one or the other would land a damaging strike. The mistake they made was approaching too close together. They needed to put more space between themselves.

Thomas judged distance, played through scenarios, then attacked. The men did not expect it, which is what he had planned on.

Rowland took a step back, opening the space between

them. Thomas filled it. He wrapped his tagelmust around his arm, and when Oswyn thrust his blade at him Thomas let it slide along the linen cloth, the thick winds of material offering protection. As Oswyn's blade slid through the cloth, causing it to part, Thomas pushed against the killing blow until he grasped the hilt of the long blade. He pushed up, twisting, and the knife clattered to the floor. Before Thomas could pick it up, Oswyn pulled a second, shorter knife from behind him. It might have gone badly for Thomas then if Rowland had not assumed his position weak and came in hard to attack.

Thomas ducked, pushed the man's arm to one side, then rose. Rowland's feet came clear of the floor, and Thomas used his own momentum to fling him directly at Oswyn. Both men slammed to the floor.

But Thomas had made a mistake. The two of them landed hard on Philippa, who was turning over so she could stand. They crashed into her, slamming her against the flagstones, and she cried out.

Thomas grabbed Rowland and flung him to one side before reaching for Oswyn, noting he had acquired a wound to his belly as the two men collided. He pulled him away from Philippa. He was reaching for her when Rowland crashed into him, sending him sprawling. Thomas rolled and kicked out as Rowland leapt at him, his knife ready to strike.

Thomas reached out, his hand finding the hilt of the knife Oswyn had dropped. As Rowland fell, Thomas twisted to one side and slammed the knife upwards. The blade slid against a rib, then further to pierce the man's heart, instantly stilling it. Thomas experienced no remorse at killing the man.

Thomas flung the body to one side, then rose to face Oswyn who was backing away, clutching his side.

"Try to run and I will kill you before you reach the door." Thomas's words drew Oswyn to a halt. "Drop your weapon and tell me why you were torturing Philippa."

Oswyn spat at him and turned to run, but his wound made him slow.

Thomas caught him at the door and grabbed his hair, causing Oswyn to squeal. Thomas wanted answers, but doubted he would get them from the man. Oswyn had been following orders. But whose orders? No doubt those of Hugh Clement.

When Oswyn struck out, Thomas avoided the thrust with ease. His own blade entered Oswyn low on the front right-hand side to pierce his liver. It was the blow Thomas intended, and he stepped back as Oswyn slumped against the wall then slid down, his knees raised as if to offer a protection that was too late. Blood streamed from the wound to pool beneath him.

Thomas went to his knees in front of Oswyn. He reached out and raised the man's chin until he was staring into Thomas's eyes.

"Did Hugh order you to do this?"

"Philippa said you were a surgeon," said Oswyn. "Can you save me?"

"If you tell me the truth, but you need to be quick. Why Philippa?"

"We were told to question her."

"About what?"

"Movements in the castle. About you. He wants to know exactly who you are and whether you are dangerous."

"As you have discovered, I am indeed dangerous. Why did Philippa come with you willingly?"

"Not me. Her man."

Thomas stared into Oswyn's eyes, which were clouding. His breath came in shallow gasps, and the blood barely pulsed from him now.

"What man? Hugh? Daniel?"

Oswyn smiled. Perhaps he knew his death was imminent and it no longer mattered whether he told the truth or not.

"Not you."

Oswyn's eyes lost whatever life they contained and his breath stopped.

Thomas rose to his feet and turned to Philippa. He had a hundred questions to ask, but not now. He went to his knees in front of her and grasped her hands. Philippa's head came up and her eyes flickered open.

"Tom, what are you doing here?"

"Taking you to safety. Can you walk?"

"I don't know. I think so." She pulled at the torn front of her dress but only succeeded in partly covering herself.

Thomas held out his arms to support her. "Try to stand, I'll help."

Philippa nodded but stayed where she was.

"I cannot move my legs." Her eyes rose to his. "What have they done to me?"

"I don't know." Thomas looked around, uncertain what to do next. He recalled when both Rowland and Oswyn fell on Philippa and wondered what damage that blow might have done. "Who knows you are here?"

"Those two and you. Nobody else." Philippa grimaced as she attempted to stand again, then slumped back to the floor.

"What about Hugh Clement or Daniel Lupton?"

"I don't know," she said, a shortness to her response.

"Who was the man who came for you at the castle?"

"What man?" Philippa rocked her head. "Help me, Tom. I hurt."

"A monk came for you. A monk from the Abbey, the guard said."

"Yes. I remember now. It seems so long ago. He was a monk, that was all. A man of God."

"Where did he say he was taking you, and to who?"

Philippa shook her head. "I cannot remember, Tom. Stop all these questions and take me home. Please. I hurt everywhere."

"I need to find something to carry you on. Stay here while I go to look."

"I am not going anywhere without you, but be quick."

"I want to check your wounds first. Can I?"

"Do what you must." Philippa was not her normal self, but that was understandable.

Thomas eased her torn dress aside and examined her flesh. Oswyn and Rowland had cut her in several places, but the wounds were shallow, intended to hurt rather than kill.

"They did this while questioning you?"

Philippa nodded without meeting his eyes. "I told them nothing, Tom. Then you came and they fell on me. I felt something break inside."

Thomas turned away and left the cottage with a glance at Oswyn's body. He ran towards the manor house but did not go up to it. Instead, he headed for the stables. It was dark inside, and horses whinnied when he entered. He stroked the nose of one to quiet it and waited for his eyesight to adjust. Enough wash of moonlight filtered in to allow him to make out shapes, and one of them was a small handcart. It held two bales of fresh hay, which he tipped out before drawing the cart to the entrance.

On the far side of the yard, voices sounded as three men appeared. One was unmistakably Hugh Clement, another Daniel Lupton. The third man's presence came as a shock as Thomas made out Jack Pook. Was this one more betrayal? Thomas wondered how he could have misjudged so many people. He wondered if his soft life in Granada had changed him for the worse if he could no longer see through such deception.

Then Thomas saw his mistake as Daniel Lupton pushed at Jack Pook and swung a punch at his head. By the time Lupton's fist reached where Jack's head had been, it had already jerked aside. Something silver flashed in Jack's hand, but instead of using the blade on Lupton, Jack jerked it at Hugh Clement, who gave a loud cry and stumbled away to fall on his back. Jack took advantage and ran off into the night as Daniel went to his master's aid. Thomas followed his example and drew the cart into the open as Daniel helped Hugh Clement towards the house.

Thomas was almost back at the cottage when Jack Pook appeared beside him.

"Bit late for harvesting, Tom," he said as he fell into step.

"Did they catch you poaching?"

"Using a net in the river. What about you?"

"I have an injured friend in the cottage. I need the cart to get her back to Ludlow."

"I can help. Four hands are better than two. You pull and I can push from behind. Is this friend heavy?"

"No, light as a feather."

Thomas pushed the cottage door open and Jack followed him in. He glanced at the dead man sitting beside the doorway, at the other on his back in one corner, but said nothing. Thomas put his hands beneath Philippa's arms and raised her up. He let the slight weight of her settle until he felt her legs buckle beneath her and lifted her again.

"Help me carry her out, Jack," he said.

Jack took Philippa's weight on the other side and between them they half-carried her to the door. They lay Philippa in the cart, then Thomas pulled while Jack pushed from behind as promised.

"I recognise one of the dead men," said Jack, his breathing normal, as though he was making no effort at all. "His name is Rowland, and he is a bag of shit. Who is the other?"

"Another bag of shit by the name of Oswyn."

"Welshman? Some are all right, but you can't trust them all. I try to stay this side of the border if I can.

Though I've seen a few crossing it these last few weeks. Who killed them, you or the girl?"

"I did. Do you know who she is?"

"Everyone in Ludlow knows Pip Gale, and they all like and respect her."

"Not everyone, it seems."

TWENTY-TWO

The heavy doors barring the gatehouse were closed for the night, but when Thomas hammered on them a small panel opened and a pale face peered out.

"I thought you were back already. Wait while I open the gate for you. Who is in the cart?"

"Pip," Thomas said, and heard the industry on the other side of the door increase in pace.

As soon as the door was open wide enough, Thomas and Jack Pook pulled the cart inside.

"I need something flat to carry her on," Thomas said to the guard.

"Would a door do? They are replacing three in the kitchen but have not hung them yet."

As they waited, Thomas considered whether it would be wise to carry Philippa up the stairs to their room on the second floor or not. He played scenarios through his head until satisfied. There was one turn on the staircase, but it was wide and two men should be able to manage. If not, he would have to examine her somewhere on the ground floor, but would prefer privacy because he needed to strip her to check every inch of her body for damage. He had no inkling yet of what was wrong with her, but feared the worst. If Rowland and Oswyn crashing into her had broken something in her spine, she might never walk again.

Thomas reached for her hand and kissed it out of habit as he pushed away his doubts about this woman. Jack Pook found something fascinating on one of the stone walls.

"How are you feeling now?" Thomas asked Philippa.

"How do you think? My back is on fire and I have lost count of how many wounds they inflicted."

"What about your feet?"

"My feet? Are you mad, Tom?"

He reached for her left foot, still encased in a leather boot that rose above her ankle. He gripped it and twisted her leg, but Philippa gave no sign the movement pained her. She gave no sign she even knew what he had done. Thomas bit back the questions he wanted to ask about why she had gone with those men. About what her involvement was with Hugh Clement. She claimed she went with her mysterious caller innocently enough, but the story did not sit right. There would be time to raise hard questions later, once she had recovered. Now she needed Thomas the physician, not Thomas the accuser. He had dealt with similar injuries when he lived in Spain. Some he had cured, some he had not. He would only know which this was when he examined her more closely.

The two guards emerged, carrying a door between

them. It looked heavy. Possibly too heavy. Even so, Thomas removed his robe and got to work.

"I expect you have a sharp knife about your person, Jack."

Jack Pook withdrew a wickedly honed knife and handed it to Thomas, who used it to cut his robe into strips. They lifted Philippa gently as the guards rested the door across the back of the cart. Thomas slid Philippa onto it, then bound her tight with strips made from his robe. He saved four, which he threaded through the door-frame at top and bottom, leaving them to hang as loops.

"I am going to need your help," he said to the guards. "Yours too, Jack."

"They rarely let me inside the walls of the Castle. Perhaps I can find something to eat before they toss me out. Tell me what you want me to do, Tom."

"Take the strip of cloth on the left-hand side I will be on the right." Thomas turned to the guards. "I want you to do the same at the other end." It relieved him when they nodded. No questions. No objections.

Between them, they lifted the heavy door, which swayed from side to side. Thomas led the way, setting his feet down softly to avoid any jarring. There was a moment of doubt at the turn of the stairs, but the guards at the back lifted their end above their heads and between them they manoeuvred the door holding Philippa up to the gallery and into Thomas's room.

"Lay the door on the floor, I can lift her onto the bed. I thank you for your help, all three of you, but I need to work now."

"Do you want any message sent?" asked one guard.

"Is Lady Pole still awake, do you know?"

"She is usually abed early, but her husband is still in the Tower. Do you want me to take a message to him?"

"Not yet. What about the kitchen?"

"There is always somebody there overnight to bake bread for the morning."

"I thought you bought your bread from town," Thomas said.

"We do most of the time, but the young Prince has some funny ideas about what he will and will not eat. He insists on rye flour and takes nothing else. The rest of us go to Agnes Baxter's shop. Best bread in town."

"Go to the kitchen and ask them to send me as much warm water as they can spare. I need soap and linen towels as well."

"I will go," said Jack Pook. "These fine fellows should return to their duty in case some wicked person tries to sneak inside the castle walls." His face remained without expression, but Thomas caught a glint of mischief in his eyes.

"Good idea. Now, if you can all leave, I need to undress Pip."

The guards stared at Thomas as though they might object, but eventually they turned and left, muttering between themselves as they departed.

"A special thanks to you, Jack." Thomas offered his hand.

Now the conversation involved only the two of them Jack laughed. "You are practically family, Tom. Might have been if things had worked out different. Bel told me you went to see her. Fair made her day, she said, to see you alive and hale."

"I thought you were the black sheep of the family."

"Aye, I am, but you know how Bel is. She holds no grudge against anyone unless they deserve it, and I've always done right by her. I'd best do right by you and get that water sent up." Jack glanced at Philippa's prone body on the door. "Good luck, Tom."

"Before you go, help me get her onto the bed. I would do it myself, but it will go better with the two of us."

Between them they lifted Philippa, managing to keep her flat, and laid her on the top of the bedclothes face down.

Once they were alone, Thomas opened his leather satchel and drew out what he needed. Three small, wickedly sharp blades; a small ball of sticky hashish resin; a stoppered bottle holding tincture of poppy mixed with raw spirit. There were other items inside, but he hoped he would not need them. All the other instruments of his trade were still on the back of one of the carts Jorge and Will were bringing all the way from southern Spain. Thomas considered the message he had received and wondered how close they might be to reaching him. The note was three days old. Could they be far behind it by now? The help of Jorge's wife, Belia, would prove useful. As would that of his own daughter, Amal. Like her mother, Amal had turned into a skilled practitioner. She might even be as skilled as Thomas himself, he sometimes thought.

He mixed the hashish with a little poppy liquor and

fed it to Philippa, aware he should have done so before turning her over.

"I am going to have to cut you out of your clothes."

"You always have some excuse, Tom. Cut all you like, they ruined this dress."

Thomas removed the top section of her dress, which came away easily with it already being half-torn open. His sharp instruments made quick work of the fine ties at the back. When a knock came at the door, Thomas laid the remnants of cloth across Philippa and went to open it. Two women stood outside, one carrying a heavy basin of water from which steam rose. The other carried a linen sheet, which he would need to cut up. Once they had set both on the floor beside the bed and left, Thomas turned the lock on the door and went to work. A calmness settled through him, and he realised how much he had missed this manner of work. It had been his living at one time, and he knew he was good at it. Many avoided his services because of his reputation as a butcher, but that came from treating men on the battlefield. Only a butcher could save as many as Thomas had. Other patients would go to nobody other than him.

He cut away more of the dress until Philippa lay naked and bruised, still face down on the door.

"I am going to examine you now. If I press too hard cry out and I will try to be more gentle."

"You know I don't enjoy gentle, Tom." Philippa's voice had softened, losing the edge of tension her pain had brought, so Thomas knew the poppy was doing its work. She might need more if he had to manipulate her spine, but for now, what he had given her would be enough for an initial examination.

Thomas took the linen sheet and ripped it into lengths before wetting it and wiping away the blood streaking Philippa's back. He ignored the exquisite nature of her. He had seen her in all states of dress and undress, but that had been different. Now he was Thomas Berrington, surgeon and physician, and he knew he was the best of those in Ludlow. Not that there was much in the way of competition.

As he worked, Thomas discovered several minor cuts on Philippa's skin where Oswyn and Rowland had pricked her. He tried not to think about what they had wanted to know. His own questions would come soon enough. The cuts were not deep, barely breaking the skin, but would have inflicted a great deal of pain. They covered her shoulders and sides and, he knew, would cover her breasts and belly when he turned her over. That act would have to wait until he knew what other damage had been done to her.

When her back and legs were clean, Thomas leaned close to examine each individual wound, trying to decide if any needed stitching. Already most had stopped bleeding and the healing process begun. It might require stitching on her front, but not her back. The wounds to her buttocks were deeper, as if made in a rage, but the flesh there would also heal without his help.

What concerned Thomas most was the deep bruise that spread from the base of her spine. The slimness of her back led his eye to the bruise, and he reached out to touch it with two fingers, not yet pressing.

"Can you feel me touching you, Pip?"

"I can, but only a little. Is that the tincture you gave me?"

"What about here?" Thomas touched her side.

"I can feel that fine. You can peck me a kiss there if you like."

"I fear I may have given you too much poppy." But Thomas smiled. If they had damaged her inside, he did not think she would act as she was. Unless he *had* given her too much, but he doubted it. Years of experience allowed him to judge the exact amount for each person.

"Give me more anytime you like, Tom. I like the feeling of being wrapped in soft feathers."

Thomas took one of his blades and turned it round. He ran the blunt end along the back of Philippa's right leg and she made a small sound.

"Is that your finger, Tom, or something else?"

"It is metal."

"Hard as iron," she said.

"You felt it?"

"I did."

Thomas repeated the movement on her left leg, disappointed to get no response. He tried again.

"What about this?"

"What about what?"

"I need to press harder on your back. If it hurts, tell me and I will stop."

Philippa made no response. After a moment, Thomas put two fingers of each hand alongside the ridge of her spine. He drew them down until he reached the bruise.

Philippa grunted. "Hurts now, Tom."

"It might hurt a bit more yet. Do you want more poppy?"

"Not yet. Later, help me sleep."

Thomas pressed harder, noting as Philippa tensed. He pressed harder still, searching for damage, a cracked bone, a dislodged vertebra, but found nothing.

When he finished, Philippa was breathing hard.

"So?" she asked.

"I am worried about your left leg. You did not feel the blade when I touched it, but I cannot find anything obviously wrong, so I am going to bind you tight then turn you over."

"Are you going to wash my front like you did my back?"

"Of course."

"I think I might enjoy that."

"I doubt it," Thomas said. "Besides, I am your doctor now, and doctors never get involved with their patients."

"Then I hope you cure me soon."

Thomas looked around then gave a sigh when he could see only one source of leather. So be it.

He took a blade and cut his best boots into long strips. Then he did the same with his second-best pair of boots.

He laid the strips along Philippa's spine, then wrapped lengths of cut bedding around them, lifting her to slide them beneath. He tied the makeshift splint as tight as he could until Philippa let out a small cry. It was the best he could do.

Thomas turned her carefully, inch by inch, until she lay on her back. He removed the last remnant of her dress, then gave her a little more poppy liquor, enough to dull the pain and bring sleep. When her eyes closed, he waited. Once small snores sounded through her parted lips, Thomas wetted more linen in the now tepid water and washed her front. He examined the wounds to her breasts which, like those on her buttocks, were deeper. He cursed the two men, suspecting they would have violated Philippa further had he not interrupted them. Thomas wondered if anyone had discovered their bodies yet, and what the reaction would be when they did.

He stood over Philippa knowing there was nothing more he could do. She would recover or not. He had done the best he could, aware that if any other doctor had attended her, she might have been crippled for life. She still might.

He covered her marred beauty with a blanket and went to the chair beside the window. As he sat, a wave of exhaustion rolled through him, held at bay until that moment only through an act of will. Thomas scrubbed his hands across his face, knowing he should have washed himself as well, but too lethargic to get up again.

He stared at Philippa, thinking of the conversation they would need to have in the morning.

TWENTY-THREE

Thomas jerked awake, not knowing why until he heard a knock at the door and someone tried to open it. He rose from the chair, stiff from sleeping there all night. Bright sunlight filled the room to tell him the day was well started. He glanced at Philippa, who continued to sleep, her chest rising and falling softly, then went to unlock the door. It surprised him to discover Lady Margaret Pole, Sir Richard's wife, standing outside with a hand raised to knock. She was the matriarch of the castle, a short woman with dark hair who was renowned for her good humour and willingness to help anyone who needed it.

"Can I come in, Thomas?" she asked. "I heard Pip has been taken ill. Also, my husband and Gruffydd need to talk to you."

Thomas stood aside and ushered Lady Margaret inside. She went immediately to Philippa and stood over her.

"What ails her?"

"I think it better I tell the full tale to your husband." He reached out and drew the sheet down to reveal the puncture marks on Philippa's chest and arms. To his eye, they looked improved on the night before, but that might have been only the daylight.

Lady Margaret looked at Thomas. "Who did this?"

"That is what I need to talk to your husband and Gruff about. Pip should sleep another hour or two yet, but I need to know as soon as she wakes."

"Shall I ask John Argentine to attend her? Those wounds look as though they may need dressing. I will ask a woman to accompany him to do that, of course."

"I am also a physician, my lady, and have already treated Pip. She has a bruised spine, which I have splinted and bound. I would prefer no other physician sees her." Thomas stared into Lady Margaret's eyes, hoping she would not try to argue.

Perhaps she saw something in the intensity of his gaze because she said, "I forget you are also a physician, Thomas, and come highly recommended. Pip is in safe hands, then."

"I would welcome a lady to sit with her and send a message if she wakes. I would like to examine her again as soon as she does. The damage to her back concerns me."

"There are cuts there too?"

"There are, but it is not that. Last night she had no sensation in her left leg. I am hoping it might be improved by now. If not…" Thomas let his words trail away, hoping Lady Margaret would glean his meaning. She was an intelligent woman and nodded.

"Of course. I will send someone at once."

When she was gone, Thomas drew the covers from

Philippa and examined her. He ran a hand down her right leg, pleased when her toes curled. When he did the same to the left, her big toe twitched. Was it coincidence or not? Thomas stroked the leg again with the same result and smiled before pulling the covers back. Just in time, as the door opened with no knock and a woman even shorter than Lady Margaret bustled in. She glanced at Philippa before turning to Thomas.

"Lady Margaret tells me I am to sit with Pip and send a message if she wakes."

"That is correct."

"How long will you be?"

"That I don't know, but I must be told as soon as she wakes."

"I said I would, did I not?" The woman looked around, then took the seat Thomas had slept in. She drew a half-completed embroidery from beneath one arm, then waggled her fingers to let him know he was of no more interest to her.

At the foot of the stairs, Thomas found Lady Margaret waiting for him.

"Are they in the tower?" he asked.

"They are with the Prince in the Council chamber. You are to join them there."

The Council chamber was across the courtyard and Thomas tried to ease some of the stiffness from his limbs as he crossed it. A guard stood at the entrance but nodded him through. The room was large, tapestries depicting hunting scenes and battles covering most of the walls. Prince Arthur sat at the head of a long table with Sir Richard on one side and Gruffydd on the other.

Gruffydd rose and approached Thomas. "Arthur heard about Pip and wants to know how she is. Do you know yet, Tom?"

"She is better than last night but has some way to go."

"Then tell him that. But also tell him you are the best man to heal her. He has heard of your reputation, as have we all, but none have seen proof of it yet. John Argentine is champing at the bit to examine her."

"I wager he is. Make sure he goes nowhere near or he will bleed her, and she has lost enough of that commodity already."

"We will do what we can. Now come and tell Arthur she is going to be well, and then we need to talk."

"The Prince also?"

"He might be young, but he knows his responsibilities." Gruffydd met Thomas's gaze. "Hugh Clement has already sent a message. He claims you are responsible for the murder of another two of his men last night." Gruffydd shook his head. "I don't know how you manage it, Tom; I really don't. Trouble follows you around like the devil's tail."

"I thought I had left such behind me, but you are right, trouble has found me again. Would you expect me to turn away from it?"

"You would lose all my respect if you did. Now come and tell Arthur what he wants to hear."

When Thomas finished his report on Philippa, he saw that Prince Arthur wanted to rise and visit her at once, but the boy also knew protocol would not sanction such action. Instead, he sat back and allowed Sir Richard Pole to move matters on.

"Pip was to be your witness today, was she not?" said Sir Richard.

"She was, and may still be once she wakes. It was her body that was damaged, not her mind. What is this about Hugh Clement accusing me again?"

"How did Pip get her injuries?" asked Gruffydd.

"Do you need to know that now?" Thomas looked at Prince Arthur. Gruffydd was right. The boy was young, but his expression showed he understood what was going on in Ludlow and the district around.

"Hugh Clement has made an accusation against you, Sir Thomas," said Prince Arthur. "Sir Gruffydd vouches for your good name and assures me Pip will do the same once she can. But we must take all such accusations seriously. How would it look if I took no action? If I failed to question an accused man simply because he is part of my retinue?"

"It would look as if you were as corrupt as my accuser." Thomas saw a spark of annoyance in the Prince's eyes, pleased by it. Arthur was no man of straw. "So I will tell you what happened and then you can question me. Is that acceptable?"

Once again, Arthur impressed Thomas because he did not look to either right or left for advice or confirmation before saying, "Tell us everything then, Thomas. Will the telling take long? Do we need to send for food? It is almost noon."

It surprised Thomas he had slept so long.

"It will not take long, Your Grace." Thomas waited for a nod from the Prince. "Philippa was not in our room when I returned yesterday evening. The guards at the gate told me she had a visitor and went away with the caller willingly enough. They claim the visitor was a monk, but I suspect he was no brother of Wigmore Abbey but one of those who tortured her. I suspect the man was called Rowland, because Pip knew the other and would not have gone with him. He was one of those who attacked us on the Lemster road. Oswyn ap Cadwallader, who accused me of the murder of his companion, as you are already aware of."

"Are you sure the monk who called for her was a deceit?" asked Sir Richard. "Or might he have, in fact, been one of Wigmore's brothers?"

"There is a great deal I do not know yet, Sir Richard, but I cannot see how one of the brethren would have any involvement in the capture and torture of a woman. I will have to question Pip to discover what really happened, and who she thought she was going with."

"You need to be gentle with her," said Sir Richard. "And I would suggest you have one of us present. Are you sure Pip cannot come here now to set matters straight, both in this and the other accusation against you?"

"Perhaps we should send for your wife. She has seen the damage done to Pip and will tell you I cannot move her. And then perhaps I can tell you what I did when I found her in such a state. After that, we have to discuss what action to take against Hugh Clement, for it must be him behind this attack on one of our own."

Sir Richard stared at Thomas with cold eyes. Before he could respond, Prince Arthur intervened, once again showing a preternatural gift for diplomacy. It made Thomas believe the boy would grow into a great king.

"I believe Thomas's suggestion is sound, Sir Richard. Let us hear about Pip's injuries from your wife, if we may."

"I will send for Lady Margaret," said Gruffydd as he rose to his feet and went to the door.

Sir Richard continued to stare at Thomas, his mouth set firm.

"Will Pip recover, Thomas?" asked Arthur.

"She will if I have anything to do with it. Today and tomorrow will be critical, but I believe there are already signs she will walk again."

"What did these men do to her?"

"I will tell you everything, Your Grace, once Lady Margaret confirms what I have said."

Gruffydd returned and retook his seat. "I have sent for her, and also asked for ale and wine to be brought, as well as a little food. I am starving, and Thomas will not have eaten since yesterday. We cannot accuse a man whose belly rumbles." He laughed, and Arthur joined in.

"May I ask you something else, Thomas?" Arthur leaned forward in his chair. He was as tall as Sir Richard, almost as tall as Gruffydd, but of slighter build.

"If it does not concern the immediate matter, of course you may, Your Grace. I am at your command."

"Is that true? In that case, tell me about my bride-to-be. I saw the painting of her you brought father, and I believe you when you say she is beautiful, but there is more to a woman than mere beauty, is there not?" Arthur waited until Thomas nodded. "So what I want to know about is her character. Is she kind? Is she intelligent? Is she brave?"

Once more the Prince impressed Thomas. Many men would look no further than a pretty face, a nubile body, and good child-bearing hips.

"She is all of those things, Your Grace. I have known Catherine since birth and she has grown into an admirable woman, firm in her belief in God and strong in her protection of her country and friends."

"Do you count yourself among those friends? You call her Catherine, not Princess Catherine of Aragon, as even a Duke of Granada should refer to her."

"I believe we are friends, yes. It is one reason Isabel asked me to return to England. Catherine will be safe under your protection, Your Grace, but her mother trusts me to ensure no harm ever comes to her."

"I hope you can make a better fist of it than you have in protecting Pip," said Sir Richard.

Prince Arthur ignored the comment. "You also call the Queen of Castile by name. Are you going to call me Arthur next week?" The boy's smile softened his question.

"I would never do so unless invited, Your Grace."

Sir Richard made a huffing sound, but Gruffydd laughed just as their ale, wine and food arrived, together with Lady Margaret following behind.

Thomas rose. "Has Pip woken yet?"

Lady Margaret gave a shake of her head. "She has stirred but remains asleep. I promise I will call you as soon as she does. Now, what do you all want of me? We have visitors, and I need to find out why they are here and whether I should admit them."

"Thomas says these men he killed tortured Pip, and you have seen her wounds."

"She looks like a pin-cushion," said Lady Margaret. "It is no doubt why she sleeps so deeply, so her body may start to heal." She glanced in Thomas's direction. "Whatever Thomas tells you, I can assure you he had nothing to do with her injuries, other than doing all in his power to heal her. Is there anything else?" She waited impatiently, a tremor running through her.

"No, go see to your visitors."

After she left Sir Richard said, "All right then, Thomas, tell us what happened, and whether you killed two men last night."

So he did.

All three listened without interruption, though the tale did not take long.

When he finished, Thomas reached for a mug of ale and drained most of it in one swallow. There was bread and cheese, slices of meat that looked like goose, as well as small pots of various sauces.

"This Oswyn ap Cadwallader is the same man you allowed to ride away with his life?" asked Gruffydd.

"He is."

"Did Pip have anything to do with that act of mercy?"

"She was not there when I made the decision, so no. I grow tired of killing. I try never to kill a man who does not deserve to die or is not intending to kill me or those I love."

"Not so tired you did not add two more to your tally last night," said Sir Richard.

Thomas glanced at Prince Arthur, who was listening intently. He sipped at his ale but had weakened it with water from a jug. Thomas liked the way the boy listened to everything in silence until he had a contribution to make.

"You have heard what they did to Pip, and Lady Margaret did not see the worst of her injuries. Those men would have killed her. They would have killed me. I had no choice. None."

"So you say." Sir Richard continued to hold his suspicions close, unwilling to let them go yet.

"Did Hugh Clement come here himself to make his complaint?" asked Thomas.

"He sent his man, Daniel Lupton."

"And his accusation is what?"

"That you killed both men in cold blood and then burned their bodies by setting fire to the cottage."

"There was no fire when I carried Pip away. I have a witness to that, though you may not be willing to take the word of Jack Pook."

Gruffydd laughed. "Richard may not, but I would. If he vouches for what he saw I would be minded to take his word on it."

"I could not have brought Pip back without his help. I intend to reward him as soon as I can."

Gruffydd offered another laugh, louder than the first. "Just leave your purse open on the table and turn your back for a second. Jack will help himself to his own reward." Gruffydd's face was serious when he turned to Sir Richard. "Do we accept Tom's word or that of Hugh Clement?"

"Thomas's, of course." It was Prince Arthur who spoke, but Sir Richard inclined his head in agreement.

"The question is," said Sir Richard, "what do we do

about Hugh Clement? He is getting beyond himself when he has an innocent woman tortured, but he also has powerful followers in the area and even beyond. We cannot strip him of his powers without sparking a rebellion."

There was a fact all three facing Thomas had missed, or failed to mention, because it implicated one of their own. Why had Philippa Gale gone with the monk last night? And what information were Oswyn and Rowland attempting to extract from her through torture? They were questions Thomas intended to find answers to as soon as Philippa was well enough to be questioned.

Thomas rose. "I would like to check on Pip, Your Grace."

"Go, Thomas," said Prince Arthur. "And my thanks for your service. I believe you are a man we can trust."

As Thomas emerged into the courtyard, fully intending to go to Philippa, he stopped dead in his tracks. A group of dusty travellers stood around three carts. Lady Margaret was talking to their leader, a tall man of unnatural beauty.

And then a smaller figure detached itself from the group and ran as fast as her feet would carry her to careen into Thomas, almost knocking him from his feet. His daughter Amal clung to him, kissing his face.

"Pa!"

TWENTY-FOUR

Lady Margaret Pole drew Thomas to one side. "They cannot stay here." Thomas's family and friends were gathered around the three carts as if for protection. "There is no room, for a start, never mind the fact they are all strangers."

"Not to me," Thomas said. "But I agree they are strangers in this land. I need to see Pip, and then will come down and sort arrangements out. Two of the women need to come with me if allowed. I will vouch for their good behaviour."

"Who is the girl who flung herself at you?"

"My daughter, Amal."

Lady Margaret looked at Thomas. "But she is... her skin is so..."

"Her mother was a Moor. Amal is lighter-skinned than Lubna, but could be her twin. It hurts my heart every time I look at her, but also fills me with joy."

"And the giant of a man with the blonde hair?"

"My son, Will."

"I see. Not from the same mother?"

"I will regale you with my family history later if you wish, Lady Margaret. Right now Pip needs me, and I need Amal and Belia's help."

For a moment Thomas thought Lady Margaret might refuse him, then she offered a nod. "Tell the others they can stay within the outer bailey, but not the inner."

Thomas walked across to the group. He touched Amal's sweet face, then embraced his son. Will returned the hug, almost breaking Thomas's ribs. He lifted his father off his feet and swung him around as if he was a child. Then Thomas went to Belia and kissed her on the mouth, the scent of her so familiar it hurt. He touched the heads of Belia and Jorge's children, three of them now, including the girl Jorge had so wanted. Only then did he turn to the last figure.

Jorge faced Thomas, waiting. For what, Thomas did not know. It had been two months since he had last seen these people, but it seemed far longer. Something more than time held him back. This was his family, blood or not. The man standing in front of him was closer than a brother.

"You did well," Thomas said.

Jorge smiled, and the smile broke Thomas's shackles and he embraced the man. They held to each other for a long time, then Jorge gripped Thomas's face in his hands and stared into his eyes.

"God's teeth, Thomas, but you look awful!"

Then he kissed him on the mouth.

"I need to steal Belia from you for a while. I want Amal with me, too. You are to wait beyond the castle moat, but I suggest you do not go into town yet. I need to talk to you about what is going on here."

"Again, Thomas?" said Jorge.

"It is not of my choosing."

"It never is, but that does not stop trouble finding you like flies find carrion. You are fortunate we are here to save you from yourself. Take my wife and your daughter if you must. I will try for patience, but you know it is not something that comes easily to me."

"Does anything?" Thomas moved away. He exchanged a few words with Belia, asking for the box his instruments were in. When she pointed it out, he lifted it from one of the carts.

"You might need your herbs if they have survived the journey."

"They have," said Belia. They spoke in Arabic, as they would at home in Granada, but Thomas knew that would have to change. He had tutored each of them in English, but it came hard to some. Perhaps hearing the strange tongue all around would make it easier.

Amal trotted ahead as they ascended the staircase. Thomas could barely take his eyes off her. She was exquisite, growing day by day into a woman of rare beauty. She dressed strangely for England, as did Belia. Thomas did not want that to change, but suspected it might have to. They would stand out too much if they continued to dress in the Moorish fashion. Not in London, perhaps, where much of the diaspora of the Spanish war had fled to, as well as exiles from other lands. But here in Ludlow, they would draw attention for the wrong reasons. Thomas knew how small-minded people in the area could be. At least he had known it once and doubted they had changed much.

Belia said nothing when they entered Thomas's room and she saw a woman on the bed, but she did raise an eyebrow. Amal went to Philippa and leaned over her. She sniffed, breathing in her scent, then turned to her father.

"Who is she, Pa?"

"Her name is Philippa Gale, and she and I were lovers." As the words came, he noted the use of the past tense and wondered if he spoke the truth or not.

Amal only nodded her acceptance.

"What is wrong with her?" asked Belia.

"Men tortured her last night, and she damaged her spine when I fought them. I gave her a draft of poppy and hashish to make her sleep, but it will wear off soon."

Belia went to the bed and touched a corner of the blanket. When she glanced at Thomas and he nodded, she drew the blanket down to reveal Philippa's pale skin, punctured by dozens of knife wounds.

"Did you punish whoever did this?" she asked.

"They are dead now." Thomas glanced at Amal to see her reaction, but she was studying Philippa intently and had most likely not heard.

"The wounds are many, but not dangerous. I take it you washed her well?"

"Of course."

"I have herbs and lotions I can use to ensure putrefaction does not take hold, but you know how to do that as well as me."

"I don't yet know where to source the herbs," Thomas said, though he realised he did. Prior Bernard would know every herb, root and fungus for miles around. It was what he used to do, and Thomas doubted the man would have forgotten the knowledge he once possessed. "Help me turn Pip over, I need you to see what else they did to her."

"Pip, is it?"

"It is what everyone calls her. Short for—"

"I am not stupid, Thomas."

"I know you are not. I apologise. Ami, help us turn her over."

His daughter stood beside Belia on the other side of the bed from Thomas and between them they rolled Philippa onto her front. She groaned as they did so, and Thomas knew she might wake at any moment.

"Ah, I see," said Belia.

Amal reached out and ran her fingers across the bruise at the base of Philippa's spine. It had spread overnight and turned darker.

"Is her back damaged?" asked Amal. Belia was a wonder with herbs, but Amal knew more about the internal workings of the human body. She had sat on Thomas's knee since she was a two-year-old as he showed her the books and drawings he possessed, continued to do so when he imparted his own knowledge to her.

"That I don't yet know. Her right leg seems to be fine, but she could feel nothing in her left last night. This morning there was a little reaction, so I am hopeful."

"If her spine is badly damaged there is little we can do," said Amal.

"I agree, but we don't know that yet. When she wakes, I want to examine her again. I need you both here with me. If she is further improved, a little manipulation might be useful, and you know how to do that, Ami."

"I do, Pa, but so do you. Even Will knows a bit, but he is more likely to snap her spine as fix it."

"Yes, like as not." All the months of missing these people seemed to melt away in a moment. It was as if they had never parted, and he did not want them to separate ever again. Even as the thought came to him, he knew he could not hold on to his children forever. Will was handsome and strong. He had eighteen years and, Thomas knew, had already lain with women. Soon he would find the one he was looking for and marry. They would set up their own household, and before too long Amal would be next. She was younger, but her knowledge and experience were prodigious. When that day came, Thomas knew what he would do. Once everyone was settled, once Catherine was Queen of England sitting alongside King Arthur, he would make the journey south, back to Spain. To Granada. He would spend whatever days were left to him in the city he loved above all others.

Philippa mumbled and tried to turn over. Before Thomas could reach her, Amal laid her hands on Philippa's shoulders and pressed her back to the mattress.

"You have been hurt," she said, speaking in accented English. "I am Thomas's daughter, Amal, and I am going to help you."

"Where is Tom?"

"I am here." Thomas moved until he was in her line of sight. "These two women are going to care for you while I deal with the men who did this to you."

Philippa tried to turn again, but Amal was stronger than she looked.

"You already dealt with them. You killed both last night."

Thomas saw Belia glance at him, but her face showed no expression. They knew each other too well for the news to come as a surprise.

"You know who I mean."

"He will kill you, Tom. I know he will."

Now was not the right time, but Thomas asked anyway. "How well do you know Hugh Clement, Pip? The guards said you went with a monk from Wigmore Abbey, but he was no monk, was he? Was it Hugh Clement in disguise, or someone else?"

"Not now," Philippa said into the pillow. "I hurt, and my leg aches."

Thomas put his questions aside with reluctance. A better time would come, once Philippa recovered.

"Which leg?"

"Both of them!"

Thomas went to the small table and brought back a blade. He did the same as he had the night before, ran the blunt edge along the back of Philippa's right leg, then repeated it on the left.

"Tell me what you feel."

"You touched me. Both legs. But I felt it more on..." she had to think a moment, then reached down and tapped the right leg, "... this one."

Thomas turned to Belia. "I want you to make up a fresh tincture of poppy and hashish and give it to her once Amal has manipulated her back." He turned to his daughter. "You know exactly what to do?"

"Apply pressure, but if I feel any movement, ease off. Keep on massaging the bruise until the patient feels the pain lessen, or stop if it grows worse. Where do I send a message if I need you, Pa?"

"You will not need me, but if you do, send it through the woman who met you outside. Her name is Lady Margaret Pole."

Amal nodded. "And the name of my patient?"

"Philippa Gale, but you can call her Pip. Everyone else does. You will need to use English with her. She claims a little Spanish, but it is meagre at best."

"I will use English, Pa. I need all the practice I can get. It is a coarse language, is it not?"

"You get used to it." And then, because Thomas knew Belia would have struggled to understand them, switched to Arabic to repeat the instructions before leaving them to work.

Thomas found Jorge and Will at the base of Mortimer's Tower. Jorge was playing with his children, some game of tag that involved a great deal of running, tumbling, and screams of delight. Will sat on the back of a cart and watched, a smile on his face. A third figure stood beside one of the other carts. Prince Arthur. He was alone, with no guards nearby, and Thomas walked across to him.

"I heard the cries of the children and came out to see what all the fun was about. I like your friend, by the way, and would never have taken him for a eunuch had he not told me." Prince Arthur's eyes caught Thomas's. "He also

247

told me how he came to be made a eunuch and who did it."

"How long have you been out here, Your Grace? A month?"

Arthur laughed. "Oh, a quarter hour, no more. Jorge can impart a great deal of information in a short time. Though being honest with you, Thomas, it was your son imparted most of it. He translated as Jorge spoke. He claims his English is improving but is not yet good enough for the explanations he gave."

"Do not take everything Jorge says at face value, Your Grace."

"He tells me he is your best friend."

"Occasionally he tells the truth."

"His children are full of mischief, are they not?"

"They take after their father."

"Is that right?" The Prince's eyes caught Thomas's again, and he wondered if Jorge had also communicated another truth to him. That Thomas had lain with Belia to set the seed for each child, but that Jorge was their father. How else could a eunuch have such wonderful children?

"I like your son, too," said Prince Arthur. "He is uncommonly tall, is he not? And possesses the broadest shoulders of any man I have ever met."

"His grandfather is taller and broader, but you are right, Your Grace."

"I will speak with Lady Margaret Pole and see if she can find accommodation for them within the castle. I would enjoy hearing about their journey. About Spain, too. Will tells me he knows Catherine well."

"They grew up together, Your Grace. They are like brother and sister."

"Then when we marry, your son will be, what, a brother to me?" The Prince laughed and shook his head.

"If they were brother and sister, but they are not. Merely as good as."

"You are close to Queen Isabel of Castile, are you not?"

"I have been, Your Grace, but less so of late. She has much on her mind with the discoveries across the great water."

"I would like to hear more of those as well. Is it not interesting that those lands lay undiscovered for centuries, but one voyage and now all the nations of Europe attempt to lay claim to territories. England must do the same. Now we are to be allied with Spain we will become an indomitable force."

"True words, Your Grace."

"I will speak with Richard Pole about you, Thomas. It is clear to me any accusation raised against you is false. You saved Pip. You are healing her." The Prince smiled. "John Argentine does not approve of your methods, but has been told you come highly recommended and not to interfere. How is Pip?"

"A little better."

"Good. Is this the end of the matter, do you think? Was Pip kidnapped by those men for some... unseemly purpose... but is safe now?"

"I trust it is the end of it, Your Grace."

"Good," said Arthur again, and walked back towards the inner courtyard.

"Is that who Cat is going to marry?" asked Will once Arthur had left.

"If he told you his name, which I am sure he did, then you know it is."

"He seems all right," said Will, making Thomas laugh. "He said you had got yourself into some sort of trouble again, Pa."

Will's face showed only amusement. He was no stranger to trouble himself. There were times Thomas believed his son was too much like his grandfather, Olaf Torvaldsson, who relished any fight as long as it was fair.

"Well?" asked Will, when Thomas said nothing. He was watching Jorge and the children, the eldest Jahan barely a child anymore at fourteen years of age.

"Yes, I have found trouble again." He smiled. "It would have been good to have Usaden with us, but I expect he will be in Africa by now. Or has crossed the great water. He told me he likes the idea of a clean land without corruption."

Will raised two fingers to his mouth and emitted a piercing whistle. When Thomas looked up he saw a man trotting towards them. The guards moved to intercept him, but the man swerved a little to one side, a little more to the other, and continued past them. Wiry, with nut-brown skin, he dressed in black with a wrap of dark cloth around his long hair.

The man stopped in front of Thomas and nodded a greeting.

"Pa's found trouble," said Will in Arabic, and the man grinned.

"Go-od," he said in heavily accented English. "Usaden is bored."

And then a black streak ran through the gate, jumping clean over the arms of a guard. Eight feet from Thomas, the dog leapt into the air so he had to catch him or be bowled over. The dog wriggled in joy, its tail drawing wild circles.

"Hello, Kin," Thomas said, grinning. The family was complete.

TWENTY-FIVE

Thomas stood in dappled shade on the side of the wooded hill overlooking Hugh Clement's manor house. Will, Jorge and Usaden stood beside him. Jorge's children were in the care of Agnes, who was delighted to amuse them. When Thomas left, they were all trying their hand at making bread rolls. He suspected the bakery might sell some strangely shaped ones that day.

The air was chill with a sheen of frost still lurking in shaded hollows as the three made their way along the side of the hill so as not to be seen. When they came to the far side of the wood and could look down on the manor house, Usaden wrapped his robe more tightly around himself, but Will seemed unconcerned. Perhaps, Thomas thought, he had inherited the constitution of his Norse grandfather.

"It looks peaceful enough at the moment," said Will, perhaps a hint of disappointment in his voice. "Tell me again what the man is planning."

"Hugh Clement wants to enrich himself at the cost of

the townsfolk. I suspect he will not content himself with only Ludlow unless someone stops him. The man is setting up an extortion scheme, demanding a small sum each month in return for protection—except the protection is from his men. They do not ask for enough to make the traders refuse, but add up all the small amounts and it becomes a large sum. A very large sum indeed."

"How many men does he have?" asked Usaden.

"It is difficult to say with any certainty. Forty, at least. They come and go, but from this distance it is impossible to pick out individuals. I also hear he is recruiting fighting men from Wales. What they are for I do not know, unless he feels in need of their protection."

As if on cue, five men rode out on horseback from the stables, heading towards town.

"What about the castle?" asked Usaden. "There are soldiers there. I saw them. Do they know what is going on?"

"The two men closest to Prince Arthur do, as does the Prince himself. They believed me when I told them about Hugh Clement, but are unwilling to commit their forces until he does something they can call him out on. At the moment all his men are doing is going around the traders and telling them what they will pay."

"Surely the attack on your new lover is more than enough to act on," said Jorge.

"It might be, yes. Everyone likes Pip, so what they did to her could be just what is needed. Except Hugh Clement denies all knowledge of it and accuses me of murder and burning his cottage down. No doubt he also claims it is me who tortured Pip."

"Does anyone believe his lies?" asked Will.

"Prince Arthur's closest advisors have to be seen to follow the law. Hugh Clement has made an accusation and they must investigate it. Gruffydd and Sir Richard believe me innocent, but there is no proof as yet."

"You appear to have made a place for yourself among these people," said Jorge with a smile. "I hope you don't forget your old friends."

"As if they would let me."

"Do you have any kind of plan? Or is this going to be the usual chaos until you come up with something?"

"I don't know enough yet to have a plan. And there is the matter of Pip. She went off with one man willingly. I have not wanted to question her while she is in pain, but will have to once she recovers. I need to know what her involvement is, if any. Perhaps you can advise me on the best approach, because it will not be easy."

Jorge only laughed.

"There is a man watching us," said Usaden.

Thomas looked around, but the woods appeared to be peaceful, deserted other than for themselves. They had seen rabbits and birds as they passed through, signs of boar and deer, but no hint of men. He could not see one now, however hard he looked.

"Where?"

"Over there," said Usaden, with a slight inclination of his head. "I would point him out but he would see me and likely run to his master."

Thomas narrowed his eyes. "I still see nothing."

"He is difficult to make out, I agree. If I run at him he

will run in turn, and then you will see him even with your poor eyes."

"There is nothing wrong with my eyes."

"Except you cannot see the man."

"I can," said Will. "Long grey hair and beard, thin and dressed like someone down on their luck?"

"That will be him," said Usaden. "So, Thomas, do I run at him or not?"

Thomas smiled. "That sounds like Jack Pook. If so, he is on our side. I think."

"It would be better if you were sure," said Jorge.

"Jack is on Jack's side, I expect, but I knew his sister once, so he considers me some kind of friend."

Jorge stared at Thomas, his eyes wide. "*Knew?*"

"Yes, knew." Thomas waved an arm in the general direction Usaden had nodded in. He saw a figure rise to its full height of five-and-a-half feet and come towards them. Jack Pook had two coneys slung from his belt and used the cherry stick even though he had no need of it. Thomas suspected it provided good camouflage.

He stopped a few paces away because he knew Thomas, but not the others.

He nodded. "Tom. Who are your friends? They are friends, I reckon, from the way you were talking. You were making too much noise even if I did not understand a single word. Gabble-gabble-gabble is all I got."

"We were speaking Arabic," Thomas said, using English now.

"Is that similar to Welsh? It didn't sound much like it."

Jack's eyes took in Usaden first, because Thomas knew he would recognise him as a kindred spirit. They were of similar height and build, and Thomas knew Jack could be fast when he needed to be. His attention turned to Jorge and he scanned him from head to foot. A faint frown touched his brow. Jack was sharp and recognised something strange about Jorge, but could not place what it was. Finally, he examined Will.

"He's a big one, ain't he? I'm glad he's with you, Tom. And that other one."

"What about me?" asked Jorge. "Do I not look dangerous?"

"Not as dangerous as these other two, no. I suspect you might be more dangerous to me if I had a pair of dugs."

Jorge smiled. "What are dugs, Thomas?"

Thomas put his hands to his chest in explanation, and Jorge laughed.

"If you had those," he said to Jack, "pretty as you are, I would have to ask you to shave first."

Jack laughed, a soft sound even though he was clearly amused. Jack did everything softly. It was how he could pass through the landscape unnoticed.

"Have you been watching the house?" Thomas asked.

"Getting my supper, is all." Jack patted the two coneys at his belt. "But I might have glanced that way once or twice. As a favour to you and to Bel. She told me if you were interested in something, I might be as well. She also told me about the men who came to the brickworks and what they wanted. So it's family business now. How is your woman, Tom?"

"A little better."

"Are you going to punish them?"

256

"That is a consideration."

"You might need a few more with you if you intend to do that," said Jack. "There have been men coming in from Wales. They are not here yet but camped out in the woods and valleys of the Teme west of here. Probably reminds them of home out that way. So yes, I reckon you will need more men, even if you have got this big one with you."

"The big one is my son, Will. The pretty one is Jorge, and the dangerous one is Usaden."

Jack examined Will again, his head cocked to one side. "I expect he does look a little like you now you mention it. I take it none of the others are yours, though."

"They are not. Are these Welshmen anything to do with Hugh Clement or here for something else?"

"Well, the Welsh have no love for Arthur, despite him being their prince. There have been raids in the past and this might be nothing more than the same, but I have seen a few of them around the manor house, so I reckon Hugh Clement has brought them here for a purpose."

"Have you been out here all night?"

"I like these woods," said Jack, as if that was the only explanation needed. "They can feed a man and there is the river down there if he needs to drink. Not ale, but good clean water, which is more than you can say for most sources. Are you staying here?"

"I have to get back to the Castle and check on Pip." Thomas hesitated, then decided that the risk of saying more might be worth it. "She went willingly to that cottage, Jack. Have you seen her hanging around Clement's manor house before?"

"Not so I've noticed, no. And I think I would notice.

She's a looker, ain't she? Half the men in Ludlow would be jealous if they knew you were tupping her, Tom. Maybe that's what this is all about. A jealous lover who doesn't like being passed over. Or someone who wishes they were her lover."

"It is a possibility, but I think not. But something does not sit right with what happened. Pip lied to me, but about how much I need to know before I decide what to do."

"Some women lie, you know that. You should have stayed with Bel, Tom. Her heart is good and true. But if Pip told you she went straight to that cottage then that was a lie too."

Thomas stared at Jack, waiting for more. When nothing came he said, "Did you see what happened? I know you were there."

"What did she tell you?"

"That a monk called for her and she went with him. I have had no chance to question her more about what happened."

"There was a monk." Jack looked off into the trees, no doubt seeing more there than Thomas could. "I was down at the river setting nets when I heard voices. A man and woman talking. The truth is there was a monk—or at least someone dressed as a monk. The other was Pip. They entered Hugh Clement's house and I heard no more, not until later. A quarter hour passed and I'd set my nets by then when the monk appeared again, alone this time. He went to the stables for his horse and rode off to the west."

"To Wigmore?"

"More than likely."

"And Pip?"

"Another quarter hour passed before she came out. Hugh was with her, together with Daniel Lupton and two other men. They spoke for a while but I couldn't hear what was said, but it all seemed friendly enough. Then Pip embraced Hugh and set off with the two men and Daniel."

"There were only two men in the cottage when I got there."

"Because Daniel Lupton came back before many minutes had passed. The next thing I know is when they came out and caught me, and then you came along."

Thomas did not know if Jack Pook's words made what happened any clearer, but he was certain the man spoke the truth. It would be interesting to compare it with what Philippa claimed when he had a chance to question her.

"Are you coming back to the castle with us?"

"I might find a soft spot here and rest my eyes for a moment or two." Jack nodded at each of them. "It's good to meet your folks, Tom, and I'm glad we're on the same side. Not sure I could take on either of those two if it came to a fight."

"Then let us not fight," Thomas said.

"I saw a lanky dog over that way." Jack inclined his head, barely a movement. "Is he with you, too?"

"His name is Kin. He is getting old now, but when pushed he fights with us."

Thomas watched Jack move away and disappear as if the woods swallowed him whole.

"I expect he was too polite to include me in the list of those he did not want to fight," said Jorge.

"No doubt," Thomas said with a smile.

"Do we need to watch that house day and night?" asked Usaden.

"Jack will do it for us. No better man for the job, and he knows how to find me. I suspect he catches those rabbits mostly for show. He'd rather they chase him off as a poacher than a spy."

"I take it this sister of his you used to know is a little better looking?" asked Jorge.

"She is." Thomas turned and started up the slope back to town. "You have all seen the house, which is all we need for now." He glanced at Jorge as he fell into step beside him. "And you are right, we need to talk about a plan."

"Do they ever ride out in larger numbers?" asked Will. "We could pick off groups of five easily enough."

"If we do, then they will come out together."

"But there will be five or ten less of them before that happens." Will and Usaden moved across the ground silently. Unlike Jorge, who seemed to find every leaf and twig there was.

"I will leave the planning up to the three of you," said Usaden. "Tell me what I need to do once you decide."

"I still have to find somewhere for you to stay tonight," Thomas said. "I have an idea for tomorrow that might prove more permanent."

When Thomas entered the room he shared with Philippa he found her with Amal, who was massaging the dark bruise on her back.

Amal raised a finger to her lips and came across to him. "She fell asleep, so the pain must be less. Belia left me a potion of poppy and hashish, but she has not needed it yet."

"Have you been massaging her all this time?"

"Apart from when she needed to use the privy. You are fortunate to have one attached to the room. It is almost like Andalusia, is it not?"

"Did you have to carry her?"

Amal shook her head. "She walked there herself with a little help, then insisted I leave her alone, but called me to help her back to the bed. She is exquisite."

Thomas examined his daughter's face for some sign of disapproval, but found none.

"Yes, she is."

"Where did you go?"

"I had something to do, and now I have something else to do. There are two men I need to speak with, but first I have to find somewhere you can all sleep tonight."

"We have slept beside the cart since coming to this land," said Amal. "If need be we can do so again, but I admit the nights are growing colder."

"I would like you to sleep in a proper bed if I can arrange it." Thomas embraced his daughter, catching the scent of the oils she had rubbed into Philippa's skin. "Leave Pip to sleep while she can. Come with me, I want you to meet someone."

The others were waiting for them in the outer court-yard. Thomas led them through town to Agnes's bakery to pick up Jorge's children, who appeared reluctant to leave. Agnes was full of questions, wanting to know who everyone was. Amal enchanted her, and Will impressed, but there was little time to talk before they left again.

The alley to the Rose and Crown was narrow, so their progress was halting as people coming the other way had to press themselves into doorways as the carts filled almost the full width. One man berated Thomas, telling him they should have come into town by Ludford Bridge so as not to cause danger to the good citizens. Thomas thanked him through gritted teeth and went on.

He entered the inn with Jorge, knowing he could charm any woman when he set his mind to it, but good-wife Constance Sparrow informed them she had only two small rooms available, even after Jorge had used his best smile on her.

"It is always the same when the Prince is in residence. People come seeking influence. Not that it does them much good because he leaves all such business to Sir Richard Pole and his wife, and he is a hard man even if she is not a hard woman. How many are you? I might manage something."

Thomas knew he had been away from the others too long when he had to count their number in his head.

"Nine in total. Four are children under the age of four-teen years, so they could share one bed. Then there are Jorge and Belia, my son Will, daughter Amal, and Usaden. So we would need four rooms, possibly five."

"Your friends have some funny names, don't they?"

"Not where we come from."

"Are they foreign?"

"They are."

"I don't hold with those who are unwelcoming to

people who flee to England from beyond our shores, but it does not make rooms magically available. I am sorry, Thomas. Not even for you or your friend there." Constance's gaze drifted towards Jorge, to be captured. She took a breath before letting it go in a long sigh. "But I might find a little space for you, sir. Do you have a name?"

"I am Jorge Olmos, my sweet, and I hope my name is not too foreign to you." He took her hand and kissed the back, bringing a flush to her cheeks. "And any small crevice you could find for me would be most welcome. My wife would need to be accommodated as well, of course."

"You are married?"

"As good as," said Jorge.

His response brought another sigh. "Come back later and I will see what I can do. There are a couple of gentlemen who told me they may leave before evening, depending how their business goes, but I can make no promise."

"I am sure whatever you manage will be most suitable, sweet lady." Jorge kissed her hand again and walked out with Thomas. "So," he said once they were back in the yard with the others, "where are we going to sleep tonight?"

"I thought you and Belia were sharing the goodwife's chamber. And she has a small room for the children. Will and Usaden might have to sleep under the stars again." Thomas cast his gaze heavenward. "Though it looks like it is going to rain before morning."

"You warned me about the weather in England," said

Jorge, "but I did not believe it could be as bad as you claimed. Now I know it is not—it is worse."

"You have not experienced winter yet."

"Do you mean this is not winter?"

"I will go into the woods again and see if I can find this Jack Pook," said Usaden. "He can feed me rabbit and tell me what he knows about the men in the house we were watching."

"You will struggle to understand a word Jack says, his accent is so broad," Thomas said.

"Then I will go with Usaden," said Will. "The cold does not bother me, and I can translate between them. Besides, I want to watch the house as well."

Thomas considered telling Will to take care, but knew the words would be both unnecessary and unwelcome. His son had eighteen years and was a man now. Stronger than almost any other man and, thanks to Usaden's years of training, more skilled than any other man. Thomas stood beside Jorge and watched Will walk away, a giant beside the much shorter Usaden, but both equally deadly.

TWENTY-SIX

The afternoon was half gone before Thomas and Jorge crossed a low rise and Lemster appeared ahead.

"Is that where we are going?" Jorge nodded towards a tower that rose above all other buildings in town, even the church spires that dotted the landscape. Every hamlet and group of houses wanted their own place of worship.

"I hope Bernard is there."

"You said he was a Prior. Does that mean he is an important man?"

"Not as important as an Abbot or an Earl, and nowhere near as important as a Prince, but yes, important enough in Lemster. People go to him when they need help, to report crimes and murders, to be fed if they cannot feed themselves. Bernard is more than his position. He has a sense about him that makes people trust him."

"Like you," said Jorge, causing Thomas to glance across to see if he was joking, only to discover he was not.

On arrival at the Priory, they discovered Prior

Bernard was in a meeting with several local business owners, but would be informed they were waiting to see him. The man who took the message returned within moments to tell them the Prior wanted them to come at once.

When Thomas entered the wide room it brought back unwelcome memories. It was the chamber where he had once been judged for murder and found wanting, for lack of anyone to speak for him. Even his father had refused. Had plague not come to Lemster, Thomas might well have hung, innocent or not.

Prior Bernard sat at the head of a long table, four men two to a side. The Prior waved Thomas forward before his eyes went to Jorge.

"Who is your companion, Thomas? A stranger to me, and England too, I wager."

"I did not think monks wagered, but you are right. His name is Jorge Olmos and he is a Spaniard, though such a simple designation does him little favour. Jorge is that and much more. He is my closest companion."

"Then welcome, Jorge Olmos. Any friend of Thomas Berrington is a friend of this Priory and its Prior."

Thomas noticed one of the man's eyes widen at mention of his name but did not know who he was. He had been away so long any of the men could be from families he knew.

"I am glad you came," said Prior Bernard, "for two reasons. I have news of somewhere that might suit you to live, and I welcome your opinion on a matter these gentlemen have brought before me. If you could tell Thomas what you told me, Mr Wodall."

The man looked across the table as Thomas sat, Jorge taking the chair next to his. He was the man who had shown surprise when Prior Bernard spoke his name. Thomas knew the name Wodall, but there was no need to bring up the reasons for that, as the man would no doubt also know of them.

"You tell him," said Wodall. "You know as much as the rest of us. And what Thomas Berrington can do, I don't know. He has not lived in Lemster these last fifty years."

"Forty-seven years," said Prior Bernard. "I value his opinion as a man with no iron in this fire." He turned to Thomas. "Men came to Lemster yesterday to inform every business, alehouse, tavern and inn that they expect a payment from them once a month. Though Wodall here told me they want payment in arrears as the month is over two-thirds gone. These men came to see what I can do to help, but I have informed them this is beyond my remit or ability. They should take their complaint to the Justice of the Peace."

"They will get short shrift there, for I believe Hugh Clement is the man behind the scheme."

"Clement?" said one man. "How can that be? He protects the peace, not threatens it."

"I believe he has ideas above his station." Thomas leaned closer, resting his elbows on the table-top. "How many in Lemster will make a stand? Those of you here, I assume?" Thomas saw two pairs of eyes look away and knew the answer was not what he might have hoped. "How many bonemen came?" he asked.

"Bonemen?" said Wodall. "What are bonemen?"

"They work for Hugh Clement. There are others in

London, and now they have come to Ludlow, and Lemster too, it seems. How many were there?"

"Five," said Wodall. "All armed, all dressed in leather fighting doublets, all wearing green felt hats. They made it clear they will take measures against anyone who refuses. One of them left this at the Star tavern." Wodall reached beneath his jacket and drew something out. He set a small fragment of bone on the table.

"What did the landlord of the Star do to be given that?" Thomas asked.

"He told them to leave. Threatened them with a beating, or worse, if they came back. One of them set it on the counter before he left."

"It is both a symbol and a threat," said Prior Bernard. "Such men are not to be tolerated in a peaceful town." He turned to Thomas. "Are you sure this involves Hugh Clement?"

"As sure as I am of anything. His men attacked me and my companion after I saw you here a week ago. And only two days since they abducted and attacked that same woman."

"Killed her?" asked Prior Bernard.

"Almost, but she will recover. They demand payment from every business in Ludlow, and now here as well. Has anyone heard from anywhere else? Hereford, Gloucester and Worcester would be ripe for such a scheme, and far richer than towns such as Lemster or even Ludlow."

"I will send brothers out to make enquiries," said Prior Bernard. "But it will take several days, and people may not admit the truth. Of all the traders in Lemster it is only these four who have come forward."

"They don't threaten households," said Wodall. "Only traders and farmers, claiming the payment is for a force to protect us from others. But they are the others. They beat some who told them they would not pay, and left more bones. Not badly beaten, not yet, but it is a sign of what will come." Wodall stared at Thomas. "I still don't see what you can do, Berrington."

"Are you any relation to Arthur Wodall?" Thomas asked, meeting the man's stare in kind.

"He was my father. Dead these ten years. But he told me about you when I sat on his knee as a child. Told me what you did."

"I expect he did. Whatever he told you was a lie."

"Not to me, it wasn't. I am still waiting to hear what you intend to do."

"I can stop Clement," Thomas said. "I have stopped worse men, more dangerous men, and I can do it again."

"He can," said Jorge, his voice soft, controlled. "You don't want to cross Thomas, for he has killed more men than I have bedded beautiful women, and that is a great many indeed."

Thomas saw Prior Bernard suppress a smile.

"What are you going to do when those men return?" Thomas's gaze remained on Wodall because he seemed to be their leader.

"Pay them. What else can we do? They are clever, not asking for more than we can afford. It will hurt, but it won't kill us. Though they might if we refuse. So yes, we pay what they ask. I will not put my trust in you stopping them, Berrington. Like as not you will run off, just like you ran from trouble before."

"I am sorry," said Prior Bernard, when only the three of them remained. "His grandfather Arthur Wodall used to bad-mouth you every chance he got, even though you were not here to defend yourself. He went to his grave believing it was you who killed his son."

"And you, Bernard?" Thomas asked. "What do you believe?"

"I believe you are a good man, Tom. Who killed Raulf Wodall I do not know, but I know in my heart it was not you."

"I know who killed him," Thomas said.

Prior Bernard stared at him for a long moment. "Then do not tell me. I prefer not to know. There have been rumours, too many rumours, but it is all in the past now. The long distant past, and best forgotten."

"Except Wodall has not forgotten, has he?" Thomas said.

"Words, Tom, only words. Forget what he said." Prior Bernard straightened. "Now, how are you fixed for a ride back north? I need to speak to the Abbot at Wigmore, and I think between us we may have found you somewhere to live."

"And the bonemen?" Thomas asked. "Is anything going to be done about them?"

"It is not my place." Prior Bernard shook his head. "I can raise the matter with Abbot John, but it is not his place either. You already know who to report such matters to."

"The Justice of the Peace."

"Exactly. Is this another fight you are about to get

yourself involved in? Have you learned nothing in all the years since you left Lemster?"

"He has not," said Jorge, making Thomas scowl because he knew the truth of the words.

The lowering sun cast long shadows across the tall grass lining the track they had followed for the last half hour. Thomas and Jorge rode a little way behind Prior Bernard, the only one of them who knew where they were going. The Prior was no longer dressed as a man of God but more like a soldier, and Thomas wondered if the clothes were those from when he once was one.

Thomas had sent a message to Ludlow so Belia and the others would know they would not return until late, or even the following morning. The distance between Wigmore and Ludlow was a little over three leagues, but Prior Bernard had made it clear the Abbot would want to question Thomas, both on the matter of Hugh Clement and on the land available for him to set up home on. The thought of settling back in England disturbed Thomas for some reason he could not pin down. He preferred to leave his mind to work at any reason on its own rather than examine it himself, in case he did not like what he found.

Jorge nodded towards Bernard. "Do you think he is regarding the wonder of God in the landscape?"

Thomas cast a puzzled glance at Jorge, relieved to see he was smiling.

"No doubt to him it is indeed a wonder."

"How much further to this place?"

"It cannot be far now."

"I thought you knew this country. It is where you were born, after all."

"It is, but other than journeys to Ludlow and Shrewsbury, I never had much call to come this way. It all looks the same around here."

"Green," said Jorge.

"Yes, green. That is because it rains, as you already know."

They crested a low rise to see a tall, extensive building fashioned of local red stone ahead. Wigmore Abbey sat contentedly with well-tended fields arrayed around it, a cluster of houses set at a small distance which would accommodate servants and lay-persons. As well as the Abbey, the squat tower of a Norman church rose on the far side of the village and on a steep hill perched a castle.

Thomas urged his horse forward to catch up with Bernard. Two white-robed monks emerged from a gateway and waited for their approach.

"Welcome, Prior Bernard. Abbot John is expecting you and your guests. I will get a brother to attend to your horses."

Thomas and Jorge followed Prior Bernard as he accompanied the monk inside the stone wall surrounding the Abbey. Inside, the layout was similar to Lemster Priory but on a larger scale. Monks worked gardens, fish ponds, and a small herd of sheep. Chickens pecked at the ground inside a fenced run and one monk was on his knees collecting eggs in a basket.

The monk led them into the main building and along a

cloister to its end. Here another man waited. It was not the Abbot but Peter Gifforde.

"Welcome, Prior Bernard. Welcome also, Thomas Berrington. Your companion, however, is unknown to me."

"His name is Jorge Olmos," said Prior Bernard. "A friend of Thomas."

"Then greetings, Jorge Olmos. I take it you understand English?"

"Unfortunately so," said Jorge.

"We were expecting to see the Abbot," said Prior Bernard.

"My apologies Prior, perhaps Abbot John's message could have been clearer. As the matter you wish to discuss involves land, he thought it better I should deal with it."

"We have another matter to discuss with him as well," said Prior Bernard.

"If you will tell it to me, I can judge whether the Abbot needs to be involved. He is not as well as he was and tires easily. He prefers not to be troubled by lay matters unless he must."

Prior Bernard stared at Peter Gifforde for a long time, and Thomas watched the Prior, trying to work out his reaction. The man's story sounded plausible, but something bothered the Prior. What bothered Thomas was the fact that Peter Gifforde's grandfather had been responsible for the death of a boy, a murder the town had accused Thomas of.

"I believe the matters I need to discuss require Abbot John," said Prior Bernard.

"In that case, I will take you to him now, but try not to

upset him if you can. Perhaps once you settle your business, you can attend Vespers with the Abbot and I will take Thomas to view the property before it grows dark."

Peter Gifforde led the way, moving as slowly as the monks they passed in the cloister, and Thomas wondered if it was a learned gait from sharing the building with them.

"What is wrong?" asked Jorge. The two of them had held back for a moment.

"How do you know anything is wrong?"

"Do you even need to ask? I watched you. That man troubles you."

"And you? I trust your judgement on men and women." Thomas started walking again, Prior Bernard and Peter Gifforde twenty paces ahead.

"His reasons are plausible. I do not know this Abbot John, but if he is as old as claimed then he might need protecting from visitors."

"Perhaps. But Bernard is the head of Lemster Priory and not some casual visitor."

"You still have not told me why you dislike that man as you clearly do."

"I don't dislike him; or at least I am trying not to dislike him. If I say it enough times, then perhaps it will be true. I cannot cast blame on the man for the sins of his grandfather. If I did, then I would have to accept the sins of my own father, which were many."

"You knew Gifforde's grandfather?"

"Oh yes, I knew him."

"Are you going to tell me what he did?"

"Not now. Bernard and the Abbot are waiting for us."

"But later?" Jorge fell into step as they started along the cloister.

"I will think about it, but more than likely I am wrong to cast suspicion on the man. He is not his grandfather, as I am not my father."

TWENTY-SEVEN

Abbot John was a man of advanced years, white-haired apart from his tonsure, clean-shaven and almost grossly overweight. He started to rise, but Prior Bernard waved him back into his comfortable chair. Wooden panels depicting Christian scenes hung on the wall behind him. The crucifixion, of which there were several; St Paul with his head in his lap, the eyes still open; Jesus walking on water. Narrow shelves held glazed boxes in which relics were lodged. Most seemed to be small fragments of bone. Some might even be genuine relics, but Thomas doubted it. The fragments reminded him of the small slivers the bonemen left as a threat, and he wondered if they held some religious significance. If so, it was a strange twisting of religion to threaten, torture and kill people. Though as the thought came to him, he wondered if it was so different after all.

"I am glad to see you looking well," said Prior Bernard.

Abbot John smiled and reached for a fine silver goblet

on the desk. "It is the wine that keeps me young, Bernard. Come, all of you, sit. Peter will join us if you have no objection. I rely on him so much these days. It allows me to spend more time in prayer. As the years pass, I grow increasingly aware that before much longer I will sit in the halls of the Lord, and prayer brings me ever closer to Him. Now, what brings you all the way out here?"

"Two matters," said Brother Bernard. "The lesser concerns Thomas, and is already being taken care of, I understand. A place to set up a home. The other is more important and also rather more delicate. Thomas, as well as a delegation from Lemster, has brought a matter to my attention that I believe should be raised with you."

The Abbot's clouded eyes narrowed as he studied Thomas. "A delicate matter? Are you sure I want to hear about it? Can Peter not deal with it?"

"I would rather Thomas tells you himself. Perhaps once you have heard it, he and Peter can discuss it further while they ride to see this land you have so generously offered."

The Abbot chuckled, the laugh turning into a cough. When it had settled, he said, "Not as generous as you might think, Bernard. It is another of those nuisance parcels that seem to have fallen through gaps in the law. They end up with the deeds stored in our library for want of any place better. The holding might belong to the Abbey, but if it does we have no record of it. All the same, I believe I can arrange a freehold or tenancy. Is that not right, Peter?"

"I have studied both canonical and royal law and

believe you to be correct, Abbot. My preference would be to sell the freehold, then it will not be our responsibility anymore. Prior Bernard has vouched for Thomas Berrington's good repute, and he is known to my family."

"Good. Good. Now, this other matter, if you must."

Brother Bernard glanced at Thomas, who took a breath and started in on his accusation of Hugh Clement. It took longer than he hoped and, judging by the expression of the Abbot, far longer than he had hoped as well. Peter Gifforde asked several astute questions, not all of which Thomas had an answer for, but he was honest in expressing his ignorance. With their meeting concluded, Prior Bernard stayed with the Abbot while Peter Gifforde accompanied Thomas outside to where their horses were stabled.

There was little more than three hours of good daylight as they rode across flat ground away from Wigmore, the lowering sun casting their shadows to one side. Ahead, a wooded ridge rose, separating the bucolic Wigmore valley from Ludlow.

"Is this all Abbey land?" Thomas asked, riding beside Peter Gifforde. Jorge followed several yards behind.

"As far as you can see." Peter Gifforde smiled. "Other than this holding I am about to show you." He gave a shake of his head. "It should belong to the Abbey, of course, but I can find no record of it. No record anywhere. It is as if the thirty acres dropped from the face of the earth."

"Or someone died intestate and nobody thought to report it," Thomas said.

"Yes, that is the most likely explanation."

"I am surprised you spoke of the freehold. Prior Bernard gave me to believe the Abbey never sold land."

"Which is true when the land has a sound record, which the majority have. This parcel is one of perhaps half a dozen that show no ownership, and it is better out of our hands. I will have to draw up a deed of ownership, but that is what I am good at, Thomas." He glanced across. "I may call you Thomas, may I? And you will call me Peter."

"As if we are friends."

"Yes. As if we are friends." Peter Gifforde turned in his saddle to look more directly at Thomas. "I want to ask you something, but it is personal. Tell me it is none of my business if you wish."

Thomas said nothing as he waited for Peter Gifforde to state his question, though he suspected he knew what it concerned.

"Grandpa told me you and he were friends but there was a big falling out. Something to do with a boy who died."

Thomas still said nothing. The question was not quite as he expected. It was far more explicit. Did Peter Gifforde know the truth or not of what had happened forty-seven years before?

"Yes, I knew your grandfather, but we were never friends, despite what he might have told you."

"I was being polite at the Abbey," said Peter Gifforde. "It would not have done to tell you what he really said about you."

"Do you believe everything he told you?"

"He was my grandpa, so of course I do." Peter Gifforde showed little expression.

"In which case, why are you helping me now?"

"Because it was all a long time ago and you are now in service to the next king of England. Men can change. And working with Abbot John has taught me a great deal about forgiveness. So I forgive you."

Thomas bit back a retort because there was nothing to forgive. Peter's grandfather, Walter Gifforde, had killed Susan Wodall's brother, but he knew the man would never believe that truth. Thomas did not care if he thought him guilty of murder. What would one more death mean in the litany of those whose lives he had taken? Except never in murder.

"Why did you return to Lemster, Peter?"

Peter Gifforde smiled as if they had amicably settled their moment of hard truth. "My father was not a man who engendered familial love. The same as your own father, I believe. Our family business had suffered of late and could no longer support us all. I was not interested in wool. I left it in the care of my two older brothers and tried my hand at other forms of commerce. In London at first, but events conspired to force me to leave." He waved his hand in the air. "Nothing serious, more a difference of opinion. My employer and myself did not see eye to eye on expansion of his business."

"You were in a senior enough position to offer such suggestions?" Thomas considered Peter Gifford an intelligent young man. Ambitious too; which was borne out by his honesty regarding the reason for coming to Wigmore. In general, business owners rarely welcomed the opinion of those they employed, however senior their position might be.

"I was his second in command. The chosen one. My suggestions for change might have been overlooked had I not fallen in love with his daughter. She was estranged from him, but that made little difference. He could not countenance what he saw as betrayal. I had to leave London, and leave it fast."

"Your grandfather was born in Lemster," Thomas said. "Is that why you returned here?"

"More out of curiosity than expectation at first, but then I found I liked the area. Liked its people and the possibilities here. I obtained my position at the Abbey almost by chance. I sought shelter there at first, then saw how my skills might be used to its advantage. To admit to a liking of administration is almost a confession in itself, is it not? I enjoy the arranging and keeping of records. The brothers did what they could, but God calls to them more than paper does. So when I suggested the Abbot appoint me as lay administrator he was more than pleased to do so, as long as I could prove to him the appointment was sound. Which I have done."

"You said nothing when I made my accusation against Hugh Clement. I am aware you know the man. I saw the two of you together the night I arrived in Ludlow."

Peter Gifforde scowled. "I recall the night in question, of course. Hugh even invited you and your companion to his table, which surprised me. Though he, like most people in Ludlow, knows Philippa Gale and is aware of her closeness to Prince Arthur."

"You are a friend to Hugh Clement?"

"I was there to discuss a business matter, nothing more. I do not know how you conduct business in Spain, but here a man sits down and shares wine with both those he likes and those he does not."

"And which camp does Hugh Clement fall into?"

"I am not a man to speak ill of anyone without proof. If what you speak is true, then something must be done. You are in a better position than am I to do that, as you also serve Prince Arthur."

"You are well informed, Peter."

"It is my business to be well informed. When I first came to the Abbey…" Peter Gifforde's voice faded away before he finished what he was about to say. They had come down from Halton Hill and below lay a wide turn of the Teme, which enclosed a scatter of fields gone wild. A stone house sat on a small rise above the floodplain. Beyond lay Ludlow and the castle.

"What were you going to say about when you came to the Abbey?" Thomas asked.

"Nothing more than I already have. The Abbey had allowed the administration of its affairs to drift. I hold a great admiration for the men of God who worship there, even more admiration for the Abbot, who is indeed blessed. But monks do not make good businessmen, and the running of a great Abbey is a business."

"I have no doubt of it."

"But that is not your concern. What lies ahead is. This is the house, such as it is, and the land is everything enclosed by the loop of the river."

"It seems strange for good river-land such as this to be left idle when it lies so close to Ludlow."

"Strange indeed," said Peter Gifforde. "I expect local farmers have grazed sheep here on occasion, but it being so close to the town means everyone can see what they are doing. Punishment for grazing on land that is not common can be harsh, and there is enough common land around Ludlow for this not to be needed. And enough woods between here and Wales to provide pannage for their pigs. Someone will have owned this land once, of course, but now it is cut adrift. Until now."

"I take it the Abbey has the legal right to assign it to me?" Thomas said.

"Of course. The Abbey is second only to Prince Arthur in this area, and sometimes not even second in matters of tenancy and freehold. Come and see what you think, Thomas." Peter Gifforde urged his horse forwards.

Rather than ride to Dinham Bridge, they crossed the Teme at a shallows. When they came to a low stone wall surrounding the house, they tied their horses to hawthorn bushes heavy with bright red berries. Thomas climbed the wall, offering his hand to Jorge, who was making harder work of it. Peter Gifforde followed behind. The man was affable, likeable, but Thomas was not sure what to make of him. If his grandfather had made a good business for himself in London why had he given it up to work for someone else? As the thought came to him, he suspected he might know the answer. Peter was unwilling to follow tradition, just as Thomas himself was. Could it be only that? But would someone with such a nature end up in an out-of-the-way backwater such as this? Except, he realised, it was no backwater when the Prince of Wales, the next King of

England, lived less than three leagues from Wigmore Abbey.

Thomas walked with Jorge around the house, judging the walls sound enough with the application of a little lime mortar. Some tiles had slipped from the roof, but a good builder could fix them easily enough.

"What do you think of this place?" he asked. "Can we make it a home?"

Jorge looked around, and Thomas saw him make some manner of judgement. The sun was lowering towards the horizon, washing the landscape in a golden light. It reflected off the river, which ran fast between pools which would hold fat trout and grayling, maybe a salmon in the autumn.

"For how long?"

"If I said we could leave for Spain tomorrow, what would you say?"

"Spain is all I have ever known, but this is where you were born."

"Not here, but close, and that is no answer."

"Catherine is coming to live in the town over there, is she not?"

"Once she and Arthur are married."

"Then this is a good enough place to live while you watch over her. I know that is what Isabel asked of you. And I know you well enough that you always do as she asks." Jorge gave a knowing smile. "I am not sure it is large enough for all of us. Thanks to you, I have three wonderful children and they are growing up."

"We can remedy the lack of space. There is ample ground to build on. We can have a house each, then my

284

own children will not have to put up with you walking around naked half the time."

Thomas knew he would have to look inside the house, but that could wait for tomorrow. He went to where Peter Gifforde stood.

"Draw up whatever papers I need to sign, Peter. This will do us fine."

"I will see if I can find someone to effect repairs for you."

"No need. I can attend to all of that. How long will it take?"

"I can have the papers ready to sign by this time tomorrow. You can make a start on the work in the morning if you wish. There is some furniture inside but I expect there is worm in it all and it will need burning."

"I have other matters to deal with in the morning, but I will return to the Abbey tomorrow evening. Can you find your way back on your own? We may as well enter Ludlow, as we are so close. Tell Prior Bernard I will see him again before long. And my thanks."

Thomas held out his hand and after a moment, Peter Gifforde shook it.

As they followed the banks of the Teme to Dinham Gate, Jorge said, "I liked that man, but he held something back from you. Of what nature I could not tell because the customs of this land are strange to me, but I suspect it was of a small nature. It was when he spoke of his reason for leaving London."

"He is hiding something, I agree," Thomas said. "I also suspect it is to do with why he left London, and why he has returned to this area. Peter Gifforde is an intelligent, educated man who could do much better for himself than administer an Abbey, however large its holdings. I expect we might find out what manner of shame he hides, but if not it is, as you say, a minor matter."

"Do you think that woman has found rooms for us yet? It is months since Belia and I have lain together in a bed, and I have missed the comfort."

"I am sure you have. If not, perhaps Lady Pole can arrange something. Though I suspect she grows tired of my demands, as does her husband."

"Do you think Peter Gifforde or the Abbot gave enough attention to your concerns about this Clement man? Did you really share wine with him and Peter when you arrived here?"

"I did, as well as Pip."

"You did not press Peter on how well he knows Clement, which is not like you."

"Perhaps I am out of practice in such things these days. But I suspect I know why he shared his table. Because Peter Gifforde administers land for the Abbey, and Hugh Clement is a man of little intelligence but great ambition. Sometimes it is necessary to deal with men you despise if the wheels of commerce are to continue turning."

Jorge laughed. "My, but you have changed. I recall no time you have ever done such."

"There have been times I would have been better doing so, but I regret nothing. I grow older and try not to seek conflict as much as I might have once done."

"Except conflict has found you."

"It has found Ludlow, not me. Hugh Clement is a matter for Richard Pole and Gruffydd ap Rhys to deal with. Or even Prince Arthur. The boy is young, but he is the power in the Marches. King Henry has his suspicions regarding Clement and will back whatever action he might take. What worries me is the small army the man is gathering around himself."

TWENTY-EIGHT

It was late by the time Thomas returned to the castle. He had spent the evening with Jorge, Belia and Amal at the Rose and Crown. Constance Sparrow had eventually found them three rooms, and once settled they enjoyed a passable wine and even more passable meal. Jorge's children had gone to their small room in the eaves earlier, and Will was still out in the woods with Usaden and Kin.

Thomas ascended to his room in the castle, surprised to find the bed empty when he entered. Belia had told him she had left a small tincture with Philippa to help her sleep, which would be the best thing for her now.

When Thomas called out a reply came from the privy. "I will be out when I have finished washing!"

"Do you need help to walk?"

"I am a grown woman, Tom. I think I can manage ten steps on my own."

Thomas smiled and kicked off his new boots. He knew he would need to pull them on again soon, but for now he luxuriated in the sense of freedom. He lay fully clothed on the bed and put his hands behind his head and wondered how Philippa might respond if he asked if she wanted to share his house at Burway. The thought brought a frown because he realised he had almost forgotten he had yet to question her about what had happened the night her found her at the cottage. He was almost asleep when Philippa emerged, dressed in a long nightgown. Thomas sat up and watched her cross to the bed, judging how she walked. He was pleased to see she favoured neither side. Even more pleased when she leaned across and kissed him hard on the mouth.

"Tomorrow," she said, "I believe I will be strong enough to greet you as you deserve. I owe you my life, Tom, and it is a debt I intend to repay over and over again."

"I may not be living in the castle much longer."

"So you have heard that Arthur leaves on the morrow to meet his betrothed? I expect you are to go with him, as am I."

Thomas sat up. "No, I had not heard. But you should not ride for at least a week, and I cannot leave tomorrow. Not with what is going on here and in Lemster."

"Did you not tell me you are in England to watch over Catherine of Aragon?"

"I am. But what good will it do her to come to Ludlow, a married Princess, only for the town to be a cesspit of corruption? I will serve her best by cleansing the corruption before she arrives."

"Do not expect me to tell her that when she asks where you are. You need to do it yourself. Face to face."

"I will send a message with... who is going, Lady Pole?"

"She will be there, of course."

"Then I will send a message with her and a copy with you, but Lady Pole is more likely to meet the princess. Catherine will understand. She knows how I am, the same as her mother does."

"Should I be jealous of this Catherine?" said Philippa.

"She has but fifteen years, Pip."

"And?"

Thomas shook his head and swung his legs to the floor. He reached for his boots.

"Try to sleep a little longer. I need to speak with Sir Richard and Gruff."

"I cannot sleep anymore. I doubt I will sleep for a week unless you have more of that tincture your friend left me. She is very beautiful, is she not? Even more so because she is so exotic."

"She is. And no more tincture. It can become a habit, and I would not do that to you."

"What would you do to me, Tom?"

Instead of answering, Thomas left the room. He considered it the safer option.

He ascended Mortimer Tower but found it deserted. He found both men he sought, together with Prince Arthur, in the Armoury. Thomas hesitated outside the entrance, stepping aside as a servant passed carrying a tray of goblets, wine, and a jug of ale. Gruffydd caught sight of Thomas and waved for him to enter.

"Come in, Tom, some of this concerns you. Have you

heard about Princess Catherine's arrival and our departure?"

"I have, Pip told me."

"Sit down, then. We are all men here, and Arthur is always telling us not to stand on ceremony. Not that it stops Richard bowing near to the ground every time the lad speaks."

Thomas watched Arthur, expecting some flicker of annoyance, but his face remained placid. Once again, Thomas thought about what a great King the boy would make. He took a chair as Gruffydd asked the servant to bring another goblet, and was one jug of ale considered sufficient for a serious conversation?

"Pip told me I am expected to travel with you when you go to meet Catherine, Your Grace," Thomas said.

"Queen Isabel's message to my father said you are to remain close to her, so I believe it is expected."

"And this matter with Hugh Clement?"

"Not again," said Sir Richard.

"Let Tom speak," said Gruffydd. "Princess Catherine takes precedence over everything, but what good will it do the Prince to return to a Ludlow infested with vermin?"

Gruffydd's words so much matched Thomas's own thoughts on the matter that his estimation of the man went up even more than it already was.

"Is Pip awake yet?" asked Sir Richard.

"She is."

"And can she walk?"

"Thanks to those who have joined me from Spain yes, she can."

"Then we should send for her."

"Yes, send for Pip," said Arthur. "I would like to see this miracle you have performed, Thomas. Lady Pole told me she was close to death's door when you brought her back to the castle. That she can now stand is miracle enough. Have her fetched, Gruff."

Gruffydd rose and went to the door to pass the message on before returning.

"When Pip confirms what Thomas has told us about Clement, what do we do then, Richard? Give him full reign while we are away?"

"Thomas will need a title, a position, if we are to leave him here," said Arthur.

Thomas smiled. "Any more titles, Your Grace, and I am likely to lose track of which to use."

"Not for you, but for your standing in this town and these counties. Hugh Clement is Justice of the Peace here and regarded as an important man. Go up against him and some people will take his side because of that. Important people, with men of their own."

"Which is why I have attempted to dissuade Thomas from this course of action," said Sir Richard.

"And if his accusations are true?" said Arthur. "Gruff is right—we will return to a town rife with crime and a brutalised population." Arthur turned to Thomas. "How many men do you need?"

"You cannot leave men here, Your Grace," Thomas said. "Your safety is of prime importance. I will make do with whoever I can find. Some of the townsfolk may fight, and I have my friends who arrived this morning." It seemed so much longer ago Thomas could scarcely believe it had been so recent.

"There is always a small guard left at the castle," said Sir Richard. "If needs be, you will retreat inside its walls for your own safety and that of your family. I met two of them earlier today and was impressed by their manner."

Sir Richard's opinion surprised Thomas. He wondered which two he meant. Belia and Amal? Or Will and Jorge?

"I do not intend any direct confrontation with Clement, not initially," Thomas said. "I will watch and judge, gather evidence and, if time permits, present it to Prince Arthur on his return."

"That may be some while yet," said Arthur. "A wedding has to be arranged, and that cannot happen overnight. There will need to be ceremony."

"Of course, but it will give me more time for my investigations."

"Do nothing hasty," said Sir Richard. "Keep an eye on matters, as you say, but do not intervene until we return. A month should do it."

"I will attempt to restrain myself."

Gruffydd rose to his feet as Philippa entered the room, dressed in a long dark blue dress with pearls at her throat. She came across and stood beside Thomas, who rose and offered his chair.

"I am glad to see you much improved, Pip," said Arthur.

"Thanks to Tom and his family, Your Grace. I fear if not for him I would lie in my grave now." She reached out and took Thomas's hand.

"True or not, we have hard questions to ask of you,"

said Sir Richard. "Are you aware of the accusations Thomas has made against Hugh Clement?"

"More than accusations. Tom speaks the truth. It was Hugh's men who questioned me. Hugh's men who would have killed me once I told them what they wanted to know, I am sure of it."

Sir Richard stared across the table at Philippa for a long time before finally offering a reluctant nod.

"What questions?"

"Hugh Clement has noted Tom's interest in him. Also his presence in the castle and well being close to you, Your Grace." Philippa's gaze met Prince Arthur's.

"Did these men threaten you?" asked Gruffydd.

"They…" Philippa seemed overcome for a moment, perhaps calling to mind her predicament. "… they showed me a sliver of bone and said if I did not tell them what they wanted to know, then the next bone would be mine."

"You are sure Hugh Clement was behind this?" asked Sir Richard. "Sure they were his men?"

"Both of them are Hugh's men," Thomas said. "I can vouch for that."

"And do you think they were working under his orders or on their own?"

"Why would they abduct Pip without his order?"

Sir Richard looked at Philippa, back at Thomas. "Why do you think? Pip is one of the most beautiful women in Ludlow. I expect there are scores of men around here willing to risk a hanging to lie with her. I apologise if my words upset you, Pip." He offered a smile with little trace of apology in it.

"You might be right," Thomas said, "but in this case

those men were working for Hugh Clement. I do not know whether they would have let Pip go after questioning her or not. The one called Oswyn is the man who wanted to take my head before Gruff rescued me. The other is even worse."

"And both are dead by your hand," said Sir Richard.

"I am still here, you know," said Philippa. "It was me they questioned."

"What questions?" asked Arthur, cutting through to the point.

"About Thomas, Your Grace. Why is he here in Ludlow. Where he came from, for Tom is a stranger, a wild card in this game Hugh plays. How close is he to you. When you might leave to meet your betrothed. What Sir Richard and Gruffydd know, or suspect, about Hugh's dealings. I don't know what else they might have asked because Tom got there before they could do so."

Sir Richard stared at Thomas the whole time Philippa spoke.

"If it is as Pip says, Thomas, then do you not think you were hasty in killing them both?"

"With respect, you were not there," Thomas said. "Both men had knives. Both men attacked me as soon as I entered the cottage. Is that the response of innocent men? It was kill or be killed, Sir Richard, and it would not have been just my death, but Pip's as well. Would you have preferred I waited to see how far they intended to go before I reacted?"

"I think we all need to keep our heads over this," said Arthur. "I am sure Thomas is not lying to us. Why would he? My father, the King, already has his doubts about

Hugh Clement. If we did not have to leave tomorrow, I would set you and Gruff to uncovering what he is doing and bring him to justice. But we do have to leave, and you both must be with me." The Prince turned his gaze on Thomas. "I take it you are happy to do as Sir Richard and Gruff have asked. To watch, but not to act?"

"Unless there is a threat to the town or its people." Thomas met Prince Arthur's gaze, waiting.

Sir Richard shook his head. "Damn it, we had enough trouble finding someone willing to be Justice in the first place. It is a thankless enough task at the best of times, and it looks to me as if these are not the best of times." Sir Richard turned to Thomas. "While you are destroying this man's life, see if you can find someone to replace him. Preferably someone honest, if you can find such a man, for there appear to be few in these parts."

Thomas walked close beside Philippa as they ascended the staircase, her hand on his arm. Amal's attentions and Belia's tonics had worked wonders. In their room, she asked him to untie the laces on her dress.

"How did you tie them?" he asked, his fingers nimble.

"A servant, how else? I am much improved, but not that much yet."

"I need to ask you something that may anger you."

"What could you ask that would anger me, Tom? Or is it a proposal?"

Thomas let his breath go, wondering why he found it so difficult to question this woman. He steeled himself and forced the words out.

"The guard at the gate that night said you appeared to be on friendly terms with the monk who called for you."

"Then he is mistaken." Philippa's voice was sharp. "Unless politeness is regarded as being friendly."

"So you did not recognise him?"

"Of course not. He told me they had sent him from Wigmore Abbey on behalf of Hugh Clement. He took me to Hugh's house before leaving. Hugh wanted to know about you, but when I told him nothing he sent me away. He asked those two men to accompany me. When we passed the cottage they dragged me inside."

"Were they acting on Hugh's orders?"

"How am I supposed to know that? He told them to ensure I reached the castle safe. What he said to them before that I know nothing of."

"But they questioned you in the cottage. Questioned you hard. On behalf of Hugh Clement, I believe, because neither are bright enough to do so on their own."

"Do you not trust my word, Tom? I am telling you what happened. I heard what Sir Richard said—you are to investigate Hugh. So investigate him, not me!"

"It is not you who is under suspicion, but I need to know if it was Hugh who ordered those men to assault you. Did you see what happened to this monk after he left?"

"Probably went to meet his accomplice."

"His what?"

"There was another man standing on the hillside behind the cottage. I assumed he was waiting to escort the monk back to the Abbey or somewhere in town."

"What did this man look like?"

Philippa thought for a moment. "Short. Badly dressed. Long hair under a felt hat. And a stick of some kind."

"Jack Pook was there?" Thomas said. The description fit, but not his actions.

"I do not know who you are talking about." Philippa's face was expressionless, and Thomas suspected she was trying to rein in her anger at his questions.

"Were you not suspicious when this monk took you to Hugh Clement's house so late at night?"

"Why would I be? I know Hugh and have occasional conversations with him, as is to be expected."

"After this man delivered you there, did you see him join the other on the hillside?"

"I was inside by then, so no. Do you have any sense where you are going with these questions, Tom? Because I am tired, and I ache."

"One of those men attacked us on the road from Lemster. Did you not recognise him?"

"You sent me into the woods before I had much chance to examine his face, so no, I did not recognise him or I would have run. As well as I could, for I am a mere woman and those men would have caught me easily enough."

Thomas still found it hard to accept Jack Pook's involvement, unless he had completely misjudged him. Or was it because he was Bel's brother? Black sheep of the family. Jack admitted as much. But just how black?

Jack Pook had told Thomas what he had witnessed, and his testimony matched what Philippa had said. Would he have come to Philippa's rescue if he saw her being dragged into the cottage? His appearance so soon after Thomas's arrival took on a new meaning if he had been part of the plot. He recalled seeing Jack at the manor house with Hugh Clement and Daniel Lupton when he went in search of a cart. They had been arguing, but had the argument been about the events of that night and not some poaching, as Jack claimed?

"What did those men ask you?"

"I have already told you, Tom. They asked about you. I grow increasingly tired of your suspicions. I am going to bed. You can do what you like, but I do not want you to lie beside me. Not tonight. Perhaps never again."

TWENTY-NINE

Thomas woke with no clue what had roused him. He was in the chair again, his body as stiff as the last time he had slept there. A single candle illuminated Philippa stretched across the bed. Thomas glanced at the small window to judge how close dawn might be. From beyond, a torch burned somewhere. Its light reflected on the beaded glass to reveal it had rained, and rained hard by the look of it. When a knock came at the door Thomas knew what had woken him. He rose and went to see who wanted him at this time of night.

A male servant stood outside, eyes downcast; no doubt well-versed in the sights he might witness on waking people.

"There is someone asking for you, Sir Thomas. A tall man with white hair."

When Thomas thanked him and turned back to dress Philippa was sitting up in bed.

"Are you going out again at this time of night?"

"I am." Thomas dressed, ignoring the fine clothes of a

man of court, choosing instead those he had worn in Granada before he became its Duke. As he drew them on it was almost as if he donned armour, and with it came a sense of assurance, and power.

"I am wondering if you are worth the trouble of my time," said Philippa. "First you throw wild accusations at me and now you intend to abandon me again."

"My son is downstairs. He would not disturb me if it was not important. And I did not throw wild accusations but questions to which I need answers. If only you—" Thomas cut himself off before they started arguing again. Not that he fully trusted Philippa yet. Her story made sense and explained what had happened to her, but now was not the time to press too hard without evidence. "Try to get more sleep. I will send a message for Amal to come and massage you again in the morning. You may feel better, but the bruising remains."

Philippa pulled a face, which Thomas ignored as he drew on his boots. He chose two daggers, one small and one large, and a sword which he strapped to his waist before covering the weapons with his robe. Finally, he wound his tagelmust around his neck and head, so he looked more as if he belonged in the northern deserts of Africa than the English countryside.

Will waited patiently below, just as Thomas knew his grandfather Olaf Torvaldsson would have done. He briefly wondered what the old Northman was doing with himself before pushing the thought aside as irrelevant.

"You need to see what is going on," said Will. "Scores of men are streaming into the grounds around the manor house. Something is about to happen, and Usaden says we need your advice."

"Do we need Jorge?" Thomas asked as he followed his son to the outer gate. They would require no horses as it would take longer to fetch them than walk into the woods north of Ludlow.

"Usaden did not mention him, so I would say leave him to sleep for now."

"I need to send a message for Amal to visit Philippa in the morning."

"Then do it, but be quick because we both believe something is about to happen, and not something good."

As they crossed the dark market square, Thomas noticed that a light burned inside Agnes's bakery. He assumed she was already awake and firing her ovens ready for that day's bread. They turned down the road to the church and then entered Linney before breaking away to enter the woods. The rain had stopped, but the sky remained dark. Progress was slow without even the benefit of starlight, but Will seemed to know exactly where he was going, and Thomas kept a hand on his son's shoulder as they wound their way between the trees until they came out onto the side of the hill where a faint wash of illumination came from starlight in the western sky.

"It is fortunate those men below are many or someone would have heard your approach." Usaden sat with his back to the trunk of a sturdy oak, his head and clothes dry. Kin lay across his feet. Off to the side, Jack Pook leaned against another tree. He appeared to be asleep. Thomas thought about Philippa's description of a man who might be him, but found any suspicion even harder to accept in his presence.

"It is too dark back there for stealth."

"If you say so, but I did not hear Will, only you."

"You can tell us apart?"

Usaden seemed to believe the question required no answer. He rose to his feet and walked silently to the edge of the tree-line. Thomas followed, trying to place his feet softly but failing, unlike his son, who came to stand at his side.

Below, a score of torches illuminated Hugh Clement's manor house. Their flickering light gave the scene a look of the fires of hell as it danced across the faces of the gathered men.

"How many?" Thomas asked, knowing Usaden would have made an accurate assessment.

"That depends how many there were to begin with. Let us assume there were three score, which I believe to be close. Their number is now twice that, with more arriving all the time."

"Do you have any idea where they are coming from?"

"I don't, but Jack says they are from Wales and camped in Bringewood, which is to the west. He disappeared for a few hours when the first of them appeared and tracked the route they took."

So Jack had gone missing for two hours. To do what? Thomas glanced across to where he had been sleeping, only to find him no longer there. Instead, he stood next to Usaden and offered Thomas a grin.

"I like Wales, but those men are not the kind I like.

Fighting men, they are. Hard men, ready to take anyone's shilling and willing to kill for it."

"If this is to do with the bonemen, then killing is counter-productive," Thomas said. "It will make people rise up."

"They cannot rise up if they are dead," said Will, offering his opinion for the first time. "Something has changed, and there are only two things I can think of that could trigger it. First, word is all over town that Prince Arthur and his men are leaving, and Ludlow will be relatively unprotected. The second is you sticking your nose into matters that are none of your concern."

"Would you rather I turned aside?" Thomas asked, annoyed at Will's judgement.

"Not at all, Pa. I like it when you stir the ants' nest. It makes for more interesting times."

Yes, thought Thomas, Will was just like his grandfather. He suppressed a smile because there was something of himself in his son as well. As he stared down over the manor house he saw more riders enter the outer yard, forcing some of those already there to move into the surrounding fields. Thomas glanced west to where the land he would make his own lay, but it was too dark to see it. Close to Hugh Clement's manor house, though; which might be a problem.

"Arthur does not leave until the morning, and on previous experience he will be slow to depart."

"Not this time," said Will. "He rides to meet Catherine, his betrothed, and any man would make all haste to greet her."

"You would know, I suppose."

"As you are well aware, Pa, Cat and myself have never strayed beyond the bounds of a deep friendship. Do not take me for a fool."

"I would never do that."

"Then speak as you mean it."

Thomas was about to ask what was wrong with Will then stopped because he knew. Catherine, the girl he had grown up loving, but knowing could never be his, was about to be someone else's. And Will was preparing to fight. Thomas knew what that did to him, and it would be the same with Will. They had fought side by side since before Will was old enough to do so, but those times had sought them out, not the other way around. Will was a force of nature, and Thomas was once again glad his son had arrived in time to stand at his side in whatever fight was coming to Ludlow.

"We are three; four if we count Jorge," Thomas said.

"Five," said Jack Pook. "If you will have me. It is a while since I killed a rich man."

Thomas wondered whether his words were boast or reality.

"You are more than welcome, Jack," Thomas said. "I would like a word with you once we have decided on what action to take. I suspect we are going to need a few more than five men and a dog, even if Will and Usaden are among our number."

"And you, Pa," said Will. "The five of us are a match for any twenty men."

"There must be over a hundred and forty down there by now," Thomas said.

"So we find more men. How many will remain at the castle?"

"Only a dozen come noon, perhaps less. Their orders are that if there is trouble to close the inner and outer gates and raise the drawbridge. It would take a thousand men, plus siege engines, to break into that place."

"Then we can make it our headquarters if they will let us," said Will. "We bring Belia, Ami, and Jorge's children inside. Your aunt and nieces as well if you think they will come. Then we go out to recruit others."

"I will go to Lemster to get my nephews," said Jack. "Bel's three boys will join us."

"Anyone else in Lemster?"

"It is a shame the Prior has turned his back on the past and now serves God. I expect he was a fearsome warrior when he fought the infidel in Jerusalem."

"My daughter is an infidel," Thomas said.

"No judgement meant, Tom."

"We need a lot more men than that," said Will. "What about those in Ludlow? Do you know any of them, and whether they might join us?"

"I don't, but Agnes will. As does Constance Sparrow. Between them, I expect they know every man in the district."

"As do I," said Jack. "There are men on the holdings around about who will fight, but they lack proper weapons."

"There are weapons aplenty in the castle," Thomas said. "Weapons will not be a problem. Hearts and minds will be the issue."

"Then let me sound people out," said Jack.

"I still need to talk to you before you go."

"Then talk, we are wasting time."

Thomas took Jack's arm and led him away from Usaden and Will.

"This feels serious, Tom." Jack's face had lost the almost perpetual smile it wore.

"I don't know. It may be. What were you doing..." Thomas had to work backwards. "Four nights since?"

"Four nights? I scarce recall what I was doing last night. What is this all about?"

"It was the night you helped me carry Pip on the cart."

"Then you know what I was doing. A bit of poaching. I saw you watching when Daniel Lupton tried to whack me. You were lucky I was there."

"I spoke to Pip tonight. She described a man standing on the hillside above the cottage and the way she did made it sound an awful lot like you."

Jack Pook's eyes caught the little moonlight that reached the floor of the wood. They stared up into Thomas's without a trace of friendship.

"You know what I was doing, watching Clement's house, and have already told you what I saw. Are you accusing me of having something to do with what happened to her?"

"I don't know. Did you?"

"Why would I help you take her back to the castle if I had been involved in taking her from it in the first place?"

"Because I saw you. I was there. I killed the other two and would have killed you as well if I thought you were part of it."

"You might have tried to kill me, Tom, but don't be so

sure you could have. Even if I was there, I had nothing to do with what happened to Pip."

"So it was you she saw?"

"Could have been, I suppose, but usually people don't see me, you know that."

"Yes or no?" To Thomas, this felt like a test of Jack's loyalty.

"I already told you what I saw, so yes I was there."

"Then I would ask two things. Why were you? And did you tell me everything you saw when Pip arrived?"

"You know why I was there. I was looking out for goings-on at Clement's place for you. And yes, I saw her arrive."

"With a monk?"

"Yes."

"Where did he go when he left?"

"I don't know. I watched as he went inside, then went to check my nets. The next thing I know, Hugh Clement and Daniel Lupton are after me. And then along you came to steal a cart." Jack stared into Thomas's eyes. "That is the truth, Tom. All of it. Can I go now?"

"I am sorry, Jack," Thomas said. "I had to ask."

"Of course you did. I am just disappointed you felt you needed to. Are we done?"

"We are done."

"Then it is forgotten between us." Jack held his hand out and Thomas shook it.

"I will keep an eye on what is going on before I go to Lemster," said Jack, before disappearing into the darkness as if he had never been there.

Thomas returned to stand beside Will and Usaden on

the low hillside and watch as even more men gathered. Most came on horseback, short Welsh ponies they could ride all day. Others arrived on foot, weapons strapped to their backs. They were short, hard men with the look of those who knew how to fight and revelled in it.

"We need to get back to the castle," Thomas said.

"I will stay to watch," said Usaden. "You need all the information you can get."

Thomas considered Usaden's suggestion, then agreed with a nod. He and Will turned away, and once again he laid his hand on his son's strong shoulder as he led him through the dense darkness beneath the trees towards Ludlow and a reckoning.

THIRTY

The sky was lightening to the east as Thomas sent a message for Sir Richard Pole and Gruffydd ap Rhys to meet him in Mortimer's Tower as soon as possible. Gruffydd was the first to arrive, his unruly hair in even more disarray than usual.

"What is so important to get me out of my bed at this ungodly hour, Tom? You know Arthur leaves today, or had you forgotten about your Prince? Is this more of your suspicions?"

"More than suspicions this time, Gruff, but I would rather wait for Sir Richard so I have to speak them only once. No doubt he will be in an even worse mood than you."

"You are wrong there, Thomas," said Sir Richard as he emerged from the stairs. "I am in the worst mood you have ever seen me in. I do not welcome being woken in the middle of the night."

"It is gone six according to the bells of St Laurence."

"In that case, I stand corrected—which only makes my

mood even worse. What is so urgent, man? The castle is waking and preparing to leave for Lady Margaret Beaufort's house at Dogmersfield. Arthur's betrothed is already there and awaits him with much impatience. So spit it out and make it fast. You are not my primary concern at the moment."

"I agree I am not, Sir Richard, but Hugh Clement should be."

"Clement again. You are obsessed with the man. He is Justice, but he is also one of the most inept individuals I have ever met. How in God's name he was appointed I do not know, but his appointment will not last long once we return, I can tell you that."

"He has recruited an army."

"You told us that before. And my answer remains the same. You are to watch but do nothing."

"Men have been streaming in from Wales all night," Thomas said. "When I left, over seven score were gathered around Clement's manor house. It could be more by now, and they are not here for the entertainment."

"You are sure of this, Tom?" asked Gruffydd, before turning to Sir Richard. "That is a small army. We should think about leaving more men at the castle when we go."

"And if this Welsh army is not here for Thomas—which is as likely as me being able to fly from this tower on wings—then they are here because they have heard Arthur is travelling south. Never mind leaving more men, we must take every man we can with us. Strip the barracks of everyone other than the tack-boys. I will arrange it now." Sir Richard stared hard at Thomas. "This is your doing, Berrington. Ludlow was a quiet backwater until you arrived. There will be a reckoning, I promise. I will have to tell the Prince what you have done. I will have to tell the King as well when I see him, and he is a man whose patience can wear thin mighty quick."

Before Thomas could defend himself, Sir Richard stormed from the room.

"That could have gone better," said Gruffydd. "You and he are chalk and cheese, Tom."

"But they cut you and me from the same cloth, I suspect"

"Aye, you might be right there. Not that it will do you any good. Richard is right—we are going to need every man we can muster to protect Arthur in case it is him this small army has come for. I make no claim to understand what Clement's place in things is, but that can wait for another day. It is who is behind him we need to worry about, because the man is not sharp enough to conjure what you claim."

"Would it not be better for the Prince and his retinue to stay inside the castle walls until you are sure what is going on?"

"Which we cannot do, for reasons Richard has already explained. Two great nations are about to be joined in marriage and nothing—nothing!—can stand in the way. Stay here, Tom, and try not to get into any more trouble, if such a thing is even possible. I will put in a word for you with both Arthur and Henry, but if you continue to stir the pot I can only do so much. Once we have gone, lock the gates and raise the drawbridge. If it is not Arthur they are after, as soon as these men of Wales discover there is no one to fight they will slink off back home, mark my words. We will deal with Hugh Clement on our return."

Gruffydd left Thomas alone in the tower. He went to the low wall and leaned on it, staring across a landscape coming alive with the new day. In the distance he made out Hugh Clement's manor house and, arrayed around it, the small army he had gathered. Not so small now, it seemed. Thomas thought he may have underestimated their number.

He did not know what he was going to do, other than what he had always done. Whatever he could, as well as he could.

Thomas washed a hand across his face before descending the spiral staircase and going out into Ludlow to start his defence of the town. Let everyone else flee. He would attempt to protect the people here, even if he had no idea how.

He found Will standing outside the castle walls with Usaden and Kin at his side.

"What is the situation now?" Thomas asked, using Arabic so all three could converse more quickly, and in private. He saw one of the guards glance at them but ignored the man.

"Men are still arriving in ones and two," said Usaden, "but Jack Pook returned to tell me no more are coming in from Wales, wherever that is."

"The land to the west," Thomas said.

"Is this land not all England?"

Thomas only laughed. "We need to get everyone together inside the castle, but not until the Prince has left. I stopped and had a word with Lady Pole, and she will arrange for us to gain access once they have all gone. It will give us some time to gather our thoughts and make a plan. Is Jack still watching Hugh Clement's house?"

"He went south. Said he needs to warn his sister and you would know who he meant."

"Bel," Thomas said. "He mentioned recruiting her sons. Three strapping lads. I am hoping he might gather others as well. I only wish I knew what Clement was planning. A siege of the castle? To take over the town? He has already set things up so most traders will pay him what he is asking. Why does he need all these extra men?"

"It is obvious," said Will. "He was not expecting anyone to fight back."

"But they are not."

"You are, Pa."

"But only me. How many men does he think he needs to deal with one man?"

"Then the rest of us arrived," said Will.

Thomas stared into space for a moment as he tried to make sense of Hugh Clement's actions. Will was right that his arrival, along with the others, made the job of the bonemen more difficult. But why the army of men from Wales? Had they come to ambush Prince Arthur, as Sir Richard Pole believed? If so, why would that involve Hugh Clement? The Welsh had no love of the English, but they would attack the prince with or without the help of Hugh Clement's bonemen. And then it came to him. A possibility, perhaps.

The Welsh were a distraction, nothing more. Hugh Clement, or more likely Daniel Lupton, had gone into the mountains of Wales to recruit an army. News of Arthur's betrothed arriving in England had come weeks before. Hugh Clement wanted to milk Ludlow's traders, but must be aware the authorities would not stand idly by while he did so. But what if there was a bigger threat to worry about? Such as a hundred and forty fighters from Wales. Attention would be on them, and when the fight was over and the Welsh defeated, as they would be, attention would return to rebuilding, not the bonemen. The departure of Prince Arthur only made the task easier, because Ludlow would be undefended. Which meant come the end of the day the defeat of the Welsh was no longer a given. It made the recruitment of local men even more critical.

Thomas wondered if Hugh Clement had followed the same logic. Was he aware that if Ludlow fell to the Welsh his plans would crumble into dust? The man was inept, but at least one of those with him was not.

"Let us fetch the others." Thomas started across the outer bailey. "We can take them to Agnes's bakery and wait for the castle to empty. It is also a good place to watch the town from. Everyone passes through Market Square."

The Rose and Crown had gathered a few customers when they arrived. Jorge, Belia and Amal sat at a table picking at a plate of unfamiliar cheese, bread and meat. Thomas asked Belia to fetch the children while he settled the bill with Constance Sparrow.

"I want you to take care today," he said to her. "I think something is about to happen in the town."

"Something is always happening," said Constance. "I have seen just about everything there is to see. A goodwife sees all, Tom." She pushed one coin back across the table. "You have paid too much."

Thomas pushed the coin back. "Not enough, Constance." He leaned over and kissed her cheek, bringing a flush to her face, but not as much as a kiss from Jorge would have.

The children were hungry, but Jorge told them they could fill their bellies at Agnes's shop. The market square was growing busy with traders setting up their stalls. One smallholder had brought in a dozen live chickens in cages, together with a crate of eggs to sell, but three of the chickens had escaped. It was a source of great amusement to the other traders and a game for the children who ran between legs in pursuit of the cackling birds. The scene was so normal that Thomas doubted himself. What if the Welshmen were not here to threaten Ludlow? It made no sense, for what did they hope to gain? Even if they attacked the town, once word reached the King he would send an army to destroy them. And if they took the town, for what purpose? Thomas had heard often enough that Ludlow was the capital of Wales, but that did not mean it belonged to it? Were these men here to claim the capital as their own rather than it be a constant threat from England? It was too late for that. Wales had fallen under English subjugation a century before and kept too weak to make any claim. Ludlow Castle was the embodiment of that domination. Perhaps they wanted only to kick the sleeping beast that was England. To prove they were men of iron. Or men of bone? Thomas shook his head, aware he was dreaming up too many connections. But Hugh Clement stood at the centre of everything.

Thomas ran across the market square to catch up with the others. It would be good to know the reasons for what was happening, but he did not need to in order to put up a defence. He only needed good men for that, and hoped there would be enough of them.

Agnes welcomed them all with kisses, which took some little time, then Thomas drew her aside and told her what he had told Constance Sparrow. Trouble was coming to Ludlow. Perhaps not today, perhaps not tomorrow, but he did not expect it to be long in arriving.

Agnes's response was identical to Constance's.

"I am a grown woman, Tom." She patted his cheek. "I know how to take care of thieves and ruffians. But you need to have a word with that son of yours. My girls have gone all doe-eyed over him and he needs reminding they are related through blood."

"I will tell him, but he has been pursued by inappropriate females before and knows how to behave."

"He is a handsome devil. Not as handsome as Jorge, but handsome enough to stand out around here. Not to mention his size. How tall is he?"

"Over six feet, but I have never measured him. Tall enough, he always says."

"Aye, tall enough. Get him a wife. It will save him from debauchery."

"I had not heard marriage was a cure for that, but I will see what I can do. I have another favour to ask."

"Of course I will look after the children. And it is not a favour when you do the asking. We are family, are we not? Besides, I sold all those misshapen rolls they made the last time. I think the customers liked them better than mine."

"Yes, we are family." Thomas kissed his sister's cheek. "It is only until the Prince leaves the castle with his entourage, then they can have the run of the chambers."

Agnes's face lost its smile. "Take care, Tom. This fight you believe coming is not yours. Ludlow is not your town. Neither is Lemster anymore. You could go with Prince Arthur and nobody would think any the worse of you."

"Except I would. I cannot do that, Agnes. You know I cannot."

"I do not know it, Tom. I know you hardly at all except it seems I have always known you. There is so much you need to tell me."

"And you me, sister."

Agnes shook her head. "My life has been dull compared to yours. A husband, children, work; but it suited me and still does. Stay long enough and you can tell me of your exploits."

"I am not sure I have enough years left for that."

"Try," said Agnes. She patted his face and turned away, calling for the children to follow.

Will was leaning on the wall outside the shop, eating a fresh roll. Agnes's two daughters were staring at him in between serving customers.

"What now, Pa?" He waved to his cousins before falling into step beside Thomas. Usaden and Jorge rose from where they had been sitting on the far side of Market Square and joined them, Kin trotting along at their heels. The dog was slower than he had been and spent most of his idle moments in sleep, but if trouble came to Ludlow, Kin would be in the thick of it.

"We wait until everyone has left the castle, then we

take our people inside and close the gates, of both castle and town. In the meantime, we split up and walk the streets. I want you to look out for strangers. You have seen how Clement dresses his men with those green hats. Watch but do nothing. Once you see the Prince and his retinue depart, come back to Agnes's bakery and we will all go from there."

"You want us to hide ourselves away?" Will's expression showed what he thought of the idea.

"Only until we know what is going on. Richard Pole thinks Clement's army has gathered to attack Arthur. I don't believe he is right, but I cannot dismiss the idea either; so we have to wait and see."

"And if they are after us?"

"Why would they be after us? After me, perhaps, but they don't even know about the rest of you. As far as they are aware I am but one man, and one man does not require an army. They almost certainly believe three men could take me."

Will laughed. Usaden said nothing. Jorge watched a woman cross the street with a basket under her arm. When he smiled at her, she caught her toe on the cobbles and almost fell.

"What are you going to do while we are watching for trouble?" asked Jorge.

"I will do the same."

"Except as you have already pointed out, they know who you are."

"I can wrap my tagelmust around my face."

Jorge shook his head. "That will be a fine disguise indeed. Go back to the castle and find out what you can.

See what weapons it has we can use if we are fortunate enough to recruit any men in the town. Should we start asking now?"

"Not yet. I am going to get Agnes and Constance Sparrow to help with that, as well as whoever else they can think of. The conversation will come better from one of their own rather than strangers."

After they split up Thomas remained in Market Square. He found an empty house with a deep entrance doorway and stood far back in the shadows. Men, women and children passed. The square filled up. Heads bobbed around like flotsam on the surface of the sea, but as far as Thomas could tell none wore the green felt hats of Hugh Clement's men. They could, of course, have removed them to pass unnoticed more easily, but Thomas did not think they would do that. The hats and the bones sent a message, a symbol of their threat, one they would discard with reluctance. The sun rose higher. Thomas's shade grew less until anyone looking in his direction would see him. And then a great noise erupted. A trumpeter led the way as Prince Arthur rode at the head of a long column of soldiers, courtiers and servants. The crowd in the square made room, most bowing deeply as the Prince passed. As he did so, he dipped his hand into a pouch at his waist and tossed small coins into the roadway, as he had on his arrival.

It took over half an hour before the last of the retinue disappeared. Thomas watched every face but did not see Philippa among them. He hoped she had taken his advice and remained in the castle. Not for his sake, but hers. She needed more time to recover from her injuries. And he wanted to talk to her again. Her explanations sounded genuine enough, but there remained unanswered questions and gaps in her narrative. The biggest of which was why did she go to Hugh Clement's house? And who was the monk? Was Wigmore Abbey involved?

The sound of the royal progress faded. The market square returned to normal.

And then the first of the bonemen appeared. Only three at first, then others until at least thirty had passed Thomas's position. Four of them went to Agnes's bakery and an argument broke out. Thomas stepped out from his cover, but Will was already running towards the altercation. Thomas cursed the impetuousness of his son, even as he knew he was about to do the same thing.

THIRTY-ONE

Will was not like his father. Thomas might have tried to talk with the men first before attacking them. Will had no such intention.

He hit the first in the small of the back and the man went to his knees. Two others turned to meet the threat and Will hit both great thumps to the side of their heads that sent them sprawling. By which time Thomas had arrived and held his son's arm as he tensed for a final blow.

"Wait, I want to talk to them."

"Fuck talking, Pa. We should kill them all. It will be four less when the attack comes."

"Will!" Thomas stared into his son's bright eyes. His mother's eyes, a deep blue. Thomas continued to stare until he saw a change in them, then turned to the last man. He had grasped him by the shoulder as he arrived, digging his fingers hard into a bundle of nerves that prevented the man from moving.

"How many are coming?"

The man spat in his face.

Thomas wiped spittle from his cheek and dug his fingers in harder. The man made a keening sound and his knees buckled.

"I asked you a question. Do you want my son to hit you harder than he did your companions? He will be happy to."

"You are a dead man, Berrington." The man pushed the words out through clenched teeth.

"Did Hugh Clement tell you my name?"

"And your family's. Why do you think we came here first—to your sister's? Hugh let us all know you are a wealthy man, so Agnes has to pay more. A great deal more."

"Why are the Welshmen here?"

"Nothing to do with me. They are Hugh's idea. And their own. The Welsh have an argument with Ludlow and it suits Hugh to have them on his side."

Thomas shook his head and stepped back. "Do it."

When Will hit the man his head snapped back. He was unconscious before he hit the ground. Two of the others were recovering, so Thomas kicked one and Will dealt with the other.

"What do we do with them, Pa?"

"Drag them into the middle of Market Square and tie them together. Put two of them in the stocks. We can pile them up with any others and add those Jorge and Usaden bring to us."

Both returned to the shop once finished. Agnes's daughters stood with pale faces, staring out at the bound men.

"Pull the shutters down," Thomas said. "Lock the doors. Keep everyone inside, we have more work to do yet."

The girls nodded and did as asked.

Will grinned. "Are we going to fight?"

"We are."

Will's grin grew.

Neither of them carried much in the way of weapons other than a knife pushed into their boots, but neither felt the need. The bonemen had made a mistake in not coming with more men, and only coming in groups of three of four. So far, they held the Welshmen back. This foray was purely to stamp the authority of the bonemen on those they threatened.

Thomas and Will moved through the town, identifying individual groups and taking care of each. They encountered Usaden and Jorge and told them to take those they had knocked out or captured to the market square. Usaden went in search of a cart, Kin trotting after him once he had snuffled at Thomas's hand.

Word must have spread because all at once there were no more bonemen. The four of them returned to the market square with the last of their victims to find the townsfolk gathered. They had surrounded the pile of unconscious bodies and armed themselves with makeshift weapons. There were a few swords, a few bows, but most held lengths of wood, sticks, pitchforks, and spades. Some of the bonemen had worked their ties loose and tried to break through, but not without receiving several blows. Thomas saw Agnes and her daughters armed with the long wooden paddles they used to slide loaves into the oven. They were whacking at men as they revived, sending some back into darkness. Thomas stepped into the circle before somebody killed one of the bonemen.

He held his arms above his head and shouted. "You have all done well, as I knew you would. The brave men and women of Ludlow town!"

This brought a cheer and a few more blows.

"Leave them be for now," Thomas said. "Let them revive and skulk off back to their master. Any man willing to fight come to the outer courtyard of the castle and I will provide weapons. The rest of you, go home and lock your doors, because this is only the start."

"Who are you to give us orders? We don't know you."

"But you know me." Agnes stepped across to stand beside Thomas. "This is Thomas Berrington, and he is my brother. Which means you all know Tom. Do as he says if you want to keep your businesses, your homes and your lives."

The crowd broke up, but not without some muttering. Thomas watched them disperse, wondering how many would gather at the castle. He suspected the number would not be enough.

Jorge and Usaden left to return to the castle. They would not be allowed access until Thomas arrived, but they said they also wanted to ensure all the bonemen had left.

Thomas walked beside Agnes towards the bakery. "I expected to see Amal out here with a stick, too. She can be hot-headed like her brother when she sees someone in danger."

"She is such a sweet thing, Tom, you are a lucky man."

"We will see in a few days how lucky I am. I expect she stayed to protect the bakery."

"She went to the castle with Belia and the children. She said it was safe enough now you were dealing with the ruffians."

"She has too much trust in me."

Agnes reached for his hand. "With justification, I would say. Trust in all of you. Will is magnificent. And I saw how that short man dealt with some of the others. He is fast."

"Yes, he is."

"I did not think I would like your dog, but he has grown on me. He has a sweet nature under all that hair and those teeth."

Thomas laughed, releasing some of the tension that flowed through him. "Not sweet all the time. Are you going to be all right if I return to the castle? Keep your doors locked. I expect they will be back later, most likely tonight once it grows dark. They want to terrorise the town, but I am hoping it will only be some beatings and nothing more."

"And what are you going to do, Tom? Stop them?"

"Yes."

As he walked with Will towards the castle, Thomas wondered if his answer had been no more than bluster. He still had no plan, nor even any idea how he could formulate one, but he knew creating one was long overdue.

Usaden, Jorge and Kin fell into step with them as they crossed the outer courtyard. The remaining guards had shut and barred the gate, but when Thomas hammered on it a small panel hinged back. A face stared out at him before offering a nod. It took several minutes to release all the bolts, but eventually, the door swung open and everyone stepped through.

"How many remain in the castle?" Thomas asked as the man closed the gate and started throwing each long bolt across.

"A dozen of us. Eight men and four women. The cooks, of course, and Pip Gale is still here."

"Did you volunteer, or were you told to stay?"

"Lady Pole asked for volunteers."

"Did she tell you what might be about to happen?"

"Gruffydd ap Rhys did. I stayed because I used to be a soldier. I am getting too old for the field of battle, but I can still fight." He looked at Thomas. "Like you, I reckon."

"Did the others arrive?"

"What others?"

"Two women and three children, two boys and a young girl."

"You are the first to knock at the gate," said the man.

Thomas laid a hand on his shoulder. "My apologies, but you need to open it again."

The man began the process as Thomas went to the others and told them Belia and Amal had not returned to the castle, so he was going to find out where they were. Will said he would come with him, as did Usaden and Jorge.

"We quarter the town," Thomas said. "It will be quicker that way. As soon as we find them come back here."

"And if we don't find them?" asked Will.

"How far can they have gone? Meet up here again

when the church strikes four. I expect one of us will have found them by then."

Thomas returned to Agnes's shop, pleased to discover the shutters down and the door locked. One of her daughters opened the door a crack at his knock. Rose or Jilly, he always had trouble deciding which was which.

"Did you see Belia and Amal leave?" Thomas asked.

"I did. The children were complaining it bored them making bread rolls." Her expression showed some sympathy. "Belia said they should return to the castle, but Amal said they ought to go to the river. The children wanted to catch minnows, and it would be safe enough now you had dealt with the wicked men."

"Which direction did they go, Jilly?"

The girl pointed. "I am Rose, not Jilly, and they went that way towards Dinham Bridge. They asked where the best place to go was, so I told them down there. There are rapids and shallow pools that way and plenty of fish. Did I do wrong, Uncle Thomas?"

"No, you did well. Now lock the doors again."

"Come and tell us when you find them so we know they are safe."

"I will."

Thomas walked fast around the castle wall and out through Dinham Gate. As he passed through, he knew it made sense to close all seven gates before night fell.

He stood on the wooden spars of Dinham Bridge and looked both upstream and down, but could not see Amal or the others. He wondered if they had wandered further, but doubted it. Rose was right. The shallow water and rapids were the perfect place for children to play.

Thomas scrambled down and walked along the gravel bank but saw nothing until he came to the top of the rapids, where there was something caught in a bush. He knelt and pulled out a length of dark material. He raised it to his nose and inhaled the unmistakable scent of Belia. It was her scarf. Thomas rose to his feet and looked around, but saw nothing else.

As he turned to search in the other direction he found several deep gouges in the gravel. As he ran his fingers across them he saw a stain on the pebbles. When he lifted his fingers, he found them red with blood and a great fear ran through him. They had been here. Belia, Amal, Jahan, Saman and Leila. Five people Thomas should have protected better.

He rose and climbed to the track that ran around the base of the town walls until he came to Linney. As he walked, his eyes scanned the ground for further signs. At one point he found a discarded toy, a small wooden carving of a dog which Usaden had made for six-year-old Leila, which she carried with her everywhere and called Kin. He could see Leila and the real Kin curled together on the floor of his house in Granada. Kin who had torn the throats from men allowing Leila to pull the long hair of his ears and tie it above his head. A little further on, he saw a small square of red cloth and recognised it as from the dress Amal wore that morning. Another hundred paces and he found a second. Thomas realised she had torn them loose to form a trail to follow.

All the signs led to Hugh Clement's manor house.

Thomas went far enough to see the host of men staining the fields around. He slipped into the woods before anyone saw him and continued under cover, but it soon became obvious the woods were no longer safe when he came across four men. They stood facing away from him, talking softly in a language he did not understand. Thomas drew the knife from his boot and considered killing them, but he had never attacked a man who did not face him before and would not do so now. Instead, he re-sheathed the weapon and stepped backwards, for once placing his feet so he made no sound.

When Thomas told Jorge what had happened, he punched him in the face and Thomas allowed the blow without retaliation. He would punch himself if he thought it would help.

"How many men?" asked Will, his expression set hard.

"Over one hundred and forty, I reckon. Too many for a frontal assault." Thomas glanced at Usaden. "I tried to approach through the woods, but they have stationed men there. You might get past them, but I could not."

"I am better staying here if there is going to be trouble," said Usaden .

"A plan," said Will. "We need a plan. Do you think they know who Belia and Amal are?"

"Why else take them? Besides, they look different enough from people around here for the bonemen to know they are with us. The question is, why take them— do they think it gives them a hold over us?"

"Of course they do, because it does," said Jorge. "I want Belia and my children back, and you need Amal." He paced backwards and forwards, punching one hand into the palm of the other. "When does it get dark?"

"Two hours yet," Thomas said. "That is when they will

come in full force, together with the Welshmen. I am sure that is why they are here, to offer backup if Ludlow rejects the bonemen. We need to be ready for them." Thomas went to the gate of the inner bailey to find the man who had admitted them. "Has there been any message for me?"

"Not that I have seen, but nobody can reach this far with the outer gate barred."

"Open the gate," Thomas said.

"And let them in?"

"What did Sir Richard Pole tell you about who was in charge while they were away?"

"They said you were, sir."

"Then open the fucking gate and let me through."

The man paled and began throwing the bolts. Thomas joined in, and shortly after Will and Jorge helped.

Once the door was open Thomas turned to them. "One of you has to stay here. You do it, Will."

"I am better being with you if there is going to be trouble."

"And you are better here if something happens to me. Jorge, with me."

Thomas passed through with Jorge at his side, the gate slamming shut behind them. They strode across the courtyard and unbolted the small door set in the outer gate. Thomas bent his head as he went through. What he saw on the far side almost turned his legs to water. Someone had pinned Amal's dress to the outer door with a knife. As Thomas worked it free he saw the torn edge where his daughter had left a trail for him to follow.

A single sheet of stained paper showed beneath the

dress. Thomas pulled the knife out and read the scrawled message.

> Thomas Berrington, as you can see, we have your daughter and the other infidel, as well as her children. Ludlow is to be made an example of. Stay inside the castle, do not interfere, and they will be returned to you at dawn.
>
> Interfere, and I will kill them. Slowly and painfully.

There was no signature. The note did not need one. Thomas knew its author.

He screwed the paper into a ball and dropped it to the ground. Then he picked up Amal's dress and re-entered the castle.

THIRTY-TWO

Thomas was sitting in the Armoury, Amal's dress clutched to his face so he could smell her scent, when Jorge came in and slapped him across the face. Will stood behind him, his own face set hard.

"Stand up and act like the man I know," said Jorge.

Thomas stayed where he was, unseeing eyes latched on the past. Amal as a baby. Amal as a toddler. Amal as a young woman; agile, loving, clever, stubborn. And then the dark memories came. Amal's mother Lubna slain in Málaga, Amal still inside her, only saved by Belia because Thomas could not bring himself to cut her out of his wife's belly, even though they would both die if he did not.

Jorge slapped Thomas again, this time on the other cheek.

"Do you forget they have Belia and my children, too? Do I not grieve? Of course I do, but feeling sorry for myself will not get them back. Now stand up before I get

Will to hit you. I wager you feel that, if you are still conscious."

Will stepped closer, his fists bunched.

"They have Ami, Pa, so get up. I have a plan."

Finally, Thomas raised his eyes. They met Jorge's, saw the pain there, and moved to his son's. His reflected that same pain.

"What plan?"

"Tell me again what they said in that note."

"We must stay within the castle while they ravage Ludlow."

"How do they intend to do that?"

"How? With men, of course. Over a hundred men. And with iron and steel and fire. That is why they recruited the Welshmen. The bonemen are thieves and rogues. The Welshmen are hardened killers. They will come with oil and lanterns to burn the houses, and they will kill men, women and children. They have no love of the English."

"They have to get into the town first," said Will. "I walked the entire wall yesterday. It is high, and there are seven gates that can be closed and barred. We need to find someone here who knows how to do that before nightfall. I reckon we have an hour at most."

Thomas felt the lethargy that gripped him start to fade, replaced by a glimmer of hope. "And Amal?"

"A hundred men, you say?"

Thomas nodded. "More."

"Coming to attack the town?"

Thomas nodded again.

"So how many will that leave to protect the manor house? That is where Hugh Clement will have them as hostages. We cannot fight a hundred men, but a dozen? A score? We have done it before, Pa, and for less reason than saving Ami."

Thomas looked at Will. His strength. His certainty. And he fed off it, trying to remember the man he used to be and what he could do. He rose to his feet, folded Amal's dress as neatly as he could, which was not very neat, and placed it on the chair. He looked around at the weapons arrayed on the walls and tables of the armoury and firmed his shoulders.

"Pick your weapons."

"I have mine." Will raised a hand and patted the shaft of the axe that hung from his shoulder and along his back. Thomas knew he was right. The weapon was an extension of Will, doing his bidding with barely a touch. "But I may take two of those fine swords and some daggers as well." He smiled, but the expression contained nothing of humour. "Just in case."

"Arm yourself, Jorge, while I go to find someone who knows how to lock the town gates, but only after we have passed through one of them."

Thomas ascended to the room he shared with Philippa, surprised to find it empty. He assumed she had gone to the kitchen. She was no doubt starving after having eaten nothing for almost two days while she recovered. He stripped and washed himself, a ritual, then pulled on a fresh set of clothes. The fighting clothes he had almost left behind in Granada, expecting never to need them again. Some last-minute whim had made him pack them, to be carried on a cart together with the chest containing his and Jorge's wealth. A not inconsiderable sum he would gladly give up to have Amal, Belia and her children safe again. His and Belia's children, conjured by their joining, but they were not his. They belonged to Belia and Jorge.

Thomas found the man who had admitted them to the castle and knew how to work the town gates. Thomas sent him out to recruit helpers while he returned to the armoury. He examined the weapons before choosing a fine sword that came alive under his touch. He selected three daggers to add to the one already in his right boot. By the time they were ready, the light was fading from the sky. Thomas led them to the inner bailey to discover Usaden and Kin waiting for them.

"Did the gatekeeper let you in before he left?"

"No gatekeeper," said Usaden. "The walls are not so high and I climb well. I admit to opening the gate to let Kin in. He does not climb so well. He can leap high, but not as high as these walls."

Thomas looked up at the wall and shook his head.

"Jack Pook is in the market square, together with three strapping lads he claims are his nephews. He has also brought two dozen men recruited from some town called Lemster. Your sister has gathered another two score from Ludlow."

"I need to tell Agnes not to get involved."

"Too late for that," said Usaden. "I can see some of you in her, Thomas. Without the beard, obviously."

Without thinking, Thomas stroked his chin, trying to recall the last time he had shaved. Then it came to him. At the barber's shop in London, where all this had started. The bonemen had been there, and now they were here.

Those in London would need dealing with, but not tonight, not this year, most likely. But dealt with, they would have to be.

"And Jack knows where they have taken your daughter, Belia and the children."

"Has he seen them?"

"You can ask him yourself when we go outside."

Thomas went to the kitchen and found someone to lock the gates behind them. He asked if they had seen Philippa, but no one had since she ate lunch with them. Thomas wondered if she was taking the opportunity of the castle being abandoned to explore the royal residence.

"They are alive," said Jack Pook, when Thomas asked him about the captives. "At least they were when I saw them being taken into the manor house by Hugh Clement and that bastard Daniel Lupton. There was someone else there as well. I didn't know him, but I'd say he was the same monk that took Pip there that night you rescued her. He went inside with them, same as before, then came out after a short while and rode off to the west; same as before. And there are six dead men in the woods. Your friend here took care of them."

Thomas glanced at Usaden, who only raised a shoulder. Killing enemies was what he did. What he had always done. When Thomas first met him he was a mercenary in Málaga, but over the years his loyalty had shifted and now lay only with Thomas and his family.

"I need men to protect Ludlow, but I would welcome you and Bel's boys with us if you are willing."

"Willing and ready, Tom," said Jack, and the boys all nodded, their faces set in determination.

"There will be killing."

"Still with you," said Jack with a grin.

"All right. Once we are outside we cannot get back into town easily, so if we get separated you and the lads head back to Lemster. I don't think anything is going to happen there tonight, so it should be safe enough. All Clement's men are going to be storming Ludlow, except they cannot get in."

"Oh, they will get in," said Jack, "but it will take them till midnight, I expect. We will have your family safe by then and the real killing can start."

"I fear there are not enough of us," Thomas said.

Jack Pook only smiled and turned away.

They passed through the Corfe Gate as the sun disappeared behind the hills of Wales, then skirted the eastern edge of the woods in case Clement's men were patrolling them. In the distance came the sound of a horde gathering, now and then the clash of metal on metal. The sound faded as they moved north to reach the Corfe, where a narrow strip of grass grazed by sheep ran between the water and the woods. Jack Pook led them because he knew this ground as well as he knew his own hand. Thomas and Jorge followed, with Bel's three boys taking up the rear. Usaden patrolled the woods with Kin, appearing only occasionally to tell them no one was watching. All Hugh Clement's men were gathered together with the Welshmen to prepare for the attack on Ludlow.

When they came closer to the manor house, they stopped and hunkered down beneath a stand of pollarded willows, waiting for the light to fade completely. The men

Hugh Clement had recruited moved off. They carried swords, knives, and crossbows. As Thomas watched through the gathering gloom he saw something that gave him cause for concern. A heavy cart appeared. Strapped to it with a series of ropes was the trunk from an oak, arranged so it could be swung.

"Is that what you meant when you said the town gates would not keep them out?" Thomas asked Jack.

"I saw them loading it up. It will break through eventually, but only after they have retied those ropes so it works. Someone might have crept up and sawn them halfway through with a sharp knife."

Thomas patted Jack on the shoulder.

They settled down to wait, a thrum of impatience running through Thomas. He watched Jorge, knowing he must feel the same. Fear for his loved ones. Anger at those who had taken them. He glanced at Bel's sons and saw only grim determination on their faces. He wondered if it was to hide their fear, but if so he only admired them the more for joining their band. Going up against over a hundred men was enough to unnerve anyone. Thomas knew if he still lived when this was over, he wanted to get to know each of them better.

He smiled into the dusk at his own thoughts.

When this was over.

If he lived…

The rump of the mercenary army gathered and headed out on foot, the journey to Ludlow not far enough to bother with horses. Hugh Clement came out to watch them and shout encouragement. Thomas grasped the hilt of his sword, his knuckles turning white as he fought the urge to run out and attack the man. Before the last of his mercenary army had left, Hugh Clement turned and re-entered the house. Thomas heard the thump as bolts were thrown across to bar the thick oak door.

"How do we do this?" asked Will.

All eyes were on Thomas.

"Is there another way in?" Thomas asked Jack, on the assumption he was the most likely to know, which he did.

"There are three doors. The one Clement just used is the main one and the strongest. There is a second on the far side, which leads to a field that runs down to the Corfe. A third is at the rear and gives access to the kitchen."

"Which is the easiest to get through?"

"They will all be locked by now, so none of them."

"Will they have barred them all inside as well?"

Jack Pook looked at the sky for a moment as he thought. "The main door will be, the kitchen probably not. I don't know about the other, but there is a second door from the kitchen that can cut it off from the rest of the house. If they are sensible, they will have locked that as well, but it has no bolts on it."

"You know a great deal about the inside of the house," Thomas said.

Jack smiled. "I may have taken a little peek inside when Clement was out hunting. Out of curiosity, you understand."

"Know your enemy," Thomas said. "So is the kitchen our best chance of getting inside?"

"Depends if they barred the door between it and the rest of the house, but I don't believe Clement has any expectation you are mad enough to try a direct assault, so I doubt if they have."

Thomas looked at Jorge. "Did you bring anything with you to pick a lock?"

Jorge shook his head. "I did not realise I was going to have to."

"Then it is lucky I thought to bring these." Thomas reached into his jacket and withdrew a velvet wrap. He unrolled it to reveal slim metal instruments which caught the last of the light in the sky, and Jorge grinned.

"Those will do nicely." He reached out and selected two. "If there is anyone in this kitchen they are going to hear me working, so how do we do this?"

"If you are attacked, call out. Usaden, Will, me and two of Bel's boys will create a distraction on the river side. Edmund and Jack will come to protect you in case someone hears you. Take Kin with you as well. He will hear if anyone approaches. If there is anyone in the kitchen with luck they will come through to find out what is going on and leave the door unbolted." Thomas looked around at everyone until all nodded agreement.

"All right, let's get our people back."

THIRTY-THREE

The Corfe ran narrow and mostly shallow but the occasional pool was deep, so cold water reached the chests of Thomas and the others by the time they saw light shining through the windows of Hugh Clement's manor house. Two rooms on the upper floor showed flickering lamplight, but the whole of the ground floor was brightly lit. As Thomas climbed to the bank, water streaming from him, he saw movement beyond the windows of the room nearest the river. He watched shadows move within. Two men at least, he estimated, but there would be others. Hugh Clement would want protection around him, even if he was not expecting an attack.

Someone came to the window and cupped hands around their face to look out, but the darkness was deep now and Thomas knew he was invisible. He was considering going on his belly and crawling closer when they all heard a sound off to the left. Men talking. At least three of them.

Thomas raised a finger to his lips, pointed at Usaden,

then in the sound's direction. He pointed at Will, telling the two of them to go.

Usaden slipped away, disappearing into the gloom. It was harder for Will, at least a foot taller, but he had wrapped a scarf over his head to cover his blonde hair and dressed in dark clothing. Thomas stayed where he was, listening, but he heard no cries, no clashes, no screams. What he did hear was the sudden cessation of conversation. And then Usaden appeared at his side as mysteriously as he had left. He held up all four fingers and thumb of one hand and drew it across his throat.

Thomas cocked his head to one side in a silent question. Usaden appeared to think about it for a moment, then held both hands up, all fingers splayed. He closed and opened them three times. So thirty men remained. They would be bonemen, not those recruited from Wales. And, Thomas hoped, easier to deal with if it came to a fight. Thirty against their seven. Long odds, but they had fought worse in the past and won. And two of their seven were Usaden and Will, each of them worth at least ten men.

Thomas glanced at Michael and James, seeing only their shapes and the whites of their eyes. He did not know if they were scared, but they should be. Will, Usaden and himself were used to this kind of skirmish; Bel's sons were brick-makers, but hopefully no strangers to a fight. Lemster would have made them that way, as it had made Thomas as a lad.

The figure had gone from the window now and Thomas could see no more movement inside. He was trying to decide on his next move, knowing it would depend on Jorge, when the man appeared at the corner of the manor house, illuminated by a torch burning in a sconce. He raised a hand to beckon them over.

Thomas turned to Will and drew him close so he could whisper in his ear.

"You stay here with Bel's boys. I need someone outside to take care of Clement's men if they show an interest."

Will drew Thomas to him until his lips touched his ear.

"Ami's my sister. I come with you. Leave Usaden here, he is the better fighter in these conditions."

Thomas was not sure that was true.

They exchanged places again.

"His English is not good enough."

"There will not be much need for conversation. I am not going to stay out here while Ami is inside."

Thomas considered Will's stubbornness for a moment, then called Usaden close and told him what he wanted him to do. Usaden nodded and tapped Bel's two boys on the shoulder. He led them, together with Jack Pook, into the shelter of the riverside bushes. As soon as he had gone, Thomas and Will dashed across the short grass of the lawn to where Jorge still waited. The third of Bel's sons, Edmund, stood beside him, and Thomas told him to join the others, but to take care not to be seen. Watching the lad run fast to where he had seen the others disappear, Thomas was relieved to see his agility and lack of fear.

"I have opened the kitchen door and found my children tied up in there," said Jorge. "I released them, but want to take them from here before we do anything else."

Thomas tried to work out some way of achieving this,

but the only solution he could think of would mean sending Jorge away with the children. He was about to dismiss the idea when he realised it might be for the best. Jorge was good with people, less so when fighting them.

"Can you take all three with you and get back to Ludlow?" Thomas asked.

"Have you forgotten there is an army between here and there?"

"Follow the riverbank. Most men will be gathered around the Linney Gate, so you may gain entrance through another. If not, cross the river and hide out in the woods. How are they all, scared?"

"Of course they are. They told me a man threatened them if they made a sound."

"Then take them now. You are the best man for the job."

"Belia is still inside. I will not leave without her."

"You have to. We cannot leave the children in there. What if we have to fight?"

"If they have hurt Belia, I will kill them."

"You may have to get in line for that. Go get your children, Jorge. Take them away from here. Make them safe." For a moment, Thomas thought Jorge would refuse. If he did, Thomas did not know who else could take the children away. Bel's boys were not known to them, and Thomas needed Will and Usaden here. Then Jorge's shoulders dropped, and he nodded.

"All right, but once they are safe inside the castle I am coming back, unless you have joined us by then."

"Go fast and be safe."

Jorge brought his three children out. Jahan already tall

at ten years of age, his normally dark face pale; Saman only a year younger, his eyes refusing to rise from his feet; six-year-old Leila came last, the bravest of them all. Thomas touched each on the head and watched as Jorge led them away, then he dismissed all thought of them as he turned back to the open kitchen door.

Will entered first, his axe hanging from his left hand on its leather strap, a wickedly sharp knife in his right. He had to duck to avoid hitting his head, but was upright again in an instant, scanning the room. When Thomas entered behind he smelled stale food and an underlying taint of corruption. The iron stove was cold when he touched it. Three chairs were set against the wall. The ropes that had tied Jorge's children lay on the stone floor.

The far door was shut, but opened silently when Thomas raised the latch, relieved someone had not barred it from the other side. Perhaps it was fortunate they had put the children in the kitchen because it meant those on the other side would want the door to open fast if needed.

Thomas heard voices, his heart lifting when Amal's was amongst them. Then he heard the anger in her voice, underlain with a note of fear.

"Touch me again and my brother and father will kill you."

A laugh came in response. "Your brother and father are too busy at the moment and will not be alive to kill me come morning." The voice was that of Hugh Clement. "Even now, they may be strung up in the market square, along with others who resist me. Now lie back and spread those pretty thighs of yours. It is Daniel's turn to sample heathen flesh now I have broken you in."

346

Thomas put his hand on Will's chest as his son tried to come past him, but was brushed aside like a fly when Amal screamed. There was nothing for it but to follow.

Eight men stood in the big front room, more than Thomas expected, and light glowed from a dozen lamps. They had strapped Belia face down on a table. Amal lay on her back, tied to another. Both women were naked. Blood streaked Amal's thighs. Hugh Clement lounged in a padded chair, a goblet of wine in one hand. He was naked from the waist down. Daniel Lupton stood in front of Amal, his hose around his ankles.

Will's axe swung, almost taking Lupton's head from his shoulders. Will turned, blood-spattered, to confront the remaining men.

Thomas took two at almost the same time. Then the rest put up some kind of resistance, but it was not enough. It could never be enough against Thomas and Will. It would not have been enough against Will alone. His face was a rictus of hate as his axe danced through the air to do its deadly work.

"Not the man in the chair!" Thomas shouted as he took a third man, his sword running him through.

The floor grew slippery with blood. When Hugh Clement rose and tried to flee Thomas had to only put a hand on his chest and push him down. He set the tip of his sword against the man's throat to draw a bead of blood, then turned away to finish the last of the resistance, only to discover Will had left none alive. The air was filled with the metallic taste of blood. Thomas put his hand on his son's shoulder, felt it rise and fall as he drew air into his lungs.

"See if you can bar the kitchen door. Put that big oak table against it in case anyone tries to get in."

When Will had gone, Thomas cut Belia's bindings first, then went to Amal and did the same. He lifted her in his arms as if she weighed nothing. She clung against him, great sobs shaking both of them.

"They hurt me, Pa," she said. "Put me down, I want to punish the man who did this to me."

Thomas set her feet on the floor, keeping a hand on her shoulder to hold her back. He removed his cloak and wrapped it around her. Amal's eyes were brown fire as she stared at Hugh Clement.

"He put his cock inside me, Pa. Give me your knife."

"Not yet. You can kill him later, once I have questioned him."

"I will not kill him."

Thomas looked at his daughter, the hate in her eyes, and nodded his understanding.

Thomas touched Belia on the arm. "Jorge has taken your children back to the castle. You will have to wait until I finish with this man, but then I will take you to him. Did they hurt you as well?"

"Not yet, but they were going to. All of them." Belia's gaze burned against Hugh Clement, just as Amal's did.

"See if you can find your clothes. They must be here somewhere."

After Belia moved away, searching the room, Thomas stood in front of Hugh Clement and looked down at him. The man cowered under his gaze, and Thomas knew the sight of him must be fearsome—blood-streaked and wild-eyed. This man had violated sweet Amal and would account for his actions. Thomas would gladly hold him down while Amal unmanned him, but even that would not be enough. A rage burned through him that brought a tremble to his limbs and he did not know if he could control himself long enough to question the man. All he wanted was to thrust a knife into his heart. That might bring satisfaction, but no answers.

THIRTY-FOUR

"You will pay for this, Berrington." Hugh Clement summoned a sliver of courage from somewhere. He straightened in the chair and tried to pull his hose up to cover his shrivelled manhood. "You cannot attack a Justice of the Peace and get away with it. I will report this calumny to the Prince and King Henry. You will hang or worse for what you have done this night."

"It is not me who will hang. You violated my daughter and will be punished for it. By her, unless you tell me what I want to know."

"Don't trade with him, Pa." Amal came to stand at his side. "He is not worth it. Just let me kill him. After I have cut his cock off." She had found a knife from somewhere, no doubt from one of the men Thomas and Will had slain. She had also stripped the hose from one of the bodies and pulled them on, together with a too-large jacket.

"Let it go, Ami. Hate will kill you in more ways than you can know."

"Says you, who has killed more men than you can count."

"Which is why I say the words to you. Do not let this change you."

Amal punched his chest. "It has *already* changed me! He put that—that thing inside me. What if I am with child?"

"Then Belia and I will take care of it. You know we will."

Mention of Belia made Thomas glance to one side to find her staring into space, her face slack. Thomas doubted she saw anything, her sight still on what had happened in this room, her thoughts on her children.

"Belia." Thomas waited until she looked his way. "I want you to take Amal and find somewhere safe. There are rooms above us. Go there and hide until either me or Will come for you."

Belia looked around at the bodies, but showed neither fear nor hatred. She had moved beyond emotion to somewhere else.

"Why can we not stay?"

"Because I want neither of you to witness what I may have to do in this room." For a moment, Thomas was sure Belia had not heard him. Then she pulled her torn clothes around herself, took Amal's hand and led her from the room. It surprised Thomas that Amal went as meekly as she did, but no doubt she, too, was still in shock at what Hugh Clement had done to her.

Thomas turned back to the man. "We can do this two ways, but both will end in your death."

"In that case, why would I tell you anything?" Hugh

Clement tried to stand again but Thomas put the tip of his sword to his throat and he sank back into the chair.

"Because tell me the truth and I will ensure your death is swift and painless. I know how to do that, trust me. Resist, and I will allow my daughter to do whatever she wants to you. Your death will be slow and agonising. She knows the ways of a human body as well as I do, and I can promise she will take her time."

"Do not negotiate, Pa," said Amal. Thomas turned to find she had returned to the room. She stood in the doorway, shoulders back and head erect.

"Go with Belia. She needs you. I will call you down when I am done. If he continues to be a fool you can do as you want to him."

"If he talks, let me kill him. I can do it as swiftly as you."

"No. It will taint your soul forever. I will kill him. I will unman him as well if you ask it, but you are too innocent to corrupt yourself."

"Not innocent any longer. *He* ripped all the innocence from me!" She spat the words at Hugh Clement.

From beyond the door came the sound of clashing swords, and Thomas knew the remnant of Clement's men had forced their way into the kitchen. He would have to trust Will to handle them, and hope Usaden, Jack and Bel's boys would attack from the rear.

"Go upstairs and protect Belia," Thomas said. "Find a room and lock yourselves in. There is more fighting to be done yet." For a moment, Thomas was sure she was going to refuse, then Amal ran from the room.

Thomas turned back to Hugh Clement. While he was

distracted, the man had found a knife from somewhere and struck out. Thomas deflected the blade with ease and it clattered to the stone floor. He put his hand on Clement's chest and pushed him into the chair once more.

"Damn it, but you are an even bigger fool than I took you for. Was it you who captured Philippa? Did you rape her like you raped my daughter?"

"All I did was ask my men to question Pip about you. I needed to know what you were planning, nothing more. Their orders were to ask questions and let her go unharmed. What happened in that cottage was not down to me."

"Who did you send to fetch her? Was it really a monk from Wigmore?"

Hugh Clement's eyes flicked to one side. "Of course not. It was one of my own men. It is simple enough to get hold of a monk's robe for disguise."

"You sent Daniel Lupton to the castle to accuse me of the murder of those men."

"Are you trying to tell me you did not kill them?"

"I am telling you they would have killed me and, I feared, Pip. Why are you doing this? You must see you will fail and hang for your actions."

Hugh Clement attempted to gather what little strength and dignity he could muster. It did not appear to be much.

"I will tell you what you want to know, but only if you give me your word I can walk away from here. I will leave Ludlow. Leave the Marches. I will even leave England if you ask it of me, for I have contacts in Spain these days." A faint smile touched his lips.

"Answer me true and I will decide, if I think you have spoken the truth."

"I need a firm promise now. Everyone I asked about you said you are a man of your word. Thomas Berrington's word can be trusted. Bel Brickenden was the first to tell me that, but others have done so since. A few even remember you from before you left Lemster. Even those who did not like you say you are honest. Most consider you a fool for it."

Thomas paced the room, trying to decide. His entire being told him Clement had to die. For what he had done to Amal, if nothing else. How could he allow the man to live after such a violation?

But could he make a pact with the devil? Could he sell his own soul for the truth, then kill the man anyway? He believed he could, so offered a nod.

"Agreed."

"In writing," said Clement. "There is paper and ink over there."

"If you try to run, I will catch and kill you before you reach the door."

"I will not run. Not if you write my pardon."

Thomas found the paper, ink and quill, and scratched words that were barely legible from his anger. As much at himself as at this man. He sprinkled sand across the paper, then tipped it off before handing the note to Clement, who read it.

"Yes, that will do." He set the paper on a small table where his goblet of wine still remained miraculously intact. "Now, what is it you want to know?" He made another attempt to pull his hose up to cover himself, and this time Thomas allowed it.

He ran a hundred questions through his mind, picking, discarding, until he had the ones he most needed to know the answers to. He pulled a chair up and sat with his knees almost touching Hugh Clement's.

"First, who are the bonemen, and why are they in Ludlow?"

"Ah, you start with an easy one, do you?" Clement shook his head. "The answer to that is long and convoluted, so I will tell you the short version. I will also offer you the name of a man who can tell you everything, though whether you can get to him, and whether he will talk is another matter."

"The name?"

Hugh Clement stared at Thomas, who could see him gathering his courage now the immediate threat was fading.

Thomas reached across and picked up the note he had just written. He started to tear the paper in two. "Don't mess with me. Tell me the name."

"The man lives in London. You need to go there if you want to talk to him. He never leaves his house."

"I am still waiting." Thomas stopped tearing the paper but continued to hold it in front of Hugh Clement.

"His name is Galib Uziel."

Thomas put the note back on the table as he searched his memory, but the name was unfamiliar.

"One of those names is Moorish, the other Jewish. Who is this man?"

Hugh Clement smiled. "Speak with him and you will

find out. And yes, he is an exile from Spain. He hates the Spanish with every fibre of his being. It is one of the reasons he created the bonemen."

"To terrorise London and Ludlow?"

"To terrorise Christians. He cannot return to his homeland because it no longer exists. But England is a devout country about to tie its fortunes to those of Spain through the marriage of Prince Arthur and Catherine of Aragon. That is why the bonemen are in both London and Ludlow. Because they offer Galib Uziel the greatest opportunity to hit back at those he hates."

"Why you?"

Hugh Clement raised a shoulder, urbane now, sure of his own power and knowledge. "Because I enjoy wealth, and I was asked."

"By this Galib Uziel?"

"Of course not. By someone far closer."

Thomas sighed. "Now I need another name." He drew his knife, which he had put away. As he did so, he heard raised voices from somewhere inside the house, then Will ran into the room.

"We have beaten the rump of Clement's men, but Jack Pook says a third of the forces sent to Ludlow are on their way back here. They will arrive in a few minutes, so we need to get out now. Someone must have escaped and alerted them."

When Thomas looked at Hugh Clement, the man was grinning.

"Amal and Belia are upstairs. I need to fetch them. Tie Clement up and drag him out with you. Flee west to the Teme, then follow its banks to Ludlow. I will follow as soon as I can, but there is something I need to do first." Thomas thought for a moment. "When you go, see if you can make some kind of diversion. Send Usaden and Bel's boys, so they are seen. It might cause Clement's men to chase after them rather than come back here."

Thomas waited in the room while Will tied Clement's hands and feet, then lifted him in his arms as if he was a child and walked to the door.

"Struggle and I will toss you into the river," he said. "And then sit on you until you stop moving."

"Like father, like son," said Hugh Clement, seemingly unconcerned.

"See if you can get back into town and the castle," Thomas said to Will. "Lock the gates in the walls and raise the castle drawbridge."

"How will you get back in?"

"I don't know, but I will. Now go, before those men get here."

When his son had gone Thomas looked around the room. There were cabinets and drawers he wanted to search, sure they would contain more information on what was happening, but first he needed Amal and Belia with him. They could help, if there was time. He went into the wide hallway and climbed the stairs. When he reached the top, he heard faint voices which led him towards where Amal and Belia were hiding. He thought to chastise them for making a noise but knew he could not after what both had been subjected to.

He followed the corridor on soft footsteps, the voices growing louder as he went. He recognised Amal, and then he recognised another voice and wondered what Philippa

Gale was doing in the house. Had she been captured again so they could continue the questioning of her? Or was she tied to a bed, just as Amal had been tied downstairs?

The voices came from a room at the end of the corridor and Thomas stepped fast through the door and stopped dead.

Belia stood huddled into a corner of the room as if the junction of walls might protect her. Amal sat on a bed where the remnant of cut ropes coiled across the covers. Philippa stood in front of her with a matchlock pistol in one hand and a burning wick in the other.

"Hello, Tom," she said, turning so the pistol now pointed at him. "I wondered how long it would take for you to find us. Where are Hugh and Daniel?"

"Daniel is dead. Hugh is captive and being taken to Ludlow for judgement. Are you going to fire that thing?"

"I think I might. You have come here and ruined everything. Everything."

Thomas leapt at her as she moved to set the smoking wick against the matchlock chamber. A tremendous explosion shattered the air, and both Amal and Belia screamed. Then so did Philippa.

THIRTY-FIVE

When the smoke cleared Philippa continued to scream. The matchlock pistol lay in pieces across the floor. Philippa grasped her arm between hand and elbow. Except the hand was no longer attached. What was left of it lay on the floor and bed. Blood jetted from the stump as her voice keened in shock and pain.

Thomas went to Amal first and grasped her shoulders. He examined her face, her body, but could find no damage. She had been so close to the explosion her cheeks were darkened from the powder, but she was unharmed.

She tapped the heel of her hand against the side of her head. "I cannot hear anything, Pa." Her voice sounded odd.

"It will get better." Thomas was unsure whether he spoke the truth or not.

He used his knife to cut the curled rope on the bed into lengths, then wrapped them around Philippa's arm. The blood continued to flow.

He went to a narrow chair and kicked the back out, then used a spar to twist a knot in the bandage until eventually the bleeding slowed. It did not stop altogether, but at least Philippa would not bleed to death before he could treat the wound. Questions ran through his mind about why she was here, why she was threatening Amal, but he knew the answer. He had been a fool to believe her lies. Too easily swayed by a woman's beauty. By her soul as well, he knew. Every fibre of his being had believed she loved him.

He grasped her undamaged arm and dragged her from the room.

"Ami, Belia, with me, I need you."

Downstairs, Thomas sat Philippa in the chair vacated by Hugh Clement. He used the remains of the ropes that had tied Amal and Belia to secure her. He went to the window and looked out into the night, cupping his hands as he had seen someone do not so long before. There was no sign of Clement's men, and Thomas hoped Will and Usaden had led them away. Only when he knew they had at least a little time did he turn to his daughter.

"What is your understanding of written English like, Ami?" he asked.

"Middling," she said.

"There may be Latin, too."

Amal gave a shake of her head. "Why?"

"I believe this room to be where Hugh Clement is likely to keep any documents he may have, and I want them all. On second thoughts, don't bother reading anything, just search out what you can and I will find

360

something to put them in. Belia, you can help as well if we only need to gather them together."

As Amal and Belia started opening drawers and cupboard doors, Thomas went through to the kitchen. He found a hessian sack that once held flour and brought it through. Then he did the same as the others. It took time. Half an hour passed. None of Hugh Clement's Welsh recruits turned up, so Thomas assumed they had either not returned or were chasing Will and the others.

When the sack was half full and he could find no more documents, Thomas finally turned to Philippa. Her face was white, her pupils wide, and he knew she would be in agony.

"Was I only a pawn in all this, Pip?" he asked.

She looked away, unwilling to meet the anger in his eyes.

Thomas crossed to the chair. He untied her bindings, but then retied the rope around her damaged arm. If she tried to run one tug would send searing pain through her entire body.

"On your feet, we are going to Ludlow."

"Are you going to punish me, Tom?" Her voice was soft, as if shock was turning her responses off one by one.

Thomas worried her heart might give out before he could get her back to the castle; he had seen such happen before with serious wounds. Even so, he gave the rope a tug and she grunted in pain before rising to her feet.

"Hugh made me do it," she said.

Thomas did not believe her. He would believe nothing she told him ever again.

Outside, the moon had risen to cast enough light to allow them to follow the Corfe to its joining with the Teme. The larger river brought them south until they stood on the shingle bank below Dinham Bridge, from where Belia, Amal and the children had been taken. With good fortune, the children would be safe within the castle by now. Thomas called a halt and told Amal and Belia to remain with Philippa, who stood with head downcast, her damaged arm clutched to her chest.

Thomas climbed to the bridge. He looked in all directions but saw none of Hugh Clement's mercenaries and wondered where they were. Not all would have returned to the manor house. Had they heard their master was captive and fled back to Wales? Thomas had not taken them for that manner of men. If they heard Hugh Clement was held in the castle, they were more likely to double their attack. Yet he neither saw nor heard anyone.

As he turned to descend back to Amal and Philippa a dark shape detached itself from the shadows and ran towards him.

"Will sent me to wait for you," said Usaden. "Who do you have with you?"

"Amal, Belia and Philippa. Did Jorge get the children safely inside?"

"He did."

"And is Hugh Clement locked up?"

"He is."

"Do you have any idea where Clement's men are? I expected them to be all around the town walls."

"They are at the northern gate in the belief it is less secure. They have brought up a battering ram and are

362

preparing it for use, but I do not believe they know how to operate it correctly. The ground there is steep and I think it came as a surprise to them. Clearly they do not know the town well."

"Will the gate hold if they work it out?"

"Unlikely. It is by far the least sturdy. Will has an idea he wants to talk to you about."

"How do we get back inside the town walls?" Thomas asked.

"Through the gate in front of us, of course. Jorge and those sons of your friend wait on the other side for my signal."

Thomas clapped Usaden on the shoulder, eliciting what might have almost passed for a smile. "Then let us get inside so I can treat Philippa and hear what this plan of Will's is. Has he told it to you?"

"He has."

"And?"

"It is a good plan. I approve."

When they reached Dinham Gate, Usaden tapped out a series of knocks and within moments the gate swung open wide enough for them to pass through before being locked again. Jorge embraced Belia and Amal, then Thomas before leading them towards the castle. Another series of knocks opened the outer gate and then the inner.

"I am going to need Belia's help with Philippa. Her wound needs cleaning and cauterising. Then I want Belia to examine Amal to make sure that man did no permanent damage to her."

"The children are going to need her," said Jorge. "They

are too afraid to be left without their mother, and she is better with them than I am."

Thomas did not believe Jorge—he adored his children, and they him.

"I will help you," said Amal, who remained at his side, the rope binding Philippa still grasped in both her hands. "I know how to treat her injury almost as well as you do, and Belia has taught me all she knows of herbs and tonics. She can examine me later. Whatever has been done is already done, an hour more will make no difference."

"I care about your injuries far more than I do Philippa's," Thomas said.

"I hurt, Pa, but I can work. Belia can examine me when we are finished, or you can, I don't mind."

"I would rather it was Belia."

"Very well, but we need to treat Philippa and get some poppy and hashish into her before she passes out from the shock and pain. You cannot question her if she dies."

Thomas suppressed a smile because his daughter of fourteen years had come to the same conclusion he had. He wondered how much longer before she overtook him in skill, for she had already done so in comforting her patients. It had not been one of his strongest features, according to many.

As they crossed the inner bailey Thomas handed the hessian sack he carried to Jorge. "Keep this safe. I need to go through its contents as soon as I can find time. And bring Will to me so he can tell me this plan of his."

"As soon as he returns," said Jorge. "He is walking the town, checking that all is secure. He said he wants to call on his aunt as well before he finishes."

Instead of heading for the apartments, Thomas went towards the kitchen. Amal tugged Philippa along behind her.

"Go to my rooms and fetch my leather satchel," Thomas told her when they entered the kitchen.

He took the rope from her and she ran off. Looking at her litheness, Thomas knew she might appear outwardly no different, but tonight had changed her forever. Losing her virginity would have happened soon enough because she was a beautiful young woman. He had seen the way boys and men looked at her, but what she had lost was meant to be done in a loving manner, not through force. He felt a fresh wave of anger roil through him and tried to divert it. Later, he promised. More men would pay for what had been done to his daughter.

Once inside the kitchen Thomas sat Philippa in a heavy wooden chair. He tied both her arms to the chair, ignoring her cries of pain, then did the same with her legs.

"I will not run, Tom. You have my word."

"You have given me your word too many times of late for me to believe anything you say. Besides, this is not to stop you from escaping, for there is nowhere you can run to. What I have to do is going to be painful. I will give you poppy, but it will still hurt."

"Why are you helping me? I betrayed your trust. Most men would have let me die back there, but not you."

"No, not me. Were you working for Hugh Clement all this time?"

Philippa tried to smile, but the pain of her wound made the effort too hard. "Not Hugh. Never Hugh. He is a pawn, just like the others. I take my orders from someone far superior to those ants."

Thomas knew this was the time to press her for answers, before the pain of what was to come.

"Is that why you were so keen to seduce me?"

Philippa's eyes refused to meet his, but she gave a nod of her head.

"I was told to get you into my bed and keep you there. You were more resistant than I expected, but I managed it in the end. It was not such a hardship, was it?"

"No hardship at all."

"I almost confessed to you when we arrived in Ludlow. When I saw how brave you were. When I realised what a good man you are. But it was too late by then. I was having feelings for you and knew to confess would drive you away."

Thomas suspected her words of love were as false as everything else she had made him believe.

"Who is this man you serve?"

"Galib Uziel."

The same name given him by Hugh Clement.

"What is his connection to you, or is the relationship purely one of greed?"

"He is my father, and head of the bonemen in London."

Thomas stared at her, thoughts swirling through his mind but finding no traction.

"You told me your father farmed in Northampton-shire. It is how you came to work with the Queen. You were friends as young girls."

"That was the truth. But... something happened. Father was accused of a crime he did not commit and was dismissed. We moved to London and he set up the bone-men. Not at first, but later after Elizabeth of York married Henry Tudor. To punish her and the King for the harm done to him by her mother."

"Uziel is a Moorish name."

"He is half Moor. My mother came from Germania, hence my pale skin, but my father is a Moor. I would say like you, but your Moorishness is nothing but an affectation."

"I don't understand why you were allowed back into the Queen's presence again if your father was exiled."

"Because we are friends and she holds no blame to me. When I went to her at Elsyng Palace she welcomed me, pleased I had returned. Everything I told you was the truth, Tom. All I did was withhold some of it."

"Did your father send you to the Queen to spy on her and the King?"

Philippa shook her head. "We fell out. Over a man I was in love with. Father disowned me. As did the man I thought loved me. I had no one else, so I went to Elizabeth."

Amal ran into the room with Thomas's satchel grasped in her hands. She was breathing hard.

"Are you all right?"

"I ran, that is all." Amal dropped the satchel on the big kitchen table and went to the fire. She used bellows to bring the coals to a white heat, then looked around for something made of iron. She opened drawers until she found what she wanted. A long rod with a wooden handle at one end. She thrust it into the flames and used the bellows again. She knew exactly what to do without being instructed.

Thomas put aside the information Philippa had given him, knowing he would have to come back to it later. The name would be enough to track this Galib Uziel down when he returned to London, but he suspected he already knew who he was and where he lived. He would have to confront the man before he broke the spirit of England. Perhaps now King Henry would believe the threat against him when Thomas laid it out. He suspected Hugh Clement had been recruited to spread the bonemen's evil to Ludlow. The only thing that made no sense is what Philippa's involvement was; because she had to be involved. The daughter of the head of the bonemen here in Ludlow when they made inroads in the town? Had she lied about the falling out or not? If so, why? What benefit would it give her now? Thomas might have believed her an innocent party had she not tried to kill Amal.

He used one of the small blades from his satchel to slice through the bandage on Philippa's stump. As he did so it started to pulse blood again.

Thomas discarded the blood-soaked linen and leaned closer to examine the wound, but it was too streaked with gore to see anything. He brought across a bowl of warm water and a linen cloth and started to wipe it clean.

Philippa cried out even though he was being as gentle as he could.

"There is poppy in your bag, Pa," said Amal. "Belia mixed the strongest dose she could. Here, change places with me, I will give it to her and clean the wound. You know I do it better than you." She smiled. "Nobody ever called me a butcher."

Thomas touched her cheek as they passed each other. He knelt and picked up the bellows. The iron rod was almost hot enough, but he could not use it until the poppy mixture dulled Philippa's pain. He wondered why he was even bothering to try. Let her scream. It would be punishment for her treachery. Yet he could not. A faint remnant of the feelings he felt for her remained.

"I have done the best I can, Pa." Amal crossed the room to him. "The poppy is working, but you have to stop the bleeding or she is going to die. She may still, and you may want her to, but I know you better and you will not let it happen."

"No."

Thomas rose with the glowing iron rod held in front of him.

"Are you able to hold her firm, Ami?"

"We should have sent for Will, but I can try."

"Apparently he is prowling the town."

"He needs a woman to soften him," said Amal.

When Thomas pressed the iron rod to the stump of Philippa's arm she screamed loud enough to wake the dead and writhed like a headless snake. Amal held her as best she could. As Thomas cauterised each of the leaking blood vessels, the stink of burned flesh filled the room. When he was finished Amal had nothing to do because Philippa had fled into unconsciousness.

Thomas doused the iron rod in a bucket of water.

He stared down at Philippa, watching the slow rise and fall of her chest, and wondered what they could do with her. There must be somewhere in the castle that could be used as a prison cell. Hugh Clement would be held somewhere secure. He would house the two of them together. It would be fitting justice.

"Clean the wound again and bandage it," he said.

When Thomas walked from the kitchen Will had returned and stood waiting for him.

THIRTY-SIX

"Hugh Clement's army has returned from his house and is gathered beyond Linney Gate," said Will.

"Usaden told me you have a plan." Thomas sat in the Armoury with his son, Jorge and Usaden. Kin lay asleep in front of the wide hearth, even though there was no fire in it. Two of Bel's sons, Michael and James, had been despatched to watch over Hugh Clement in his makeshift cell. Philippa had been carried to the same room and laid on the bed. Amal was with Belia so she could be examined.

Midnight struck from the tower of St. Laurence's church as they gathered. The night outside was pitch-black, clouds scudding across from the west to obscure the moon. Thomas was bone-weary but knew none of them could rest until the attack on the town was over.

"Tell it to me," he said to Will.

"I spent some time walking the top of the town walls looking down on the gathered men. They could see me and fired arrows, but it was simple enough to avoid them.

It angered them they could not get to me, so I strutted around some more on purpose as I counted them. They are around a hundred and fifty, but no more, and I think we should open some of the town gates and let them in."

Thomas stared at his son. "Are you mad?"

"No, not mad. Usaden agrees with me."

Thomas glanced at him to receive a nod in return.

"And you, Jorge?"

"You know I am not someone to ask about warfare," he said. "But Will needs to explain more to you."

Thomas turned his attention back to his son. "Yes, you do."

"The gates are narrow, so they will be forced to enter no more than three abreast. I have talked to several men in the town and enough are with us. We have archers, swordsmen, and others who can wield a weapon. We set the archers atop the walls and they fire down on the men as they come through the gates. Most will enter through Linney because that is where they are gathered. We should be able to take at least a score or more of them that way, and when we do, there will be closer to a hundred to concern us."

"Still too many," Thomas said.

Will acknowledged with a nod. "The alleys that lead from the gates are narrow apart from three. We set more archers on the church and houses on either side and fire into them as they try to get into the market square. I propose we keep the other gates shut because then some attackers will try to open them, to assist their own escape, if nothing else. But we open Dinham Gate because that offers the easiest access to the castle, and the roadway up is steep. It will split their forces and we take more of them as they enter. Each of us stalks the alleys and take men as we find them. If we stay in the narrowest streets they cannot rush us, and I know you, me and Usaden are a match for any five men, and only that number can move easily through the alleys of the town."

"God's teeth, Will, how many will we need to kill for this plan of yours to work?"

"Reduce their number by half and I believe the rest will run back where they came from."

"You think so, do you?" Thomas looked around at their group. "These are men of Wales. Hard men. Cruel men. Go find someone in Ludlow who has fought them before and ask whether these men will retreat. They will fight to the last."

"No, they will not," said Will, "because this is not their fight. They are mercenaries. They came here for money. That and bloodshed. But when the blood on the ground is theirs, not ours, and they hear we have Hugh Clement captive and there will be no payment, they will flee."

"Half of them?" Thomas said with a shake of the head.

"More if we can manage it. I was erring on a smaller number, but I think we can kill more than that. You know Usaden can, and so can I. I have seen you fight, Pa. You are not as young as you used to be, but you are still good enough."

"And me?" asked Jorge.

"We need someone here to let us back in if we have to retreat."

"I thought we were going to kill men, not retreat," Thomas said.

"Better to have a complete plan than half of one," said Will with a smile. "And there is one more part to it. Once they are all inside the town walls, we close the gates. There is a man who knows how to bar them from outside and has offered to take a group of men to do that. We trap them within the walls and kill as many as we can."

Thomas could scarce believe what he was hearing. He knew Will was headstrong and that his son was enamoured of battle… but this?

"How long to prepare?"

"An hour, but I say we make it two. They will grow frustrated by then. If they break through Linney Gate sooner then we bring the plan forward. We set cauldrons of hot pitch over the gates we intend to open. We recruit as many archers as we can, as many men willing to fight." Will glanced at Edmund. "I assume you and your brothers are with us?"

"We are, and we can all draw a longbow if you can find us one each."

"We are standing in the Armoury of Ludlow Castle," said Will. "I don't think finding weapons will be a problem. You can choose from the best bows, swords and knives. Once you have done that, two of you come with me. You know the men of Ludlow better than I do. We need to recruit as many as we can."

Men of this town will die, Thomas thought, but kept it to himself. Perhaps it would not come to that, but he did not expect every man who fought on their side to survive the night. He decided to carry his leather satchel with him so he could treat the wounded.

Thomas rose to his feet and motioned Will to follow.

Bel's sons were selecting weapons, commenting on the quality of each.

"While Edmund and James are attempting to recruit men to fight, make sure they only ask those who can be trusted. I expect the bonemen will have spies inside the town walls."

"I agree, but not enough to cause havoc unless they have a store of black powder." Will slowed. "Now that is a thought, Pa. Do you think there is any in the armoury?"

"More than likely, but nobody who knows how to use it. Even if there is, best to leave it where it is."

"I expect you are right. I need to go into town with Edmund and James now."

"Are you sure you know what you are doing? Why not leave the attackers outside the town walls? They have had no luck breaking through yet, and when dawn comes I expect them to retreat."

"They will break through," said Will. "I watched that battering ram they have and it is going to do the job. When is the question. Trust me, Pa. Usaden has trained me well, so has *morfar*. Olaf might be a giant of a man, but he has the best tactical brain I have ever known. This will work, I promise you."

"At the expense of how many lives?"

Will stared at his father. "You know as well as I that no fight comes without casualties. I will make that clear to those who agree to fight. I am forcing no one to join us if they don't want to, but this is their town. These are their houses, their businesses, their wives and their children. A man deserves to fight for what is his. You have done the same, I know you have."

And, Thomas thought, that was the problem with Will's plan. It was better than anything he could have come up with himself. He wondered if he was getting too old for such challenges. If he wanted to stay locked inside the castle protected by three layers of stone. The man he had once been would never have contemplated such cowardice.

In the courtyard, the dull, heavy sound of a large tree-trunk hitting the Linney gate came clear through the air. The entire town would hear it as well, a countdown auguring the fight to come. Some would cower in their homes. Others would come out despite their fear to protect what was theirs. Few of them would be like Will or Usaden, men with no trace of fear. Men sure of their own abilities. Thomas had been like them once, but worried he was no more.

So perhaps it was time to fight. Time to discover if he still could, or if a fear lay within him that never had before. He thought back to the barber's shop on Ludgate Hill. He had not hesitated to protect the barber and his daughter. His reaction that day was instinctive.

He thought of the men on the road between Lemster and Ludlow. He had reacted the same way there, without hesitation. The first time had been to protect strangers. The second to protect a woman he had feelings for. Feelings she had betrayed, but he would do the same again because that was his nature.

He thought of protecting Amal and Belia, and knew he would protect the townsfolk of Ludlow in the same way. To the best of his ability. That ability had been impressive at one time, but the last ten years had been easier for him.

The Duke of Granada was not expected to fight his own battles. Or even any battles. It had been a great deal of argument and diplomacy, and often enough following orders he did not agree with. Now Thomas put all that behind him, as well as thoughts of his three-score years. He had never contemplated growing so old, but even now he did not feel the weight of his years.

"Go, do what you must," he said to Will, before pulling his son into an embrace. "There is something I have to do first, but I will join you before you put your plan into action. Know I will be at your side."

"There is no need, Pa, not if you want to stay here with the women."

Thomas stared at his son, a hard stare, and Will looked away.

"All right. I will come for you before the fighting starts. But I want you to stay close to Usaden."

"I can fight, Will. You know I can."

"I have seen little of that of late, but I admit you looked more like your old self at Hugh Clement's house."

"I will fight alongside you." Thomas turned away before he started an argument. He only hoped he spoke the truth.

He found Amal with Belia, who had finally calmed the children enough for them to sleep. All three lay tumbled in one bed, arms and legs tangled. Belia sat in a chair, looking as if she was about to join them, her eyes heavy-lidded. Amal sat in another chair, but her eyes were bright. Thomas hoped she was not reliving her ordeal but suspected he hoped in vain.

"Is Ami all right?" he asked Belia, his voice low.

She gave a nod. "She is sore and bruised, but otherwise undamaged. I have washed her, so with luck nothing will set in her, but if it does I can take care of that too." Belia lowered her voice so Amal could not hear. "Her body will mend, Thomas, but her mind dwells on what happened."

"You were there as well."

"I am older, and have experienced more of men, even men like that. Ami has not. She needs time to come to an accommodation with what happened to her."

"We might not have time." Thomas turned away, hoping he might find some distraction for his daughter. "What did you do with that sack of papers, Ami?" He put a hand on the back of her chair, leaning on it for support.

"Over there on the table."

The room was the one Belia and Jorge had chosen and was finely appointed. Thomas wondered who had used it before everyone left with Prince Arthur. It was large enough to have been Sir Richard Pole and his wife. There was a wide bed with heavy drapes, together with two smaller beds. The children had chosen the larger one, or been put there.

"I have a job for you if you are not going to sleep."

"How can I sleep after what happened, and with those men outside the town walls? And that crash-crash-crash on the town gate. They will break in and create havoc. They are…" Amal took a deep breath before letting it out, fighting to find some stability in her thoughts. "Will told me he has a plan." Amal's eyes met her father's. "Don't stop him, Pa. He is ready. You know he is."

Thomas offered a sharp nod. "Yes, he is."

"I know what you want," said Amal. "To go through

those papers and search for something that might offer a clue to who is behind all of this. That man who raped me will not be. He is too weak, even if I could not fight him off."

"Daniel Lupton held you down."

Amal nodded, her eyes not meeting Thomas's.

"You could not fight them, Ami. You did the right thing."

"It does not feel like the right thing. But I will look through the papers for you and hope it stops the thoughts I cannot push away." Amal waved a hand in dismissal. "Go do your fighting, Pa. It is what you are good at."

"Not for a while now."

"You are still good enough." Amal rose to her feet and embraced him, kissing his mouth. Then Belia was there as well, clinging to him.

"Take care of Jorge, Thomas," she said. "He likes to think he can fight, but you know he is not like the rest of you."

"I will bring him home safe."

"Make sure you do, or I will have to marry you myself."

Thomas laughed. "Is that a threat or a promise?"

"I will leave you to decide. You are supposed to be the clever one."

Thomas went to check on Philippa and Hugh Clement, locked in the same room. He needed to question Philippa again, but morning would be soon enough. Perhaps Amal would find what he sought in those papers. There were enough of them.

One of the remaining guards had been set to keep watch on the room, his face familiar to Thomas, though he could not recall from where. He knew he was remiss in not learning the names of those who made the castle function. The man was slumped on a chair, barely awake. He jerked upright when Thomas tapped his foot with his own.

"Any sound from inside?" he asked.

"They were talking earlier, but they spoke too softly for me to make out their words. Is it true Pip betrayed Prince Arthur?"

So that was the story going round. Good.

"It is true. The Prince and Ludlow both."

"Will she be punished?"

"That is not up to me. Sir Richard, Gruff and Prince Arthur will make that decision when they return. They will have a new princess with them by then."

The man smiled and settled back in his chair. Thomas considered asking him to at least make some attempt to stay awake but knew it would not be heeded. Philippa and Hugh Clement could not escape, and even if they did, the castle was locked tight.

Thomas descended to find Will standing in the inner bailey with Edmund and James. Usaden had returned and Jorge stood beside them. He was dressed in a chain-mail vest of excellent quality, if a little tight. Thomas wore his ordinary clothes. Or rather, the clothes he was most comfortable in; those of Moorish Spain.

Will looked at him and offered a nod.

"I am ready," Thomas said. "Let us go defeat some evil men."

THIRTY-SEVEN

It was the Welsh who tipped the balance when they broke through Linney Gate. Men streamed in to be constrained by the narrowness of the entrance. As they did so, the leaders were allowed to get forty paces inside, more men pushing from behind, before those placed on the walls above tipped vats of boiling pitch onto those below. A great scream rose and as it did, the archers arrayed along the walls fired down into those who had nowhere to run. As men tried to escape along Linney into town other archers perched on the buttresses of the church aimed their arrows and took more victims. It was a start. A skirmish. Thomas knew the fighting to come would be closer at hand and more savage. He had never fought the Welsh, but even when he lived in Lemster as a boy their reputation was fearsome. It was said they never gave ground and never gave up. He stayed long enough to watch the first attempt at slowing them, then stepped back and tapped Jorge on the shoulder, who had stood watching in horror as dying men collapsed to the ground and others walked over their bodies.

"This way." Thomas turned into a narrow alley between two houses. He knew enough of Ludlow to have at least a little knowledge of its passages and secret places, and intended to make all the use of them he could. It surprised him to hear nails on stone as Kin came to join them. Thomas had assumed the dog would be with Usaden, but perhaps Kin knew they needed him more. Thomas dropped his hand and stroked the dog's narrow head and Kin twisted to offer his ears.

Behind them came the clash of sword on sword. More screams as arrows found fresh targets, but the archers could only hold the Welshmen back for so long as they continued to stream through the gate. The more attackers who entered the town, the more its defence would rely on individual bravery.

Thomas heard a shout from behind. When he turned, half a dozen men were running at them.

He pushed Jorge behind him and turned to confront the attackers.

The narrowness of the alley meant that only two abreast could come at him, and even then they struggled to wield their swords as they clashed against stone and wattle. It was one reason Thomas had pushed Jorge behind him because it left him free to attack.

He took the first man before he even saw the strike coming. The second barely lasted any longer. Their bodies made an impediment to the progress of the others, so Thomas turned things around and went at them. Kin leapt past him, a harsh snarl coming from lips pulled back to reveal sharp teeth. The dog was so fast no man could react in time to avoid his snapping lunges.

Six men were easy in the confines of the alley, and when they were dead Thomas believed that Will's plan might work. Then Jorge shouted for him, and when he turned four more were coming from the other direction. They must have come around into the market square and found an entrance that way. Thomas felt disappointment they had reached that far already. He stepped past Jorge, but then heard something from behind. Glancing back, he saw another eight men enter where the six had before, and cursed.

"Do what you can," he called to Jorge, then turned back to the larger force. "Kin, wait."

The attackers approached more slowly, aware they faced stronger opposition than they had counted on. One man came ahead of the others, swinging his sword from side to side. Almost too late, Thomas saw another raise a crossbow and fire. He flung himself to one side. As he did so, the lead man came at him at a run. Kin leapt at him, his jaws opening a deep wound in the attacker's thigh and he went to the ground, where Kin continued his attack.

Thomas raised his sword as two more men leapt over their fallen comrade. Blades clashed, while from behind Thomas heard Jorge's own ring against that of an attacker. The men coming at Thomas were skilled, fast, and ruthless. One had discarded his hat and his long hair hung past his shoulders. He was short, wiry, with a black beard and skin dark from living in the open air. Another had become a new target for Kin. The others held back, afraid of the mad dog.

The man spat curses in Welsh, which Thomas failed to understand, but their meaning was clear enough.

The man danced on nimble feet, advancing to strike out, parried, parrying in turn as Thomas made his own attack. The other men behind waited, cheering their champion on. Thomas was relieved they were doing so because it meant he had only the one man to worry about for the moment.

When someone slammed into his back, he assumed it was Jorge, because if not he would already be dead. As the Welshman saw him lose balance he came in again, fast as a snake, and the tip of his sword cut into Thomas's arm. While the man was still grinning Thomas heaved himself forward, feeling the sword slide through his flesh, and ran the man through. The Welshman fell to his knees, then toppled onto his back, lifeless eyes staring at the dark sky.

"Are you still alive?" Thomas shouted to Jorge.

"Just about. They are falling back. How about you?"

Thomas watched the remaining men packed into the alley.

"Afraid not. Keep close, I am going to go at them."

"I am a little busy right now," said Jorge.

Thomas's eyes scanned the group, picking out who would be brave enough to attack him. He found his man and ran at him. Instead of falling back as some others had, this one stood his ground, setting his feet and raising his sword.

Thomas threw the knife he held in his left hand at him, watching as it twisted through the air. It struck the man's chest hilt first.

The man laughed and took a pace closer.

Thomas pulled a second knife and threw it. This time he had more skill, or more likely luck, and the shaft thudded into the man's belly. Lower than Thomas had hoped, but the pain would be intense. He stepped forward and used his sword in a great blow from above, almost taking the man's head from his shoulders.

The sight of another of their number killed unmanned the few remaining attackers, who retreated. Soon only two remained, and Thomas knew they were dead men too stupid to realise their mistake.

"How many do you have now?" he shouted to Jorge.

"Two, but they are being annoyingly stubborn."

Thomas made an instant decision.

"Kin, kill!" He released his dog to attack before turning to push past Jorge. He struck out at the two men facing him, taking both in a heartbeat that stilled their own.

"With me," he said, and ran along the alley, uncaring if the rump of Welshmen followed or not. Out on Linney, attackers passed but only in ones and twos, and the archers and other defenders were taking care of them.

When they came into Market Square Thomas found a different battle taking place. The attackers had formed themselves into a circle in the wide space, swords facing outwards, while the townsfolk made darting attacks. Thomas saw men fall, but most of the injured were those of Ludlow. He caught sight of Will on the far side of the square, towering above everyone else. Usaden was at his side, but only the top of his head was visible. Thomas tried to calculate how many of the attackers were in the defensive circle, but it was difficult to tell in the dark and melee. He estimated between sixty and eighty, which left almost half that number still prowling the streets.

When Thomas saw Will give a great bellow and run at the circle, his axe swinging free, he did the same on the other side. His sword flashed. His knife struck out. Men were injured or died.

Thomas pulled back, his attack lasting only a few seconds, too fast for the defenders to react. On the far side, he saw Will do the same and his son offered a nod.

The next time Usaden ran in beside Will, even more deadly. Jorge joined Thomas, and they injured another two before drawing back. Kin prowled the edge of the defensive circle, darting in now and again to savage legs and feet.

The circle of men grew tighter. Their defence was sound, but they had never come up against the likes of Will or Usaden before and did not know how to deal with them.

Other men of Ludlow gathered. Edmund Brickenden punched Thomas on the shoulder, a grin on his broad face.

"I killed three, Tom," he said.

"How do you feel about killing three more, and then another three?"

"Sounds fine to me."

The next time Thomas ran at the defensive line, Edmund was with him on one side, James and Michael on the other, and a sense of rightness settled through him. These were the boys of a girl he had once loved above all others, and they were defending what was theirs. Had life taken a different turn they might have been his sons.

They were only average fighters, but Thomas deflected two or three blows that might have struck them, and their own blades did damage. The attackers had become defenders, and as the night progressed their number grew less.

Thomas made his way around to Will, whose face was blood-spattered so only the whites of his eyes showed, together with his pale hair.

"We should offer them a chance to surrender," Thomas said. "To retreat and scurry back to Wales."

"No—we kill them all."

"We could do that, yes, but it will mean men of Ludlow will die as well. You have seen they are not skilled fighters. Already a dozen will never see the dawn, and twice that number will need my attention before then. How many attackers still roam the town?"

"There are a few left," said Usaden. "This group is the bravest of them. Most of the others fled when they had the chance. We can take them all, Thomas."

"I am tired of killing men for the sake of it," Thomas said. Usaden did nothing but stare at him. Killing is what Usaden did. But he also respected those who employed him, and those he liked. Thomas was relieved he was one of that tiny number. Will was another. So was Amal. Thomas hoped if Usaden stayed in England he might add a few more to his list.

"Do we talk, then?" asked Will.

"They are watching the three of us. You have scared them and they believe you our commander. It should be you."

"You are better with words, Pa. You do it."

"Then stand beside me so I can pretend I am following your orders."

Will walked a little behind Thomas as he made his way to the gathered attackers. Thomas had watched them as the fight progressed and estimated he knew who their leader was. A man no taller than the others but better dressed, still wearing a green hat, unlike most of the Welsh. He stood unprotected by the others in the front rank, and it was to him that Thomas strode.

The man raised his sword, ready for an attack, but none came.

"Do you speak English?" Thomas asked.

"Better than you by the sound of it. What is it you want?" The man spoke to Thomas, but his eyes were on Will, a judgement in them.

"You were sent here on a false errand, but we have no wish to punish you for following the orders of an evil man. We offer you this one chance. We will withdraw to the edge of the square. Linney Gate remains open. Leave England and return to Wales and you can die old men in your beds."

"You make it sound so attractive," said the man.

"Then die with a beautiful woman riding you, but die you will, the same as us all. The difference is you can choose whether it is tonight, or in your homeland many years from now."

"I need to speak to the others."

"Then do it."

Thomas withdrew at Will's side.

"If they refuse, we attack hard and fast," he said. "No

mercy. None. Send men out to call everyone here. Get the archers to circle the square, swordsmen closer in."

Will offered a nod and went to speak with Edmund, Michael and James, who ran off into the dark. When he returned he stood at Thomas's side as the Welsh leader spoke to his men in their own language. There was some argument, but as time passed Thomas saw there would be no more fighting. When the man returned to the edge of the defensive circle Thomas walked across with Will and stood in front of him. He lowered his sword and slid it back into the sheath at his waist. It was not much, but it was something.

The man did the same.

"No archers to pick us off as we go?"

"No archers."

"We can take our dead with us?"

"Those you can carry. Any left when dawn comes will be given a Christian burial here."

The man gave a nod. "Then it is agreed." He took a step out from the circle, spat in his hand and held it out.

Thomas was about to do the same when Will came past him and shook the hand.

"You fight well," said the man.

"So do you."

"What is your name?"

"Will Berrington."

"I am Llewelyn ap Gwyrdd. May we hope to never face each other in battle again."

"Stay on your own side of the border, then," said Will.

The men of Ludlow stood back against the edge of Market Square and watched as the Welshmen gathered into cohorts before marching away through the streets and out through Linney Gate, where they had come from.

"That will need fixing come morning." Will stared at the shattered wood of the gate.

"I am sure there are fine workmen in Ludlow." Thomas slapped his son on the back. "Come on, I need to eat, and I need to sleep. I also need to talk to Ami about what happened to her tonight. It fills her head to the exclusion of all else."

"Let Jorge do it," said Will as they started back towards the castle. "He is better at that kind of thing."

As they passed Agnes's bakery the door opened and she emerged from inside. She ran to Thomas and embraced him so tightly he could hardly breathe, then she kissed his face.

"Thank you, brother. You have saved me all over again." She wiped tears from her face.

"I wish the fight had never come."

"But it did, and you were ready. You too, Will. We watched you from the windows upstairs. The girls wanted to come out and fight but I stopped them." She kissed Thomas again. "Come to see us tomorrow. Or today, I expect it is now. Ludlow owes you a great debt."

Except, as Thomas walked back to the castle, he wondered if she spoke the truth. He knew matters were not yet concluded. This battle was just the beginning. And the head of the enemy remained to poison England.

THIRTY-EIGHT

Once inside the walls of Ludlow Castle, Thomas looked around to ensure everyone had returned safely, but he could not see Will or Usaden.

"Did you see where Will went?" he asked Jorge, who looked as if he could barely stand. "He was with us at Agnes's house and I assumed he had come ahead."

"I think he went with Usaden and Kin to follow the Welshmen. He said something about wanting to make sure they kept to their side of the bargain and did not sneak back."

"They were beaten," Thomas said. "And their leader gave us his word."

Jorge laughed and shook his head. "Despite all you have been through over the years, you are still too quick to trust the word of others—even that of your enemies."

"They were mercenaries, not enemies. There is a difference. Usaden was a mercenary when he came to the siege of Málaga. I still recall watching him walk off the galley that brought him and his companions from Africa."

"And?"

Thomas tried to remember if he had been trying to make a point, but was too exhausted to follow his own thread. Then it came to him. "Usaden was loyal to those who recruited him, but he had no enmity for those he fought. It was a transaction, nothing more."

"Except he has changed," said Jorge. "His loyalty is now to you, to Will and Amal."

"You also," Thomas said.

"Belia and me and our children, yes, but it is you he follows without question."

"More so Will these days."

"As it should be, perhaps. Our children grow up and, if we have done the work of raising them right, then they are better than we are. Now, I am going to find somewhere to bathe the stink of death from me and then I intend to sleep until noon." Jorge slapped Thomas on the back. "I suggest you try to do the same."

"Soon."

When Jorge had gone Thomas stood in the courtyard, swaying a little, his mind failing to gain traction. He knew he should take Jorge's advice and sleep, but there were things he needed to do first. Once he remembered what they were.

He found Amal sitting at the table when he returned to the room he had left her. Belia was curled on the bed with her children, sound asleep. A single lamp burned where Amal studied the documents from the hessian sack. Thomas watched her, head bowed, a frown of concentration on her brow. Only when he crossed the room towards her did she look up.

"You are still alive, Pa. Good. And Will?"

"We all survived the night. Even Jorge. He has gone to bathe, so we will need to move to my room when he arrives. No doubt he will be naked when he gets here."

Amal laughed. "I think I have seen him naked more times than I have seen myself." For a moment she was the old Amal; carefree, positive, a little wicked. And then, watching his daughter, Thomas saw the moment when the memory of what had been done to her returned.

He reached across the table and took her hand, enclosing it in both of his. She offered a smile, but it came and went too fast.

"It will get better," he said. "I thought losing your mother would scar my soul forever, but now when I think of her, which is every single day, the pain recedes little by little and I recall more of the good times, of which there were many. The pain of her loss will never leave me, but we make accommodations."

"Am I like her? Will tells me I am, but you never say so."

Thomas stared at his daughter, and in doing so, it was as if he was looking at her mother, Lubna.

"You could be her reborn. She was only three or four years older than you when she came to my house in the Albayzin. It is as if she has been returned to me. And you are like her in more than just how you look. You are like her inside as well." Thomas gave a smile. "Like her, but like yourself as well."

"Are you like your father, Pa? You never talk about him."

"I am nothing like my father. Nothing at all. I never

speak of him because he was a bully and a coward. I recall nothing good about the man. Nothing at all."

"Then you are not like him. Will is like you, isn't he?"

"Some of him, yes, but he is more like Olaf than me."

Amal shook her head, her dark hair covering her face, so she had to push it back. "You always say that, but you are wrong. Will is more like you than *morfar.*" Amal used the northern word for her grandfather, as she always did.

"Do you miss him?"

Amal frowned. "Will?"

"Olaf."

"Of course, but I know the life we led in Granada would end. *Morfar* transferred his loyalty to Isabel, but he was never used in the same way as he was under the Sultan. I don't think Fernando trusted him, even if Isabel did. Now we are gone, he told me he will travel north to his homeland. There is nothing to keep him in Spain since Fatima passed." Amal raised her eyes to stare into Thomas's. "He told me he feels his age these days. That he never thought he would, but the years accumulate and take their toll. His life has been hard, just as yours has, Pa. Do you feel your age?"

"Tonight more than ever."

"Are we to stay in England now?"

"I gave my word to Isabel to protect her daughter, so yes, we stay as long as Catherine needs us."

"I used to think Cat would rather marry Will, but I know that is impossible. Just as I used to dream something would happen to Fernando and you could marry Isabel. Even if he had died, you would not have been allowed to, though I know it is what you both wanted. What you both deserved. Each other."

Thomas smiled. "Why are you so clever, Ami?"

She shrugged. "My father does not allow me to be anything else, and I never want to be anything other than his daughter. Even now."

Jorge came in. He was naked and damp. He stopped and stared at them until Amal laughed and gathered the papers together.

"Am I so funny, Ami?"

"You know you are, *tio*, but I love you anyway. We will be gone in less than a minute."

"Not on my behalf. I am too tired to ravish Belia, and besides, I would not want to shock my children."

Amal laughed again and rose to her feet. "I think it is a little late for that, don't you?" She clutched twenty or thirty pieces of paper. The rest remained scattered across the table.

"These are the ones you need to read for yourself, Pa, the others are of no importance."

Thomas heaved himself to his feet and followed her to the door. He trusted her word.

When they entered his room Amal asked, "Is this where you and she slept?"

"It is."

"I don't really know her, but I assume you must have trusted her to sleep with her, to share this room."

"I did."

"And she betrayed you."

"She did." Thomas lit a candle and set it on the small table near the window. Beyond the glass, night continued to hold hard to the dark. "Now show me what you found, and then we can sleep."

"Can I stay with you, Pa? I cannot sleep alone, not tonight."

"Of course you can." Thomas thought of all the other nights they had slept three to a bed, Will, Amal and him. It had been some years since they had done so. Will was too big now, and Amal was growing into a woman. But tonight he would allow her to sleep in his room because his protection would be important to her. Even if he had failed in his duty and allowed her to be defiled by Hugh Clement. For a moment, anger surged through him and he had to fight the urge to rush to the room where the man slept alongside Philippa Gale and kill them both. Tomorrow, he would think of a suitable punishment. Tonight, he would read the papers Amal had selected, and then he would sleep.

Before Thomas could start, Amal reached for the papers and re-arranged them into a stack.

"Start at the top and work your way to the bottom. They tell a story, and you will not see it unless you read them in order."

"So how did you see it?"

"You already said it—I am clever. Now, if I can, I am going to lie on your bed and go to sleep."

Thomas started with the top sheet, as instructed. It related to a land transaction in London. The location appeared to be in the middle of the river Thames, but when he set it aside he saw the next sheet held a drawing of London Bridge with a building circled. The name on both sheets of paper were the same.

Four sheets further down, he came across the first mention of the name Galib Uziel. It related not to any transaction in England but in Spain. The document was written in Spanish, which Thomas could read well enough. The man had sold his extensive holdings in Málaga for a tenth of what they were worth. However, even a tenth proved to be a considerable sum, and Thomas knew many conversos and moriscos had been forced to sell for much less.

The next sheet identified where a portion of the money had gone. The house in London used some, but much of the rest went on recruiting men. It puzzled Thomas why anyone would record the details of such transactions, which would prove their guilt. He could only suppose these papers were never meant to be found. Which raised another question: why did such an inept man as Hugh Clement have them in his possession?

The next was a personal letter from Galib Uziel to his daughter, also written in Spanish. The letter was addressed to Philippa by name and assigned her the deeds of a house just off Cheapside in London. Thomas looked across the room, wondering if that was where she had been living when he first met her. The date of the transaction was fifteen years before.

He set the sheet to one side with the others and continued.

Eventually he sat back, then stood and stretched to ease the ache in his body, knowing only a bath and twelve hours of sleep might cure him. Amal was right. The papers told a story. A story of corruption, of bribery, and murder.

What puzzled Thomas was that they contained nothing to directly link Hugh Clement to the bonemen in London. Yet there should be. It was beyond belief two such organisations could spring up by accident. Only the man's name on a few documents made a loose link, but nothing mentioned both Hugh Clement and Galib Uziel.

The man was a fool to keep the papers, but no doubt he never expected them to be found. The trail to his involvement was clear and all the proof King Henry would need to have him removed from his position. More than removed—there was enough here to hang the man.

There was nothing about the recruitment of the Welshmen, but it was possible they had missed some more recent documents. What did interest Thomas was how the trail implicated Wigmore Abbey. The connections hinted at by the last pages were less clear, but reading them, Thomas saw the Abbey was involved in some manner. Abbot John was beholden to Hugh Clement. He was named on the documents. He had allocated Abbey lands to the man. More than likely it was he who had sent a monk to take Philippa to Hugh Clement's manor house. What was not clear was why the Abbot had done so. It made no sense, but it might once Thomas talked to him. Except he knew he could not do so alone. He needed someone the Abbot trusted, someone closer to the church, and Thomas knew exactly who that was. He glanced at the bed where Amal slept then left the room.

Jorge was not pleased when Thomas shook him awake.

"That is not ten hours," he grumbled.

"I need you, now."

Jorge glanced at the window. "It is still dark!"

"What has that got to do with anything? We have to ride south to Lemster, and then ride north to Wigmore."

"Go south, then north? Are you mad?"

"I wish I was. Get up, get dressed, and meet me outside. We need two horses so I will arrange that."

Jorge rolled over and put his arm over his head. "Can you not take Will?"

"He is not back yet, but even if he was he is not the man for this task. I need you. I need your skill with people."

Jorge rolled onto his back and stared at Thomas. "You are mad. Tonight has been too much for you, so I had better humour you."

THIRTY-NINE

Night still cloaked the town as Thomas and Jorge rode into Lemster, but in the east a faint band of grey showed a promise of the coming day. Thomas left the horses with Jorge and entered the Priory grounds. There were no monks to be seen, but a sharp rap at one door brought it open soon enough and Thomas asked for Prior Bernard.

"He is preparing himself for Prime, but I will tell him you are here, Thomas Berrington."

After the man had gone Thomas wondered how he knew his name, but supposed it was no great secret. No doubt if he remained in the area it would become even less of one.

Thomas walked back to where Jorge was leaning against a wall with a sulky expression on his face.

"We might have to wait for him. He has to pray."

"Monks pray all the time. You should have known that and let me sleep another two hours at least."

"Enjoy the coming morning. The air is fresh and we are going to end matters today."

"I am sure you said the same thing last night. Who are we going to kill now?"

"Nobody, I hope, but there may be a man who will lose his position. Are you hungry?"

"I could eat something, but where will we find anything at this time of night?"

"It is an hour until sunrise, but Lemster has two bakeries as I recall and both will be baking bread at this hour. There is also a surfeit of taverns and inns where we might break our fasts."

"I am not altogether sure I will ever get used to the food in England. At least in Spain there is spice, even if there is less than under the Moors. Here there is a great deal of salt and fat and not much else."

"I will ask Belia to find you spice. There are some in this land that can be used, just not by most cooks. We can —" But what they could do would have to wait because the gate in the Priory wall opened and Prior Bernard emerged.

"What is it now, Tom? I was about to go into prayers."

"I need to talk to you about the Abbot of Wigmore. He has been plotting against King Henry and Prince Arthur."

"Abbot John?" Prior Bernard shook his head. "Are you an idiot? I never took you for one, but you must be if you accuse that man. He is almost as holy as God in Heaven Himself."

Thomas reached beneath his jacket and pulled out six sheets of paper. "Take these and read them where you have better light, then tell me if I am mistaken."

Prior Bernard took the papers and peered at them, but Thomas was right about there being too little light.

"Come with me. You can explain what you think they say, which will save us both time. Bring the tall one with you as well. Has he ever considered taking the cloth?"

"Only from a woman's body," Thomas said, which brought a smile to Prior Bernard's lips before he closed the expression down as inappropriate.

It took less than a quarter hour, at the end of which the sky had lightened further, and the monks of the Priory were making their way into the chapel.

"I am going to have to accompany you, Tom. An accusation such as this cannot be made by you alone. I will need to speak with the Abbot first."

"Do you believe me?"

"I neither do nor do not. I have to discuss the matter with Abbot John before I can decide. Wait outside while I change into more suitable clothes and find a horse."

They were a mile outside Lemster, the light allowing them to ride a little faster, before Thomas said, "If you talk to the Abbot and you reach the same conclusion as I did, what will be done?"

"There are channels for such things. They will involve the Bishop of Hereford, possibly even the Lord Chancellor and Archbishop of Westminster."

"And the King?"

"The King appointed those men to act on his behalf. A ruler cannot make every little decision."

"This is not a small decision though, is it?"

"Not if what you say is true. But I have already told you I am yet to make my decision on it. Do not press me, Tom. You always were a hasty boy."

"And now I am a man of sixty years and have left haste behind me. How old are you now, Bernard?"

Prior Bernard flicked a hand towards Thomas in chastisement at not using his title, but it came nowhere near, unlike some blows he had given Thomas when he was young.

"I have seventy-five years. I believe I told you that the last time we spoke, but a man of my age is apt to forget such things."

Thomas laughed. "Other men your age, perhaps, but not you. How long will all these prominent men take to decide?"

"I believe the last time an Abbot was found guilty of a crime—and that was not a crime as heinous as this, if you are right—it took a little over a year."

"Will Abbot John remain in post while the investigation goes on?"

"He will be offered accommodation in another house. Even if he is found innocent of all charges it is unlikely he will ever return to Wigmore Abbey. He is not in good health, and already has more years than most are allotted, so it would surprise me if he lived long enough to be disrobed."

Thomas wondered if he ought to feel guilt should that happen, but was sure the papers Amal showed him offered little evidence to the contrary. Money and favours had passed between Galib Uziel and the Abbey at Wigmore. The documents showed Hugh Clement as a vassal of the Abbot, bent to his will and that of his master. Abbot John would burn in the fires of hell if such was true, but would not be the first man of God to do so. If,

Thomas thought, I believed in the fires of hell, or the gardens of heaven.

The day had fully arrived by the time they stabled their horses at Wigmore and entered the abbey grounds. Morning prayer had ended, and white-robed Benedictine monks made their way out to perform morning duties. The Abbot stood talking with Peter Gifforde, still dressed in his expensive black clothes, clearly taking no part in the religious acts of the abbey.

Prior Bernard marched directly across and spoke with the Abbot. Both men looked back at Thomas, then they walked together into the accommodation wing of the abbey. Peter Gifforde strode across to Thomas and Jorge.

"What do you think of that land I showed you, Thomas? Fine arable land, and the house can be repaired swiftly enough, I am sure."

For a moment, Thomas was unsure what he was talking about. Their visit to the derelict house felt more like two years ago than two days.

"It would suit, I agree, but the conversation Prior Bernard is having with Abbot John might make it a problem."

"Abbot John assured me the freehold is yours if you want it. He said any friend of Prior Robert is also a friend to Wigmore Abbey."

Thomas wondered why the Abbot would stipulate such. He knew enough about canon law to be aware abbeys rarely offered freehold. In this instance, did the Abbot believe by gifting land to Thomas he would be in his debt? Just as Hugh Clement was in his debt?

"Was it you who assigned the lease to my old home?" Thomas asked.

"That was before my time, but I looked up the records after meeting you. As far as everyone was concerned the entire Berrington family no longer existed. You went away and never returned."

"Yet here I am." Thomas glanced across at Jorge, who was watching the slow work of the brothers as they went about their business. He would hear everything, Thomas knew, and judge what truth or untruth lay beneath the words. "And my sister Agnes still lives in Ludlow."

"The only Agnes I know there is Agnes Baxter, the baker."

"I left her with my aunt when she had but three years. She took her aunt's family name, then reverted to it again after her husband left her. But she is my sister, or do you doubt my word?"

"Perhaps the lands and house will make up for any oversight. Do you know what Prior Bernard's business is with the Abbot? Is it something I should involve myself with?"

"Not unless you are also corrupt," Thomas said. He saw Jorge give a brief smile before suppressing it.

"In that case, I think I need to protect the Abbot from any false accusation. Excuse me, both of you."

Thomas watched Peter Gifforde strut away across the grass. He noticed his feet had a tendency to stick out like those of a duck. His dark hair combed at the back also resembled the rear end of the same bird.

"He is involved," said Jorge, coming to stand beside Thomas.

"It would be difficult for him not to be. The Abbot might give the orders, but Peter Gifforde carries them out. His name is not on any of those papers, but I wager he and Hugh Clement are as close as you and me."

"But without the love," said Jorge.

Thomas ignored the comment.

"I would suggest you might be wise to follow him inside the Abbey," said Jorge. "I listened closely to the tone of his voice and, try as he might, I heard the strain in it grow as your conversation went on. I would not put it past him to attack your friend Bernard."

"Prior Bernard," Thomas said.

"Indeed. Well, are you going?"

Thomas sighed and started across the grass. He had almost reached the doorway when a high-pitched scream shattered the silence and he broke into a run. He pushed past monks rushing to find out who had cried out.

Thomas grasped one man by the shoulders. "Where is the Abbot?"

"At the end of the cloister. You went there the last time you came. I saw you."

Thomas released him and ran on. He slammed into the large room at the end to find one man lying in a pool of blood, another standing over him with a knife in his hand which, when he saw Thomas, he dropped to the stone floor.

Thomas went to one knee and turned the body over to see if there was anything he could do, but the eyes that stared back at him lacked any trace of life.

He looked up at Prior Bernard.

"You did this?"

"I thought I had put all violence behind me, but look, here it is again." He shook his head. "It was all instinct. I suppose that always remains with a man once he has fought, as we have."

Thomas rose to his feet and went to the Abbot.

"How do you feel, Your Grace? This must have come as a shock."

"I am a little breathless, but..." The Abbot looked at Peter Gifforde's body. "He came at me with a knife in his hand. He planned to thrust it through my heart. I could see it in his eyes. Peter would have killed us both, but Bernard... Bernard moved faster than I have ever seen a man move. He took the knife from him and he... he used it to..." The Abbot reached for the back of his chair. "Excuse me, I must sit."

Thomas helped him, then laid two fingers on his throat to feel his heartbeat. It was fast and thready, but shock could do that. He would monitor the man in case he grew worse, but knew there was little he could do if he did. The Abbot was not a young man, and grossly overweight.

"I must pray for forgiveness," said Prior Bernard.

"You are forgiven, my son," said the Abbot, crossing himself. "You protected me first, yourself second. Why did Peter do it?" The colour was returning to his face, bringing back its usual floridity.

"He was allied with a man called Galib Uziel, who lives in London," Thomas said. "He intends harm to the King and all his family. Intends harm to all of England. I need to see where Peter Gifforde lived, to search his rooms to discover if there is evidence there." Thomas looked into

407

the Abbot's eyes. "My apologies, reverend father; I suspected your involvement. But it is clear now Peter included your name in the documents I read in order to protect himself. I will leave you to recover."

"I still wish to pray," said Prior Bernard as he accompanied Thomas from the room. "A brother will show you where Peter's rooms are. I owe you an apology for doubting you, Tom."

"I had the wrong man, though."

"I see how you believed as you did, but talking with Abbot John it became clear he had nothing to do with it. He is growing old and more than a little forgetful. He is incapable of involvement in a plot such as the one you outlined to me. What are you going to do now?"

Thomas smiled. "I plan on returning to Ludlow and sleep for a week. Hugh Clement is under arrest, his compatriot dead at your hand. Soon, Prince Arthur will return with his new bride and I will have more than enough to do."

FORTY

Peter Gifforde's accommodation was a small cottage on the edge of the village beyond the confines of the Abbey. On the steep hill behind it stood Wigmore Castle, home to the Mortimer family for centuries, though none of that name lived there anymore and the building had an air of neglect.

Thomas thanked the brother who showed them where the cottage was and tried the door. It was unlocked and he entered, Jorge coming in behind. Both had to duck to avoid hitting their heads.

There was one large room with a small cooking area beyond an arch, but no smell of food, and when Thomas went through, he found no food at all. He suspected Peter Gifforde ate with the monks. A narrow door led to a small bedroom with an equally small bed. The covers were unmade, the shape of the man who had lain there clearly visible. Thomas thought of how short the span of time between a life lived and a life ended. The strike of a blade. A moment's carelessness. Peter Gifforde must have known he was found out as soon as Thomas told him his concerns regarding the Abbot. He had gone to kill them both, Prior Bernard and Abbot John, but had not counted on Bernard's training as a soldier coming back when attacked. Thomas thought of those he had killed the night before and knew his conscience troubled him far less than Prior Bernard's would now. What he did not know was which reaction was the right one. Bernard and he were too far separated to decide on the matter. One was a man who worshipped God every waking hour, more than likely in his dreams too; Thomas a man who had lost all belief in any deity years before. Thoughts flitted through his mind as he conducted a swift but thorough search of the contents of the cottage. Clothes and bedding in the bedroom. A Latin bible in the main room. And then, pushed far back into the single cabinet, he found a file of papers. Thomas skimmed them, saw more names, more properties, more monies changing hands and favours asked and offered. Sometimes, he knew, the favours were more important than the money. The papers were not even well hidden. They showed an arrogance in Peter Gifforde that indicated he never expected to be found out. Thomas read a note of promise for five hundred shillings for the hiring of Welsh mercenaries, made out to Llewelyn ap Gwrydd—the man who had led them into Ludlow. Five hundred shillings that would never be paid. It was a small fortune for a Welsh warlord, more than a small fortune for a man such as Peter Gifforde to pay. It hinted at the wealth that lay under his control. Wealth and power.

As Thomas returned to the main room, he discovered

Jorge standing there wearing a white robe, the hood pulled over his head.

"I doubt it suits me, does it?" said Jorge, pushing the hood back to reveal his face. "But I wondered if it would make me feel different. And it did. I feel stupid."

"Where did you get it?"

"Over there." Jorge nodded at an open chest. "There are two more, but this was the cleanest."

Thomas went to the chest and drew the other robes out. He held one up and saw a smear of dirt on the hem, and saw how it had been, but not why. Peter Gifforde had come for Philippa and taken her to the cottage before going to Hugh Clement's house. The man had been at the same table in the Rose and Crown. Had they been plotting then? It seemed likely. But had Philippa been a part of the plot? That also seemed likely, particularly considering her attempt to kill Amal. Thomas knew he was missing something, but did not know what. He glanced at the papers still clutched in his hand and wondered if they would fill in the missing pieces of the tapestry that made up the bonemen.

Had Peter Gifforde represented the bonemen in Ludlow? He told Thomas his father had lived in London as a child. Is that where he fell in with Galib Uziel? Thomas wondered if he was a man who would also need to be dealt with, or would naming him to King Henry be enough? He hoped it would.

"Are we finished here?" asked Jorge. "I want to return to my bed and Belia. The children will be awake and playing by now so we will have privacy."

"I was not aware privacy was ever required where you and she are concerned."

Jorge smiled.

"Yes, we are finished. I will take these papers with me and let Amal run over them. She sees better than I do these days, both with her eyes and her mind."

"Don't make me feel sorry for you. I saw you fight last night, remember. As did others. You will have little trouble now from those who might have considered you had grown too old and too slow."

"There are times I fear what I have created in Will."

"He has a good heart. Beneath all that strength he remains the sweet boy he always was."

"I want to take another look at that house the Abbot offered us on the way back. It will not take long, only a slight diversion."

"If the death of Peter Gifforde does not halt the transfer."

Thomas smiled and held up one of the papers. "This is the deed of sale made out to me, signed by the Abbot with his seal attached."

"Will we all live there?" asked Jorge.

"Ride with me and we can look it over again. You stayed talking with that man the last time, as I recall. The property is a good size and there is ample land to build on." Thomas smiled as they left the house. "Perhaps we can even build a bathhouse like we had in Granada. Heat water with the sun. Stone pipes to carry it where we need it. And homes made with small bricks."

"Small bricks?" Jorge looked at Thomas as if he had lost his wits.

"Like my house on the Albayzin. I want a house with small bricks. And arches. Lots of arches."

"In England?"

"Yes, in England."

"And water heated by the sun?" said Jorge. "Again, in England?"

When they reached Burway Thomas went inside the abandoned house. It was partly built of stone, with sections of wattle and daub that had weathered less well to expose gaps in the walls. It would take some work to make it habitable again, but Thomas was not afraid of hard work, and Will would relish the opportunity to use his strength. Thomas would ride south to Lemster tomorrow or the day after and talk to Edmund, Michael and James about crafting bricks of a very specific size. He would sit and talk with Bel too, about her life, her hopes for the life left to her. Left to both of them. Thomas had no expectation, but believed a conversation might be worth the while.

"Will it do?" Jorge asked when Thomas emerged from the house.

"Yes, it will do."

"It will feel strange to live in the countryside. Even stranger to live in a green countryside where it rains all the time."

"Not all the time," Thomas said.

"Really? When does it not rain?"

"Two days in August." Thomas laughed. "Every third year."

"Ah, I look forward to those two days, then. We might even manage a dribble of warm water."

Thomas smiled as they started back towards Ludlow. It felt like the start of something. The end of something, too, but a new life for them all.

At the castle Thomas bathed, then fell into bed, asleep before he could pull the covers over himself. When he woke it was to discover almost an entire day had passed and Amal was sitting on the bottom of the bed, her beautiful face serious.

"Do you hurt?" Thomas asked, sitting up.

"No. I mean yes, a little, but not as much as I did, and Belia has given me a salve, which helps. She has examined me and said there will be no permanent damage and I will be able to have children."

Amal with children of her own. It was a thought Thomas was reluctant to explore at that moment.

"So why the serious expression?"

"I read those fresh papers you brought."

"I did not give them to you. They were over there on the table." When Thomas looked the papers were still there and he frowned.

"I sat and watched over you while you slept. I opened the folder out of boredom. You are a very boring sleeper, Pa. You don't even talk in your sleep."

"I was tired."

"I know. The papers contain even more damning evidence than the others. Who do they belong to?"

"A man named Peter Gifforde. He is dead."

"Was he tall, slim, and wears dark clothes?"

"He was. Why?"

"There was another man in Hugh Clement's house when they dragged us in. He was tall, slim, and wore dark clothes, but he left before they... before they..." Amal's voice trailed off and she stared into space for a moment. Thomas thought of what Jack Pook had told him that night. Of a third man in the house who had not been there later. A man dressed as a monk when he left. Peter Gifforde, come to give his orders.

Amal gave a small jerk and returned from whatever memories had drawn her away. "Did you kill him?" There was no accusation in her voice. She knew what her father used to do, what he had done again only two nights since.

"No. Another man did. A man of God."

"I thought they were meant to turn the other cheek."

"Prior Bernard is no ordinary man of God. I believe the act of killing again has made him sore guilty. He will pray even harder than before, if such a thing is even possible."

"Is becoming a monk not a strange profession for a man who used to be a soldier?"

"Not as strange as you might think. Soldiers are used to taking orders, to having their lives controlled and constrained by duty and the needs of their masters. Being a monk is not so different. And it soothes the souls of men who have killed, even if the killing was just."

"Do you think Usaden might become a monk?"

Thomas laughed. "I doubt it. Tell me what is in those papers, and who they accuse."

"Only after you put some clothes on; you are not as pretty as Jorge."

It took an hour for Amal to explain the connections she had drawn from reading the papers. She had made notes which she passed to her father only once she had completed explaining them.

"It is important you understand the logic before you see my conclusion," she said. "Otherwise I expect you will just dismiss it."

Thomas reached out and touched her cheek. "Do you have so little faith in me?"

Amal said nothing. She is growing up, Thomas thought. Becoming her own woman. Overtaking her father.

"Are you going to confront her with it all?" asked Amal once she had explained her findings, and Thomas was dressed.

"I am."

"Then I will come with you. I want to see her face when you do."

Thomas considered saying no, then realised Amal deserved to get what she asked for. When they approached the cell where Philippa and Hugh Clement were held Thomas cursed because the guard was not on duty. He cursed again when they drew closer and he saw the door open.

"What does he think he is doing going inside?"

Amal stopped two paces from the doorway and Thomas turned back. "I thought you wanted to see her face when I tell her we know everything."

"Can you not smell it, Pa?"

Thomas turned back to the door. He could not see

inside yet, but when he inhaled he discovered why Amal had stopped.

"Stay where you are." He started forward, but when he entered the room Amal was at his side and witnessed the same as he did.

Hugh Clement hung from a rope tied to a metal hook set high on the wall. His feet were a bare six inches above the floor, but six or sixty inches would have made no difference.

His death had not been easy. There had been no sudden drop to break his neck. He had hung until the breath went stale in his lungs and his heart ceased beating. A small stool showed how he had been raised up, but it now lay on its side two feet from the wall.

The guard who was on duty lay on one of the cots, his throat cut from ear to ear. It was his blood Amal had smelled.

Of Philippa Gale, there was no sign.

"We should take him down," said Amal, who stood in front of Hugh Clement. She stared up at the man's mottled face, bulging eyes, but there was no fear or disgust on her own face.

"I will send someone up. We should look for Pip first."

Amal stepped closer to Hugh Clement. She reached out and touched a hand that hung down. After a moment, she turned to her father.

"He is cold. Three or four hours, I would say. What about yours?"

Thomas touched the dead guard and nodded. "The same."

As he stared at the grey face, he recalled where he had

seen him before and what happened here made more sense. He was the soldier Philippa had gone to at Tenbury bridge, before she and Thomas rode to Lemster. When he asked, she said a message had been sent to let the castle know Arthur was on his way. Except the message had not been for the castle but, Thomas suspected, Peter Gifforde. Was he the man who had ridden after Philippa into the woods? Had the confrontation been pre-arranged so the two could plot? And was the attack on Thomas deliberate or a mistake? If deliberate, it told him how cold-blooded Philippa Gale was. She had wanted Thomas dead. And then, when he was not, she had seduced him instead.

"She has gone," said Amal. "You will not find her now."

"But I can try." What Thomas did not say was that he had to find Philippa before she found him, or his children.

FORTY-ONE

Thomas stood naked in a room at the Bell Savage as he looked through a small window onto the street below. It was busy with people coming and going, but most were entering London. The marriage of Arthur, Prince of Wales, to the beautiful Catherine of Aragon was due to take place tomorrow in St Paul's Cathedral. Today, Catherine was to enter London, making passage across London Bridge which had been decorated to welcome her, the roadway strewn with rose petals in both red and white. Where they had been found in November had been a topic of much conversation until someone discovered most were fashioned from cloth or paper. With the window open, Thomas could hear Catherine's approach. A blast of trumpets. The roar of the crowd. A hubbub of voices from the street. He had worried about her passing the house of the bonemen on the bridge and had gone to check on it earlier, satisfied no attack could take place. Not there.

"Are you going to watch them arrive at the Cathedral tomorrow, Tom?"

Thomas glanced at the bed where Peggy Spicer, good-wife of the Bell Savage, sprawled as naked as he was. Her skin was pale, her body buxom, and they had spent the morning indulging themselves in the pleasures each could offer to the other. It had been less a matter of seduction than commerce, but Peggy had put her heart, soul, and body into meeting her side of the bargain. Thomas also suspected her wantonness might have been some manner of apology for her duplicity the last time he stayed at the inn. If so, she was forgiven.

"I expect so," he said.

"What plans have you for today? Will you go to the bridge to watch her? I hear people who have seen her say she is most beautiful."

"She is."

"How do you know so, Tom?"

"Because I have known Catherine since she was a babe."

Peggy stared at him, her expression giving no sign of whether she believed him or not.

"I intend to go to the bridge, but not until the crowds have thinned. I have other plans for today. Plans for tonight too, I am afraid."

"Perhaps tomorrow," said Peggy. "For an older man you made an excellent account of yourself."

Thomas smiled. "My thanks." He went to the bed and kissed her, then dressed. The sound of the celebrations told him that Catherine had passed across the bridge and would be making her way to Baynard's Castle on the riverside, where a grand party had been arranged.

Thomas waited until Peggy had slipped her own clothes back on and left before opening his leather satchel and taking out the message that had brought him to London. It was short, direct, and could not be ignored.

Princess Catherine of Aragon insists you attend her wedding to Prince Arthur. Come at once and report to Baynard's Castle. Fresh horses have been arranged for your journey.

There was a florid signature and the seal of the King, though Thomas expected he had never set eyes on the note. It was possible Prince Arthur had, or more likely, Queen Elizabeth.

The request did not surprise him. Catherine had been promised he would be there by her mother, Queen Isabel of Castile. Apart from which, Thomas's might be the only friendly face at the ceremony, and the only person she might converse with. Other than the Spanish ambassadors, of course, but their faces would not be so familiar or so friendly. Thomas had heard they argued between themselves, each vying for advancement in this new England about to be joined with Spain. Just as Arthur and Catherine were about to be joined. Thomas smiled at the thought, and at the memory of Jorge instructing Catherine in matters of both the heart and the body. There was no one better suited to the task, though Isabel had not allowed the two to have their conversation in private. Thomas had been there, as had Amal. Isabel had listened through an opening in the wall, thinking none of them knew she was there, but Thomas had glimpsed her eyes and knew it could be no one else.

On receipt of the note, Thomas had ridden hard from Ludlow, taking no sleep to arrive a day earlier than the ceremony. Which gave him time to do what he had really come for. He had tried to put Galib Uziel from his mind and failed. There had to be a thousand rogues in London, ten-thousand or more scattered throughout England. Did he expect to have to take care of every single one of them? But the trying had failed, and thoughts of what the man had brought about continued to plague him.

Galib Uziel was the reason men and women had died in Ludlow and Lemster.

Galib Uziel was the reason Peter Gifforde had died.

Peter Gifforde had been Galib Uziel's man in Ludlow, behind the corruption of Hugh Clement. Though Thomas suspected not so much corruption had been needed. And Philippa's role in everything had been laid clear in the papers Amal showed him. Amal had told him she understood what Philippa had done. A daughter scorned. A daughter banished. Amal said she understood, because she was also a daughter who loved her father very much indeed.

"But I would never banish you," Thomas had said.

"I know, Pa, but reading those letters I felt sad for her. And there are times you have been far away from us all, and not just physically. Sometimes you do that, you know. You go away inside your own head."

Thomas was not so sure he did. Nor sure he understood the reason for Amal's sadness. But he accepted he was a different person to her. Less forgiving. Less intelligent in matters of the heart. It was one reason he had bedded Peggy Spicer—to erase the final memories of what he and Philippa had shared. He determined in future never again to lose his heart to anyone beyond those he already loved, but suspected he might fail because the need to be loved lay within him. Lubna had given him that ultimate gift.

Galib Uziel, Peter Gifforde and Philippa Gale were the reason sweet Amal had been subjected to pain and hurt, and the taking from her that which could only be taken the once and which should have been gifted to a man she loved.

Peter Gifforde lay dead, buried in an unmarked grave.

Philippa Gale had fled and may herself be dead without someone competent to treat her wound.

Which left only Galib Uziel who could be punished.

The man had to die. Or Thomas would die in the attempt.

He had not come alone. Will and Usaden were walking the streets of London with his dog, doing their own work. They would meet later, after the pomp and ceremony had been attended to.

Thomas stopped on his way out to tell Peggy Spicer he would not be back tonight but to keep his room for him, also to reserve two others, which he paid for.

"Where are you spending the night, Tom? Have you got another woman in town?"

"I expect I will have to sleep in Baynard's Castle."

"Or a cell in the Tower, you rogue."

"There is always that possibility."

Thomas walked along Ludgate Hill to St Paul's, where the spire rose higher than any other in London, and a crowd had gathered in some vain expectation they might glimpse someone important. He worked his way around their edge and went along Cheapside until he reached the gate to London Bridge, which stood open. The King had decreed no payment was needed to pass through that day.

The house Thomas sought was almost half-way along and he recalled it from his earlier visit, unaware then he would ever return. A little further from it lay a stall selling eels. Thomas bought a pot and picked at them, pretending to eat his lunch, but his eyes were on those who came and went.

Most were bonemen, recognisable by their russet headwear and arrogant manner. Thomas ate his eels slowly, his eyes taking in how often men arrived and departed, what manner of security there was, and how heavily defended the house itself was. It rose to four storeys, each with at least three windows facing the street. A narrow gap lay along one side, but Thomas had noted that the other end butted up against a high wall with no doorway in it. The alleyway had a man stationed at its entrance to stop anyone from gaining access to whatever lay to the rear of the house.

Thomas set his empty pot back on the stall he had bought his meal from and made his way along the bridge until he emerged in Southwark. Here he went in search of a wherry to take him back across the river. He found one easily enough, for the traffic was sparse with the bridge being open without payment. Thomas paid the owner and sat in the back as they moved out across the Thames.

"What is it like closer to the bridge?" he asked. He had already seen that between the central pillars white water showed and sounded as the river emptied following high tide. He knew enough of tides to know the situation would be similar in the small hours of the coming night.

"Depends on the time of day, sir. At the moment, you would not want to get too close. At ebb and flood a man might climb onto a buttress if he had a mind to, but why he would ever want to is another matter. Why do you ask, sir?"

"Casual interest, nothing more. Can we get a little closer, do you think?"

"A little, but not much. The rapids are like to turn a small wherry like this upside down and drown us both."

"I can swim," Thomas said.

"I never learned, but the Thames will take you whether or not you can swim. She is a savage mistress, so she is."

As the wherry-man brought them closer, it allowed Thomas to view the bonemen's headquarters from the waterside. Its wooden walls jutted out almost twenty feet from the bridge, as did those of most of the other houses. Wherever the narrow alley led he had seen from the bridge, it would offer no access to the rear. But what Thomas saw offered him hope.

Running along the side of the bridge, ten feet down from where the houses and shops and church rose, ran a narrow walkway. There was no handrail, and it would take someone with good balance to walk along it, but it was possible. The walkway must be used for maintenance and would likely be blocked at both ends to stop fools from trying to use it and falling into the river.

Back on the northern bank, Thomas walked to the end of the bridge and searched until he found where the narrow ledge emerged behind a heavy iron gate, which was padlocked. Thomas stood back and studied the gate. He thought an agile man might climb it and drop to the other side. Then he wondered if someone could do the same in the dark. It would have to be in the small hours because London always seemed to be busy, and he wanted nobody to see what was happening. He had a plan, and two companions to help him carry it out. As he walked to his next duty he tried to decide whether he wanted to attack the bonemen or not. He would see King Henry shortly and might tell him what he had learned. Except he had already tried that and the King appeared uninterested, or considered it work for someone beneath him.

Any attack on the bonemen did not come without risk. Thomas wondered if he was willing to take that risk. Willing to give up his life. And then he thought of what had been done to Amal, what had been done to the people of Ludlow, and knew he had to. Tonight, either Galib Uziel or Thomas would die.

FORTY-TWO

Thomas made his way to Baynard's Castle, where he was admitted as soon as he gave his name. Inside, an air of merriment reigned. Musicians played, sometimes their tunes clashing one over the other to create a cacophony. Well-dressed men and women wandered around clutching goblets of fine wine, some with ale, others with stronger spirits. Then Thomas saw Catherine.

She stood close to the entrance of the main building talking to King Henry with Prince Arthur at his side. The King stood closer to Catherine than did his son, his arm protectively on her shoulder. As Thomas approached, Prince Arthur caught sight of him and came to greet him.

"Thomas, thank goodness you have come. My betrothed was sore concerned you would not be here. I promised her you would, but I am not sure she believed me." Arthur's words emerged in one long rush, then he came even closer. "You lied to me, Thomas. She is even more beautiful than you claimed. Far, far more beautiful."

"I thought it would be a pleasant surprise for Your Grace."

"Come and see her. She will be pleased to know you are here. Did you bring Pip with you?"

"I did not." There would be time later to explain to the Prince what had happened in Ludlow, but that time was not now. Let the boy enjoy the festivities and his wedding first.

"A faster journey, I suppose. An excellent decision made, Thomas. She will like Catherine when she comes to the castle."

As they made their way through the crowd towards the small group gathered around the King, Catherine turned to see who he was looking at and broke into a wide smile, which she tried to suppress as she came to greet Thomas.

"I am pleased to see you have arrived at last." She spoke in Spanish, as they had conversed the entire sixteen years she had walked the earth. "I told Prince Arthur I could not marry him if you were not here. Mother promised you would be with me. I want you near when I enter the Cathedral tomorrow. I think Arthur likes you." She looked beyond Thomas. "Has Will come?" She attempted to make the question sound of no importance.

"He is in London, Your Grace, but it would not be seemly to meet him before your wedding." Thomas gave a laugh. "Or even after your wedding."

Catherine punched his arm with a small fist. "Do not Your Grace me, Thomas. You have never done so and I will not have you start now. And who I meet is my decision."

Thomas leaned closer and spoke softly. "I think it may be expected, Cat. You are to be the bride of the next King of England, and know well enough what that means. You have lived your entire life in the shadow of power. I expect I will need to Your Grace you always from now on."

Catherine laughed, covering her mouth with her hand. "Not when it is only us, then. What say you to that?"

"If you insist, Your Grace." Thomas glanced at Arthur, who was watching their conversation, unable to understand even if he could overhear the words. "He is a good man, Cat. He will make a good husband and a great King. You are fortunate in who your mother chose for you."

Catherine gave a great sigh. "Nothing is ever my choice, Thomas, but I expect that is how it will be from now on. But yes, Arthur is a good man. We have spoken a little, though it appears we have learned different dialects of Latin. I have tried the little English you taught me and I think it pleased him, but I find it hard to follow long conversations."

"You will pick it up soon enough. It is not a hard language to speak badly."

"But I want to speak it well."

"Then you will. Now I must speak with the King, but I will see you later. I will be close tomorrow, I promise."

King Henry's eyes were on Thomas as he approached. There was little of welcome in them. He never offered friendship to interlopers, but for Thomas, acceptance would be enough. What the King would make of the news he had to impart was a different matter.

"I hear there was trouble in Ludlow but you took care of it," said the King.

"As best I could, Your Grace."

"Good enough is what I hear. Well done. Well done indeed. Now, you are to eat at the top table at tonight's banquet, and the Princess has said she wants you close to her tomorrow."

"It is not my place, Your Grace."

"I saw you talking to her. Did she ask you the same?"

"She mentioned it, but I made no promise to her. But I will do as you ask, Your Grace."

"I spoke with the Queen, and she is of a mind that you can follow her into the cathedral. She suggested we list you as a Spanish Earl." The King almost smiled. "What say you, Thomas? Yay or nay?"

"If you ask it of me, Your Grace, then I say yes. It would please Princess Catherine, I know, and her mother also when she hears of it."

"I am sure it will. Now tell me about this trouble in Ludlow. I heard Hugh Clement was involved. Is the man dead?"

"He is, but not at my hand. When the room he was held captive in was opened he had been hanged."

"Someone taking justice into their own hands, eh?" The King stared into Thomas's eyes. "Good. The man will not be missed. He was a coward, so good riddance. A new Justice will have to be appointed, and soon in order to send a message. Can you think of anyone in the area who might take his place? Someone reliable, someone clever, but most of all, please God, someone honest."

"In Ludlow?"

King Henry offered a rare smile. "Yes, in Ludlow. I can think of only one man who might fit the bill but am unsure he would accept. He is new to the area."

"You should ask him, Your Grace."

"I believe he already knows my mind on the matter. I will have Arthur do the asking when he returns to the town. It is his place to make appointments."

"There are two other individuals whose treachery was uncovered, Your Grace. One was employed by Wigmore Abbey and is now dead. The other is someone you and the Queen know well—Philippa Gale."

"Pip?" King Henry shook his head. "Not possible. She has been employed by my wife these past fifteen years and a friend since both were children. You must be wrong in this, Thomas."

"I trusted her too, Your Grace. We became… we had a relationship. But I have uncovered information that puts her guilt beyond doubt."

"I will need to question her myself before I can believe her a traitor."

"That might be difficult, Your Grace."

"God's Teeth, don't tell me she was hanged as well."

"The man assigned to guard the room she and Hugh Clement were held in was in her employ. Pip escaped, but only after she cut the throat of her accomplice. I suspect money and other favours changed hands, though as you know Pip can be very persuasive, particularly where men are concerned."

King Henry glanced around at the gaiety in the room, none of it reflected in his eyes. The news Thomas had imparted had scrubbed all such from him.

"Tell me what you found out, if I cannot hear it from her."

"She is the daughter of the man who runs the bonemen in London. I believe he wants them to operate in every large town of England, and she has helped him with that. She has been close to your power all these years and I am sure she has fed information and secrets to her father for some time, until they fell out. It is another sad tale of fathers, daughters, and the men they love."

King Henry stared at Thomas. "I had people investigate these bonemen when you came to me before. As you know I was not aware of them, but I am now. Those same people are looking at ways to neutralise them, but they have brought nothing to me as yet."

"I know how to neutralise them, Your Grace. Cut off the head of their leader. A man by the name of Galib Uziel. Pip's true name is Gala Uziel."

"I had received no information on who their leader is until you gave it to me just now. Are you absolutely sure of this, Thomas?"

"I am, and I intend to kill him tonight."

The King took a step back. "Do not say that to me. I do not want to know, because if I know I will have to arrest you. So you said nothing to me of this matter, did you?"

"What matter, Your Grace?"

"Explain to me about Pip, for I can still scarce believe what you accuse her of. Why would she do such a thing? Have not myself and my queen treated her as part of our family?"

"There was a man at Wigmore Abbey by the name of Peter Gifforde, Your Grace. I am in receipt of documents that show how he worked for Galib Uziel and ascended to a senior position within the bonemen. He was trusted, until he and Pip fell in love. Whether it was a genuine love on Peter Gifford's part or a pretence, I do not know, but for Pip it appeared to be so. She was besotted with the man. Besotted enough so that when he asked her to seduce me, she did. But I am getting ahead of myself." Thomas reached out for a glass of wine as a servant passed with a tray.

"Did her father object to the relationship?" asked the King. "Was the man she fell in love with not good enough for his daughter? Pip was truly exquisite, as everyone who met her could see. She was entertaining and bright. I do not believe she would fall in love with someone unworthy." He shook his head.

"I do not wish to burden you with the details, Your Grace. If you will accept my word then the matter is at an end."

"Burden me, Thomas. At least a little." The King looked around. "These events bore me. Come, let us retire to a private room and you can tell me what you will."

Thomas followed the King through the melee and into a small room. A fire burned and chairs were drawn up in front of it. There was nobody else there, and Thomas suspected the room was reserved for either the King or Queen should they need privacy.

"Sit, Thomas," said the King. "More wine?"

"A little, Your Grace, but only one. I have more to do tonight."

It was Henry who poured dark ruby wine into fresh glasses. He brought them across and handed one to

Thomas before taking the seat across from him. He offered a nod for Thomas to start.

"I understand Pip used to play with your wife when they were children?"

"They did, which is why when she came to us we had no hesitation in employing her."

"When was this?"

The King stared into the fire for a moment before replying. "Forty-six or forty-seven. There will be a record, but that is near enough. She was taken on to tutor Arthur, then the others when they came along. She never gave us a moment's doubt, Thomas. Not one."

"She would not, Your Grace. Did you notice any change in her two years ago?"

Once again Henry looked into the fire. This time it took him a little longer before he said, "She told Elizabeth she was ill. She was away from court for a week or two. When she returned she was different. More inward looking, which was commented on by all who knew her. I asked John Argentine to look her over in case she still carried any sickness that might affect the children, but he said there was nothing." Henry's gaze met Thomas's. "What happened two years ago?"

"Understand that I have not heard this first-hand, Your Grace, only deduced it from correspondence between Pip, her father, and Peter Gifforde. Mostly with Gifforde. Love letters, many of them, but also conspiracies."

"We have had too much of damned conspiracies!"

"It is the bane of rulers, I understand. Queen Isabel and King Fernando suffered from the same. In the spring of 1499 Philippa fell in love with Peter Gifforde, who worked for her father and the bonemen." Thomas saw the King scowl, but continued. He needed to present only the bare facts, enough to convince him. "Gifforde was someone with more ambition than was good for him, as I believe Pip was as well. She had asked her father for more involvement with the bonemen and was refused, so she went to Gifforde. Between them, they hatched a plot— one dangerous to both of them if it was ever discovered— to oust her father. But he uncovered their plan, as well as the fact that Gifforde was stealing from him."

"So why are both not dead?"

"Because Pip pleaded for their lives. She is Galib Uziel's daughter. No doubt it was difficult to forgive her, but forgive her he must have. I suspect one reason you have never heard of the bonemen is because Pip started spying for him, feeding back information, which enabled him to continue operating without your knowledge. I also believe, but without proof, I admit, that she used her beauty and her body to further her ends. Gifforde was banished and returned to where his family came from. The same small town south of Ludlow where I was born, but that is of no relevance. He obtained a post at Wigmore Abbey and the two of them implemented their plan. Had Abbot John not been so old, or so keen to hand over the responsibility of managing the Abbey to a layperson, their plotting would have come to nothing. When Hugh Clement was appointed as a Justice of the Peace Pip already knew his weaknesses, and the pair exploited them for their own ends. This year the bonemen came to Ludlow. Not those of her father. These men were beholden to Pip and Peter Gifforde." Thomas stared at the

King, who took a long swallow of wine and went to refill his glass.

"Is that everything?" he asked when he returned to his seat.

"Not everything, but enough for now. You have other responsibilities at the moment."

"That I do. How do you manage it, Thomas? To get involved in matters that are nothing to do with you?"

"I do not know, Your Grace, but it seems it must be a part of me because it keeps happening to me over and over again. I do not seek trouble, it seeks me."

"Thank God it did in this instance. I am indebted to you, and your family. Sir Richard, Lady Margaret and Gruffydd have told me a little about them. You are a fortunate man, Thomas, as am I. Family is everything."

"It is."

King Henry rose. "We have been absent too long, I suspect." He smiled. "Once more into the fray, eh?"

As they entered the main room, the King nodded towards where the young Harry was entertaining Catherine with a song. "That boy is too full of his own importance."

"Is that not essential in the son of the King, Your Grace?"

"Perhaps in a Prince. Arthur is not like that."

"No, he is not. I admire your son a great deal, Your Grace."

The King looked at Thomas as if searching for false flattery, but found none. "England will be safe in his hands," he said. "But Harry has far too much energy. It makes me feel old just looking at him."

"All young men have too much energy. It will not last."

"You are right in that. We will see you at the banquet?"

"You shall, Your Grace."

"Say nothing to the Queen about Pip, it will only upset her."

"I would never mention it to the Queen, Your Grace. I leave it up to you what to do with her when she is found, and found she will be."

The King offered a heavy sigh. "One day I will not have to make hard decisions."

"Hard decisions are expected of a King, Your Grace. You may have to wait a long time for the day to arrive when that is not the case."

"I expect you speak true, Thomas." The King patted him on the shoulder. "Now talk to Catherine again, for I saw the smile she gave you. And while you do, see if you can find some other object for my youngest son to obsess over. He has been this way ever since I agreed he could walk her along the aisle when the ceremony is concluded."

The King turned away, no doubt more decisions expected of him. Thomas watched Catherine and Harry, then looked beyond them to see Arthur's eyes on the pair. He started across the courtyard to do as asked. It would take his mind off what must be done later that night, for he did not want to consider the danger he was about to place himself, Jorge, and Usaden in. Thomas also knew he might not be alive come morning to accompany Catherine to her wedding.

FORTY-THREE

It was late before Thomas managed to sneak away from the banquet. He had spoken with the two Spanish ambassadors, kissed the hands of a score of fine ladies, all of who were intrigued by the Englishman who spoke not only Spanish but Arabic. All the while his mind was on other matters. Queen Elizabeth had led him around, her arm through his as she introduced him to a dozen men she said could help him and whose friendship he should encourage. Thomas had disliked every single one of them.

Now he stripped out of the heavy ornate jacket he had worn and dressed in more suitable clothing he had sequestered in a side-room earlier in the day. The streets were still thronged with people celebrating as Thomas approached London Bridge, and he was concerned there would be too many for what he planned. It was almost midnight, but still men, women and children celebrated the coming wedding.

Instead of going onto the bridge, Thomas steered a course along the riverside until he saw an unmistakable

438

shape loitering at the entrance to a narrow alley. Will stepped out into the street. Usaden followed with Kin padding at his side. It was quiet here and they would not be overheard, and definitely not understood, even if they were.

"Did you find out what we need?"

"We did," said Will. "As you know, Usaden can be persuasive when he needs to be. And Kin's snarl usually convinces even the bravest."

"Did you kill anyone?"

"You told me I could not," said Usaden.

"He came pretty close, Pa, but it got us what we wanted to know. The house has four floors, as you can tell from the front. The ground floor is one big room, and is where all the money the bonemen collect comes into at the end of each day. Above that are offices, then living quarters. At the very top is a room Galib Uziel has turned into a fortress. If the house is ever attacked he retreats there, together with a dozen of his best men. There is only one entrance from below, a trapdoor set in the floor and reinforced with iron. Even if someone broke through, there is an escape route using an opening on the river side with a rope to take him down."

"You did well. Do you believe what this man you captured told you?"

"Of course not, so we took eight prisoners and questioned each. Some yielded at once, others took more persuasion, but between them, what I have told you is as close to the truth as we are going to get short of going in there. When do we do that, Pa?"

"Soon enough, once Usaden does his part." The information Will imparted confirmed what Thomas had guessed when examining the building from the riverside. He had seen the door on the upper floor. A wide opening with a pulley set above, exactly like others that lined the river to haul goods up and down through.

"How likely do you think it Galib Uziel will flee to his eyrie if he is under attack?"

"That is what it is there for, according to those we questioned."

A thought occurred to Thomas. "What did you do with the men? What is to stop them running back to their master to tell him what happened?"

"They may be tied to each other in a damp cellar. They will live, as you asked, but will be cold and stiff come morning before they are discovered."

"So the plan should work." Thomas said. "Even more so if those men are missed and he worries where they are. How many will he have inside the house with him?"

"A score, I reckon. Those we questioned confirmed the number varies between a score and two score, but never less. There are four-hundred bonemen, but most are foot-soldiers doing his bidding. He has a core of well-trained men around him, and there are always some of those inside the house. We spent the rest of our time watching the building to see men enter and leave. My best guess is he has twenty in there with him at the moment."

"Too many?"

"For us?" said Usaden.

"I ask again—is it too many?" Thomas looked at Will, expecting no sensible answer from Usaden.

"It depends what your plan is," said Will.

So Thomas told them. When he was finished, there was a look of doubt on Will's face, but Usaden showed no more expression than he ever did.

"When?" asked Will, putting any reservations he might have aside for now.

"On the strike of four, give or take. I will drop Usaden off, then join you. We watch the house until someone enters or leaves. It will be just you, me and Kin to begin with. Are you ready for that?"

"Of course. The timing is good. They will be asleep, or if not, they will want to be. We go in hard?"

"As hard as you like."

"Prisoners?"

"If any try to cut and run let them go. Otherwise you know what you have to do." Thomas had no sense of mercy. Too many had suffered under these bonemen for that.

The bells of the many churches struck the call for Matins, each of them slightly earlier or later than the others. The noise of the last was fading as Thomas stood beside Usaden in front of the iron gate blocking the path to the narrow ledge that ran along London Bridge.

"Can you climb it carrying what you need?"

Usaden patted the sack slung over one shoulder on a length of rope.

"But you can give me a lift if you like."

Thomas stood with his hands on the bars and let Usaden climb along his back, then stand on his shoulders. He tilted his head up to see that Usaden could just reach the top of the gate. Without help, he would have been capable of climbing it, but there was no need. The weight left Thomas as Usaden hauled himself up. He teetered on the top, balancing so the spikes tipping each iron shaft lay below him, then with a single motion he tipped head-first over the far side. As he turned his hands came out and gripped the top railing where his feet had been. In the darkness, Thomas saw his teeth flash white in satisfaction, then he dropped down and moved off along the side of the bridge. Thomas turned away, checking the area to make sure no one had seen Usaden cross over, then walked back to join Will, who remained watching the house with Kin at his side.

"How long until Usaden is ready?" asked Will.

"However long it takes. He says we can start when we think he has reached the window. We should walk slowly to the far end of the bridge and back. That should give him enough time."

"And if it does not?"

"Then our task will prove more difficult, but you have seen Usaden climb. He will be half-way up the side of that house by now."

They walked to the far gate, which was now closed, as was the one on the northern bank, but Thomas had simply climbed over it. There were meant to be guards, but they were almost certainly asleep. The night was quiet other than for a slowly growing roar as the full tide turned and the buttresses of the bridge funnelled the ebbing water through their narrow channels. The sound grew as they made their way back towards the bonemen's house. So loud did it grow that Thomas almost missed the sound of footsteps coming from behind, only aware someone was there when Will pulled him hard into a narrow opening, just in time as four men came fast from the south. Thomas made out their fixed expressions in the light cast from occasional torches set in sconces on some buildings.

"They don't look happy about something," said Will, once the men had passed, the sound of their footsteps slowly fading.

"It cannot be anything to do with us if they came from the south bank of the river. Did you and Usaden go that far in your search?"

"We did, but soon came back when we saw no bonemen."

"What about others who might work Southwark? It is possible they have rivals that way."

"Not that we saw, but then we were not looking for them. If they have rivals, then that is good for us."

"Unless they decide to attack at the same time as we do, but that is unlikely." Thomas stepped out into the roadway and looked both ways. It was empty as far as he could see. "Come on, let's see if we can catch them up. If they enter the house, we can storm the door when they do so and start matters off."

Will grinned and drew his axe from his shoulder and let it swing from his wrist. Both of them ran.

Thomas slowed when he caught sight of the four men ahead, then slowed again when they gathered at the door of the house. One man gave a coded knock. Three slow taps, two fast, four slow. A minute passed, then the door opened, spilling light out onto the road.

"Now?" whispered Will.

"No. We wait."

"For what? The door is standing wide open."

"You heard that knock. We give them a little time and try the same thing. When the door opens, we rush them and trust Usaden hears the noise and does his part."

"And if this Galib Uziel does not follow your plan?" asked Will.

"You questioned his men. Do you think he will not retreat to his safe room?"

"No, I think that is the most likely. All I am saying is what if he does not? What if he stands and fights with his men?"

"Twenty, you said?"

Will nodded. "Yes. Twenty."

"Then when Usaden sees the room is empty, he will come inside and attack them from above. That might work even better."

"Or we will be dead."

Thomas looked at his son. "I thought you liked to fight against impossible odds."

"I am thinking of you, Pa; I don't want you to die. You fought well in Ludlow, but Usaden told me afterwards you were slower than you used to be. Good enough, he said, but not as good as you were."

"I am sorry to disappoint both you and him, but is it not a little late to be bringing this up?"

Will shrugged. "I suppose I will have to keep you safe."

Thomas fought against his annoyance. He stepped to

the door and rapped on it. Three slow. Two fast. Four slow.

He heard bolts being thrown from within. As soon as the door opened a crack Will barged past him, using his weight and strength to slam the door back against whoever stood on the other side. A man went down, blood streaming from a broken nose, and Thomas followed his son. Kin padded in behind him, waiting patiently to see what happened next. Eight men faced them, all with expressions of surprise on their faces. Only eight men. Thomas could not believe their luck.

Then he heard loud steps crashing down an open staircase on the far side of the big room and ten more appeared. Still, he thought, that only made eighteen. Nineteen if he included the unconscious man by the door. It was a start.

"What do you want?" Another man stood at the top of the staircase, half in shadow. Thomas believed it was the man he had seen taking the money on the first day he observed the house. The man took two more steps down and the light showed him more clearly. Definitely the same man. And there was a faint family resemblance to the woman Thomas had been seduced and betrayed by.

"If you are from south of the river, then do not start a war you cannot finish."

"We are not from south of the river," Thomas said. "We are not even from London."

"Then who the fuck are you? Do you even know where you are and who you are dealing with?"

Thomas saw that as the man spoke, his men formed a circle that moved closer to him and Will. Knives appeared

445

in hands, others held swords. Thomas was aware the door to the street remained open and hoped there were no other bonemen nearby who might have heard the commotion.

"Are you Galib Uziel?"

"How do you know that name?"

"A man in Ludlow told it me."

Galib Uziel frowned. "Ludlow? Nobody knows my name in Ludlow, wherever that is."

"Don't pretend ignorance. Everyone knows the home of the Prince of Wales. And there is another in Ludlow you know well. Your daughter. She told me you are a clever man."

"Gala?"

"She told me her name was Philippa Gale, just before I removed her clothes, but she also told me her Spanish name as well... later." Thomas hoped to anger the man by referring to Philippa, but saw he had failed.

Galib Uziel turned away as if uninterested. "Kill them both and throw their bodies into the river. The ebb tide will take them halfway to Holland by morning." Uziel continued up the stairs until he disappeared, only the sound of his footsteps as he crossed the floor. Which is when his men ran at Thomas and Will.

Kin, who had waited at Thomas's side because he had been commanded to do so, launched himself. He offered no bark, but his lips were drawn back in a vicious snarl, and a deep rumble sounded from his chest. Two of the men turned on what they saw as a weak dog and swung their swords at him. Kin leapt across the scything blades and took the throat out of one of them. The other retreated so fast he lost his footing and landed on his back. Kin was on him in an instant.

Thomas saw all this from the edge of his vision as he fought three of the attackers. He also saw Will swinging his axe to stunning effect. Then, as Will advanced on another of the attackers, his foot slipped in the blood on the floor and he fell sideways, tangling himself up with Kin, who gave a loud yelp as Will landed on top of him. Thomas struck out at the nearest attacker before turning to protect Will. As he came close Kin wriggled from beneath him and caught Thomas's feet, bringing him down as well. A moment later, ten men fell on the pair of them and Thomas could not move.

Galib Uziel appeared at the top of the stairs again and looked down.

"Tie them both and bring them up here. I need to find out what they know and who they might have told. And someone kill that dog."

"Kin, run!" Thomas ordered. Before any of the men could approach him, Kin turned and dashed out through the still open door, far too fast to be captured. Thomas knew he would wait outside, unseen, until he and Will emerged. And if they did not, Kin would probably wait forever.

FORTY-FOUR

As the bonemen bound a rope around Will he almost broke free, but one of them struck him with an iron bar and Will fell unconscious to the floor. Thomas made no attempt at escape. Galib Uziel could have had them both killed on the spot, but had not. The man was not finished with them yet, and Thomas was curious why. If Will had not lost his footing, if Kin had not tripped Thomas, their attackers would be dead by now, or fled.

It took four of them to carry the comatose Will, only two for Thomas.

He wondered where Usaden was, and if he knew what was happening. The thought of him raised a flicker of hope.

They were manhandled up three flights of stairs and dragged into the upper chamber. It comprised one enormous space with the trapdoor that could be slammed shut to prevent anyone entering from below. In the far wall was a wide opening that gave out into darkness. A pulley system was arranged above it, a wooden cage hanging beneath. No doubt it was used to bring contraband items up from the river at ebb or full tide. Or to drop enemies down into the racing water. Thomas could hear it now. He believed he could feel its power as a tremor through the floorboards.

One man pulled at the wooden cage until it sat on the floor just inside the doorway. Thomas's captors dragged him across to it and flung him in head first, making him strain under his bindings to work himself upright again. When he did, he saw Will being tied to a series of metal hooks screwed into the wooden wall. His arms, his legs, another rope around his neck so he could scarcely breathe. He was still unconscious and Thomas feared for how hard the man had struck his son. He knew he had made a mistake. Had been too confident. Had believed the three of them would be a match for the bonemen. Just as they had during the attack on Ludlow. And no doubt they would have been if not for that single stroke of bad luck. Thomas knew he should have taken such an event into his calculations, but had been overconfident. It was a lesson to be learned. If he lived long enough.

The wooden cage was lifted, swinging from side to side before being pushed out through the opening where it continued to swing, but this time sixty feet above the roaring waters of the Thames.

Galib Uziel walked to the doorway and stared at Thomas for a long time without expression before speaking.

"Nobody attacks the bonemen," he said. "Did you not know that? Or are you a fool?"

"There is always a first time for everything."

"Yes. Always a first time. And a last time. This will be both for you, Thomas Berrington. Your last act will be when I release the cage you are in and the river carries you away. Then I will toss your giant son after you."

Thomas stared at the man, wondering how he knew his name, though he had no need to search far for the source of such information. Philippa. Galib Uziel was not tall, not thin, but neither fat. He was nondescript. People would walk past him without note. Just another man. Not handsome. Not ugly. Nothing made him stand out. Unlike his daughter. Even so, the shadow of familial resemblance remained. Something about the eyes. Something about the high cheekbones.

To Thomas's left something moved, and he tried not to look in that direction. From the edge of his vision he glimpsed Usaden clinging like a spider to the vertical wooden wall. He did not know how the man could do that. Then he saw two knives in his hands, their blades pushed between the horizontal planks of wood.

Usaden inched closer.

"How do you know my name?"

"My daughter wishes to return to good favour with me, so sends frequent reports on those she believes might cause me problems. Most are no threat at all. You, she claims, may be different." Galib Uziel smiled. "Did you think she fell into your arms because of your good looks?" He tilted his head to one side. "No, I thought not."

"Did she tell you what she and Peter were doing in Ludlow?"

"Of course. Both want my forgiveness. Gala may received it. Peter, never."

"Then it is a good thing he is dead, for I suspect he would have suffered more at your hand than he did at another's."

"You killed him?" There was no inflection in Galib Uziel's voice.

"Not me. A friend. Are you claiming the bonemen in Ludlow are nothing to do with you?"

"They are not, but I was willing to take them under my control if they set themselves up. Though it is a long way from London."

"Why are you here, not in Sevilla or Granada or Córdoba?"

"Because the Spanish Queen's daughter is here to marry the next king of England. Spain and England will be united. We exiles have made a new life for ourselves here, but how long will we be allowed to stay once a Spanish Queen sits at the side of King Arthur?"

"Catherine is not like that."

"Which is what the Catholic King and Queen also claimed when Granada fell. I hear you shared Queen Isabel's bed. Do you do the same for her daughter? Or both together, perhaps? Such debauchery would not surprise me."

Thomas tried to lunge at the man, a pointless gesture which sent the cage swinging wildly, and he sat rigid until it settled. Galib Uziel smiled as he watched him struggle.

Usaden had climbed higher and now perched above the open doorway, hidden from sight from those within. He could reach the rope from which Thomas's cage hung, but it would do little good. Try to stop the cage's fall and they would both plummet to the raging water below.

Thomas knew Usaden had many skills, but the ability to fly or swim was not among them.

"I cannot understand what you hope to achieve. Do you believe you can bring down the King?"

"I do not need to bring him down. All I need to do is stir up the population. The bonemen are but one part of my plan. I also have influence among the clergy. England is run by monarchs and bishops. The little men and women are nothing to them, and with enough manipulation they will rise and overthrow their cruel masters."

"But you do not care for the little men and women, do you?"

"Of course not; only in so far as they can help me meet my aims. A just England, ruled with compassion and not raw power. A beacon of light to the rest of the world. England has seen enough kings this last hundred years to welcome a just ruler."

"Do you expect that to be you?" Thomas saw from Galib Uziel's expression that he did and laughed to show his contempt. "What manner of compassion is it that steals from every trader and goodwife in London? Ludlow as well, if your daughter had her way. Do you know we defeated the bonemen in Ludlow?" Thomas smiled. "Ah, I see from your face you do not. I have documents in my possession that lead directly to you. Documents I intend to hand to King Henry."

"Do you mean these documents?" Galib Uziel clicked his fingers and held out a hand.

Thomas was annoyed the man's eyes remained locked on him crouched in the cage, because above him Usaden had a slim knife in his hand ready to drop to him.

A man approached and placed papers in Galib Uziel's outstretched hand.

"Goodwife Spicer allowed my men access to your room. She also told me what you and she had been doing before you came here. I hope the experience was pleasurable, for it will be your last ever pleasure before you die. Possibly goodwife Spicer's as well. She has served her purpose now and it does not profit a man to leave alive those who have knowledge of what he does."

"Not when that man follows your profession, I agree. But Peggy Spicer is a businesswoman. She pays your tax regularly. She is not stupid enough to say anything about you, so you can let her live."

Galib Uziel smiled and stepped forward. He flung the papers out into the air past Thomas, where they were sucked away by the wind.

"And now I cannot let her live, for the simple reason you have asked it of me. It would never do to agree to the request of a man such as yourself, one who has given me so much trouble. Now, Thomas Berrington, if my ears do not deceive me, the ebb of the tide nears its peak. Time for you to die. Time for—" A bellow sounded and Galib Uziel glanced aside as Will came to his senses.

Thomas took his chance. He looked up at Usaden and offered a nod. The slim blade dropped straight down to embed itself point first in the wood between Thomas's bound hands.

He leaned forwards and sawed the rope along the blade until it parted against the razor-sharp steel. Thomas pulled the knife free and slid it underneath himself, working on the bindings around his legs. He did the work blind, his eyes still on on Galib Uziel, who turned away and disappeared from sight.

Thomas worked harder, rewarded when his legs came free. He remained crouched in case Galib Uziel returned.

A second enormous bellow sounded, followed by a loud crashing and tearing, and Galib Uziel reappeared, but now he was going backwards fast. A moment later Will came into view. Ropes continued to hang from his wrists and ankles, but he had torn the iron rings clean out from the wood.

"Cut it. Cut the rope now!" shouted Galib Uziel. "Send him into the river."

Thomas could not see if anyone did as ordered, but he felt the cage swing again as someone hacked at the thick rope from inside. It was too late to pretend he was still captive. Thomas stood and swung the cage. Further and further, swinging far out away from the doorway and then back. On the fourth swing, he steadied himself, then leapt. For a moment, he was sure he would not make the distance. His jump pushed the cage away, weakening his attempt with nothing for it to hold against. Then he grasped the edge of the opening. For a moment he hung on one hand, his fingers uncurling. Then Usaden dropped down beside him and grabbed his wrist. The man might weigh a third less than Thomas, but he was more than a third stronger. He pulled him over the lip.

They turned to confront the remaining men. Fourteen of them, plus Galib Uziel. The man had retreated to a corner of the room, as far from Thomas as he could get, and a sword now hung from his hand. He was a prisoner in his own safe-room; the trapdoor barred his exit.

Thomas saw Usaden stalk one of their adversaries. Will rounded on two others. Thomas saw uncertainty in the men facing them. There might be fourteen against three, but some of the fourteen had seen how Thomas and Will had fought downstairs. Except then they had made mistakes, which was not like them. Everyone, Thomas thought, is allowed one mistake. They had made theirs for tonight. There would be no other. He turned to confront Galib Uziel, ignoring the others. He assumed Will and Usaden could deal with them without his help.

As he approached him, the man raised the sword he grasped, but it was not a convincing gesture.

"Have you ever fought before, or have you always had men do it for you?"

"I am no coward."

"That was not my question. I have fought since the age of thirteen. I have lost count of how many battles I fought and how many men I killed. You will be one more, and then your scheming ends."

Galib Uziel laughed. "If you think it ends with me, then you are mistaken, Thomas Berrington. I have sent men to all the major cities and towns of England. I have contacts in France, Holland, Spain, Italy, Germany, in Scotland and in the Northlands."

"But they all pay allegiance to you. When you are gone everything you have built will fall apart. Oh, some may continue to threaten the population of their own towns, but without you there will be no central control, no master plan. And I will make it my job to ensure each of their organisations, each of the bonemen, comes to justice."

As Thomas spoke Galib Uziel crept along the wall, his sword held out in front in an empty threat. Thomas used his own knife against it, knocking it from one side to the other, backwards and forwards. From around him, he heard cries and screams as men fought and died.

"Are you going to end it here? You might as well throw yourself into the river. Can you hear its roar? It sounds like thunder, does it not? It calls for you."

"My daughter will find you and cut your throat."

"Not with her right hand, she won't." Thomas saw a sudden anger spark through Galib Uziel.

The man made a fast attack, a flurry of strikes that told Thomas he was not unskilled. Or had been skilled at one time. Now his moves were rusty, too slow, and Thomas countered each without effort. He glanced back to check on Will and Usaden to discover that the men opposing them had formed some kind of defensive wall while others worked to open the trapdoor. As Thomas continued to watch, countering Galib Uziel's weak thrusts as he did so, he saw them get it open. The defensive wall retreated towards it. And then a black streak dashed into the room as Kin returned to his masters.

Galib Uziel saw the dog and a snarl contorted his face. He turned and ran at the opening in the river wall. When he reached it he threw himself out, clutching at the wooden crate until he could clamber inside.

Thomas saw him reach down for a lever he had not seen when he had been bound there and knew exactly what was going to happen. The crate would descend and Galib Uziel would make good his escape.

Thomas hesitated only a moment before throwing

himself after the man. He had come too far, encountered too much resistance, to let the man escape now. His feet found a hold on the outside of the crate, which swung wildly from the force of his landing. Galib Uziel tried to impale Thomas with his sword, but he evaded the blow with ease. His hand closed on the hilt and with a single twist it fell away into darkness and the raging river below.

The crate swung out, then back. It crashed into the side of the opening before swinging out again. Galib Uziel pushed at Thomas and tried to punch him, but his blows were weak. The crate swung again and then, with no warning, the rope holding it aloft gave way. Only afterwards did Thomas recall the man's instructions to cut the rope to send Thomas to his own death. Now both plunged through darkness, the roar of the river growing louder with each moment.

They hit the white water raging between the buttresses. The force of the fall threw Thomas away and he sank beneath the surface, tossed and tumbled so he could not tell which way was up and which down. He let the current take him, knowing it was impossible to fight, hoping it would slacken before the air left his lungs. His eyes were open, but all was darkness. He had chosen this hour because the city would be asleep and no light would show. He had chosen this night because there was no moon and clouds obscured the stars. And now that choosing might bring his death.

Thomas's lungs burned. He kicked his feet and moved his arms, hoping he might rise to the surface rather than sink deeper. There would be boulders, jagged wood and metal littering the river bed. There would be fish to feast on his corpse before morning if he did not find a breath soon. Then his head broke surface and he took a great gasp before the torrent dragged him down again. Except now he had his bearings and a few hard kicks brought him back to the surface. He could see a little now. Yes, it was dark. There was no moon, but lamps burned on the bridge, and torches flared on either bank, casting a weak illumination across the water.

The buttresses of the bridge lay a hundred paces upstream from where Thomas surfaced and he kicked out for the shoreline. He saw the walls of Baynard's Castle rising and thought of the meal he had eaten there a scant few hours before. He thought of Catherine sleeping in a strange bed, and wondered if she lay awake, excited or afraid about tomorrow and her marriage to Prince Arthur.

Thomas's feet touched the bed of the river and slipped away on the mud. He stroked harder until he could kneel, then worked his way to a narrow shingle beach. Only when he was safe did he turn to look for Galib Uziel, but there was no sign of him, nor the crate in which they had both plunged to the river in. Had he lived or died? Thomas tried to work out if he cared one way or the other, then decided he ought to. But not right now.

He put his head back on the shingle and closed his eyes.

He did not know how much time passed, but when a hand shook him awake the sky above was bright with the coming of dawn. The clouds of the night had cleared and a pale blue sky showed to the south. Today was a day for a wedding. Two great nations united. And Thomas was expected to attend.

He reached up to his son and Will hauled him to his feet as though he were a rag doll.

"How many did you kill?" Thomas asked.

"As few as we could. We let the others run. Usaden was not pleased, but agreed with me it was the right choice."

"Kin?"

"Gone with Usaden. They are on their way back to Ludlow. Neither are interested in a wedding ceremony, but Usaden said to give his regards to Cat when you see her."

"He can give them himself when she comes to Ludlow. Do you have better clothes?"

"Of course."

"You cannot enter the cathedral, but if you stand at the front of the crowd Cat might see you. She will like that."

"Then that is what I will do, Pa. I hope you have some better clothes as well. The Duke of Granada needs to make an impression."

"I am going to see if men can search both banks of the river for any sign of Galib Uziel. I would like to know whether he lived or died."

"He is dead, Pa. Has to be. I thought you would be as well when I saw you fall, but I searched the river anyway." Will embraced his father. "I am glad you are not. Ami will be too."

FORTY-FIVE

"You look tired, Thomas. And what have you done to your hair?" Catherine of Aragon reached out and tried to put his hair tidy. She pulled out a small twig and gave a sigh.

"I had a haircut that was interrupted, and an argument with a river." They stood close, a dozen others around them. Thomas was the only man other than the young Harry, who shifted from foot to foot. Young the prince might be, but his gaze lingered on the slim figures of Catherine's ladies and a smile played across his lips.

"Then you should have gone back and had it finished. Mother always said you are hopeless. You care nothing about your appearance."

Catherine was nervous, Thomas could tell. Normally, she listened without speaking until she had something to say. Today, she chattered like a young girl. Which, he admitted, she was not much more than. Sixteen years of age and about to be wed to a boy half a year her junior. Such were the ways of the royal families of Europe. Such, he supposed, were the ways of the world for all.

Marriages were rarely a matter of choice; even less so for women.

Catherine was dressed in a lavish dress, pinched hard at the waist but with voluminous skirts. She wore layers of pearls at her throat, her budding breasts made more prominent by whalebone stays. Her ladies-in-waiting wore similar, though less opulent, dresses. Prince Harry wore hose and a vibrant jerkin. A tilted cap sat on his red hair, a long pheasant-tail feather cocked to one side.

Catherine looked as though she could scarcely breathe.

"You will stay near to me, Thomas? Mother would want it."

"As near as I am allowed, Your Grace."

Catherine leaned close, her breath warm against his ear, though he had to duck his head for her to whisper into it.

"Do not Your Grace me again, Thomas. Not here. Not now. Call me how you always do, just this once."

"Then only once, Cat," Thomas said, returning the whisper. "And for the last time. By sunset you will be a princess of England, and in not so many years you will sit beside its king with you as queen. I believe Your Grace will be required by all your subjects then."

"Never from you, Thomas. Never. Nor Will or Amal. I saw him in the crowd as I entered this grand cathedral. I could not wave, but I think he saw my gaze on him. He looks even more of a man than when last I saw him. Where is Amal?"

"In Ludlow, where you will soon be."

"King Henry is trying to make his mind up whether or

461

not I should travel there with my husband, but I have made it clear I want to be with Arthur. Is Jorge in London?" Catherine tried to make the question sound casual.

"He is also in Ludlow. I was there when he had his talk with you, so know you are well prepared for what comes next."

"I would have liked to hear his explanations and encouragements one last time, but am aware he will not be allowed near now. I do not suppose you can tell me them, can you?"

Thomas suppressed a laugh. "I am not Jorge, Cat, as well you know. He is the master of love and loving, but fear not, you and Arthur are young and everything will come naturally to you."

"I pray you are right, and will pray again before we are bundled together in our bed. It is rather a social affair at the start, I hear. I hope it does not become too rowdy."

Thomas glanced at Harry, who was attempting to beguile one of the younger Spanish ladies. He appeared to be having some minor success in bringing blushes to her cheeks.

"I expect I will still be present and shall attempt to prevent it becoming too much so."

A door opened and robed churchmen stood waiting. The arrangements were known to all, though the timing had become a little vague.

"Stay as near to me as you can, Thomas. Not just here, but afterwards." Catherine touched his hand briefly. "I need your sage advice and wisdom. England is your country and I am a stranger here. Help me, for I need all the help I can get."

"You know I will."

Thomas kissed Catherine on both cheeks, then watched her walk to the door. Slim, elegant, regal. Her ladies followed her, and then it was only Thomas and Harry.

"Arthur is a lucky man, Tom. She is exquisite, is she not?"

"She is, Your Grace. I am sure you will find someone just as beautiful when your time comes."

"Or even before. I am not sure I can wait until I am fifteen. For marriage, perhaps, but the other thing…"

"The other thing, as you call it, Your Grace, is not always love. And love often as not does not mean only that other thing. You will learn soon enough."

"Stop calling me Your Grace, Tom. I heard Catherine say the same to you. Heard too when you called her Cat. I liked the sound of it. So you are to call me Harry, the same as those close to me do because I think we shall also be close. Ah, look, you are needed. I am to stay here to emerge when the wedding is done, then to walk beside Cat," Harry smiled, "when she leaves the cathedral. So what say you, Tom, do we have an understanding?" Harry held out his hand. He was tall for his age but still half a foot shorter than Thomas, so the boy had to look up to meet his eyes.

"Yes, we have an understanding, Harry." Thomas shook the hand.

"The house is yours if you want it."

Prior Bernard was dressed as an ordinary man. He claimed it made it easier for him to travel because few recognised him without his robes of office. They stood on a slope close to the woods and looked down at the manor house that once belonged to Hugh Clement.

"I thank you, but the house at Burway suits me better. That house holds too many memories for my daughter and Belia."

"Belia is Jorge's wife?"

"Something like that."

"And he has three sweet children. A miracle for a eunuch, I would say."

"Indeed."

"Belia is skilled in herbs," said Prior Bernard. "When we talked of them I thought I knew everything there was, but she is far more knowledgeable than I am."

"She is. So I don't have to take Hugh Clement's manor house?"

"Not if you don't want it. I will have to find another tenant, though."

"You can leave the matter with me if you wish. It is a fine house for someone who carries no memories of what went on inside it."

"You are, after all, Justice of the Peace for the district now, Tom. Who better to find an honest tenant?"

"It was not a position I sought, but neither King Henry nor Prince Arthur would take no for an answer. I am less sure Sir Richard Pole was much pleased, though. I suppose I have to make it work now. At least the appointment is only for a year."

"An honest Justice," said Bernard. "It is a bit of a departure, but I am sure you can manage." He clapped Thomas on the shoulder. "It is good to have you back in these parts, Tom. I cannot tell you how good it is."

Thomas made no reply, believing none was required, but Prior Bernard was not altogether finished.

"Have you seen Bel since your return?"

"Not yet."

"But you will?"

"I need to talk to her boys about bricks."

"Well, they are the men to talk to about bricks, I agree. And you can say hello to Bel at the same time."

"Are you trying to be matchmaker, Bernard?" Thomas smiled when he received a light slap on the back of his head at the dropping of the title. "I suspect we are both a little too old to consider taking up where we left off. A great deal of time has passed, and we are not who we were."

"She is still a handsome woman, and you a handsome man."

Thomas laughed.

"Whatever happened to Hugh Clement and that woman you used to have a relationship with?"

"Philippa Gale. Are you telling me you don't know her name? She has worked for Prince Arthur for many years."

"I may have heard the name, but as you know my order discourages me to think too much on women. Particularly beautiful women with fine figures."

"Hugh Clement was murdered by her. Prince Arthur had a mind to pardon Philippa Gale, but she disappeared the same night Hugh Clement died. Pip tried to kill my daughter, but the matchlock she used misfired and removed her hand. I have explained all of this to him but the boy has a soft heart."

"Your daughter is Amal."

Thomas nodded.

"And your son Will."

Thomas nodded again and turned away from the manor house. Prior Bernard fell into step at his side. The day was sharp with frost and soon the year would turn. Dark clouds gathered to the west. They would either bring a rise in temperature and rain, or snow, which already touched Clee Hill to the east.

"Your daughter is both exquisite and exotic. She stands out around here, and there will be boys, men too, who want her. Take good care of her."

"A father can only do so much." Thomas was about to tell Prior Bernard about what had gone on in the manor house then stopped. It would do no good to confess, and Bernard did not need to bear the pain of the knowledge. "One day, and not so far off I suspect, she will find someone she loves and I will have to accept her leaving, but she will always be my daughter. Nobody can take that from me."

"And she would want it no other way. Children are our legacy, Tom. We must care for them and love them and, when the time is right, let them go." He closed his hands together, then opened them, as if releasing a small bird.

"Did you ever have children, Bernard?"

This time there was no attempt at chastisement. "Not that I know about, but there is a possibility that some-where out in the world children of mine walk the earth. I was a soldier, you know I was, and not always a good man." Prior Bernard smiled, a mixture of pain and hope. "They may even look a little like Amal if they exist, for I fought in both the Holy Land and Spain." They walked on for a while in silence. The trees to their left were denuded of leaves, which lay thick on the frozen ground. "Has the Princess arrived in Ludlow yet?"

"Soon, I hear. King Henry was reluctant to send her. He thought it too remote, too dangerous, but she insisted."

"They need to be together as husband and wife. They need to consummate their marriage and have children."

"The consummation was done their first night together." Thomas smiled. "And several times since, I hear. So there may be children. It does not always happen at once, but eventually it will."

"I shall pray for a son."

"Jorge says he prefers daughters, but then he is not a normal man."

"Indeed he is not. He could live in the manor house if he wants it."

"He says he will live with me. Him and Belia and their children, as well as mine."

"Your son is of an age to take a wife, is he not?"

"More than an age."

"Is there room in that house at Burway for all of you?"

"Not at the moment, which is why I need to visit Lemster and talk to Bel's boys."

"In that case ride south with me, Tom. It is not yet noon, and if darkness falls early there is always a bed for you in the Priory if Bel throws you out."

"My thanks, but no thanks. I remember that cell from when you locked me in it."

"That was a long time ago now, was it not? And look, here you are, Justice of the Peace for Ludlow and Lemster districts. A friend of the Prince of Wales and his bride. To King Henry as well is what I hear. Ride with me, Tom, and you can tell me what you intend to do in your new position. It is unpaid, of course. I hope you know that?"

"I do, but I need no payment, Bernard. I have enough to last me ten lifetimes."

"Then a donation to the Church might ease your passage to heaven when the time comes."

Thomas said nothing. He did not want to disappoint this man he felt so close to by telling him he did not believe in either heaven or hell. Only in what lay in the world. Both good and bad. Despite his lack of faith, Thomas considered himself on the side of good. There had already been delegations from local landowners and nobles, not all of them friendly, not all of them honest. Thomas knew he would have to gather all his strength if he wanted to make a difference. And despite not wanting the job given him, he had decided he wanted to do it as well as his ability allowed.

HISTORICAL NOTE

Men of Bone is the first in a planned series of *The Thomas Berrington Tudor Mysteries*. It can be read knowing nothing of Thomas's history detailed in the earlier series of books set during the fall of Moorish Spain.

For those unfamiliar with Thomas Berrington, Jorge, and their extended family, this is their first book set in England. Thomas has spent over forty years in southern Spain, learning the trade of physician in the finest infirmaries in Europe during the Medieval period. Nine books in *The Thomas Berrington Historical Mysteries* tell his story from 1482 to 1492, during the final battles to expel the Islamic Moorish invaders, who had settled there for over seven centuries.

Bringing Thomas back to Tudor England has been a challenge. For one, far more historical fact is known of the period, and many readers are often more aware of these facts than the authors of fiction set in that period. If I have made errors, I apologise. I will make every endeavour to improve.

As with all historical fiction, *Men of Bone* is foremost a story set in a historical context. As such, some of it will be pure fiction rather than fact. In this book, the primary conceit is also the driver of the plot—those named the bonemen, spreading from London to other parts of the country.

The marriage of Prince Arthur to Catherine of Aragon is well known, but their life together is poorly documented. The next book in the series will detail more of their lives together, as well as the death of Arthur, only six months after their marriage, and the moving of Catherine to Durham House in London.

REFERENCES

For most of my research, I relied on the excellent *Catherine of Aragon*, by Giles Tremlett. For details on Ludlow and the surrounding area, much of my research was carried out on foot, but I also consulted *The Concise History of Ludlow*, by David Lloyd, which provided a wealth of detail on the history and development of that town. In addition, I have referred to *Ludlow Castle: its History & Buildings*, edited by Ron Shoesmith and Andy Johnson - an exhaustive but excellent book holding probably far more detail than I needed, but was grateful for all the same.

For a detailed picture of the London of 1500, I obtained a copy of the excellent (if scarce) *Old London Illustrated* with drawings by H.W. Brewster. My copy was printed in 1962 and contains 16 plates of drawings depicting various views of London together with detailed descriptions of each location.

ALSO BY DAVID PENNY

The Thomas Berrington Historical Mysteries

The Red Hill

Breaker of Bones

The Sin Eater

The Incubus

The Inquisitor

The Fortunate Dead

The Promise of Pain

The Message of Blood

A Tear for the Dead

The Thomas Berrington Tudor Mysteries

Men of Bone

A Death of Promise

The Thomas Berrington Prequels

A Death of Innocence

The Thomas Berrington Bundles

Purchase 3 full-length novels for less than the price of two.

Thomas Berrington Books 1-3

The Red Hill

Breaker of Bones

The Incubus

Thomas Berrington Books 4-6

The Incubus

The Inquisitor

The Fortunate Dead

Thomas Berrington Books 7-9

The Promise of Pain

The Message of Blood

A Tear for the Dead

Unit-13: WWII Paranormal Spy Thriller

An Imperfect Future